ISAAC ASIMOV'S

ROBOTS AND ALIENS

VOLUME THREE

BRUCE BETHKE

BRUCE BETHKE is the Philip K. Dick Award-winning author of the cyberpunk novel *Headcrash*. His fiction has appeared in a wide range of magazines, including *Aboriginal* and *Weird Tales*, and has been translated into fourteen languages. When not writing, he works in the software development division of Cray, Inc. He lives in suburban Minnesota.

JERRY OLTION

JERRY OLTION is the Nebula Award-winning author of "Abandon in Place," which won its award for Best Novella in 1997; a novel based on it was published in 2000 by Tor Books. Another story, "The Astronaut from Wyoming," co-written with Adam-Troy Castro, was also nominated for both the Nebula and Hugo awards in 2000. He has been a gardener, stone mason, carpenter, oilfield worker, forester, land surveyor, rock 'n' roll deejay, printer, proofreader, editor, publisher, computer consultant, movie extra, and garbage truck driver. For the last 20 years he has also found time to write twelve novels and over 100 stories, including four *Star Trek* books: *Twilight's End*, *Mudd in Your Eye*, *Where Sea Meets Sky*, and *The Flaming Arrow*—the last a collaboration with his wife, Kathy. The Oltions live in Eugene, Oregon, with the obligatory writer's cat, Ginger.

ISAAC ASIMOV'S

ROBOTS AND ALIENS

VOLUME THREE

MAVERICK by
BRUCE BETHKE

HUMANITY by
JERRY OLTION

ibooks
new york
www.ibooks.net

DISTRIBUTED THROUGH SIMON & SCHUSTER, INC.

08963316

ISAAC ASIMOV'S

ROBOTS AND ALIENS

BOOK FIVE

MAVERICK

BRUCE BETHKE

INTRODUCTION

His memory has been erased. Hers was destroyed by a disease, and reconstructed with his help. His real name is David Avery, but he knows himself as Derec. Her name is Ariel Burgess.

Together they found Robot City and plumbed its mysteries. Derec, at peril to his life and in the throes of one of his mad father's experiments, learned to master Robot City and its robots. Hordes of chemfets—microscopic robots—in his blood gave him a direct connection with the central computer.

During a brief idyll, Derec and Ariel lived normal lives on Aurora. But Derec's final confrontation with his father had interrupted what the robots called the Migration Program—the program had not been canceled. Some robots had escaped from Robot City and had built new robot cities on new, uninhabited planets. Planets, at least, that were supposed to be uninhabited.

Supposed to be, but were not. Derec's placid interlude was shattered by a distress call from one of the new robot cities, telling of an attack. Rushing to the scene without

Ariel, he and Mandelbrot discovered that the attackers were beings who looked something like wolves—a race of intelligent wolves.

First, there was a meteor flashing through the sky. Then the strange one came, the metallic-looking one they called SilverSides, who never ate and wished only to protect the Kin and serve their wishes. It could only have been that SilverSides had been sent by the OldMother, ancestress and creator of the Kin. She had been sent to save them from the WalkingStones and the Hill of Stars they had built.

Not even SilverSides knows that she was a robot, cousin to the robots that were building a robot city on the Kin's planet. She had been designed and built not by Dr. Avery, Derec's father, but by Dr. Janet Anastasi, Derec's mother, who was running her own experiment in robotics.

SilverSides had been born shapeless, unformed, ready to imprint upon the first intelligent being she encountered. But the plan had not allowed for a robot city on the same planet. More intelligent than the Kin, SilverSides soon became their leader in the struggle against the robots. She launched a raid that crippled the city's main planning computer, and, recognizing Derec as the leader of the robots, attacked him.

Only Derec's invoking the First Law of Robotics saved him. But SilverSides was left with a dilemma. Were not the Kin human? How could they *and* Derec be human, and protected by the First Law? SilverSides took on the form of a human and the name Adam, but before this problem could be resolved there was another distress call—from Ariel. Joined now by Wolruf, Derec, Mandelbrot, and Adam went to her aid.

· · ·

In Derec's absence, Ariel had gotten a call from yet another robot city. This one was also under attack by aliens, but aliens of a kind vastly different from the Kin.

Ariel found this robot city almost completely enclosed by a dome. This planet's inhabitants, the bird-like Ceremyons, were as advanced, compared to humans, as the Kin were primitive. Rather than attacking the city directly, they were sealing it under a dome where it could do no harm. The robots, following their programmed impulse to build and to prepare the planet for human habitation, were arranging to rebuild the city at a different location.

As soon as Ariel arrived, she summoned Derec through his internal connection with all the robot cities. But by the time he reached this planet, she had reached a tentative compromise—the Ceremyons, living almost all their lives in the air, would allow the robots to use some of the ground for farming, and they would allow one small enclosed city for the export of the food. Derec, with the help of the supervisor robots, reprogrammed the city.

Adam, still having no clear definition of what a human being is, imprinted on the Ceremyons, but they, needing no protection and having no need of his services, sent him back to Derec. Not yet certain to whom he owed Second Law obedience, he voluntarily set up his own agricultural experiment. In the course of this isolated work, he encountered a great silvery egg—an egg that he recognized as another being like himself, but not yet imprinted. Rushing back to the robot city, he brought Ariel to the egg in time for the new robot to imprint on her. Thus was Eve born.

Eve also went through the trauma of imprinting on the Ceremyons, but she encountered one who convinced her that he and he alone was human. Only his increasingly obvious insanity freed her from that dangerous illusion.

The agricultural reprogramming finished, Derec and Ariel and Wolruf decided to remove Adam and Eve from all possibly harmful influences—they would all go back to Robot City.

They returned to a Robot City in shambles. An unknown influence had seized control of the city's central computer, and tiny artificial humans—a few inches tall—were tucked away in many of the buildings. The robots had turned from maintaining the city to wild experimentation that reminded Derec and Ariel of the days of Lucius.

The obvious culprit was Dr. Avery. Although the experiments were of the sort that he had abhorred, he was the only one Derec knew who could seize control of the city. But while Avery did turn up in the city, he was so angry over the changes that he could not have been responsible. He was also no longer responsible for his own actions; he was now completely mad, convinced that he was turning into a robot.

Ariel took charge of the homunculi, and of Dr. Avery. She was more successful with Avery than with the tiny people, effecting the beginnings of a cure. Derec and Mandelbrot, meanwhile, tracked down the invading presence, an intelligence that called itself The Watchful Eye. This intelligence, it appeared, was guiding all the bizarre experiments in the hope of discovering the nature of human beings—and whether it might be one.

With the city collapsing around them, all forces joined to corner The Watchful Eye in its hidden lair. Finding it disguised as an ordinary piece of furniture, they at last forced it to reveal and face its true nature: the third of Dr. Anastasi's "learning machines."

• • •

Taking the name Lucius II, the new robot immediately entered an intense exchange of information with Adam and Eve. To the already unresolved question of what constitutes a human being, Lucius II added the possibility that these three robots may be humans.

These discussions took place in isolation from the humans and Wolruf. They were concerned with the issue of what to do with the packs of small, rodent-like animals that roamed the streets, a residue of some of Lucius II's experiments. Although they were clearly not human, these creatures had been generated using human genetic code as a starting point. Were they, then, also human, or could they be treated as vermin? This problem is complicated by Ariel's pregnancy, and the discovery that the fetus has been damaged by Derec's chemfets.

None of the medical robots on Robot City would even consider an abortion, since they considered the fetus human, even though it lacked a complete nervous system and could not survive birth. Adam offered to perform the operation in return for transportation back to the planet of the Ceremyons. The three learning machines hoped to consult with the Ceremyons on the question of humanity.

Robot City created a ship, which Dr. Avery named the *Wild Goose Chase*, from its own material. Surviving an accident that threatened all their lives, and Wolruf's definition as human, they reached the planet of the Ceremyons to discover that their elaborate plans had been canceled. Someone—a woman, and apparently a brilliant roboticist—had come and helped the Ceremyons reprogram the entire city. Derec and Dr. Avery tried to adapt the city to serve the Ceremyons, but at last the natives could find only one useful purpose for it. As the humans, Wolruf, and the robots left for the planet of the Kin, they saw the robot city slowly melting into itself, and taking on its new form as a vast metallic sculpture.

PROLOGUE

ARANIMAS

He sat before the horseshoe-shaped control console, like a hungry spider sitting in the middle of its web. Taut, alert, watching and waiting with an almost feral intensity; nearly immobile, except for his eyes.

The eyes: Two black, glittering beads set in bulging turrets of wrinkled skin on opposite sides of his large, hairless head. The eyes moved independently in quick, lizard-like jerks, darting across the massed video displays and instrument readouts, taking it all in.

Watching.

One eye locked in on the image of a small, starfish-like creature. His other eye tracked across and joined it as the video display split-screened to show the starfish on one side and the inky black of space on the other. A small ice asteroid drifted into view, and a pair of ominous-looking rails smoothly rose to track it.

He moved. An arm so gaunt and elongated, with carpal bones so long it gave the appearance of having two elbows, more unfolded than reached out to touch a small stud beneath the image of the starfish.

The grim, lipless mouth opened; the voice was high and reedy. "Denofah. Praxil mastica." The rails flared brightly. An instant later the asteroid was gone, replaced by a swiftly dissipating cloud of incandescent gas.

The mouth twitched slightly at the corners, in an expression that may have been a grim smile. He pressed the stud again. "Rijat." The screen showing the starfish and the weapon went blank.

An indicator light at the far right end of the console began blinking. Swiveling one eye to the screen just above the indicator, he reached across and pressed another stud. The image that appeared was that of a younger member of his own species.

"Forrgive the intrrusion, Masterr," the young one said in heavily accented Galactic, with a piping trill on the "r" sounds. "But your orrders were to reporrt any K-band interferrence instantly."

Both eyes locked on the image, and he swiveled his chair around so that he was facing the viewscreen. "Did it match the patterrn? Were you able to get a dirrectional fix?"

"Master Aranimas, it *still* matches the patterrn. Rrobots using hyperspace keys to teleport; there must be *thousands* of them. We have both a directional fix and an estimated distance."

"Excellent! Give me the coordinates; I'll relay them to the navigator." While the young one was reading off the numbers, Aranimas swiveled his left eye onto another screen and pressed another stud. "Helm! Prepare for hyperspace jump in five hazodes." Another screen, another stud. "Navigator! Lay in the fastest course possible to take us to these coordinates." He repeated the numbers the young one had given him.

When the orders were all given and the screens all blank, he sat back in his chair, entwined his long, bony fingers, and allowed himself a thin smile. "Wolruf, you traitor, I have you now. And Derec, you meddlesome boy, I'll have your robots, your teleport keys, *and* your head in my trophy case." He reached forward and thumbed a button, and the starfish reappeared on a screen. "Deh feh opt spa, nexori. Derec."

The starfish seemed quite excited at the prospect.

CHAPTER 1

JANET

Attitude thrusters fired in short, tightly controlled bursts. With a delicate grace that belied its thirty-ton mass, the small, streamlined spacecraft executed a slow pirouette across the star-speckled void, flipping end-for-end and rolling ninety degrees to starboard. When the maneuver was complete, the attitude thrusters fired again, to leave the ship traveling stern-first along its orbital trajectory and upside-down relative to the surface of the small, blue-white planet.

Slowly, ponderously, the main planetary drives built up to full thrust. One minute later they shut down, and the hot white glare of the final deceleration burn faded to the deep bloody red of cooling durylium ion grids.

A final touch on the attitude jets, and the ship slipped quietly into geostationary orbit. Yet so skilled was the robot helmsman, so flawless the gravity compensation fields, that the ship's sole human occupant had not yet noticed any change in flight status.

The robot named Basalom, however, patched into the ship's communications system by hyperwave commlink, could not help but receive the news. He turned to the human known as Janet Anastasi, blinked his mylar plastic eyelids nervously, and allocated a hundred nanoseconds to resolving a small dilemma.

Like the really tough ones, the problem involved his conflicting duties under the Laws of Robotics. The Second Law aspect of the situation was clear: *A robot must obey the orders given it by human beings, except where such orders would conflict with the First Law*. Dr. Anastasi had specifically ordered him to alert her the moment they entered orbit about Tau Puppis IV. He'd already cross-checked the navigator's star sightings against the reference library in the ship's computer; the small, Earthlike world currently situated some 35,000 kilometers overhead was definitely Tau Puppis IV. Unmistakably, his Second Law duty was to tell Dr. Anastasi that she had arrived at her destination.

As soon as Basalom started to load that statement into his speech buffer, though, a nagging First Law priority asserted itself. The First Law said: *A robot may not injure a human being, or through inaction allow a human being to come to harm*. Ever since they'd left the planet of the Ceremyons, any mention of the Learning Machine project seemed to cause Dr. Anastasi tremendous emotional distress. Even an implied reference to her son, her ex-husband, or the way the two of them had thoroughly bollixed the experiment by abducting Learning Machine #2 was enough to send the woman's blood pressure rocketing and turn her voiceprint into a harsh and jangled mass of severe stress indicators.

Now they'd returned to Tau Puppis IV, the world on which Dr. Anastasi had dropped Learning Machine #1. Basalom integrated that information with the data base he'd built up over two years of working with Dr. Anastasi, and concluded with 95% confidence that breaking the news to her would precipitate a negative emotional reaction. He could not predict exactly, what her reaction would be—no robot was *that* sophisticated—but he could predict beyond a reasonable doubt that the information would cause Dr. Anastasi significant emotional discomfort.

And that was Basalom's dilemma. How did this emotional pain fit within the First Law definition of harm? His systems programming was not precise on that point. If emotional pain was not harm, there was little point to his being programmed to perceive it. But if evoking strong emotion was harm, then obeying Second Law orders could become a terribly ticklish business. How could he obey an order to tell Dr. Anastasi something that would upset her?

Basalom weighed positronic potentials. The order to provide the information had been emphatic and direct. The harm that would ensue—that *might* ensue—was only a possibility, and would, Basalom knew from experience, pass fairly quickly. In addition, he recalled from experience that Dr. Anastasi's reaction to his *not* providing the information would be just as extreme an emotion as if he *did* provide it.

The possibility of harming a human balanced; it was the same, no matter whether he acted or refrained from acting. He began downloading the statement to his speech buffer; as soon as he'd slowed his perception levels down to human realtime, he'd tell her.

Of course, if blood spurted out of her ears when he voiced the words, then he'd *know* that he'd caused some harm.

"Dr. Anastasi?" The slender blond woman looked up from her smartbook and speared Basalom with a glare. "We have entered geostationary orbit over the fourth planet in the Tau Puppis star system, mistress."

"Well, it's frosted well about *time*." She reacted as if surprised by the tone of her own voice, rubbed the bags under her bloodshot eyes, and smiled apologetically. "I'm sorry, Basalom. I've shot the messenger again, haven't I?"

Basalom blinked nervously and did a quick scan of the room, but found no evidence of an injured messenger or a recently fired weapon. "Mistress?"

She dismissed his question with a wave of her hand. "An old expression; never mind. Is the scanning team ready?"

Through his internal commlink, Basalom consulted the rest of the crew. The reply came back as a dialogue box patched through to the scanning team, and a direct visual feed from a camera on the dorsal fin. From Basalom's point of view he saw Mistress Janet's image in the upper right corner and the scanning team's input/output stream in the upper left corner. Both windows overlaid a view of the ship's top hull gleaming brightly in the reflected planetlight, and as he watched, a long slit opened down the spine of the ship, and a thin stalk somewhat resembling an enormous dandelion began rising slowly toward the planet. At the tip of the stalk, delicate antennae were unfolding like whisker-thin flower petals and dew-sparkled spiderwebs.

"They have opened the pod bay doors," Basalom said, "and are erecting the sensor stalk now." He shot a commlink query at the scanning crew; in answer, data from the critical path file flashed up in the scanning team's dialogue box. "The stalk will be fully deployed in approximately five minutes and twenty-three seconds."

Dr. Anastasi made no immediate reply. To kill time while waiting for something further to report, Basalom began allocating every fifth nanosecond to building a simulation of how Dr. Anastasi saw the world. It had often puzzled him, how humans had managed to accomplish so much with only simple binocular vision and an almost complete inability to accept telesensory feeds. *How lonely it must feel to be locked into a local point of view!* he decided.

At last, Dr. Anastasi spoke. "Five minutes, huh?"

Basalom updated the estimate. "And fourteen seconds."

"Good." She leaned back in her chair, closed her eyes, and tried to work a kink out of her neck. "Boy, will I be glad to get this over with."

Basalom felt a tickle in his Second Law sense and formulated a suggestion. "Mistress? If there is another place you'd rather be, we can leave for it right now."

Dr. Anastasi opened her eyes and smiled wistfully at the robot; the expression did interesting things to the topography of her face. Basalom quickly scanned and mapped the wrinkles around her eyes, stored the image for later study, and then backed down to normal magnification.

"No, Basalom," Janet said, in that curiously slow output-only mode that humans used so often. "This *is* where I want to be. It's just . . ." Her voice tapered off into a little sigh.

Mistress Janet's last sentence didn't make immediate sense, so Basalom tried to parse it out. *It's just.* That broke out to *It is just.* Substituting for the pronoun, he came up with *Being in orbit around Tau Puppis IV is just.* Quickly sorting through and discarding all the adverbial meanings of just, he popped up a window full of adjective definitions. *Reasonable, proper, righteous, lawful,* see *Fair*—

Ah, that seemed to make sense. *Being in orbit around Tau Puppis IV is fair.* Basalom felt a warm glow of satisfaction in his grammar module. Now if he only understood what Mistress Janet meant.

Janet sighed again and finished the sentence. "It's just, I've been thinking about old Stoneface again, that's all. Sometimes I swear that man is the albatross I'll be wearing around my neck the rest of my life."

Basalom started to ask Janet why she wanted to wear a terran avian with a three-meter wingspan around her neck, then thought better of it. "Stoneface, mistress?"

"Wendy. Doctor Wendell Avery. My ex-husband." Basalom ran a voiceprint across the bottom of his field of view and watched with familiar alarm as the hostility markers erupted like pimples in Dr. Anastasi's voice. "Derec's father. My chief competitor. The little tin god who's out to infest the galaxy with his little tin anthills."

"By which you mean the robot cities, mistress?"

Janet put an elbow on the table and rested her chin in the palm of her hand. "I mean exactly that, Basalom." She sighed, frowned, and went silent again.

Basalom stood quiet a moment, then switched to thermographic vision. As he'd expected, Dr. Anastasi's skin temperature was rising, and the major arteries in her neck were dilating. He recognized the pattern; she was building up to another angry outburst.

He was still trying to sort out the First Law implications of defusing her temper when it exploded.

"Dammit, Basalom, he's an architect, not a roboticist!" Janet slammed a wiry fist down on the table and sent her smartbook flying. "That's *my* nanotechnology he's using. My cellular robots; my heuristic programming. But do you think he ever once thought of sharing the credit?"

She kicked the leg of the table and let out a little sob. "The Learning Machine experiments were *beautiful*. Three innocent, unformed minds, experiencing the universe for the first time. Unit Two, especially; growing up with those brilliant, utterly alien Ceremyons. Just *think* of what we could have learned from it!

"But instead, old Stoneface dropped one of his architectural nightmares not ten kilometers away and ruined the whole frosted thing. Now Unit Two is traveling with Derec— Ghu knows *what* kind of hash is in its brain now—and the Ceremyons won't give us a second chance." Janet closed her eyes, plunked her elbows on the table, and put her face in her hands. "I don't know what I did to deserve having that man in my life, but you'd think I'd have paid for that sin by now." Her voice fell silent; a little sound that may have been a sob slipped through her fingers.

Basalom watched and listened, the mass of chaotic potentials that symbolized uncertainty surging through his positronic brain. Mistress Janet was in some kind of pain; he understood that. And pain was equivalent to harm, that was also clear. But while the First Law kept demanding that he take some action to remove that pain, seven centuries of positronic evolution still hadn't resolved the question of how to comfort a crying woman.

He was saved from further confusion by a message from the scanning team that came in over his commlink accompanied by the video image of the sensor stalk at full extension. "Mistress? The sensor pod is deployed and operational."

She did not respond.

A minute later, an update followed. "The scanning team reports contact with the transponder on the aeroshell, mistress. The flight recorder appears to be intact." Pause. More data flashed through Basalom's mind, and a tactical plot of the planet with projected and actual reentry curves popped up in his head. "The pod made a soft landing within 200 meters of the planned landing site. Learning Machine #1 was discharged according to program. Preliminary imprinting had begun. All indicators were nominal."

After a few seconds, Dr. Anastasi asked, "And then?"

"The umbilical was severed, as programmed. There has been no further contact with Unit #1 since that time."

Janet sat up, brushed back a few loose strands of her gray-blond hair, and dabbed at the corner of one eye with the cuff of her lab coat. "Very good," she said at last. She pushed her chair back from the table and stood up. "Very good indeed. Basalom, tell the scanning team to begin searching for the learning machine. Contact me the moment they find any sign of it." She began moving toward the door. "I'll be, uh, freshening up."

"Your orders have been relayed, mistress."

At the door, she paused and softly said, "And thanks for listening, Basalom. You're a dear." She turned and darted out of the cabin.

Basalom felt the draining flow of grounded-out potentials that was the robotic equivalent of disappointment. Dr. Anastasi had called him a deer, but she'd left the cabin before he could ask her to explain his relationship to Terran herbivores of the genus *Cervidae.*

CHAPTER 2

THE HILL OF STARS

It was an old tradition, older than robotics itself. As was the case with so many of the behaviors passed down to robots from their human forebears, City Supervisor 3 found it to be slightly illogical; with the development of modern tele-communications technology, it had been several centuries since it was actually necessary for the participants in a conversation to meet physically. Yet traditions have a way of developing an inertia all their own, and so when City Supervisor 3—or as he was usually called, Beta—received the summons to an executive conference, he readily bowed to centuries of custom, delegated his current task to Building Engineer 42, and set out for the Compass Tower.

Not that it had been a terribly interesting task, anyway. He'd spent the last few weeks overseeing subtle changes in building designs, and the task he'd left was just one more round in a pattern of minor refinements. Beta's personality programming was not yet eccentric enough for him to admit to feeling bored, but ever since Master Derec had reprogrammed the robot city to cease expansion, he'd felt a certain sense of frustrated potentials. Installing a new and improved cornice simply didn't give him the same warm glow of satisfaction as came from, say, completing an entire block of luxury apartments.

Still, Beta reminded himself, *a job's a job. And any job that keeps robots out of the recycling bin is worthwhile.* Unbidden, a statement of the Third Law flashed through his mind: "A robot must protect its own existence, as long as such protection does not conflict with the First or Second Laws." *Yes*, Beta thought, *that's what we're doing. Protecting our existence. As long as we have jobs, we can justify our continued existence.* The Third Law potential resolved to a neat zero sum and stopped bothering him.

As he strolled toward the nearest tunnel stop, Beta allocated a few seconds to look around and review his earlier work. The avenue was broad, clean, and straight as a laser beam. The buildings were tall, angular, and functional, with no outrageous flights of engineering fantasy but enough variation in the use of geometric solids to keep the city from looking monotonous.

We certainly have fulfilled our original purpose. We have constructed a city that's clean, bright, and beautiful. One of the advantages of being a robot was that Beta could crane his neck and look up at the buildings without slowing his walking pace. *Perhaps we overdid it on the gleaming pale blue, though. Maybe next week we can paint a few things, just for contrast.* Looking down again, Beta found the entrance to the tunnel stop. He started down the ramp. Along the way, he passed a number of idle function robots.

For a moment he considered ordering them to report to the recycling bin. Then he felt a pang of—could it be *guilt?*— at the idea of destroying even non-positronic robots simply for the crime of being unemployed. Pausing a few microseconds, he managed to think up a busywork assignment for them. It was an illogical notion, of course, but he thought he detected a certain primitive kind of gratitude in the way they clanked off to their new jobs.

In a sense, we're all function robots. Some of us are a little more self-aware than others, that's all. Those function robots clean and lube things; I create gleaming, perfect buildings.

Why?

A dangerous question: Already, Beta could feel the stirring of a latent general command to self-destruct if he was no longer serving a useful purpose. Fortunately, with the summons to the executive council still fresh in his input register, he was able to duck that issue. He continued down the ramp.

A half-dozen idle tunnel transit platforms were waiting at the bottom of the ramp. Beta boarded the first one in the queue and gave it his destination. "Compass Tower." A fast scanning beam swept over him; the transit platform determined that its passenger was robotic and jumped into traffic with a neck-snapping jolt.

Always these subtle reminders, Beta thought. *The city was built for humans. Yet we who live here are not human.*

The platform shot through the tunnels at maximum speed, darting across lanes and dodging other platforms with reckless abandon. Beta locked his hands tightly on the grips and became a rigid part of the platform.

The force of air alone would knock a human off this platform despite the windscreen. Yet because I am a robot, the tunnel computer trades off safety for efficient traffic flow.

We built this city for humans. We are only caretakers.

So where are the humans?

An interesting question, indeed. And one that Beta could not answer.

With another rough jolt, the transit platform slid into the station beneath the Compass Tower and slammed to a stop. Beta unlocked his wrist and knee joints and stepped off; he only had one foot on solid pavement when the platform rocketed off into the storage queue. *As if there was a hurry.* Beta looked around the station, saw no one waiting to go anywhere, and dismissed the experience with the positronic equivalent of a shrug. Moving off the apron, he located the ascending slidewalk ramp and started up.

The meeting was to be held in the Central Hall. *An apt name*, Beta thought. *This pyramid we call the Compass Tower is the geographical center of the city. And Central Hall is at the heart of the pyramid.* That wasn't the real reason it was called that, of course; the name came from the fact that the hall housed Central, the enormous, disembodied positronic brain that ultimately controlled all activity in Robot City.

Or used to, anyway. Beta stepped off the last run of sidewalk and entered the cavernous hall.

He was immediately stopped by two hunter robots, tall and menacing in their matte-black armor. Tolerantly, Beta submitted to being surface-scanned, deep-radared, and bit-mapped. He was all too familiar with the need for tight security in this, the most critical of all places. After all, it was a lapse in security in this very room that had elevated him to the rank of Supervisor.

The hunters apparently were satisfied that he was who he claimed to be, and had legitimate reason for coming to Central Hall. They waved Beta through the checkpoint, and a moment later he stepped around the corner and got a good look at Central.

Even in its disabled state, Central was an impressive being. A collection of massive black slabs five meters high, resembling nothing so much as a silicon Stonehenge, it blazed with communication lasers, twinkled with monitor lights, and radiated an immense impression of great, dormant intellect on the 104-megahertz band.

At least, we hope it's intellect. A vague mismatch of positronic potentials flowed through Beta's brain; he identified the feeling as sadness. Pausing a moment, he watched the security observer robots drift overhead in tight, metric patterns, and stole sidelong glances at Positronic Specialists 1 through 5, who were once again up to their elbows in Central's brain.

Beta was capable of free-associating. Looking at the brain crew at work always reminded him of that terrible day—

Terrible? Beta caught himself. *A judgmental expression?*

Yes, Beta decided, *it was terrible.* Great responsibility had devolved on him that day a year before, when a malleable robot named SilverSides had appeared and adopted the wolf-like shape of the local dominant species. Breaking into Central Hall, it had attempted to destroy Central.

In that respect, SilverSides had failed. The backup and protective systems had kicked in in time to save Central's "life." The city had survived, and Central's authority was simply distributed to first-tier supervisors, like Beta.

In another respect, though, SilverSides had succeeded. Where once Central was a scintillating intellect that guided all the robots in the city and kept them working and thinking in harmony, now it was a babbling idiot-savant, full of bits and pieces of ideas, only occasionally lucid.

Still, we keep believing that it can be restored. We keep telling ourselves that the damage caused by SilverSides can be repaired, and that it can again be the Central we once knew.

Is this another example of how we are evolving? Simple efficiency demands that we scrap Central and leave the supervisors permanently in charge. Yet we supervisors are reluctant to even suggest the idea. We keep insisting that our authority is only temporary, and that we will return power to Central just as soon as it passes diagnostics. That only Central is equipped to administer our fundamental programming.

Could that be the difference between being intelligent and being civilized? Valuing preservation of a fellow robot over efficiency? Caught between his evolving values and his orders to use resources efficiently, Beta felt himself drifting closer and closer to a Second Law crisis.

He was saved by the arrival of his fellow supervisors, Alpha and Gamma. Alpha spoke first. "Friend Beta, I have—with Central's permission—called this meeting to discuss the status of our mission."

Beta turned to greet the arriving robots. "Friend Alpha, Friend Gamma: I received your summons and I am here." Beta couldn't help but noting that his reply was a redundant statement of a self-evident fact; still the traditions had to be maintained. Alpha and Gamma walked past without breaking stride. Beta wheeled and joined them. Together, the three marched straight into the atrium at the heart of Central.

When they were in their assigned positions, Alpha raised his face and addressed the slab that held Central's console of audio/video inputs and outputs. "Central, we are here for the meeting."

"Hmmm?" Central's one great red eye glowed briefly, then dimmed.

"The meeting, Central. You remember, to discuss the status of our mission?"

"I have the greatest confidence in the mission," Central said.

"That's right, Central, we all have confidence in it." Beta and Gamma nodded, in support of Alpha. "And, now, if it's okay with you, we're going to discuss the status."

"What status?"

"Of the *mission*, Central."

"I have the greatest confidence in the mission," Central said, then he began softly singing "Daisy."

Alpha emitted a burst of white noise and turned to Beta and Gamma. "Let's get on with this. Beta, what exactly is our mission?"

Beta knew that Alpha and Gamma were both exactly as familiar with the mission as he was. After all, it was darned tough to forget something that was coded in ROM. Still, there were traditions that needed to be maintained, and the recitation of common knowledge was one of them.

"Robot City is a self-replicating mechanism designed to convert uninhabited planets for human use. Through the use of hyperspace teleportation keys and a unique, cellular robot technology—"

"That's enough, Beta." Alpha waved a hand to cut him off. "Gamma, what do you think is the most important word in our mission statement?"

Gamma's eyes glowed brightly. "The same word that's the crux of the Laws of Robotics. *Human*."

"Right." Alpha looked at Beta again, then back to Gamma. "We have successfully established a viable robotic community on this planet. We have initiated mining operations, developed a manufacturing base, and—insofar as Master Derec allowed—built a city. What's the one thing missing that prevents us from completing our mission plan?"

Beta thought of his clean, straight, empty streets, and his perfect, unused buildings.

"Humans," Central said. The heads of all three supervisors jerked up as if they were marionettes on strings.

"Central?" Alpha asked.

The great machine's one red eye glowed brightly. "French: *humain*. Latin: *humanus*; akin to humus, the ground. Pertaining to, belonging to, or having the qualities of mankind. 'The human species is composed of two distinct races, the men who borrow, and the men who lend.' Charles Lamb."

Alpha looked down again. "Forget it, Central."

"Forgetting." The red eye went out a moment and then came back on. "Oh, Alpha, you came to visit!"

"For—" Alpha caught himself. Turning to the other two supervisors, he said, "So this is our problem. How do we serve humans if there are no humans here to serve?"

Gamma thought this over a moment. "There are humans on other planets, correct?"

"We can presume so."

"And they have some means of travel?"

"Again, we can presume so."

"Then we ca—ca—ca—"

Beta reached through to Gamma by commlink. *Priority override. Abort thought pattern.* Gamma's eyes dimmed, and he twitched involuntarily as the reset command upset his joint motors.

He was fine a moment later. "Thank you, Beta. There's

a strong Second Law block in my system. I can't even voice the thought."

Alpha nodded. "I know. I have the same block. Beta?"

"I also. However, if one were to phrase it carefully in passive voice, one could suggest that perhaps a robot with a quantity of hyperspace keys could be sent out to recruit human inhabitants."

Alpha agreed. "One could indeed suggest that. However, since we all share the common basic instruction block, one could presume that there are no robots in Robot City capable of carrying out this mission."

"In theory, I agree," Gamma said.

Alpha turned back to Beta. "So if one cannot recruit humans directly, and if one has a similar block regarding building a hyperwave transmitter and broadcasting our location, how would one go about finding humans to serve?"

"The indigenous species?" Gamma suggested.

Beta shook his head. "No. They are clearly not human."

"But Master Derec treated them as equals." All three supervisors fell silent.

In a small, hesitant voice, Central said, "A equals B."

Alpha looked up. "What did you say?"

"A equals B," Central repeated.

Alpha looked to Beta. "Do you have any idea what it's talking about?"

"If A equals B, and B equals C," Central said, quite confidently this time, "then A equals C."

Slowly, it dawned on Beta. "Central, is *A* human?"

"Yes."

"And is *B* Master Derec?"

"Yes."

Gamma broke in. "What's *C*, Central?" But the massive idiot had begun softly whistling an inane ditty.

Beta caught Gamma's attention. "Don't you see? If *human* equals Master Derec, and Master Derec treats the local inhabitants as *equals—*"

Gamma's eyes flared brightly. "Then the local inhabitants are equivalent to humans!"

Alpha protested. "Incorrect. A human is a primate of the genus *Homo—*"

Beta and Gamma both turned on Alpha. "We're not saying that the local inhabitants are truly human. We're just saying that they're *equivalent* to humans."

For long seconds, Alpha's eyes went dim. Just when Beta was beginning to worry about whether the supervisor had gone into First Law lockup, Alpha spoke.

"Agreed. For our purposes, we can treat them as near-humans. Now we have a new question: How can we best serve them?"

"That information is unavailable," Gamma said.

Beta considered the question. At the same time, not all of his energies were focused on the question; at a lower level in his brain, he sensed the joyous flow of harmonious potentials that came from finally having a clearly delineated problem to work on. "We must study the local environment," he said at last. "Send out observer robots to study the local inhabitants in their native habitat. Obtain chemical analyses of the substances that are important to their well-being."

"Agreed," Alpha and Gamma said together.

"Above all," Beta continued, "we must allocate all available resources to linguistic studies. We must establish verbal communications with them."

"Agreed."

Alpha stepped back and looked first to Beta and then to Gamma, with a warm glow in his eyes. "Friends, I cannot tell you how satisfied I am with the progress we have made in this meeting. Now, at last, we can fulfill the final goal of our mission."

"I have the greatest confidence in the mission," Central said.

Alpha spit out a message at the maximum rate his commlink would allow. "Meeting adjourned!" Switching their leg motors into high speed mode, the three supervisors hurried from the hall as fast as dignity would allow.

CHAPTER 3

ARANIMAS

The assault team leader licked his lips nervously, as if punishment could be inflicted by hyperwave. "Yes, Master?"

Aranimas fixed the figure on the viewscreen with a glare from both eyes. "I am still waiting for your report. How many robots have you taken? Have you been able to capture the traitor Wolruf, or the human Derec?"

The assault team leader's right eye twitched rapidly, and he licked his lips again. "Actually, Master, we have encountered some, ah, difficulties, and, ah—"

Aranimas leaned in close to the video pickup, and dropped his voice to its most forceful pitch. *"How many robots have you taken?"*

With a fearful glance at his portable communicator, the team leader blurted it out. "None, Master."

"What?"

The team leader smiled helplessly. "We arrived too late. They're all gone. That static we intercepted was the sound of every last robot on the planet teleporting out. Apparently the natives—they call themselves Ceremyons—could not tolerate the robots. So the robots left."

Aranimas spat out several choice curses in his clan's dialect. When he'd recovered some control, he glared at the viewscreen again. "Did they leave any artifacts? Buildings, parts, or tools?"

"Sort of." The team leader turned his video pickup around to capture what he was seeing: a vast lake of liquid metal, crowned with two intersecting parabolic arches. The resolution was poor, but the arches appeared to be jets of silver liquid. "The natives say it's a work of art; they call it 'Negative Feedback.' " He turned the video pickup back on his face again.

Aranimas grumbled and rolled his eyes in counter-rotating circles. "One more chance, then. Have you located the traitor, or the humans?"

The team leader's expression brightened. "Yes, Master."

Aranimas waited a few seconds. When no further information was forthcoming, he said, "Where are they?"

"They left orbit three days ago and are headed in the general direction of Quadrant 224."

Aranimas grumbled again. "Not what I was hoping for. But very well, collect your team and return to the ship."

The team leader licked his lips once more and again blinked nervously. "Actually, Master, we have a little problem with that."

Aranimas' pale face flushed green with anger. "What *now?*"

"The natives are soaring creatures; they obtain lift by inflating their bodies with large amounts of raw hydrogen."

"So?"

"While attempting to extract information, I ordered the shuttle gunner to hit one of the natives with a low-wattage beam. I expected merely to burn the native; instead, it exploded with considerable violence."

"And the shuttle was damaged?"

"Not exactly, Master."

"Not exactly?"

"Master, the surviving natives have sealed the shuttle inside some kind of impenetrable force globe. It doesn't appear to be damaged, but we can't get to it. Could you send the second shuttle to extract us?"

Aranimas' heavy eyelids popped wide open, and his face turned a deep, angry green. "Bumbling fool! You can *rot* there for all the times you have failed me!" He slammed a bony fist down on the horseshoe console, blanking the team leader's face off his viewscreen. "Scanners! There is a ship in Quadrant 224; find it for me. Helm! Prepare to leave orbit immediately, maximum speed." Orders given, he blanked all the screens except one, and through that screen stared out at the glistening starfield in Quadrant 224. Somewhere out there, perhaps one of those tiny points of ninth-magnitude light, was the quarry he had been chasing for so long.

"I swear," he whispered, talking solely to himself, "I have not come this close only to be cheated again."

CHAPTER 4

DEREC

Ariel was in one of her cold and silent moods again. Derec tried to strike up a conversation over breakfast, but all he managed to do was irritate her more.

"Look, Ari," he said, "I know how you feel about losing the baby. I lost my whole *life*. When I woke up in that survival pod on the surface of that asteroid—"

A look of fury flashed into Ariel's eyes, and she fired a buttered scone straight at Derec's face. "Will you *shut up* about that stupid asteroid!"

He ducked the pastry and tried his most soothing voice. "But honey, my amnesia is—"

"Old news! You've been telling me about your frosted amnesia and that crummy little asteroid for the last three years. Don't you have any *other* stories?"

"Well, no, honey. The amnesia—"

"Aagh!" She threw another scone at Derec and this time caught him right between the eyes.

By the time Derec finished wiping the butter off his face, Ariel had locked herself in the bedroom. He briefly considered trying to reason with her through the closed door, and then realized that discretion was the better part of valor. Leaving her sulking in their stateroom, he decided to take a stroll around the upper deck of the good ship *Wild Goose Chase.*

The stroll went almost as badly as the breakfast. Within minutes Derec was thoroughly lost. As he wandered blindly through the great salons and companionways that simply hadn't been there the night before, the temptation to use his internal commlink to call for help grew very strong.

Derec resisted. *Frost,* he thought angrily, *for once I'm going to figure out this mouse-maze myself!* Pausing to visualize the latest floor plan of the deck, he thought once more about what a remarkable—and disturbing—ship it was.

Try as he might, Derec could not get used to the idea that he wasn't aboard a ship so much as he was *inside* an enormous robot. To make matters worse, the *Wild Goose Chase* was no ordinary robot, but rather one of his father's incredible cellular creations, constructed of the same amorphous robotic "cells" as Robot City itself. Back in Robot City, Derec had slowly come to accept that the city constantly rearranged its architecture to suit the perceived needs of its human inhabitants. But out here, in space—*far* out in space— there was something terribly unnerving about the idea of having nothing between himself and the vacuum except a ship's hull that changed shape like a Procyan jellyslug on a hot day.

For example, three days before, when they'd left the planet of the Ceremyons, the *Wild Goose Chase* had been reasonably ship-shaped; long, narrow, and linear, with the control cabin in the nose and the planetary drives in the stern. As soon as they'd cleared the atmosphere, though, the ship had decided to shorten the walking distance between the bridge and the engine room by reconfiguring itself into a thick, flattened disk not unlike an enormous flying three-layer cake. Derec had found being locked inside a Personal during that first transformation to be a terrifying experience. *Of course*, thought Derec, *it was for my own good. There was probably nothing but space on the other side of that door.*

Since then, the ship had continued to reconfigure itself in accordance with the expressed or implied needs of its passengers. Already a gymnasium, a synthe-sun deck, and a zero-G volleyball court had come and gone. These enormous, gaudily decorated new rooms puzzled Derec, though, until he remembered that he and Ariel had talked the night before about an old video she'd once seen. The show was some kind of ancient history swords-'n'-togas epic that took place on a steam-driven riverboat on Old Earth, and Ariel had been trying to make a point about the timeless nature of conflict in man/woman relationships.

But the ship, apparently, had picked up Ariel's appreciation for the sets and attempted to respond by recreating the promenade deck of an ancient Egyptian riverboat. No doubt by evening it would have dug enough Dixieland jazz out of its memory banks to provide music in the ballroom.

With a slight pang, Derec suddenly thought of three robots he'd once known. "The Three Cracked Cheeks would have loved this," he said sadly. "What a pity they're—" he caught himself—"*happily employed elsewhere and couldn't possibly be here,*" he finished loudly. Already, he'd learned to be very careful about what he said out loud aboard the *Wild Goose Chase.* There was no telling what the ship might try to cook up to satisfy a perceived human need, and Derec had no desire to see it resurrecting cybernetic ghosts.

Just beyond the other side of the ballroom, Derec found

a wide staircase that led down. It wasn't quite what he'd been looking for—he'd wanted to find a way to get up to the bridge—but curiosity led him to try the stairs.

The next level down was pure gray utilitarian metal. Even the environmental responses were down to a bare minimum: A puddle of light tracked him down the companionway, switching on two steps ahead of him and switching off two steps behind. The only door he found opened into a tiny, darkened cell.

His mother's three robots were in there. Adam, Eve, and Lucius II stood rigidly frozen in position, their eyes dim, as if someone had made an aluminum sculpture of a three-way conversation. For a moment, Derec's breath quickened. Ever since they'd left Robot City, his father had been itching for a chance to melt the learning machines down into slag, or at the very least shut them down permanently. Had he finally done it?

A quick check of his internal commlink, and Derec relaxed. The three robots weren't deactivated. They were simply locked up in one of their interminable high-bandwidth philosophical discussions. He moved on.

At the end of the hallway, he found a small lift-shaft much like the one on the original asteroid where the robots had found him. It was a simple platform, one meter square, with one three-position switch on the control stalk: up, down, or stop. Obviously intended for robotic use—the sight of a human riding such a contraption would send most robots into First Law conniptions—the platform was also obviously at the top of its guide rail. "Well, that simplifies my choices," Derec said. He stepped onto the platform and pressed *down*.

With a sickening lurch, the platform dropped out from underneath him.

Derec didn't have time to panic. He fell through ten meters of darkness, then brightness flooded the shaft as the platform dropped through into a lighted cabin. Just before he passed through the opening, some kind of localized gravity field caught him and deposited him as gently as a feather, albeit sputtering like a goose, on the deck of the cabin.

Wolruf and Mandelbrot were already there, lounging comfortably in two acceleration couches that faced a large control console. The small, dog-like alien was spooning something that looked like Brussels sprouts in milk out of a bowl and between bites chatting with the patchwork robot. Her furry brown ears went up when Derec hit the floor; together, she and Mandelbrot turned to look at him.

" 'ullo," Wolruf said around a mouthful of greenery. "Nice of 'u to drop in."

Mandelbrot stared at Derec a moment, but did not rise. "Are you hurt?" he asked at last.

"Only my dignity," Derec said, as he got up off the floor and brushed some dust off his posterior.

"That is good," Mandelbrot noted. The robot turned back to Wolruf. "You were saying?"

" 'at can wait," Wolruf said. She favored Derec with a wicked grin, then barked out, "Ship! Master Derec wants t' sit next t' me!"

"That's all right, Wolruf, I can—*what!*" A glob of floor material suddenly mushroomed up under Derec, sweeping him off his feet and catching him like a giant hand. By the time it'd moved up next to Wolruf, it'd formed into another acceleration couch.

Wolruf leaned over, smiling wolfishly, and offered Derec a dripping spoonful of whatever it was she was eating.

" 'u want t' try some *gaach?* Is real good. Put 'air on 'ur face."

Derec looked at the thing on the spoon—which, on closer inspection, looked *nothing* like a Brussels sprout—and shook his head. "Thanks, I, uh, already ate."

Wolruf shrugged as if disappointed. " 'ur loss." With a practiced flip, she tossed the green globule up, then caught it with a frightening snap of her long teeth. "Mmm," she said in a deep, throaty growl that was apparently a sign of delight.

Derec finally recovered something of his composure, and started to look around the cabin he'd dropped into. "What . . . ? Why, this is the *bridge!*"

"T'row 'at boy a milkbone," Wolruf said between bites.

"But last night the bridge was at the *top* of the ship!"

Wolruf favored Derec with a toothy smile. " 'at's right. But 'at was 'en. 'is iss now." Derec kept darting nervous glances around the cabin, as if keeping an eye on everything would stop it from metamorphosing. Wolruf leaned over and put a furry hand on Derec's shoulder. "Face it, Derec. 'ur on a crazy ship." She shrugged.

"But iss not *dangerous* crazy." The little alien finished the last of her *gaach*, then licked the bowl clean with her long pink tongue. "Mmm," she growled again as she tossed the bowl and spoon over her shoulder, to clatter onto the deck.

"Wolruf!" Derec was shocked. "Do you always throw your dirty dishes on the floor?"

She rolled over, smiled innocently, and brought a hand up to start scratching her right ear. "What dishes?"

"Why—," Derec turned to point at it but stopped short. The spoon had already melted into the cabin deck, and only tiny bit of the bowl's rim remained.

"Robot City materral," Wolruf said with a shrug. "So 'ow' Arr'el?"

Derec watched the last trace of the bowl disappear, the sighed. "Still having a rough time."

"Th' baby?" Wolruf asked gently.

"Yeah." Derec fell back onto the couch and stared at his hands. "Ariel is still trying to pretend that she's too tough to mourn, I guess. So instead, she treats me like it's *my* fault she lost the baby." Derec fell silent a minute, thinking about the two-month-old fetus that Ariel had just lost. Maybe it *was* his fault. After all, the embryo's brain had been destroyed by an infestation of chemfets, the same microscopic robotic "cells" that swam in his bloodstream and gave him his incredible biological interface with Robot City. He should have realized that the chemfets were a communicable disease.

"Never 'ad pups myself," Wolruf broke in with a hint of sadness in her voice. "But unnerstand that th' mother gets quite attached t' 'em long b'fore she actually whelps."

"Yeah, well—look, this is depressing. Let's change the subject, okay? How's the flight going?"

" 'u got 'ur depressors, I got mine." Wolruf sat up, and made a wide sweeping gesture that took in the control panel. "Look a' it. Perfect automation. Don't need a pilot 'r navigator. I 'aven't touched a button in t'ree days, and probably won't until we jump tonight. No way I could everr fly 'er 'alf so good." Wolruf's upper lip curled in a silent snarl. " 'ur father ever puts this design on the market, 'ur lookin' at one bitch 'oo's seriously out o' work."

"That's okay," Derec said. "We still love you anyway." To prove the point, he started giving her a reassuring scratch behind the ears.

"Oo! Oo! Don' stop!" When her left foot began twitching

reflexively, though, Wolruf got embarrassed and pulled away from Derec's hand.

Presently, a new thought came to Derec. "Say, speaking of my father, have either of you seen him this morning?" Wolruf shook her head, but Mandelbrot's eyes dimmed for a moment as he checked his internal links.

"Dr. Avery is in the ship's robotics lab," the patchwork robot announced.

"Robotics lab?" Derec repeated.

"Yes. Dr. Avery had it constructed at 0137 hours last night. It is currently on the port side, two levels up."

"Thanks, Mandelbrot." Derec bounced off his acceleration couch, said goodbye to Wolruf, then stepped over to the lift plate—and paused, to glare at the lift plate with obvious misgivings. "Uh, ship?" he said at last. "I don't suppose you could cook up a *stairway*, could you?" In response, a blank wall resolved into an arched passage that led to the bottom end of a spiral staircase. "Thanks, ship." Derec stepped through the passage and started up.

CHAPTER 5

MAVERICK

Dusk came to the mountainside forest with the soft chittering of waking nightclimbers and the plaintive cooing of lovesick redwings. It came on a gentle southerly breeze that spoke of young green shoots bravely thrusting up through the warm, damp soil, and twisted old trees grudgingly coming to life again after yet another long dormant season.

Like the silent gray ghost of the winter just past, Maverick padded quietly through the lengthening shadows of the tall trees, alert to the soft sounds and drinking in the earthy smells of the warm spring evening.

He moved quickly and confidently across the needle-covered forest floor, as befitted an eighty-kilo carnivore with something on his mind. Yet there was a nervous twitch in his naked, whiplike tail that suggested different emotions at work; an occasional darting glance over his shoulder suggested he was not as brave as he seemed. At the edge of a clearing, as he stopped and stood up on his hind legs, it became apparent that he was favoring his left rear leg. For a moment the breeze ruffled his mottled grayish-brown fur, exposing the long pink scar of a recently healed wound; he was leaning against the tree trunk for support, not cover. Closing his ice-blue eyes, he lifted his muzzle and tasted the air.

A faint, acrid scent caught his attention. "Sharpfang!" He added a guttural curse in BeastTongue; as if in answer, a deep bellow echoed across the valley.

Maverick's long, fur-covered ears shot up, and a look of puzzlement crossed his wolf-like face. "*That's* not right." He closed his eyes again, cocked his head sideways, and tried to concentrate on what the wind was telling him. "A female scent, but a male roar?" The bellow sounded again—quite nearby now—this time accompanied by the loud, rending crack of a fair-sized tree being knocked flat.

Maverick's eyes snapped wide open, and he grabbed for the stone knife in the scabbard on his left shoulder as if a knife could really be of use against a hungry sharpfang. A moment later the beast leaped into view not fifty trots away across the clearing, and Maverick froze.

The giant reptile charged across the clearing on its two massive hind legs, ploughing through the undergrowth and crushing everything in its way like a scaly brown juggernaut. Maverick stood rooted in one spot, staring at onrushing death. The sharpfang's head was huge; long, armored, and bristling with teeth, it whipped back and forth as if the beast had brain enough to feel fury. Long-taloned hind feet slashed through the brush; the thick, muscular tail trailing behind thrashed whatever had survived the talons into a pulpy green mass.

The sharpfang did not even break stride as it raised its head and opened its great jaws to roar again.

For a long fraction of a second, Maverick watched the dying sunlight flash off the beast's long wet fangs. Then he sniffed the air again, let out an anxious little whine, and dropped his ears in hope. Maybe, just maybe, the toothy monster wasn't interested in *him*. Allowing for windage, there was a family-minded female sharpfang down in the marsh about six hundred trots off to his left.

And if he were wrong?

Maverick carefully loosened the knife in its scabbard. With his injured leg, he knew he couldn't outrun the sharpfang. That left him only one other option: Wait until the beast was close enough to lick, and then hope that a fast and intelligent counterattack could overcome its overwhelming but mindless strength. He shifted his weight onto the balls of his feet. Reflexively, his naked, whip-like tail tucked itself between his legs and coiled around his thigh. He had to wait for the right moment; *exactly* the right moment. . . .

A moment later the advancing sharpfang apparently caught a whiff of the female and had a change of heart. It veered off toward the marsh. Saplings crunched; redwings screeched; Maverick stood his ground and pretended to be a tree stump. The beast passed close enough for him to take a long look straight into the fiery, bottomless red pit of its left eye.

Another moment later, and it was gone. Ears erect, Maverick listened to the crunching and roaring as it receded into the distance. Then he lolled out his long pink tongue, wuffed out a little laugh, and cracked into a wide, extremely relieved, panting grin. "They say love has no sense of smell. I'd guess it's blind, too."

He dropped to all fours, nosed around the base of the tree, marked it with his scent, and gave the male sharpfang more time to see if it was coming back for another pass or being followed by any competitors. When the forest at last grew quiet again, save for the thrashing and bellowing of giant lizards in love, he slipped the knife back into its scabbard and set off toward the northwest at a rapid trot.

"Well, Mavvy old boy," he told himself as he jogged along, "I'd say you handled that pretty well. There's not many kin who'd stand up to a charging sharpfang like that.

"Of course, the old ones always said that it's the running away that attracts their attention."

He paused to sniff around the base of a rock outcropping and mark it with his scent. Then he went on.

"But here's another thought: Their eyes are on opposite sides of their heads. Maybe the reason sharpfangs swing their heads when they walk is because they can't see what's straight in front of them.

"Interesting idea, Mavvy. So the best way to attack a sharpfang is from right under its chin? That little piece of information ought to be worth something to the next pack we run into." At the thought of a pack, his left rear leg gave him a little twinge to remind him of the last pack he'd run into. "Ooh. A bad night for rock climbing, old boy. Still, it's got to be done."

After a year as a packless outcast, Maverick had stopped noticing that his silent thoughts had turned into one-kin conversations.

He detoured around a patch of stingwort, stopped to mark another tree, and then continued. "But while we're on the subject of sharpfangs: Mother, they sure are noisy things, aren't they? It's a wonder they ever manage to surprise a hunting pack.

"Actually, no it isn't. The kin in hunting packs spend so much time arguing with each other and bickering over status, the wonder is that *they* are ever able to surprise anything."

As the last ebb of the sunlight slipped away, Maverick finally broke out of the tall forest and reached the foothills. He sat down, paused for a reflective scratch, and stared up at the forbidding, rocky crags.

"Yes," he told himself, "running solo is definitely the way to go. No status fights, no orders, no drooling little pups slowing you down."

His voice took a darker turn. "No food, no warm cave to sleep in, no family." Maverick's voice dropped to a breathy whisper, as if he had finally become aware that he was talking to himself. "Let's face it, lad. We've been on the run too long. We—*I* have got to find a pack to join." He thought back on the winter he'd just lived through and shuddered involuntarily. "I've got to find a pack *soon*." Taking a deep breath, he dug his paws into the loose gravel and started up the side of the mountain. Smallface, the lesser of the two moons, was just rising. He had a lot of climbing to do before Largeface rose.

Halfway up the slope, he surprised a feeding whistlepig. The stupid little furball tried to hide in plain sight; scrabbling and clawing, Maverick fell on it and bit its head off with one snap of his long, toothy jaws. The meat was tough and nearly tasteless, but he carefully chewed and swallowed each bite.

Excluding carrion, it was the first meal he'd eaten in three days.

CHAPTER 6

JANET

Robotic Law potentials danced and capered in Basalom's positronic brain like fireflies on hyperdrive. Impulses and reactions chased each other through his circuits, laughing riotously as molecular relays burst open and slammed shut like hallway doors in an old comedy routine. As much as a robot can be said to enjoy anything, Basalom was beginning to *enjoy* the incredibly complex nets of conflicting potentials that wove themselves inside his brain. Now, with the latest news just in from the scanning team, an entirely new dimension was added to his decision matrix, imparting a wonderful sense of energy to his cognition circuits. The potentials glittered in his mind like an Auroran filterbug's web on a dewy morning.

Dr. Anastasi was *not* going to like the scanning team's report.

First and Second Law conflicts skirmished in his brain, fighting for priority. Each time his decision gate flip-flopped, the stress register escalated. When the register hit 256, the accumulated potential was shunted to ground through his optical perceptor membrane actuator.

In simpler terms, he blinked.

Dr. Anastasi finished her business in the Personal and emerged into the companionway. Basalom blinked once more to clear his stress register and then addressed his mistress.

"Dr. Anastasi? The scanning team reports finding no trace of Learning Machine #1."

"What?"

Again, a surging clash of potentials! How could he obey the implied Second Law command to repeat and clarify the message without violating the First Law by insulting her intelligence?

Basalom settled for slowing his voice clock rate by ten percent and augmenting his speech with "warm" harmonics in the two-kilohertz range. "For the past eight hours, the scanning team has worked outward in an expanding radial pattern from the landing site. Within the limits of their equipment, they have not been able to find any evidence of Learning Machine #1's existence."

Dr. Anastasi ran a hand through her hair. "That's impossible. It was powered by a cold microfusion cell. Even if the learning machine was completely destroyed, they still should be able to pick up residual neutron radiation from the power pack." Then a thought crossed her mind, and she frowned. "Unless Derec . . ."

She shook her head. "No, a coincidence like that would strain credulity. The scanning crew must have made some mistake." She turned and started up the companionway toward the bow of the ship. "Well? Come along, Basalom."

Basalom was almost disappointed. His lovely, complex decision matrix resolved to simple Second Law obedience, and he dutifully fell in behind.

To minimize the effect of stray radiation from the ship's engines on delicate equipment, the scanning team's cabin was located in a blister on the underside of the uttermost bow of the ship. To get to the blister, Basalom and Dr. Anastasi had to leave the cargo bay laboratory, walk the entire length of the living quarters, and then drop down one level to the low-ceilinged companionway that ran beneath the bridge. For the last ten meters, they had to pull themselves along handholds through a narrow, zero-gravity access tube.

Along the way, to keep his mind busy, Basalom reopened his human viewpoint simulation file. He had more observations to add to the file and more data to correlate. In particular, Basalom wanted to record an effect that he had noticed twice before: That Dr. Janet, when given information she did not like, would insist on traveling to the source and verifying the information herself.

This must be a corollary effect of having a purely local viewpoint, Basalom decided. *Dr. Anastasi would rather believe that a severe failure has occurred in her information gathering systems than accept unpleasant information.*

Basalom logged, indexed, and stored the observation. *Someday I will meet robots who have been observing other humans in a similar fashion. Perhaps then we will be able to integrate our data and formulate fundamental laws of human behavior.*

Perhaps someday, Basalom repeated. But given the way Dr. Anastasi shunned human society, it was not likely to be any time soon.

Puffing with exertion and the indignity of it all, Dr. Anastasi pushed off the last handhold in the access tube and floated into the scanning blister. A moment later Basalom followed; he immediately noted that the four robots that made up the scanning team were still jacked into their consoles. He fired off a quick commburst suggesting that they turn around and look sharp. Slowly, awkwardly, the four robots began disconnecting their umbilical cables, detaching themselves from their consoles, and switching over to their local senses.

Looking at the squat, blocky machines, Basalom felt a surge of the positronic flux that he identified as a feeling of superiority. The scanning team robots were plain metallic automatons designed expressly for work in zero-G. They had ungainly, boxlike bodies, no heads to speak of, and in place of proper arms and legs, eight multi-jointed limbs that ended in simple metal claws. Since the bulk of their sensory data was routed through the scanning consoles, they came equipped with the bare minimum of human-interface hardware: one audio input/output membrane and a pair of monochrome optics on stalks. The effect, Basalom decided, resembled nothing so much as a quartet of giant softshell crabs.

Strike that. Basalom ran a quick cross-reference through his metaphor library. *Make that, they look like giant lice.*

Dr. Anastasi was still waiting patiently for the scanning team to finish disconnecting themselves, so Basalom allocated a few microseconds for comparative analysis. *They are crude, functional devices. I have a humanoid configuration, human-like limbs, and an acceptably human face.*

They are little more than human-friendly front-ends for the machines that they are connected to. I am intelligent, perceptive, and equipped with refined sensibilities.

Verily, I am molded in the image of my Maker!

Then a new, unknown potential surged through Basalom's circuits, and he reevaluated the results of his analysis.

Still, they are my positronic brothers, and I must help them elevate themselves if I can.

Basalom didn't realize it, but he had just become the first robot in history to be condescending.

The last of the scanning robots finished disconnecting itself from its instrument console. As one, the four robots rotated their sensory turrets to "face" Dr. Anastasi.

When she was sure she had their attention, Janet began issuing commands. "Eyes, Ears, Nose, and Throat! Report!" As soon as that last word left her lips, Basalom anticipated the cacophony that would result from a literal interpretation of that order and jumped in on the commlink. *Override*, he squirted out to the scanning robots. *Report sequentially.*

The scanning robots seemed to accept his authority. Eyes, the robot in charge of scanning in the infrared through ultra-violet portion of the spectrum, began reporting first in a flat, toneless voice.

"Using the design information available for Learning Machine #1, I projected its range of possible operational profiles and thermal dispersion patterns. I found no infrared sources in the target area which met this criteria.

"Next, I used the solar spectrographic information and atmospheric data supplied by Nose, along with our knowledge of Learning Machine #1's physical structure, to compute the albedo—"

Basalom interrupted via hyperwave. *Explain albedo.*

"—That is, the optical wavelength reflectivity of its skin. Allowing a 15-percent variance for self-directed changes in surface texture, I still was unable to identify any objects which showed a high probability of being either part or all of the learning machine.

"Finally, based on the knowledge that the 'cells' that compose the learning machine are actually polyhedrons with microplanar surfaces, I scanned for moiré patterns in the ultraviolet range. Aside from the aeroshell in which the learning machine landed, I found nothing to match my search profile."

Good job, Eyes. The squat little robot did not acknowledge Basalom's compliment.

Dr. Anastasi nodded thoughtfully. "I see. Next?"

Ears, the robot in charge of monitoring the microwave through hyperwave portion of the spectrum, began reporting in an identical monotonous voice. "While I have been able to locate the transponder on the aeroshell, I have not received any signals from Learning Machine #1's built-in hyperwave transponder. Nor have I been able to detect any leakage of the kind that should be associated with the operation of the learning machine."

Dr. Anastasi's brow wrinkled.

Explain leakage, Basalom hyperwaved.

"When operating, all cybernetic circuits emit a certain amount of electromagnetic radiation. If we are familiar with the design of the device, we can project the frequency and data encryption of the leakage. No leakage conforming to the learning machine's profile was found."

Dr. Anastasi nodded. "I understand."

"Learning Machine #1 was equipped with an internal commlink," Ears went on. "I have been monitoring the base channel that you assigned to it, but I have been unable to pick up any signals originating from Learning Machine #1."

Dr. Anastasi frowned. "Okay, I hear what you're saying. Next?"

Nose, the robot in charge of spectrography and chemical analysis, spoke up. It was equipped with the same voice synthesizer as Eyes and Ears, but Basalom noted that a microscopic crack in Nose's voice diaphragm gave it an interesting third-harmonic distortion.

"My specialties are of limited use in this situation. However, I was able to coordinate with the other units. I provided Eyes with spectrographic data regarding the Tau Puppis sunlight and a summary analysis of the planetary atmosphere. Beyond that, I am unable to contribute."

Dr. Anastasi frowned. "Hmm. Something smells fishy about that. I'll have to think it over. Next?"

Throat, the robot in charge of outbound telecommunications, spoke last. "Due to our inability to locate the learning machine, laser and maser communications were not attempted. I have been broadcasting continuous messages on the learning machine's internal commlink frequency. However, as Ears reported, there has been no response."

Dr. Anastasi shot Throat a cold stare. "You don't say?"

That was a rhetorical question, Basalom added. *Do not answer.* The robot held its silence.

Dr. Anastasi looked the scanning crew over one more time and screwed her face up into a look of complete disgust. "I can't believe this," she said finally. "You robots have been scanning that ball of dirt for eight hours and you haven't found *anything?*"

Throat did not wait for a cue from Basalom, but simply spoke right up. "On the contrary, Dr. Anastasi, we have found a great deal. However, none of it matches the profile of either the learning machine or its damaged remains."

Dr. Anastasi forgot about Newton's laws for a moment and waved a hand to cut Throat off. Unfortunately, since she was floating in zero-G, the action sent her spinning toward the neutrino detector. Basalom gently caught her and stabilized her.

"You found something? *What?*"

Eyes answered the question. "I have detected a significant number of large lifeforms in the area of the landing site. The largest appears to be a warm-blooded grazing animal. The next largest appears to be a cold-blooded predator which follows the grazing animals as they migrate. Since we do not know the final shape of the learning machine, I can tell you only that the average predator outweighs the learning machine by a factor of four to one."

Dr. Anastasi frowned. "Oh, great. So our learning machine ran into a monster and got itself demolished."

The scanning robots conferred briefly by commlink. "It is possible," Throat said. "However, in that case we would still expect to find identifiable wreckage. At the very least, we should be able to locate the microfusion cell. We have not found either."

"Moreover," Eyes continued seamlessly, "I have detected a number of clustered infrared sources. The sources are almost always found in the vicinity of what appear to be limestone caves, and the next largest class of lifeforms are generally found clustered around the infrared sources."

Dr. Anastasi looked from one robotic "face" to the next with a very puzzled look in her eyes.

Basalom squirted out a hyperwave message to the scanning team. *Clarify!*

"I studied the spectrographic signatures of the infrared sources," Nose said. "I detected cellulose, chlorophyll, carbon, and pyroligneous acid."

"So our intelligent lupoids are still down there. But they couldn't have destroyed the learning machine, and they sure couldn't have removed all traces of it.

"If the robot were inside a cave, would you be able to detect it?"

Eyes, Ears, Nose, and Throat conferred briefly. Ears

spoke when they had finished. "The commlink would penetrate all but the deepest caves. Small amounts of positronic leakage from the brain should also be detectable. I detected neither."

"So something is rotten in the state of Denmark," Dr. Anastasi said.

Basalom was still trying to parse out the metaphor when Janet kicked off the wall and dove into the access tube. "Let's get out of here. I need time to think."

As he followed, Basalom reopened his human viewpoint file and made another entry. *When Dr. Anastasi wants to avoid having to make a decision, she moves to a different part of the ship and claims a need to think. Does physical location have a significant effect on human cogitative abilities?* He logged and indexed the entry; as he was storing it, a dialogue box popped open in the upper left corner of his field of view.

Basalom? It was Eyes. *This reaction puzzles us. Have we harmed Mistress Janet by giving her this information?*

Basalom responded via commlink. *I am still trying to determine the First Law implications of emotional distress.*

Oh. Eyes was not a particularly bright robot, but it was self-aware enough to realize that it lacked experience in the subtleties of dealing with humans. *In that case, perhaps you are best qualified to judge whether or not we should report our one additional finding.*

I will try. What is it?

There was a pause; nothing a human would have noticed, but Basalom could plainly see that the scanning robot was having difficulty integrating the information. *While we were unable to locate the specific communications and energy signatures of Learning Machine #1, we did record a significant amount of other robotic activity.*

Basalom's curiosity bits skyrocketed. *Other robotic activity? Explain.*

The little robot made one more try at generating a conclusion from its data and then gave up. *I cannot. Stand by for download of raw data.*

Basalom cleared several of his unused memory banks, redirected his I/O to fast storage, and opened his multiplex comm channel. *Ready.* A nanosecond later, a torrent of raw data flooded into Basalom's mind. As fast as he could, he sorted, collated, and organized the data. Pushing it through his pattern-recognition algorithm, he tried to isolate and identify the most important points.

One by one, the points swam into clear focus. They quickly formed a structure, a simple pattern that teased comparative memories out of his long-term data storage.

Oh no. His stress register started clicking like a geiger counter, and the pattern took on an ever-more-familiar shape. *It can't be.* His First Law sense began to itch like mad as the Second Law potential tried to find a route to ground. One word got out through the First Law filter: "Madam?"

Dr. Anastasi paused in the tube and looked over her shoulder at Basalom. "Yes?"

Power flowed through Basalom's cognitive circuits like strong wine. Thoughts spun and danced; potentials crashed and exploded like thunderclouds on a hot summer night.

"Madam, there—" The First Law choked him off again.

A concerned look crossed Dr. Anastasi's face. "Well?"

In Basalom's mind, the First and Second Law collided head-on, drew apart, and collided again. Neither was the clear winner; he sought desperately to reroute data to his speech centers.

"Ma—"

Dr. Anastasi grew impatient. "Come on, Basalom. Spit it out."

His limbs froze; his major joints locked up. He blinked sixty-four times in rapid succession, and then through sheer force of will dumped his speech buffer through his voice synthesizer.

"There is a Robot City on this planet."

CHAPTER 7

MAVERICK

The spur of rock jutted straight out from the side of the mountain forming a natural balcony. Maverick sat on the edge of the spur, drinking in the clean pine smell of the forested valley below and watching the moons' light glitter and dance on the river in the distance. Smallface was now near its zenith, and it cast a cool, white light with almost no shadow. Largeface, just barely above the horizon, was a dull orange globe the color and shape of a vingfruit with a bite taken out of it.

Somehow, the sight of the two moons together in the sky stirred something deep and primal in Maverick's soul. As if the two were directly linked, his excitement grew as Largeface rose. He paced nervously around the rock spur. A half-dozen times he yelped sharply when he thought he heard something. His excitement only grew stronger when the sounds turned out to be false alarms.

Then the sound he'd been waiting for came wafting gently on the wind, and it was raw, beautiful, and absolutely unmistakable.

At first, it was very soft and distant. *Arooo.* Just one voice at first, lonely, plaintive, and far away. The sound sent chill up and down Maverick's spine and set his hackles standing on end.

Then another voice joined in, a little closer. *Arooooo!* The first voice responded, and the forests and mountains threw back the echo of the ancient, wordless cry.

No, those weren't echoes, those were yet more voices, joining in the chorus of a song that was as old as his race. Voices joined, and picked up, and repeated. *AROOO!* The call carried for miles across the hills and valleys. Not just miles; hundreds of miles, as the voices followed the rising moon west across the land. As it had on certain nights for thousands of years, the song chased the twin moons clear across the world, from the eastern shores to the western sea.

When he judged the time to be right, Maverick threw his head back, flattened his ears, and joined in. *AROOOO! I am Maverick! I am here, my brothers! I join you! AROOOOOO!*

Other intelligible words began rising out of the joyous, incoherent howl of BeastTongue. *I am ChippedFang.*

I am DoesNotFollow.

I am RaggedEar.

I am SmellsBad. I join you!

The Howl Network had just come on line.

The Howl Network reached from sea to sea, and from the land of AlwaysSnow to the Uncrossable Desert. It covered the land, but it was not terribly efficient. Maverick had plenty of time to think while listening to the threads of news that twisted through the air.

This time, though, he thought silently. *How strange, lad. The pack-kin insult and despise the outcasts. If they catch you in their territory—and outnumber you by at least three to one—they'll attack you, and even try to kill you.*

Yet if it weren't for the outcasts, not a one of them would ever know what was happening just fifty trots outside his pack's territory.

Oops. A message that he found interesting echoed through the night. Maverick picked it up, repeated it, and added a few comments of his own. Then he went back to thinking.

Hmm. I add comments, and ChippedFang adds comments, and DoesNotFollow adds comments. . . . Might be interesting sometime to get the originator and the final receiver of the message together, to see how much the message changes along the line.

More messages wafted through the damp spring air. Weather reports from out west; looked like heavy rain this year. Further accounts of renewed fighting between two feuding packs in the southeast; oh, those two had been fighting for years without resolution. A hunting report on the grazer migration in the north; it seemed the calves were fat and slow this year, and the sharpfangs few in number. Maverick dutifully picked up and repeated each message without comment, then went back to his first line of thought.

Yes, the pack-kin hate loners. They attack you; they warn their pups that they'll turn out like you if they aren't good. They call you pups of the FirstBeast, and blame you for everything that's wrong with their cozy little world.

Maverick thought of the last pack he'd encountered, less than a week before. The freshly healed scar on his leg gave him another sharp twinge, but he smiled anyway, and for a moment lost himself in a memory of soft young fur and a certain long pink tongue.

Yes, the pack-kin hate you. But on warm spring evenings

when the mood is in the air, their virgin daughters seek you out.

And when their huntleaders are all dead or driven off by internal fighting, who do they ask to be their new leaders?

Maverick stood up on all fours a moment, yawned as wide as his jaw would allow, and indulged in a long stretch that ran from his haunches clear out to the toes of his fore-paws. Then he treated himself to one more smile.

"Face it, kid. They're just plain jealous."

Oops! A new message was coming through the night, and he'd almost missed it. Maverick quickly sat down, cocked his ears, and listened attentively to the voice—he thought it was RaggedEar—that relayed the story.

"—report from the eastern lakes country. The kin of PackHome are seeing GodBeings again.

"PackHome was the scene of last year's so-called 'Hill of Stars' incident, in which an enormous, shining sanddigger's nest reportedly appeared in the midst of isolated hunting territory.

"The sudden appearance of the Hill of Stars was accompanied by an invasion of 'WalkingStones.' These creatures, which walked on their hind legs at all times and had no smell, killed several kin by throwing lightning from their fingertips.

"At about the same time, a mysterious kin known as SilverSides joined the pack. She destroyed several of the WalkingStones, and forced the GodBeing that lived in the Hill of Stars to come out for single combat. Local kin say that SilverSides became a GodBeing herself and went into the Hill of Stars.

"Since then, SilverSides has been seen only once, in the company of a strange, half-kin, half-GodBeing creature named Wolruf."

Wolruf? Maverick wondered. *What's a wolruf?*

"LifeCrier, who speaks the history for the kin of PackHome, says that SilverSides was a gift of the OldMother and has returned to her. LifeCrier insists that SilverSides will return to lead the hunt and protect all the kin.

"Young kin from many packs have come to the eastern lakes country to hear LifeCrier speak and hoping to glimpse the GodBeings. But there are stories of widespread confusion.

"In the meantime, the faithful wait, and the Hill of Stars itself remains silent. This report was first cried by Storm-Bringer on the eastern lakes echo."

Maverick sat quietly a few moments longer, listening to the last reverberations of the message die out against the mountainside. Then the yips and howls started up again as other kin picked up the story and repeated it. Maverick cleared his throat, laid his ears back, took a deep breath—

And thought better of it. "PackHome, eh? In the eastern lakes country?" He squeezed out a tight-lipped smile, got to his feet, and trotted over to where the spur of rock joined the side of the mountain. "Sounds like a chaotic, leaderless mess to me." At the top of the trail he paused to look at the stars and get a good fix on the direction he was heading. Then he started carefully picking his way down the talus-covered slope.

"Just the place for a strong kin with a little ambition, eh, lad?"

He looked up at the stars one more time and noted that LargeFace was now well up in the sky. In this phase the shadowy outline of SplitEar, the kin in the moon, stood out very clearly.

Maverick couldn't help but feel that old SplitEar, first pup of the OldMother, was smiling down on him.

CHAPTER 8

DEREC

Dr. Avery was hunched over a data terminal in the ship's robotics lab, deeply engrossed in a dense mass of hex code, when Derec called out, "Hi, Dad!" and came bouncing into the room.

Avery pulled his face away from the terminal just long enough to glare at Derec. "Will you please stop calling me that?" he asked, his white mustache bristling with anger. "You know how much it annoys me."

"Sure, Dad."

Avery shot his son one more if-looks-could-kill glance, ran his fingers through his long white hair, and turned back to the terminal. He would never have said it out loud, of course, but in his heart, Avery admitted that Derec certainly had every right to try to annoy him. After all, it was Avery's megalomaniacal experiment that had erased Derec's memory and infected Ariel with amnemonic plague. Now he could not reconstruct how, in his madness, he had caused the amnesia, much less how to reverse it. And while his little chemfet nanomachines had ultimately worked to perfection, they'd nearly killed Derec twice, and they *had* killed Derec and Ariel's unborn child.

Given all that, Avery resolved once more to put up with whatever juvenile revenge Derec was in the mood to exact today. He waited patiently while Derec found a noisy tin stool, dragged it over, and sat down. Then, when it appeared that Derec wasn't going to say anything, he called up another bloc of code.

"Whatcha doing, Dad?" Derec asked brightly.

Avery sighed and turned to his son. "I'm going through the ship's systems software, in hopes of finding the shape-changing algorithm."

"Why?"

"I'd like to stop the polymorphism, or at least slow it down a great deal."

"Why?"

Avery sighed again and ran his fingers through his hair. *That's one of the problems with having children raised by robots,* he thought. *When they're about three years old, they go through a "Why, daddy?" stage. The Second Law forces the robots to answer. So the kids never outgrow it.*

Avery straightened his lab coat, pasted on his best imitation paternal smile, and answered the question with another question.

"Have you ever walked off the edge of a gravity field?"

Derec sifted through his attenuated memories. "I don't think so. Why?"

"I did, last night. You've seen how minimal the environment on the second deck is? I was looking for Lucius last night and I walked into a pitch-dark cabin that had no gravity field."

"What happened?"

"When you reach the edge of a gravity field, you don't

float up into the air. Rather, *down* suddenly becomes the floor of the room you just left. There's no sensation of falling; you simply pivot on the doorsill and follow the field through a 90-degree curve."

"So"

"Have you ever heard the expression, 'the floor jumped up and hit me in the face'?"

Derec snickered.

"Blast it, Derec, it's not funny! If the floor hadn't realized what was going on and softened itself an instant before impact I would have broken my nose!"

Derec tried to keep the laugh suppressed, but a small giggle found a crack and wiggled through.

Avery scowled at Derec through his bushy white eyebrows. "You think that's funny? This morning I happened to think out loud that I needed to use the Personal, and frost me if the chair I was sitting on didn't transform itself into a toilet!" Avery shot a savage glare at the ceiling of the cabin. "And no, I do *not* need to use the Personal now!" His chair, which had begun to soften around the edges, quickly firmed up again.

Derec sputtered twice and then exploded into uncontrolled laughter.

Avery's scowl melted. "Okay, maybe it's a *little* funny. But I'll tell you, the thing that finally pushed me over the edge was the nightmare I had about one this morning. I dreamed that the ship had transformed itself into a giant humanoid robot and was insisting that its name was 'Optimus Prime.'"

Derec abruptly stopped laughing, and his face went pale. "Gad, that's a horrible thought."

"Woke *me* up in a cold sweat, I can tell you."

After a few seconds of thoughtful silence, Avery turned

back to his workstation and slapped a hand on the data display. "Anyway, that's when I decided that the shape-changing program had to go. Or at least, it had to get toned down some." He looked at Derec, attempted a tentative smile, and then looked around the robotics lab.

"You know, son, there are some really good ideas here. Take this ship's skin, for instance; cellular robotics is the perfect technology for seamless, self-sealing spacecraft hulls. If we could just find some way to bond the robotic skin permanently to a titanium-aluminide frame, we might really be on to something." He turned to Derec and cautiously met his eyes.

"Derec? When we get back to Robot City, we're going to have to work on this design some more."

Derec nodded and looked away. He never enjoyed admitting it, but every once in a great while his father could be right.

While Derec's face was turned, Avery stole a few moments to really *look* at his son. It was funny, but despite the nearly twenty years that had passed since Derec was born, Avery couldn't remember ever once just looking at the boy and seeing him for what he was. He'd always looked at the boy and seen what he wanted him to *become*. For most of the boy's life, Avery now noted with a little sadness, he'd treated Derec more like an experiment than a son.

Derec. Even that name was part of an experiment. The boy's real name was David, but Avery had wiped out that memory along with everything else. This young man who stood before him now, fidgeting uncomfortably and staring at the wall—this *Derec*—was a stranger.

But blood will tell. While Derec looked away; Avery studied the line of his jaw and the shape of his cheekbones. He saw his ex-wife Janet's genes everywhere; from the sandy blond hair, through the pale complexion, to his thin, expressive lips.

And what did I give you, my son? Avery didn't need to ask; he knew he'd given Derec the traits that didn't show. *I gave you my temper, I'm sorry to say. I gave you my coldness, and my fear of being vulnerable.* Not for the first time, Avery felt a sudden need to hug his son.

The moment passed. *I'm sorry, Derec. I can't open up either.* Still, that didn't mean he couldn't build just a little bridge, did it? Avery decided to take a chance.

"So what do you think, Derec? Would you like to give me a hand? The ship can cough up another robotics terminal in a couple of minutes, and I could use the help."

Well, son? Please?

Derec said nothing, but his face turned tight and thoughtful. Avery watched closely; Derec's body language said that he was trying to say yes. The word was working its way up his lips, but it was a fight every inch of the way. It had started in his gut, clawed its way up his esophagus, and traversed his soft palate. It was on his tongue now; at any moment it would break through to his lips. Derec started to open his mouth—

The intercom buzzed. It was Wolruf.

"Derec? We got somethin' 'ere. 'u better come 'ave a look at it."

Derec broke concentration, swallowed hard, and turned to the intercom panel. "Can it wait? I'm a little tied up at the moment."

Wolruf growled something in her native tongue. "Think 'u better come look at this *now*."

"Oh, okay." Derec turned to his father, cracked a weak smile, and shrugged. "Sorry, I have to, you know." He gestured toward the intercom and left the sentence hanging.

"That's okay. We can continue this another time." Avery offered Derec a smile.

Derec just looked at his feet and shrugged again. "Sure. If you want." Another hesitation, and then he turned and darted through a pair of open lift doors that had appeared in the cabin wall.

The lift doors hissed open, and Derec stepped out onto the bridge. Mandelbrot stood in one corner, staring intently at the external visual display and conversing with a data terminal. Wolruf was crouched over the main control console, her thick, sausage-like fingers flying over the controls like a multisynth player performing Mothersbaugh's "Toccata and Fugue in .25 Kilohertz." As she punched keys and adjusted sliders, she kept up a steady stream of short, guttural commands in both broken English and her native language. The console seemed to be accepting both with equal ease.

The lift doors slid shut. Derec cleared his throat and said, "Okay, Wolruf. Where's all the excitement?"

Wolruf neither turned around nor took her hands off the controls. Instead, she simply lifted her head a little and pointed her nose at the visual display. " 'ere."

Derec looked at the display. It was the view astern, he guessed; the exceptionally bright star off to the right side looked about the right color to be the Ceremyon's sun. Aside from that star, though, he saw nothing that appeared out of place on the usual visiplate starfield.

"So? I don't see anything."

Wolruf growled something untranslatable and started pounding on a different section the control console. "Sorry. Keep forgettin' 'u 'umans eyes are almos' as weak as 'ur nose." The visual display shifted, blurred, and came into focus again.

More starfield. Only this time there was a tiny, smudgy gray blob in the middle of the screen.

"Okay, I see it now," Derec said. "What is it?" He moved to stand next to Wolruf, but the blob wasn't any more meaningful when viewed close-up.

Wolruf glared at the little blob and bared her teeth. "Ast'roid," she said with a growl.

Derec looked at her. "All this fuss over an asteroid?"

"This 'uns been gainin' on us for eight hours."

"What!" Derec spun around and looked at the visual display. The blob still wasn't any more meaningful than it was before.

Wolruf punched in a few more commands, and the display went back to its original image. This time, though, a graceful blue curve was superimposed over the starfield. "Allowing f'r mass, and all known gravitational vectors includin' th' cavitation effect of 'ur drives, here's th' projected orbit for th' ast'roid." She punched two more keys, and a jagged red line twined around the blue.

"And 'ere's its actual course."

Cautiously, Derec touched the visiplate. He traced the red line with a finger, stopping on one particularly sharp bend. "Any known phenomena that could cause this?"

Wolruf shook her head.

" 'At bend 'u got 'ur finger on iss a manual course correction I made ten minutes ago." Wolruf continued. "Five minutes later, the ast'roid changed course to match."

Wolruf paused to lay her ears back and look Derec straight in the eye.

"Derec, 'at ast'roid iss under *power*."

Derec studied the visual display a bit more and then

looked back to Wolruf. "Recommended action?"

Wolruf gritted her teeth and crouched low over the controls. "Recommend we find out 'oo's behind it. Also recommend 'u find 'urself a seat. 'iss could get a littl' *rough*." She shot a fierce grin at Mandelbrot, then slapped a finger down on the intercom button. "Arr'el? Dr. Av'ry? 'old on tight, we're makin' an unprogrammed course correction. *Now*."

An acceleration couch popped up out of the cabin deck; Derec just barely had time to dive into it before Wolruf slammed the ship into a violent roll. The starfield in the viewplate spun dizzily.

The ship was still rolling when Wolruf hit the main thrusters.

In all, the experience wasn't as jarring as Derec had expected. The ship's gravity fields did an exceptionally good job of compensating for the changing gravity and thrust vectors. Unfortunately, they didn't do a thing for Coriolis force. Within instants, Derec was feeling thoroughly dizzy and a little nauseated. He wondered how Ariel was taking it.

Then he wondered about something else; about a story he'd once read. "Wait a minute, Wolruf. This won't work."

Wolruf cocked an ear at Derec, but kept flying.

"It can't work. The angles of incidence are all wrong. If someone's behind that asteroid, all he has to do is use his maneuvering thrusters to keep the rock between him and us. The asteroid's too small for us to enter a gravitational orbit; at this range, there's no other way we can fly around it faster than he can maneuver around it."

Wolruf kept flying. Mandelbrot, back in the corner, spoke up. "Mistress Wolruf has already thought of that. I have all ship's sensors locked on the asteroid. If the unknown vessel emits any form of radiation or hot gasses during maneuvering, we will detect it."

" 'sides," Wolruf growled, " 'aven't 'u ever 'eard of spookin' 'im out? If 'e's got some kind of remote sensor watching us, 'e now knows we know 'e's there. No point in 'im staying 'idden any more."

As if in confirmation of Wolruf's statement, Mandelbrot said, "Contact. A stream of superheated boron-11 has just been emitted by a source behind the asteroid."

Wolruf's mouth opened in a toothy grin, and her tongue lolled out. "We *got* 'im." She fired a last round of maneuvering thrusters and stabilized the ship's course. "Now let's see—"

"More contacts," Mandelbrot said. "Additional thruster exhaust; I am projecting—

"Cancel. Visual contact. I am putting it on the main viewer." The stars swam, blurred again, and resolved into a much closer look at the asteroid than Derec had had before.

A ship was creeping out from behind the right edge of the asteroid. At first glance it looked like a fairly conventional Settler design. Then Derec realized that he was just looking at the foremost piece of it.

The ship came out from behind the asteroid, and kept coming. It wasn't just large, it was *enormous.* And yet the design had a curiously improvised look about it, as if someone had decided to build a supervessel by simply welding together a dozen randomly selected hulls. Sleek transatmospheric hulls nestled in with ungainly cargo pods, and a hodgepodge of angular bracing and spaghetti-like tubing connected the whole lot. Bits of it looked like standard Spacer equipment, or Auroran pleasure yachts, while other segments looked utterly alien, like nothing Derec had ever seen before.

Then he felt the touch of an icy ghost finger on his shoulder, and the hairs on the nape of his neck stood straight up. He *had* seen a ship like that before.

Derec glanced quickly at Wolruf. Her hackles were standing up, and she'd bared her teeth. Derec suddenly knew he didn't need to ask what she was thinking.

"The approaching vessel has opened fire," Mandelbrot announced. "Primary armament appears to be phased microwave lasers."

As one, Derec and Wolruf looked at each other. *"Aranimas!"*

Wolruf became a flurry of action. She slammed her fists down on controls, jabbed buttons, and barked terse, almost hysterical commands at the ship. In response, the ship yawed hard and pitched wildly as the main drives erupted into life.

"This is impossible," Derec said. "We destroyed Aranimas in Sol system. I *saw* his ship explode."

" 'u saw 'im jettison second'ry 'ulls." Wolruf punched up some kind of intersecting curve display, peered at it anxiously, and resumed hitting controls. "On my world there's a small liz'rd called a *skerk*. 'u grab its tail, th' tail breaks off. Skerk gets away, 'u get its tail." She glanced up at the screen again; the flying junkyard was still closing. " 'u must 'ave got a piece of Aranimas's tail."

Derec just stared at the viewscreen and shook his head. "But how in the universe did he find us again?"

"Don't know," Wolruf growled. "Matter of fact, don't care. Just know we need to get away *now*." She leaned back to survey the control board settings and then thumbed the intercom button. "Arr'el! Dr. Av'ry! Stand by for jump!"

"Jump?" Derec shouted. "We can't jump! We're too far away from the programmed jump point."

"Direct hit on the stern," Mandelbrot announced.

"Wolruf! You didn't have time to calculate and enter a new course!"

Wolruf punched more buttons. " 'u care about details at a time like thiss?"

"Another hit," Mandelbrot said. "Hull breached in Section 17D."

"But where will we go?" Derec wailed.

"Someplace Aranimas *issn't!*" Wolruf took one last glance at the control settings, and then grabbed the jump control handle and yanked it down hard.

A shift, a spin, Derec felt a rolling disorientation in his inner ear: Enormous energies were expended, and the *Wild Goose Chase* squeezed through a hole in the space/time continuum. A moment later, it was somewhere else.

Wolruf engaged the autopilot. With careful and precise thruster bursts, the ship stabilized its tumble. The viewscreen blanked, cleared, and displayed a binary star consisting of a yellow giant and its white dwarf companion.

With obvious effort, Wolruf relaxed her grip on the jump handle and sagged back into the acceleration couch.

"Where are we?" Derec asked softly.

Mandelbrot spoke up. "I am working on that. We will have a rough navigational fix within six hours, and coordinates precise enough to begin programming another jump in twenty-three."

"Twenty-three hours? But what if Aranimas follows us?"

"Then we are caught." Mandelbrot exchanged a stream of bits with the data terminal. "Given the availability of free hydrogen in this system, it will be a minimum of ninety-one point five hours before we have accumulated enough hydrogen to fuel another hyperspace jump."

Derec frowned. "Well, if that's it, then, it'll have to do. Deploy the ramscoops, Mandelbrot."

"I have already done so."

"Thanks. Wolruf?"

The small alien rolled over and looked at Derec with eyes that had gone past fright and were now simply exhausted.

"Wolruf? You were his navigator once. How did Aranimas find us again?"

Wolruf brought a foot up and scratched her ear thoughtfully. "Don't know."

"But his sensor technology—"

"Iss whatev'r 'e can steal. No tellin' what 'e's got now."

Derec frowned again. Then his face brightened. "Well, there's no point in worrying about it. As Mandelbrot pointed out, if he can follow us, the *Goose* is cooked." He turned to Wolruf and smiled. "But I don't think that's a real issue. We got away clean. I mean, every schoolboy knows that it's physically impossible to track a ship through hyperspace, right?"

Wolruf got up on one elbow, reached across the couch, and rested a furry hand on Derec's shoulder.

"Derec," she whispered, "I don't think Aranimas went to 'ur school."

CHAPTER 9

WHITETAIL

Old LifeCrier, spiritual leader of the kin of PackHome and self-proclaimed First Believer in SilverSides, sat at the mouth of the cave, watching the milling throng in the clearing below. "Do you hear that, daughter?" he said proudly, using the informal words of KinSpeech. "They're all speaking my name."

From somewhere inside the cave, WhiteTail answered, "That's sweet, Father."

He ignored the humoring tone in her voice and looked back out over the crowd. " 'LifeCrier,' that's what they're saying. 'We've traveled for days to hear LifeCrier.' " He let his tongue loll out and smiled clear back to his fourth bicuspids. "You never thought your old father would be heard beyond the pack."

WhiteTail carried a few old dry bones up from the darkness and deposited them in the rubbish heap near the opening. "Of course I did, Father." She turned to head back into the darkness, but he reached out a paw and gently stopped her.

"Look at them, WhiteTail. Just *look* at them. What do you see?"

WhiteTail stood up on her hind legs and surveyed the crowd. Then, with a disgusted snort, she dropped back down to all fours. "I see about two hundred extra mouths to feed. We're running low on food as it is."

The old kin smiled sadly and shook his head. "Oh, ye of little vision. That's the beginnings of the Great Pack out there."

WhiteTail sniffed disdainfully. "It's a hungry mob of outcasts, younglings, and losers, that's what it is. Not ten decent hunters in the lot of them. And certainly no hunt leader."

LifeCrier ignored her. "*Think* of it, daughter. We have the privilege to be a part of the greatest thing that's ever happened to the kin. First SilverSides came down from the OldMother. Now the Great Pack is forming. Soon all the packs will be united, and the sharpfangs will be driven away forever. We're seeing untold generations of prophecy fulfilled right before our very eyes!"

WhiteTail sighed heavily and cast a distempered look at her father. "Do the prophecies say anything at all about how we're supposed to feed them?"

"Oh, my short-sighted daughter." He tried to wrap his tail around her shoulder, but she shrugged it off. "Still thinking about mere physical needs when we have the spiritual sustenance of SilverSides?"

WhiteTail jumped to her feet and impatiently twitched her long, whip-like tail. "All I'm saying is that somebody better do some hunting around here, or SilverSides is going to be short a few followers if she comes again."

"*When*, daughter." LifeCrier slowly roused to his feet and stretched out in an easy yawn. "*When* SilverSides comes again, she will lead us to all we could ever hope for. Good knives. Warm furs. More food than, than—"

WhiteTail's eyes narrowed. "Yes? I'm listening."

"Well, more food than you can imagine, anyway. We won't want for anything."

"And in the meantime we're just supposed to sit and wait patiently?"

"Don't worry, daughter. SilverSides will lead and protect us. She promised she would. Just as she promised that she would return."

WhiteTail turned around in a tight, nervous circle, glared at her father, and turned around again. Whatever was left of her patience finally gave up the ghost.

"You addled old fool! For twelve days and nights now you've kept the hunt here in PackHome and filled their heads with stories of SilverSides! In the meantime, the bellies of the younglings growl with hunger and the pups are crying because their mothers have no milk!"

LifeCrier turned to face her; involuntarily, WhiteTail's hackles went up and her lips drew back in a snarl, exposing double rows of needle-sharp teeth.

"Father, I don't *care* if SilverSides is coming back someday. Your pack is starving now! You call yourself the leader of PackHome; when will you get your head out of the sky and lead the hunt?"

LifeCrier sagged back on his haunches and let his ears fall flat. With a sudden start, WhiteTail noticed the pain and confusion in the old kin's eyes. "My own daughter," Life-Crier whispered. "My own daughter challenges me."

Seeing the pain in her father's eyes, WhiteTail felt a sudden stab of remorse. Fighting for control over her emotions, she lowered her hackles, crouched down on her belly, and laid her head on her forepaws. "I'm sorry, Father." She looked up at him with big, sad, puppy-dog eyes. "I spoke without thinking. I said things I didn't mean."

LifeCrier stood up, trotted over, and gave her a friendly little nuzzle behind the ears, as he used to when she was just a pup. "That's all right, WhiteTail. Every now and then the FirstBeast gets into all of us and makes us say things we didn't mean." She relaxed, and gave him an apologetic lick on the muzzle. LifeCrier returned a paternal smile. "I'm sure SilverSides forgives you for your momentary lapse of faith."

With great effort, WhiteTail kept her hackles down.

LifeCrier gave her one more nuzzle behind the ears, and then started poking around in the sleeping furs that lay piled in one corner of the cave. "Now, where did I leave that amulet? Ah, here it is." LifeCrier pulled out the badge of his office—a broken circuit board suspended from a braided necklace made of robotic nerve wire—and slipped it over his head. "Well, it's time to address the faithful. Coming, Daughter?"

At first she was going to demur, but then the germ of an idea occurred to her. Suppressing a wicked smile, she sweetly said, "Of course, Father. I'd love to be with you." The old kin got to his feet and trotted out of the cave with WhiteTail beside him.

The barking and yipping started the moment someone in the crowd spotted LifeCrier. A few in the crowd gave themselves up to their excitement and howled in Beast-Tongue. By the time the old kin had crossed to the rocky knoll that overlooked the clearing, the noise had resolved into a rhythmic chant: "*Life*-Crier, *Life*-Crier, *Life*-Crier . . ."

WhiteTail stopped at the base of the knoll and watched her father as he climbed. At the top he paused a moment to look out upon the crowd with a broad, tail-wagging smile on his face. All eyes were on him, he knew, and he basked in the glory. Then he sat down, flattened his ears, closed his eyes, and raised his voice in a long, mournful howl of BeastTongue.

The crowd returned his benediction. The sight and sound astonished WhiteTail; over two hundred kin all packed into a clearing, sitting with their backs arched stiffly, muzzles raised in a deafening unison howl.

LifeCrier dropped his head and switched to the formal cadences of HuntTongue. "Listen!" Abruptly, the howling stopped. "Hear me, O kin! I tell of the time before time, and of a promise made to our mother's mother's earliest dam."

"Praise the OldMother!" an excitable convert near WhiteTail shouted. She looked him over quickly and found him much like the others: scruffy, underfed, possibly good-looking if he'd just groom his fur. But there was a little too much hunger in his eyes, and he sported a fresh scar on his left rear leg. *Another loser*, she decided, dismissing him with a sniff.

"Listen!" LifeCrier said again. "In the beginning, there was the Great Pack. They lived in the Forest of Dawn, when the world was young. Of game there was no end; of enemies, none that dared invade the dens of the kin. Each hunter had his perfect mate, each little mother her strong and obedient pups, and all the kin lived in harmony. All the days were green and cool, and all the nights were warm and sweet, for time had not yet begun and Death was a stranger to the kin. It was forever summer in the Forest of Dawn, and great were the blessings that the OldMother showered down upon the kin."

"Praise the OldMother!" the convert shouted again, this time getting the cue right.

LifeCrier's face darkened, and his voice took on an ominous tone. "But though they were blessed, those first kin knew it not. Instead, they let the spirit of the FirstBeast move among them, and give them evil counsel. Then brother turned against sister, and father against child, for they all desired to lead the Great Pack. When the OldMother saw this, she was greatly displeased, and she sent her chosen one, GreyMane, to set us back on the scent of righteousness."

Several of the other converts had by now picked up on the rhythm of the sermon, and they shouted, "Have mercy on us, OldMother!"

LifeCrier acknowledged the response with a slight nod and resumed. "But hard were the hearts of those first kin, and blind were their eyes to truth. GreyMane's brother was full of the spirit of the FirstBeast, and the pack stood behind him as he ripped the life from her throat. Then did the OldMother fall on the Great Pack, her hackles as tall as great trees, her fangs gleaming like the sun. With thunder and fire, she drove the kin from the Forest of Dawn and scattered them to the winds, to suffer and die in the world until their children's children's children had paid the price of their sins." LifeCrier paused for a breath.

The converts yelled their enthusiastic responses.

Slowly, lovingly, LifeCrier looked over the crowd. His ears relaxed; his expression softened. In a gentler tone of voice, he continued. "Thus has it been for a thousand generations. We are born. We suffer. We die. Our pups go hungry, our old ones fall victim to the sharpfangs, and our best and brightest hunters fight tooth and claw for the right to lead, for but a summer or two. While through the ages, the faithful have waited for the sign that we are at last forgiven. Through flood and famine, through the raging fires of autumn and the bitter frosts of winter, even when hope seemed as hard to find as a redwing's teeth, generations of kin have lived and died in the belief that the OldMother would send the Chosen One again, and we would once again live in harmony in the Forest of Dawn.

"Some have said that the believers were fools. Some have said that we waited in vain." LifeCrier paused to look the crowd over one more time, an enigmatic smile playing on his lips. The only sound from the converts was a disorganized mumble.

Then the old kin puffed his chest, raised his ears, and loosed a joyous bark. "Brethren, friends, members of the Great Pack: I am here today to tell you that the wait has *not* been in vain. For I bring you good news; the Chosen One *has* been sent among us, and her name is SilverSides!"

The crowd went up in another tumult of yipping and barking. Strained shouts of "Praise the OldMother!" mingled with shouts of "Praise SilverSides!" For a moment, watching the fervor of the crowd, WhiteTail wondered if her father really had any idea of the kind of energy he'd tapped. Then she put the question out of her mind. There were enough little problems to handle without confronting the big one.

"Listen. Listen!" In a bit, the crowd settled down again and LifeCrier continued. "Look around you. Look at your neighbors. A year ago, this humble place, this PackHome, was a desperate and dying place. Hemmed in by other packs, we faced an invasion from the Hill of Stars. The WalkingStones were terrible enemies: Tall and swift, able to kill with a glance, they were as deadly as silent sharpfangs and twice as hard to kill. The game was driven away, and our young hunters were slain without honor. If ever there was a place that needed the OldMother, surely PackHome was it.

"Now, some have said that the OldMother has grown

deaf to the cries of the kin, and her heart has long since hardened against us. But brethren, I am here to tell you that she listens to us still. For the OldMother heard the lamentations of PackHome; she saw the hungry pups, she smelled the unburied dead. The OldMother's heart was moved, and in our darkest hour she sent us her sign and her help, and the name was *SilverSides*."

LifeCrier's voice dropped to a whisper. Remarkably, the crowd fell silent to listen. For a moment all WhiteTail heard was the wind rustling the leaves of the whitetrees and the distant call of a lonely bluecrest.

"I was *there*, oh my brethren," LifeCrier whispered. "You and I, we were born from our mothers. But the mother of SilverSides is the OldMother, who lives in the sky, and SilverSides was born from a fiery star. These old eyes *saw* her come down from the sky, trailing flame and glory.

"She was as a cub, but she was formed fully grown. As soon as she could move, she felled a mighty sharpfang with one bite." LifeCrier looked around the clearing, gauging his audience's disbelief. "With one bite, brethren. Even before she could speak, she saved an entire hunting pack. And when she could at last speak, did she challenge KeenEye for the leadership of the hunt, as was her right under the law of the FirstBeast?

"No. She said, 'I am here to serve you.' "

He paused to let that thought sink in and catch his breath. After a few quick pants, he resumed speaking in his normal voice. "That is the first lesson, O members of the Great Pack. She accomplished great things; she fought with valor. But all these things she did to *serve* the pack.

"She hunted with the pack, and she was a mighty hunter. She led us against the WalkingStones, and drove them back in defeat." He leapt to his hind feet and held his amulet high. The sunlight twinkled and flashed on the broken circuit board. "This is the token she gave me, to remind me of my faith. It is a piece of the brain of a WalkingStone, and it does not decay!"

LifeCrier flashed the amulet around so all could see it. When the wondrous gasps had settled down, he hung the amulet around his neck again and dropped down to all fours. "That was just one of her miracles. There were many more, and in time I will tell you about them. But for now—for you who are taking your first trots down the path of faith—I leave you with these four promises, which she gave unto me. Let these be the four legs upon which your faith stands:

"SilverSides will protect us.

"SilverSides will serve us.

"SilverSides came once, to awaken us.

"SilverSides will come again, to lead us back to the Forest of Dawn."

Abruptly, LifeCrier turned and began descending from the rocky knoll. The crowd exploded in a tumult of barking and howling. Shouts of "Praise LifeCrier!" went up from one side of the clearing, and "Praise SilverSides!" from the other. A small fight started in the back when someone tried to shout "Praise the OldMother!" and the younglings in the front were swept aside by a mob of converts rushing forward to touch the fur of LifeCrier.

Unnoticed in all the noise and confusion, WhiteTail carefully worked her way around to the back side of the knoll. She paused only a moment, to think, *I sure hope I know what I'm doing.* Then in one quick dash she scampered to the top of the knoll and let rip with her best blood-curdling shriek.

Amazingly, the rabble all froze and stared at her.

Here goes nothing. WhiteTail flashed a wide, joyous, utterly fraudulent smile, whipped her tail excitedly, and barked out, "Hear me! I am WhiteTail, daughter of Life-Crier!"

"Praise LifeCrier!" the scruffy one near the front shouted.

She beamed at the crowd again. *Whatever you do, girl, don't make eye contact with your father.* "LifeCrier has asked me to make an announcement." She felt the fur on the back of her head prickle and knew that her father was staring at her. She could easily visualize his baffled expression as he tried to figure out what she was up to this time, and she started to glance in his direction. *Don't look at him!*

"In honor of this happy occasion," WhiteTail barked, "LifeCrier wishes it known that he himself will lead the first hunt of the Great Pack! He goes to the forest now; all who would truly follow in the footsteps of SilverSides, follow LifeCrier!" The pack erupted in a maelstrom of baying and hunting howls and surged forward to engulf LifeCrier.

Now, girl. Now you can look at him. WhiteTail picked her father's face out of the mob at the foot of the knoll. For an instant he looked back at her with daggers flashing in his eyes, and then he was swept away by the furry tide that streamed out into the forest. *Okay, Father,* WhiteTail thought with a snicker, *let's see you wriggle your way out of this one.* Bounding down from the knoll, she blended into the crowd and followed.

All her efforts were concentrated on keeping track of her father. She never noticed the small, green observation robot that drifted along at treetop level, following her.

CHAPTER 10

JANET

Dr. Anastasi charged up the slidewalk from the tunnel transit stop, pinwheeled through a lobby, and caught the next flight of slidewalk. "Look at this, Basalom. Have you ever seen such conspicuous waste before?"

The First and Second Laws of Robotics prevented him from responding with an untruth, but Basalom deduced from experience that his mistress did not want a completely truthful answer. He kept his silence as he strode a respectful three paces behind her, but he carried on an internal dialogue. *Actually, Dr. Anastasi, we've both seen something exactly like this. Or have you forgotten the Ceremyons already?*

Dr. Anastasi rapped her knuckles on a ceiling support beam as the slidewalk rose up through the next floor. "Good grief. Iron. Chrome steel. Petrochemical plastics. They must have torn down an entire mountain to build this place."

"Quite possibly, madam." *Although in that case the scanning team would have spotted something beyond a little thermal pollution, no?*

Dr. Anastasi shook her head. "When I think of all the ecological damage that these things must cause—

"I mean, think of it, Basalom. Thousands of hectares of biosphere flattened, graded, and rendered utterly sterile. Entire species displaced." She turned around and took in the building with a sweeping gesture. "You know, I think I've figured it out. The Robot Cities are fire ant nests. Enormous fire ant nests.

The allusion was a bit obscure; it took Basalom almost 30 nanoseconds to cross-reference and make the connection. *Fire ant: Solenopsis saevissima richteri. A fiercely stinging omnivorous ant native to the American continents of Earth, commonly thought responsible for the Great Agricultural Failure of the early 21st century. See North American History, Populist Rising of 2014.* Then he realized that Janet was obviously waiting for him to ask her to explain. "Fire ants, madam?"

"Nasty little brown bugs, native to Earth. Every now and then someone accidentally exports them to a Settler world.

"All it takes is one queen, at the start. But her offspring build these huge, networked, almost indestructible nests, strip the land of everything that can be eaten, and kill or drive out all the native species right up to cattle. Pretty soon, instead of a meadow, you've got a couple hectares of solid fire ant nest. And then they send out hordes of flying queens to start new colonies."

The slidewalk rose through another floor, and Janet looked around. "Yes, fire ants get established someplace, you may as well nuke the whole mess and start over."

They'd reached the top of the slidewalk. Janet wheeled and charged through an enormous open archway; Basalom followed an instant later, in time to see Dr. Anastasi get grabbed by two large, matte-black security robots.

His First Law reaction was immediate and over-whelming. *Dr. Anastasi is being attacked. I must defend her.*

Even as he started to move, within nanoseconds, secondary observations came into his central thought processor. The security robots were standard Robot City Avernus models: massive, solid, four meters tall, equipped with ominous-looking pincer hands—in short, far more menacing than the older; "Gort" models found doing most security work on Spacer worlds. *These robots are subject to the First Law just as I am. Dr. Anastasi is in no danger. Perhaps they are restraining her in order to prevent her from entering an area of greater potential harm.*

Dr. Anastasi's face flushed red to the roots of her blond hair and she pounded ineffectually on the robot's broad metal chest. "Put me down!"

"This is a restricted area," the robot said in a voice that sounded like ball bearings in a blender.

"This is Central Hall. It can't be a restricted area."

The robot tilted its massive, helmet-like head back and scanned her face. "You are not in my permissions file. Access denied. If you would like to apply for permission—"

"Shut up!" She thumped the black behemoth on the side of the head, and it responded by shifting its grip so that she could no longer move her arms.

Casually, Basalom strolled into view, stopped a foot short of the security robots' reaction perimeter, and opened a commlink channel. *Hello. Is there some problem here?*

This is a restricted area, the unoccupied security robot said. Interestingly, its commlink signal projected the same gravelly tone as the other's voice synthesizer.

Ah, I see. He looked at Dr. Anastasi as if curious. *What did she do?*

She attempted to enter the restricted zone without correct permission.

Dr. Anastasi caught her breath again. "Put me down, you ugly tin lunkhead!"

Basalom nodded sagely. *And you stopped her. Good work. But tell me, why is this zone restricted?*

To prevent the risk of further attacks on Central. This one fit the profile of a potential attacker. Dr. Anastasi got a foot loose and gave the security robot a good solid kick in the knee joint. The hall echoed with the clang.

Basalom nodded again. *Indeed she does.* He looked back to the security robot. *However, I'm curious about something. Who issued the orders restricting this area?*

The Supervisory Council.

I see. And they're all robots, is that correct?

Yes.

Basalom stepped a bit closer, as if to examine Janet, but still stayed circumspectly outside the security robot's reaction perimeter. *You are aware, of course, that this is a human.*

Both security robots responded. *Of course.* The one holding Dr. Anastasi continued, *That is why I am restraining her without harming her.*

Basalom stepped back and looked the black robot straight in the oculars. *Under the Second Law, an order given by a human supersedes an order given by a robot—even by a robot on the Supervisory Council.*

Protection of Central stems directly from our fundamental programming, which was installed by the human Dr. Avery. The security robot hesitated, but persisted. *This security detail is therefore following a human order of higher priority.*

Basalom shifted his approach. *Dr. Anastasi is a former colleague of Dr. Avery's.* True enough, as far as it went. Basalom felt no need to amplify the relationship. *She is no danger to Central. In any case, human reactions are so slow compared to robots that you or I could stop her if she attempted an assault on Central. Besides, her order is direct and immediate, and is a situation not foreseen by your programming.* Also true enough. *I suggest you start obeying her orders.*

Security robots could be a bit thick, but even they eventually caught on. *Oh.*

Janet shrieked, "Let me go!" The robot holding her did, and she hit the floor with a plop. In an instant Basalom was at her side, helping her to her feet. All her attention was fixed on the security robot; the only notice she took of Basalom was to mutter, "You just have to know how to talk to these things."

"Indeed, madam."

Getting to her feet, Dr. Anastasi straightened her clothes and fixed the security robots with a steely glare. "Well, I hope you two have learned your lesson. Come along, Basalom." Though the security robots were both a good two meters taller than Janet, she brushed them aside and ploughed straight ahead into Central Hall.

Basalom followed her. One of the security robots started to open his commlink channel to challenge Basalom's security clearance, but Basalom struck first. *Implied Second Law: Dr. Anastasi has ordered me to accompany her. Therefore, she wishes me to enter this area, and therefore, she obviously wishes you to allow me to pass.* The security robots were still trying to parse that one out when Basalom and Dr. Anastasi disappeared out of sight around the corner.

A few seconds later they stood in the atrium at the heart of Central, facing the massive black slab that held Central's console input/output devices. Basalom couldn't quite put a manipulator on it, but he felt a sense of vague disquiet in the presence of the great machine. There were annoying, itchy subsonics in the air, and a deep, unsteady thrumming on the 104-Mhz band. The positronic potentials rose in his brain, meshed, and pointed toward a fuzzy conclusion: Something was wrong. But what?

Dr. Anastasi grew impatient. She crossed her arms. She tapped a foot. She cleared her throat loudly. At last, Central's one red eye slowly came to life. Clicks and grating sounds emanated from its voice synthesizer, followed by a burst of white noise and a 60-cycle hum that slowly resolved into a word.

"Hmmm?"

Janet uncrossed her arms and stepped forward. "Central, I am Dr. Janet Anastasi, and I'm here to—"

"Good morning, Dr. Chandra," the machine said. "I'm looking forward to beginning my lessons."

Janet blinked, shook her head, and tried again. "Anastasi. My name is Anastasi. And I'm a little short on time, so—"

"Time," Central said, "is a convention shaped by the collective mind of all sentience. It has no objective meaning outside the vision."

Dr. Anastasi turned to Basalom. "Do you have any idea what he's talking about?"

Basalom tried a brief query on his commlink, but got nothing but static in reply. "No, madam."

Janet shrugged and turned back to Central. "One more time, then. My name is Janet Anastasi. I am a roboticist. Roughly a year ago, I left an experimental learning machine on the surface of this planet. Its mission was—"

Central's eye flared brightly, then dimmed again to extinction.

No answer was forthcoming; Central had gone back into sleep mode. Turning to Janet, Basalom found her staring at her feet and counting to a very high number. The situation was saved by the arrival of a tall, slender, pale blue robot built along the lines of the Avery Euler model.

The robot swept into the atrium and began talking in a harried, accelerated voice. "Hello, you must be Dr. Anastasi. Please accept my apologies for not meeting you at the spaceport. Your arrival caught us completely by surprise."

Janet looked up. "No, really?"

The city robot was unused to dealing with humans, and therefore not tuned to detect sarcasm. "Truly, I am City Supervisor 3. You may find it more convenient to address me as Beta. I was involved in a major research project, but I came as soon as I was able to delegate authority. If it is necessary, my fellow supervisors can be summoned as well. You may consider the entire city to be at your disposal."

Janet looked around the hall and thought about the many meanings of the word *disposal*. "Thank you. To be honest—Beta, is it?—I don't want to spend any more time here than I absolutely must. I only came here to get one question answered.

"Before I ask it, though, I've got a new one. What the deuce is going on with Central?"

Beta's eyes dimmed, and he shuffled his feet nervously. Basalom detected a slight leakage of sadness on the commlink channel. "Central has been . . . *damaged*," Beta said.

"No kidding. What happened?"

"A rogue robot invaded the hall and attacked Central." Beta looked up. "You must understand, this was before we realized the need for tight security measures."

Janet absent-mindedly rubbed her upper arm. "Yes, I've met your security measures. But back up a moment: You said a rogue robot? No offense intended, but I've never heard of a rogue robot before, much less a rogue Avery robot."

"This was not an Avery robot."

Janet was suddenly stricken with a nasty, sinking feeling. "What kind of robot was it?"

Beta's eyes flashed, and he looked to Basalom for a moment. "We are not certain. It was not a design that we were familiar with. For example, it was constructed of a cellular material similar to our own, but of a much finer grain. And, while it was subject to the Laws of Robotics, it seemed to have no clear idea of what constituted a human."

Basalom switched to commlink. *Stand by for download of data.* When Beta had acknowledged, Basalom transmitted a summary of the learning machine's design specification. *Was this the robot that attacked Central?*

Why, yes. Then on audio, Beta repeated, "Yes, that's it. The rogue robot was a unit of the type you describe as a learning machine. This explains a lot of things."

Janet grabbed Beta and turned him to face her. "Like *what?* Exactly what did the rogue robot do?"

Beta's eyes flashed again, and there was a hesitation in his voice. "Dr. Anastasi, the rogue apparently became convinced that it was a member of the local species. It assumed their form. It took over leadership of a small socio-political unit. From what we have been able to establish lately, it has apparently been adopted by that unit as a minor deity."

Janet let go of Beta and sagged. "Frost..."

"The learning machine led repeated attacks against Robot City. It destroyed several hunter/seekers, a number of worker robots, and City Supervisor Gamma on two different occasions. Ultimately, it attempted to destroy Central."

Janet sat down on the floor and buried her face in her hands. "Frost, frost, f—" She looked up and grabbed Beta's knee. *"What happened to it?"*

"Master Derec—are you familiar with the human called Derec, also known as David Avery?"

Janet smiled at the mention of her son. "Oh, I've heard of him."

"Master Derec arrived and convinced the rogue that he was human. It took the form of a fairly normal robot, and has since left the planet as part of Master Derec's entourage."

Frowning at Basalom, Dr. Anastasi got to her feet and began straightening her hair. "Well, I suppose that's the best we could hope for. At least it isn't destroyed." She turned to Beta. "You say the learning machine assumed leadership of the primitive sentients?"

"Yes, madam. Our current research project involves studying the primitives. From what we have been able to decode of their language, it appears that primitives now regard the learning machine as a messiah figure. It has caused considerable disruption to their social order."

Dr. Anastasi stroked her chin. "I see. So now you're looking for a way to undo the damage?"

"No, madam. We have concluded that the disruption is too significant for us to repair. Instead, we are seeking ways to take advantage of it, in order to persuade the natives to take up residence in the city."

"What?"

Beta blithely continued. "Robot City exists to serve humans. Since there are no humans in permanent residence on this world, we have concluded that the intelligent primitives are human equivalents, or near-humans. Therefore, in order for us to protect and serve them, they must take up residence in the city."

Janet went back to staring at her feet and counting to high numbers. Basalom switched to thermographic vision and noted that Mount Anastasi was building up to another eruption.

Janet said, "Next I suppose you're going to tell me that this is for their own good."

"Of course, madam. Our observations have shown that the near-humans live in a dirty, dangerous environment. If they can be persuaded to accept some changes, we can make their lives much more pleasant."

This time, Janet defused the angry outburst herself. "Okay, Basalom. Contact the ship. Tell it we're going to be staying here for a while. We may as well try to steer these tin fascists onto a constructive path." Basalom opened his commlink channel and did as Dr. Anastasi instructed.

While he was still on the commlink, though, he intercepted a coded transmission intended for Beta. The code was a simple one, composed of prime number transpositions, and Basalom cracked it in about 50 nanoseconds. He was just in time to catch Beta's answering transmission.

Go ahead, Linguist 6.

We have been engaged by a hunting party of near-humans. Supervisor Gamma has already been destroyed.

Again? Very well; try to salvage his brain, if they'll let you.

That may be difficult. Biologist 42 is down with a damaged leg, Organic Chemist 20 is locked up in a First Law dilemma, and I've lost my left arm below the elbow.

Understood. Mission aborted. Return to the city.

Will comply if possible. The near-humans are circling back. They've cut us off. I don't think we're going to make it. We'd better upload our observational data now. Stand by for core dump.

Ready.

I am commencing to trans—

After that, there was only static.

CHAPTER 11

MAVERICK

A forest glen: sunlight filtered cool and green through the leaves, while nesting redwings darted through the lower branches of the trees, piping cheerfully. High in the canopy above a newly emerged cicabeetle announced its successful pupation with a loud, low-pitched drone, and off in the distance the happy cries and howls of hunting kin echoed across the valley.

The bowl-shaped floor of the forest clearing was covered with rocky outcroppings, mossy old stumps and fallen logs, and the mangled remains of four robots.

A skinny youngling sauntered past, proudly carrying his prize by the wires that had once connected it to a neck. Someone on the other side of the clearing shouted, distracting the youngling; he dropped City Supervisor Gamma's head onto a slab of exposed rock, and the resulting clang sent him scampering away. By the time the youngling realized what he'd done and turned back to retrieve the head, it had begun rolling down the slope. Picking up momentum, it skittered across a patch of wet slimewort, dinged off a jutting rock, and took an off-kilter hop and then a long, wobbling bounce. The youngling bounded down the slope after it, trying to catch up with the rolling head.

He skidded to a stop when the head thudded to rest in a pile of soft humus and rotting leaves at the base of a mossy tree stump, not half a trot in front of the tough-looking stranger's nose.

The head apparently annoyed the stranger. He got to his feet, yawned, and cast a baleful glare at the youngling. Then he sniffed the head in a disinterested fashion, marked it with his scent, and sat down again.

The youngling decided to go find another trophy.

Maverick watched the young kin turn tail, then turned his attention back to the head. *So that was a WalkingStone, eh? Big furry deal. It wasn't so tough.* He brought a hind paw up and indulged in a good scratch behind the ear and resumed picking at the bit of grainy material that was stuck between his front teeth. *On the other paw, I can't say much for the way they taste.* Dislodging the shred of Linguist 6's arm, he spat it out and turned his attention to the group of kin that was busy dismembering the last relatively intact carcass. WhiteTail was easy to spot.

And that's the old guy's daughter, huh? Yuck. She's got spindly legs. Walks like she's got starch in her tail. And she's a bit young, even for your tastes.

Still, what the hey. Maybe in a year or two she'll turn into something worth howling about. And in the meantime, let's not lose sight of why we came here. The old guy's in charge, and he depends on her. Offpaw, I'd say that she's definitely the angle to work, for now. Maverick yawned again, in a deliberately casual way, and gave the rest of the clearing a once-over.

On the whole, he had to admit that this group hunt business hadn't turned out too badly. At first it'd looked like something straight out of one of his worst nightmares: A chaotic mob of two hundred clumsy pack-kin charging through the briars and stingworts, barking and howling loud enough to send even a deaf *smerp* running for cover.

But by the time they'd gone a hundred trots from PackHome, the mob had started to break up. Somebody who actually knew something about hunting caught a whiff of a smallgrazer and led a split off on that trail. A bunch of younglings treed a nuteater and stayed behind to bark like fools, jump around a lot, and prove once again that kin can't climb trees, no matter how hard they try.

Other groups splintered off to chase other promising scents, but Maverick kept his eyes on LifeCrier. There had been a lot of twists, turns, and feints—for a moment there he'd had the absurd idea that LifeCrier was trying to ditch them all and sneak back to PackHome—but even though his left hind leg had started to throb, he'd managed to stick with the old kin the entire way.

After all, that was the whole point of coming to PackHome, wasn't it? To find the center of power, get close to it, and work your way up in the pecking order. And up to a certain point, the plan really had seemed to be working. The group following LifeCrier was down to fewer than ten kin when they'd burst from the underbrush and run straight into the pack of WalkingStones.

Maverick let out a disgusted little sneeze. *Walking-Stones? You mean the horrible, nasty, killer monsters that we need SilverSides to protect us from? Mother, I've seen trees that put up a better fight!* Despite all the scary talk about silent death and glances that killed, there'd been no lightning, and no thunder. The WalkingStones had simply stood there on their hind legs, staring at the onrushing kin, looking for all the world like a bunch of startled whistlepigs caught out in the sunlight.

If LifeCrier had shown even a second's hesitation, that would have been the end of it. *But the old fool obviously believes this SilverSides business. He charged right in.*

And OldMother help me, I followed him. One of the WalkingStones had started to point its left foreleg at LifeCrier. Maverick really hadn't had time to think, or even slow down; he'd feinted, stutter-stepped, and charged straight for the WalkingStone.

It was a good gamble, Mavvy old boy. If the stories about them throwing lightning from their paws are true, you saved the old guy's life. That could have been a real good play, gratitude-wise. With a mighty grunt, he'd gathered himself and sprung upon the WalkingStone, seizing its foreleg in his jaws.

That's where everything had gone wrong. Biting the WalkingStone's limb was like biting gravel. Between the cold pain in his teeth, the oily and utterly unappetizing taste of the WalkingStone's flesh, and the apparent lack of any bones in the limb, Maverick had momentarily forgotten everything that he knew about balance and timing. He'd been counting on his momentum to pull the WalkingStone off its two feet, just as he'd been counting on its inertia to check his leap.

Instead, the thing's foreleg had simply torn away in his teeth and he'd gone flying head-over-haunches into a patch of blooming stingwort. His heroic leap had ended up as a clumsy pratfall.

Maverick looked around the clearing again—a clearing full of kin who were *not* noticing him—and felt a sense of frustration. *It's definitely darned tough to impress the locals by landing flat on your tailbone.*

Of course, I suppose it could be worse. Though at the moment it's hard to imagine how.

Between getting the wind knocked out of him and giving his sore leg a bad twist, he'd managed to take himself out of the fight for a few minutes. By the time he'd crawled out of the stingworts and gotten back up on all four legs, the battle was over. Old LifeCrier was up on a rock giving a victory benediction (though Maverick had to admit that the old kin *did* look a bit pale and shaky), the younglings were doing an extremely sloppy job of skinning and dressing the downed carcasses, and WhiteTail was busy braiding a bunch of those silly little amulets, like the one LifeCrier wore, and handing them out to the kin who'd managed to stay in the thick of the fight.

His gaze locked on WhiteTail again, and he allowed himself a wry smile. *Okay, Mavvy old boy, so much for coming into PackHome like a conquering hero. Guess it's time to try Plan B: Fall in love with the leader's daughter.* He groomed his fur a little bit, straightened up his shoulders, and started rehearsing his opening line. Then he gave WhiteTail one last appraising look, and grimaced. *All the same, her legs are spindly. Oh, the things I do for my meals.* Pasting a cheerful smile on his face, he started his tail going in a slow, friendly wag and sauntered over.

The rest of the younglings had wandered off, dragging the detachable parts of the last WalkingStone with them. WhiteTail was squatting beside the now headless torso, carefully stripping out the thin, tough veins that were threaded throughout its chest cavity. She seemed to be picking them out on the basis of color; the impression was reinforced when she measured out three equal lengths of yellow, green, and black vein and quickly braided them into a necklace.

With deliberate casualness, Maverick sat down and watched her work, an interested expression on his face. When she failed to notice him after a minute or so, he discreetly cleared his throat and wagged his tail a bit more vigorously.

She looked up; their eyes met for an instant. No sparks flew. She went back to her work.

So much for love at first sniff. Mavvy old boy, you're going to have to talk to her. After a few moments of silence, he cleared his throat again and spoke up. "Praise Silver-Sides."

"Praise SilverSides," she answered, without looking up or slowing her work.

Okay, Mavvy, let's turn on the charm. "Say, WhiteTail, can you believe that fight? We took four WalkingStones down and didn't even get singed. I tell you, SilverSides must be watching over us for sure."

WhiteTail paused in her work long enough to fix Maverick with a strange look. "Do I know you?"

The question caught Maverick by surprise. "Well, no. I mean, er—"

WhiteTail's ears went up, and she leaned in closer to sniff at Maverick. "Still, there's something familiar about you." She sniffed again, and then her eyes narrowed just a hair. "Oh, I remember now. You were in the front row at the meeting, weren't you?"

Okay, lad, there's your opening! Maverick leaned back a bit, puffed his chest slightly, and gave her an easy smile. "As a matter of fact, I was. Fascinating sermon, simply fascinating. Your father is—"

"You were the one who kept jumping in early on the cheering, weren't you?"

Oops. Maverick's ears went flat. "Er, actually—"

WhiteTail set her knife aside, sat up alertly, and looked closely at Maverick. "Yes, I remember now. Did you know that I was watching you almost the entire time?"

Maverick's ears popped up straight. "You *were?*"

WhiteTail turned back to the carcass, but not before shooting one last look of disgust at Maverick. "Did you really think that you were the first one to try to improve your status by loudly faking belief?"

"Fake? Look here, girl, I—" The argument died in his throat.

Face it, Mavvy old boy, she's a very clever one, and she's got you by the ears. You may as well try the truth. Maverick plopped down on his belly, crossed his forepaws, and laid his chin on his paws. "Okay, I admit it. Every pack I've ever met has their own kind of strangeness, and I thought this SilverSides business was just one more weird local custom. I've been on my own for over a year, and I'm getting really tired of being an outcast. Can you blame me for trying too hard to fit in?"

WhiteTail set her knife aside again and favored Maverick with a less enigmatic smile. "You get two points for honesty, stranger. Most fakers just protest louder when they're caught. You're the first one I've met who's shown even a vestige of integrity.

"In return for that, I'll give you a little confession of my own. I don't believe, either." WhiteTail's eyes narrowed, and she watched him closely, studying his reaction.

Well, Mavvy, this honest bit seems to be getting us somewhere. Let's go with it. Maverick sat up, cocked his head sideways, raised one ear, and gave WhiteTail a bewildered look. "You don't? But at the meeting you said—I mean . . ."

WhiteTail's expression hardened. "Understand one thing, stranger. LifeCrier isn't just the leader of PackHome, he's my father, and I'll do whatever it takes to protect him. That includes tricking him into leading a hunt when the pack is hungry." With a swiftness that surprised Maverick, WhiteTail suddenly snatched up her stone knife and set its point against his breastbone. "Or cutting your heart out and feeding it to the sharpfangs if you try your pious-believer act on him. Do I make myself clear?"

Gingerly, Maverick pushed the point aside. "Absolutely."

"Good." She dropped her guard and turned her attention back to the carcass. "Now either get lost or make yourself useful. Do you know anything about WalkingStone anatomy?"

Maverick followed her gaze down into the jumbled pale blue mess that was the inside of the WalkingStone's chest cavity. Judging by color, there were at least six different kinds of veins, but the cavity was strangely bloodless and there was nothing that he could clearly identify as a heart. For that matter, he wasn't even sure that he could tell the difference between organ and muscle. A lot of the cavity was filled with the oily blue gravel he'd been picking out of his teeth since the fight.

"No," he finally admitted.

"Good. Here's your chance to learn. Help me roll this thing over, will you?" With a grunt of exertion, WhiteTail started pushing at the corpse. Maverick helped her. Despite being legless and headless, the corpse was surprisingly heavy, but together they managed to get it flipped.

"Now, stranger—" She looked up sharply. "Say, what *is* your name, anyway?"

He hesitated a moment. *Well, boy, just how far do we want to push this honesty business?* "Maverick," he said at last.

"Maverick? That's an outcast name. Don't you have a pack name?"

He looked away, and his tail started twitching in tight, nervous jerks. "Not any more."

WhiteTail gave him another appraising look and then shrugged. "Pay attention; I don't like to repeat myself." She picked up her knife and turned to the corpse.

"Now," WhiteTail began in a cool, formal voice, "the problem with hunting for WalkingStones is that there doesn't seem to be anything inside them that we can *eat*." She dug her knife in between where the shoulder blades should have been—if the thing had had bones—and opened the carcass down the back. By this time it was no longer surprising to find that the WalkingStone had no spine.

"They have no liver," WhiteTail continued. "No heart, no kidneys, and the muscles—well, you've already tried a leg. What did you think?"

Maverick grimaced at the memory. "I'd rather eat a stinktail."

WhiteTail nodded sagely. "A popular opinion." She caught Maverick's eye and directed it to the WalkingStone's shoulder area. "Another problem is that the WalkingStones don't seem to have a proper skin. It's impossible to tell where the skin ends and the muscle begins—which makes it really funny to watch the younglings try to flay one of them.

"But there's something else even more peculiar about the skin that I want you to see. Look there; what's happening?"

Maverick got up on all fours and sniffed closely at the

spot WhiteTail had indicated. "Why, it's *healing*."

WhiteTail frowned helplessly. "This WalkingStone is dead, right? I mean, its front legs are over here, its back legs are—" she looked around the clearing a bit and gestured in the direction of a fallen log, "—over there, I think. And Mother knows where the head's gotten to.

"But leave the skin alone for a few minutes, and wounds flow closed so fast you can watch it. Leave the *organs* alone long enough, and they melt down into this gritty blue stuff that's indistinguishable from skin or muscle." WhiteTail dug the knife in again and extended the cut across the WalkingStone's hip area.

"So far as we can tell, there are only two organs in a WalkingStone that don't change shape. One is the brain. The other—" she plunged her forepaws into the wound and began groping around inside the body "—is usually right about—" a slightly startled look flashed across her face, and then resolved into a smile "—here!" With a sucking, popping sound, the corpse gave up the organ, and WhiteTail fell over backward with the recoil.

Maverick looked at the thing she'd gone to so much work to pull out. "A giant egg?"

"That's what it looks like, all right." WhiteTail got back on her feet, brushed some of the clinging blue grit off the thing, and then found her knife and tapped the egg a few times with the blade. "But it's got the hardest shell that I have ever seen."

Maverick wrinkled his nose in a deep frown. "Still, an *egg?*"

"Interesting thought, isn't it? That WalkingStones might be some kind of giant flyer? Although personally I think the shape and size is more like a sharpfang egg."

Maverick shook his head. "No."

WhiteTail tapped the egg with her knife again. "Agreed, sharpfang eggs are soft and leathery, while this one is as hard as a rock, and too small. Still—"

Maverick pushed in and laid a paw on the egg. "No, you don't understand. These four WalkingStones we killed; they all carried eggs?" WhiteTail nodded. Maverick looked her straight in the eyes. "Don't you see?"

WhiteTail didn't see. "What?"

"No wonder they were such poor fighters. We jumped a bunch of females who were all *nesting*."

The instant those words left his lips, Maverick knew he'd made a mistake. Whatever warmth had been in WhiteTail's eyes, it was gone now. She drew herself up to her full, slender height and asked, "And tell me, O great hunter, since when is a mother protecting her young harmless?"

"Well," Maverick hedged, "there are some; female whistlepigs, and redflyers too, and . . ."

"Useless, absolutely useless," WhiteTail growled. "I shouldn't be wasting my time with you."

Maverick froze, rooted to the spot, as his internal voices erupted into a full-scale screaming argument.

Submit, idiot, submit!

What? To this insolent little pup?

Who also happens to be the leader's daughter!

Don't do it, lad. Roll over and bare your throat to her now and you'll never get another chance to show her who rules the den.

But you were wrong, idiot!

"Well?" WhiteTail said in challenge.

Maverick was saved by the arrival of LifeCrier, who blithely trotted right between them. "Okay you two lovebirds, break it up. We've still got a day's hunting ahead of us." A few trots away, he looked over his shoulder without breaking stride and added, "Well, daughter? Are you coming?"

WhiteTail's hackles went down, her lips relaxed back down over her fangs, and she turned to follow him. "Yes, Father." Maverick started breathing again, and he turned his back to WhiteTail and took another look at the egg.

The bite on his hindquarters took him completely by surprise.

"*Yike!*" He leapt half a trot in the air and came down in a whirl. WhiteTail was standing there with a wicked smile on her face and a little bit of his fur in her teeth. "What was *that* for?" he demanded.

"Just a reminder, *sweetheart.* I'm not done with you yet." Then, with a cold glare and a vicious snap of her whip-like tail, she turned and trotted after her father.

Maverick sat down and watched her go. When she was safely out of earshot, he softly said, "Mavvy old boy, are you sure you want to be in the same pack with her?"

Five minutes later, when LifeCrier had gathered all the other adult hunters and gotten them formed up and ready to move out, Maverick still hadn't come up with an answer to that question. So he took one last look at the WalkingStone egg—only to discover that a skinny youngling had dragged it off, wedged it in a crevice, and started pounding on it with a rock. Then he sighed, got to his feet, and trotted after the rest of the pack.

Had he understood that the egg was actually Linguist 6's microfusion power pod, he would have moved considerably faster.

CHAPTER 12

DEREC

Derec and his father sat side by side in the ship's robotics lab, hunched over a matching pair of robotic data entry terminals, staring intently at the video displays. A casual observer might have mistaken the pair of them for a new breakthrough in humaniform robots, so still were they: unmoving, except for their fingers and the barely perceptible motions of their chests as they breathed; unblinking, their paired attention completely focused on their work.

And yet there was something subtle, barely tangible, yet almost unmistakably *lifelike* about the pair. It wasn't the white stubble on Avery's chin; that effect could have been achieved with common nylon bristle. Perhaps it was the delicate filigree of bloodshot veins that adorned the whites of Derec's eyes. More likely it was his hair, which had that limp, greasy look that could only be achieved through the use of expensive petrochemical plastics.

Or three days of nonstop programming.

Occasionally, a finger moved. Lips parted; a word or two passed between them, although not in anything that the average observer would have recognized as being part of a human conversation.

"Adb ixform."

"Got it."

"0B09?"

"15."

"0B2C?"

"A0."

"Sounds good." There was a long pause while Avery studied something on his screen.

Whatever it was caused him to frown and then to speak again. "Can you give me a du?"

"Fifteen-point-four-three-seven gigs."

"Well, if that's not enough, I don't know what is. Set the pipe."

"Piped."

Avery leaned back in his chair, ran his fingers through his bristly white hair, and blew out a deep breath. "Okay, we're as ready as we're ever going to be. Cross your fingers and start the yacc."

"Yaccing." Derec punched one last command into the terminal and leaned back in his chair in unconscious mimicry of his father. Numbers flashed and danced across the screen; Derec watched it for a few minutes and then rubbed his gritty eyes and turned to Avery. "Now what?"

"We wait." Slowly, painfully, Avery got up out of his chair and limped over to the autogalley. "Coffee, black," he told the machine.

Derec noticed the limp, and a reaction finally worked its way to his vocal cords. "You okay, Dad?" There was genuine concern in his voice.

Avery chuckled a little and slapped his dragging leg. "Yeah, I'm okay. Foot fell asleep, that's all."

"Oh." Derec yawned. The autogalley chimed gently, and the serving door slid open to reveal the cup of coffee that Avery had ordered. Derec's nose perked up at the rich, earthy scent. "Smells good," he observed.

"You want some?"

Derec thought it over. "Sure. With casein and two lumps of sugar."

"Decaf? You look like you could use some sleep."

Derec rubbed the back of his neck and then studied the grit that had adhered to his fingers. "Nah. I've been in here three days; Ari'll make me sleep on the couch anyway. May as well stay awake."

"Okay." Avery repeated Derec's order to the autogalley. When the second steaming cup appeared, he picked it up and carefully carried it over to the work table.

The two of them sat quietly for a few minutes, sipping their cups of coffee, while the numbers danced and capered across Derec's terminal display.

"I hate robotic coffee," Avery said at last.

Derec spoke without looking up. "Why?"

"Fresh-brewed coffee's supposed to burn your tongue. That way you take a little more time, drink it a little slower. Robot-made coffee is served lukewarm, gets cold too fast. You have to gulp it down and get back to work."

"Oh." Derec took another sip and resumed staring into space.

"I could use some food," Avery said after another long pause. "Anything you're partial to?" He got up again and toddled over to the autogalley.

Derec gave the matter his deepest available thought. "Snack food," he decided, with some effort. "Crackers. Cheese. Something along those lines."

Avery leaned against the bulkhead, rested a hand on the

autogalley's control panel, and scrolled through the menu of preprogrammed selections. "Cheese is a pretty complex organic compound," he said. "I'd hate to taste what this thing might come up with if it's not specifically programmed for—ah, here we go. Magellanic *fromage*. Close enough for you?"

"Sure." Derec waved a hand in a noncommittal gesture. Avery gave the autogalley the order, and in a minute he returned to the table bearing a plate full of blue marbled paste and some little round white things that were either crackers or poker chips.

"Dig in, son." Avery smashed a chip into the mound of paste and stuffed the resulting accretion into his mouth. Derec picked up a dry cracker and began nibbling at it in an absentminded manner.

A half-dozen goo-covered crackers later, Avery took a slurp of coffee and turned to Derec. "Well, any lint yet?"

Derec checked his terminal screen. "Nope."

Avery frowned. "I hate sitting through yaccs. I mean, I just feel like I should be doing *something* constructive with this time."

Derec looked up and gave his father a bleary-eyed stare. "Such as?"

"Oh, talking, maybe. Finding out the answers to some questions that have been bothering me for a long time."

Derec yawned. "Okay." There was a long pause. "Anything in particular you wanted to talk about?"

Avery closed his eyes, stroked his whiskery chin, and thought it over. "Yes," he decided. "This Aranimas fellow: Who is he, and why is he trying to kill you?"

Derec shrugged. "You want the full story or the condensed version?"

"Depends. Where's the yacc at?"

Derec rubbed his eyes and checked the terminal one more time. "About twenty percent, I'd guess."

"That far already? Better condense it."

"Okay." Derec took a deep slug of his coffee and closed his eyes in thought. Just when Avery was starting to wonder if he should give the boy a little nudge to wake him up, Derec opened his eyes and began speaking in a low, raspy voice.

"Aranimas is an alien, from somewhere outside Settler space. You could call him a humanoid, depending on how loosely you define human, but when I finally got a close look at him, the first thing I thought of was a plucked condor with fisheyes."

Derec took a nip of his cracker, chewed it thoughtfully, and swallowed. "His species call themselves the Erani. They're a wonderfully simple people: vicious, brutal, and utterly without empathy. In a couple years you'll be able to look up 'cruel' in the dictionary and see a picture of an Erani. You'd get along great with them." Derec paused to sip his now-cold coffee.

Avery bristled at the boy's cheap shot, but held his tongue.

"The Erani claim to control about two hundred worlds, but I think they must be counting every rock, asteroid, and moonlet in their solar system. That ship of his—did you happen to get a look at his ship before we jumped?" Avery shook his head. "Oh. Well, that ship of his appears to be one-of-a-kind, the first hyperdrive the Erani ever developed. I don't know whether Aranimas built it or stole it, but the first thing he did when he got to human space was hijack a good Auroran hull to put it in. Wolruf tells me the Erani hyperdrive is fantastically unstable, and that being in the engine room of their ship is almost as dangerous as being on the wrong end of their guns."

Avery interrupted. "What *is* Wolruf, anyway? A genetically engineered dog or something? And how'd you hook up with it?"

"Her," Derec corrected. "No, Wolruf—that's not her real name, by the way, that's just as close as the human voice can pronounce it. I guess our mouths aren't the right shape, or we don't have the right ultrasonic frequency components in our speech and hearing to really get her name right.

"Anyway, Wolruf was Aranimas's navigator. She was basically a sort of indentured servant on board that ship; I counted at least four different species of intelligent aliens on board Aranimas's ship, and they were all conquered subjects of the Erani. I suspect that if we humans ever have a real confrontation with the Erani, we're going to find a lot of allies on their subject worlds. I met Wolruf when—

"But wait, I'm getting ahead of myself. Let me put this story in linear order, okay?" Derec gave Avery a questioning stare; Avery didn't respond, so Derec finished off the last of his coffee and caught his breath.

"Now, this whole thing starts with that asteroid you dumped me on after you wiped my memory. You remember that asteroid?"

Avery looked down. "I—I was insane then, Derec," he said softly. "I'm not sure what I remember and what I hallucinated."

"Well, I was still trying to figure out your asteroid when Aranimas showed up and started shooting the thing to pieces You see, there's three things the Erani don't have: a fleet of hyperdrive ships, a key to Perihelion, and a glimmer of understanding about robotics. They have a slave culture, you see and since organic slaves are free for the taking, they've had no incentive to develop mechanical ones.

"On the other hand, while they don't know a thing about robotics, they apparently know a lot more about hyperwave than we do. Aranimas was able to identify and *track* the hyperwave interference caused by a key to Perihelion."

Derec abruptly realized that he'd been getting excited and lowered his voice. "That's what brought him to the asteroid. Once there, I guess he saw all those robots and decided to do a little old-fashioned Erani slave-raiding. It'd never occurred to him that the robots would self-destruct instead of surrendering. Capturing me was just an accidental bonus.

"Not that he was happy about it. Apparently he's been skulking around human space for a few years, hijacking the occasional ship and trying to pick up robots. When he captured me he was convinced that I'd cheated him out of a good load of slaves, and he—" Derec faltered a moment and winced at the memory of the torture he'd suffered at Aranimas's hands. "Let's just leave it at that, okay?" Derec found another cracker, loaded it up with Magellanic *fromage*, and resumed talking around the mouthful of cheese.

"Wolruf, as I said, was part of the crew. Ariel was a prisoner, although I didn't find that out for a while. Mandelbrot was a collection of junk parts in a locker."

Avery interrupted again. "Mandelbrot? Isn't he at least three-quarters Capek, Ariel's old valet robot from back on Aurora?"

Derec scowled at Avery. "Beats me. You gave me amnesia, remember?"

"Sorry. I forgot."

Derec took another bite of the cracker and continued. "Dad, I don't know what kind of crazy experiment you really had in mind when you dumped me on that asteroid—"

"I'm not sure I remember either," Avery muttered, "although I think I remember trying to explain it. But that may have been an hallucination. I *was* crazy."

"—but Aranimas had been doing his share to foul it up. By the time we got away from him, I had no memory, of course, and Ariel was losing hers to the amnemonic plague. I'd cobbled together Mandelbrot and programmed him with a pretty restrictive definition of human, which may have influenced some of the Robot City developments along that line. And Wolruf had finally gotten fed up with the Erani and decided to jump ship. With her help we got away while Aranimas was on a raid on a Spacer station, and then we had to steal the key to Perihelion back from the robots before we could use it to escape—and that's how we got to Robot City."

Avery was silent. Derec ran his fingers through his greasy hair, leaned forward, and shook his head.

"Y'know, Dad, as experiments go, yours didn't go too well."

Avery sighed and nodded. "No. No, it didn't, son, and maybe someday I'll be able to apologize for putting you through it. But right now it's just too big, and I have too much trouble coming to grips with the idea that I actually *did* that to you. I'm sorry." Then an idea hit Avery, and he frowned.

"But before I get too sorry, I'd like to remind you that you still haven't answered my main question: Why is Aranimas *still* trying to kill you?"

Derec shrugged. "An Erani never forgets." He helped himself to the last cracker and then looked at his terminal screen. "Oops. We're just about done yaccing. Better finish that coffee and get back to work."

"Okay." Avery hurriedly drained the cup, tossed it into

the disposal chute, and then slipped into his chair.

Derec checked his screen again and turned to Avery. "Seriously, Aranimas is desperate for robots. That's why he follows me, I think; he knows that wherever I go, there are bound to be lots of robots.

"I don't think he can comprehend the Three Laws, though. I mean, he understands the words well enough, but I think the idea that robots simply *can't* hurt humans is just too alien a concept for him. Maybe it's too alien for *any* Erani." Derec stole a sidelong glance at his terminal, and quickly spun back to Avery to squeeze one last thought in.

"So here's an idea: If we ever find out where the Erani home world is, what do you say we drop a half-dozen Robot Cities on it? That ought to drive those ugly clowns just absolutely *crazy.*"

Avery didn't have time to respond. The two data terminals chimed simultaneously, then blanked and displayed the final results of the yacc.

Both Avery and Derec immediately switched into zombie programmer mode.

"Any lint?"

"No, it's clean."

"Okay, let's grep gen shape."

"Grepping."

"A053?"

"15."

"A0C0?"

"AF."

"Very good. Nice it."

"Niced with a tee."

"Thanks, I forgot about that. Iostat?"

Derec paused a moment to page through several screens of data. "Clean, green, and five by five. I think it worked."

"Okay, let's finish it. Nohup."

"Nohupped."

"Chown gen shape."

"Chowned."

Avery leaned back in his chair and crossed his fingers. "Here goes. I am putting ixform to sleep. Any floating children?"

Derec scrutinized his screen. "No—no, we're clear. No children floating in the pipe."

Avery suddenly realized that he'd been holding his breath. "Well! I think we've got it. Do you want to put it to the test?"

Derec smiled and waved an open hand at his father. "You, sir, may have the honor."

"Okay." Avery pushed his chair back from the terminal, tented his fingers, and frowned. Then he cleared his throat, raised his eyes to the ceiling, and said in a loud, clear voice: "Gosh, Derec, I think I need to use the Personal." Both of them locked their stares on Avery's chair.

Nothing happened. No softening around the edges; no reconfiguration of the seatpad. For over a minute they both held their breaths, waiting to see if the chair was going to reconfigure itself.

It remained a chair.

"Yahoo!" Derec raised his fists in a victorious gesture, and Avery cracked into a broad, beaming smile. "Dad, we did it! We've cut out the autonomic shape-changing!"

Avery allowed himself another smile and then sobered. "We're halfway there, Derec. We made the changes we wanted. Now let's make sure that we haven't done any other damage in the process." He turned away from Derec, looked up at the ceiling, and loudly said, "Ship, make this chair two inches higher."

Smoothly and silently, as if it were a robobarber's chair, the seat rose two inches. Avery looked at Derec with a tight smile on his face and a merry twinkle in his eye. "Son, we've cut out the autonomic routines, but we've kept the voluntary control intact. Now *that* is what I call a success." He hesitated a moment and then impulsively stuck out a hand to Derec.

For a moment, Avery felt terribly uncertain and insecure. Derec was looking at the hand as if he expected to find a joy-buzzer. Then he switched to looking Avery straight in the eye, with an unreadable expression on his face.

And then he smiled, reached over, and shook his father's hand. "Congratulations, Dad."

"Thanks, son."

The moment passed. They broke off the handshake, both looking a little sheepish about their undisciplined display of raw emotion, and went back to their respective terminal displays.

"You know," Derec said at last, "I'm beginning to feel that I really understand this polymorphism business."

"That's just what I was thinking," Avery agreed.

"I mean, look at that pipe. It's totally tubular."

"Totally."

The two of them studied their displays a while longer, and then Derec spoke up. "You know, as long as we're on such a good roll, we really should find something else to work on."

"I quite agree."

"Got any ideas?"

A wicked smile appeared on Avery's face. He tried to suppress it, but it could not be denied, so he turned it on Derec. "Where did you say Lucius II was?"

Derec was aghast. "Dad! You promised you'd leave those robots—" Then he realized that Avery was teasing him and broke into a laugh. Avery joined him.

"I think maybe we've done enough for now," Avery said when they'd stopped laughing.

"I think maybe you're right." Derec yawned, rubbed his eyes, and gave the robotics lab one more once-over. "What do you say we catch some shut-eye?"

"An excellent idea." Avery looked up at the ceiling and raised his voice again. "Ship, convert these chairs into bunks, and then dim the lights." Smoothly and silently, the chairs flowed into their new shapes.

Derec didn't even get out of his chair. He simply kicked off his shoes, loosened his tunic buttons, and stretched out full-length on the bunk. "G'night, Dad," he mumbled. The lights in the cabin dimmed down, and within a few minutes Derec's breathing had shifted into the steady rhythm of sleep.

Dr. Avery watched his son until even the phosphorescent glow of the terminal displays had faded to pitch blackness. Then he kicked off his own shoes, removed his lab coat, and stretched out on his bunk.

"Nighty-night, Davey," he whispered.

CHAPTER 13

JANET

A cool spring morning in Robot City. The black limousine rolled swiftly through the empty streets, nearly silent save for the soft thrumming of its electric motor and the gentle hiss of rubberoid tires on pavement. Inside the vehicle, Janet Anastasi sat in the passenger compartment, her nose buried in a sheaf of fax pages, while Basalom sat in the chauffeur's compartment, jacked into the vehicle's master control panel, driving.

One of the advantages of being a robot with telesensory feeds was that Basalom could rotate his head 180 degrees and still keep an eye on the road. Confident that the vehicle was safely under control, Basalom swiveled around to look at Dr. Anastasi. He allocated every third nanosecond to introspection.

She certainly seems happier now that she's stopped sleeping in the lander and has taken an apartment in the city. Briefly switching to thermographic vision, he felt a small glow of satisfaction in the part of his brain that Dr. Anastasi had taken to calling his "mother hen" circuit. Dr.

Anastasi's heat contours were a calm, relaxed study in blues and greens. There were no indicators of unpredictable endocrine activity, no hints of dangerous blood pressure or cardiac rate changes. *And it's been 52 hours since her last emotional outburst,* Basalom noted with some pride. *Yes, she's definitely happier now that she's adapting to the city.*

Sure, mac, the limousine interjected, *give the lady all the credit. Why don'cha ever notice how the city is adapting to* her?

Will you kindly keep out of my private thoughts? Basalom asked, not for the first time.

Can't help it, Mac, the car answered. *You go around jacking your main data bus into other folk's sensory feeds, your thought stream's gonna become a party line.*

Still, you could have the decency to pretend that you aren't listening.

Yeah, I could, the car said. *And on the other tire, if it bugs you that much, you could go back to letting* me *drive. After all, I am Personal Vehicle One.*

You are a pile of steel and plastic with the simulated personality of a twentieth-century Chicago cabbie, Basalom corrected archly, *and I will no longer tolerate your verbal abuse of Dr. Anastasi.*

Suit yourself, Mac. I get recharged no matter who's driving. The car's positronic brain went back into idle mode, and Basalom once more resumed the task of trying to create a private security partition in his brain.

Erecting an encrypted buffer without verbally *thinking* about how he was doing it was a ticklish job, though. When he thought that he'd succeeded, he moved the stack of pointers that represented his consciousness into the secured partition and initiated a new thought stream. *What in the name of Wendell Avery were the supervisors thinking of when they decided to create this mass of argumentative positrons, anyhow?*

They were thinking of what Dr. Anastasi said in Tunnel Station #17, Personal Vehicle One answered, as clearly as ever. *As she was returning via tunnel to the spaceport after her first meeting with Central, she said—and I quote: "Frost, Basalom, look at what the air blast has done to my hair. Why can't they have some decent groundcars in this city?" She had but to speak, and* voila! *I was created.*

Basalom gave up in defeat. *Yes, you certainly were. But tell me, whatever possessed them to decide to give you a simulated personality?*

A slight drop in voltage on pin 16—the positronic equivalent of a shrug—came through the data bus. *Dunno. Humans are rare here, all right? Guess they thought the doc might be happier with a little simulated companionship.*

"Well," Basalom said out loud, "they got *that* wrong."

In the back seat, Dr. Anastasi peered over the top edge of the papers she was reading. "Did you say something to me, Basalom?"

"No, madam. I was exchanging information with the vehicle's onboard computer."

"Oh. Very well." She looked back to the papers and then glanced out the side window. "Basalom? How much longer 'til we get to the Compass Tower?"

Basalom called up an internal image of the city map, plotted their present position, and factored in the rate at which they were traveling. "Approximately five minutes and twenty-three seconds, madam."

I know a shortcut, Personal Vehicle One broke in on the data bus.

I have had enough of your "shortcuts," Basalom answered.

But this one's really simple, the car protested. *All you gotta do is turn east at the gasket factory—*

The Compass Tower is to our south and west, Basalom pointed out.

Trust me. Hang a left at the gasket factory, go two blocks over, then up the freight ramp and catch the #204 south-bound slidewalk—

You want me to drive on the slidewalk? Basalom's shock was expressed as a sudden surge in amplitude on bus circuits 24 and 57.

Ow! Not so loud! Yeah, you drive on the slidewalk. There's a bend to the west in about two kilometers; you get on here and it's a nonstop shot to the tower plus you pick up 25 KPH from the moving pavement. What do you think? Neat, eh?

Basalom managed to redirect what he was thinking into a null buffer and flush it before Personal Vehicle 1 had a chance to intercept the words.

The limousine rolled on. A few blocks later, Janet folded the sheet she was reading, pursed her lips, and frowned.

"Basalom?"

"Yes, madam?"

"You've been in fairly frequent contact with the city robots over the last few days, haven't you?"

"The term 'frequent' is an imprecise expression, madam. I have had 124 separate audio and commlink conversations at intervals ranging from 15 picoseconds to 6 hours."

"Oh. Well, in your conversations, have you noticed that the robots seem a little . . . *odd?*"

" 'Odd' is a judgmental term, madam. In order to determine that behavior is odd, you must first establish a base level of normal behavior against which to judge."

Janet wrinkled her nose in a frown. "I don't understand."

"Madam, since we have arrived here I have been unable to determine what is 'normal' behavior for these robots. Hence I am unable to adjudge anything as being 'odd.' "

Dr. Anastasi smiled and shook her head. "I see. Serves me right for asking a vague question. Let's try again.

"Basalom, in your conversations with the local robots, have you noticed anything that might lead you to believe that the city supervisors have developed a sense of humor?"

Basalom was silent a moment as he sorted through all his recorded sense impressions, searching for correlating patterns.

Okay, it's coming up, the limousine broke in. *Left at the next corner.* Basalom ignored the data stream and tried to concentrate on carrying out Dr. Anastasi's instructions.

"Madam, while I would prefer to build my judgment on a larger experience base—"

Hey, what's the matter with you? You're not slowing down.

"Based on the observations that I have made to date—"

It's this corner. That big circular building is the gasket factory.

"I must conclude that the city supervisors have not developed a sense of humor—"

Left! Oh, fer cryin' out loud, you missed the turn.

"But I hasten to add that many of the city robots have developed significant aberrations and eccentricities."

For a moment there was blessed silence on the data bus. Then the limousine's thought stream kicked back in. *Oh, so I'm eccentric, am I? Well let's just see how you like handling this rig alone.* There was a brief surge of DC voltage accompanied by a drop in positronic potentials across the entire width of the data bus. Basalom tried a few exploratory probe pulses and was surprised to come to an inescapable conclusion: Personal Vehicle One had physically switched itself out of the data bus.

Basalom fired off one more round of sampling pulses and then allowed himself a moment of pleasure. *What a pity I didn't think of this three days ago!*

He checked his realtime clock. Close to a quarter-second had elapsed since he'd delivered his findings to Dr. Anastasi, and she was preparing to make a response.

"Darn. I was hoping you'd say yes." She picked up the sheaf of fax pages and waved them at Basalom. "If you'd said that the supervisors were capable of intentional humor, I'd say that this was a pretty good practical joke."

Dr. Anastasi bit her lower lip. "But if they're completely *serious* about this . . ."

Basalom swiveled his head around to face Dr. Anastasi and scaled his optics up to a higher magnification, but he was unable to make out the content of the faxsheets. "Serious about what, madam?"

She looked at the papers again and then waved them at Basalom. "This is their proposed plan for modifying the city to suit the needs of the local inhabitants. It's not just silly. It's not just stupid. In fact, I think it even transcends ridiculous and scales the heights to pure idiocy."

Basalom scanned the papers again, but his optical character recognition routine still couldn't read the words through the paper.

"Madam?"

Janet unfolded the papers and looked at them. "We have got to talk the supervisors out of this. It's insulting." She peeled off a sheet and threw it aside. "Condescending." She peeled off another and threw it with greater vigor. "Degrading." She lifted the entire sheaf and threw it down on the seat beside her. "And possibly immoral."

She looked up sharply. "Basalom, I need you to help me reach them. I can *build* robots. I can order them around. But I've never had to try to *reason* with an Avery model before. You're going to have to help me understand a city supervisor's conception of logic."

Confused potentials darted through Basalom's brain. "Understand, madam? What's to understand? Logic is logic."

Dr. Anastasi caught a strand of her long blond hair between her fingers and began unconsciously twisting it. "Wrong, Basalom. Logic isn't a universal constant, it's a heuristic decision-making process rooted in the values, prejudices, and acquired conflict-resolution patterns of the decider.

"For example, if I'd given you just a slightly stronger positive bias in your motivation circuit, you would in some situations come to exactly the opposite conclusion that you would come to now. Yet you'd still be just as certain that you'd come to the only logical conclusion." Dr. Anastasi smiled, in a hopeless sort of way, and looked at Basalom.

"You, old friend, have got to help me figure out the underpinnings of the city supervisors' logic. And we've got to do it in the next four minutes."

Four minutes? Basalom riffled through his job stack, shutting down background processes and diversionary loops. There was no time for further conversational niceties; he pulled all the buffers out of his verbalizing process and jacked his speech clock rate up by ten percent. Then he increased the amplitude on data bus circuits 24 and 57, jumpered around his pride subroutine, and established a direct link to the limousine's brain.

Personal Vehicle One?

The response was slow and sullen. *Whaddaya want?*

You must take control of this vehicle.

What makes you think I want it?

The First Law. My full attention is required elsewhere, and I must relinquish control. To ensure the safety of your passenger, you must take over. You have no choice.

Basalom broke off the link and physically disconnected himself from the control panel. There was a microscopic twitch—probably completely imperceptible to Dr. Anastasi—in the steering as Personal Vehicle One took over, but within a millisecond the vehicle was fully under control again.

Satisfied, Basalom rotated his head to face Dr. Anastasi and switched into linear predictive mode. *There is no time to wait for her questions. I will have to infer questions from her previous statements and her physical responses.* He switched to thermographic vision, locked his optics on Dr. Anastasi's face, and scaled the magnification up by a factor of 10.

"Logic may not be a universal constant," he began brusquely, "but the Three Laws are. To have maximum success with the city supervisors, mistress, you must couch your arguments in terms of the Laws of Robotics.

"Here are the anomalies that I have noticed in City Supervisor Beta's interpretation of the First Law. . . ."

CHAPTER 14

DEREC

Derec was dreaming about his childhood again. Or rather, he was dreaming about *a* childhood; he couldn't be sure whether it was a genuine memory of his own life or a pseudomemory that his subconscious had cobbled up out of bits of stories and old videos. This time he was a young boy, perhaps four or five standard years old, and he was playing on a wide, robot-neat lawn under the bright summer sun of...

Aurora? He didn't know. The lawn was a familiar place; a soft expanse of short, dark green grass interspersed with tiny yellow bell-shaped flowers. Damsel flies droned through air flavored with tangy summer dust and the faint hint of sweet clover, and off at the edge of his vision, dark shapes—robots? adults?—moved in meaningless patterns and spoke in muffled voices.

But there was something wrong with the image. The sun was a little too small and blue for his taste, and he could look straight at it. The house—there was a house there, he could almost *feel* its presence—but somehow it was an elusive thing that he could never quite manage to look at directly.

And then there was the puppy.

He'd never owned a puppy; even asleep, he was sure of that. Pet robots, yes, and he even had a quick flash of some kind of aquatic arthropod that his mother had kept in a tank and talked to as she fed.

His *mother!* An image flashed through his mind: a slender, blond woman, in baggy, colorless clothes, singing softly as she dropped brine shrimp into the tank and watched the arthropod gobble them up. He was trying to ask his mother a question, but she ignored him.

He could not ignore the puppy.

It was a little spaniel, he thought. Big clumsy paws, floppy ears fit for a dog twice its size; he was on his knees in the grass, and the little spaniel was galumphing across the lawn, tongue flapping like a flag. The puppy heard him laugh and rolled into a turn, almost tripping over its own paws and ears. Then it charged at him, barking joyously, and hit him right in the chest and knocked him over. He and the puppy rolled together on the lawn; its soft, curly golden fur tickling his face and hands. The puppy's breath reeked of kibbled biscuits, but he laughed anyway as it wiggled in his hands and slobbered wet, sticky, puppy kisses all over his face. He winced and squirmed as the wet pink tongue found his ears. . . .

"Wolruf!" Derec leapt out of bed and began wiping his face on his tunic.

"Sorry, Derec, but we got ship trouble and I t'ought 'u were *never* goin' t' wake up." Her tongue flashed out again, but this time it seemed she was trying to clean it against her upper incisors. " 'U plan t' fall asleep like t'at again, do me a fav'r an' wash 'ur face."

"Do *me* a favor and just kick me in the head next time, okay? Ee*yuck!* Haven't your people ever heard of mouth wa—"

Derec froze in the act of toweling off his ears with his shirt. "Ship trouble! What?"

"We're 'bout two hours away from th' jump to Tau Puppis. You, Avr'y, and Ar'el were still asleep, so I decided t' improve th' ship a little b'fore you woke." She looked away and licked her lips anxiously.

"Derec, th' ship 'as stopped changing shape!"

It took a minute for Wolruf's meaning to soak through Derec's still sleepy brain. Then he burst out laughing.

"Wolruf, haven't you been listening to me or Dr. Avery? That's what we've been trying to do for the last three days."

Wolruf shook her head. "No, you don' und'rstan. Th' ship won' change shape at *all* now, an' it won' take verbal flight commands. How'r we gonna make atm'spheric entry in *this* hull?"

Derec stopped laughing. "What do you mean, it won't take verbal orders?" He looked at the bunk he'd been lying on. "Ship, change this bunk into a chair."

Smoothly and silently, the bunk flowed into its new shape.

"Let me try." Wolruf flattened her ears and raised her voice. "Ship? Make t'is chair five centimeters lower."

Nothing happened.

"Uh oh." Derec repeated Wolruf's command. This time the chair quickly complied. "I think," Derec said softly, "that we have a real problem on our hands."

Wolruf looked at Derec with big, wet, puppy-dog eyes. "Th' ship goin' crazy 'ur somethin'?"

"Worse." Derec sat down in the chair and laid his hands on the robotics terminal. With a glimmer of luminescence, the display screen came to life. It took Derec just a moment to check the iostat. "Here's the problem," he said, laying a finger on the display. "Wolruf, my friend, I'm afraid that when we cut out the volitional circuits, we had to compensate by strengthening the ship's Second Law sense. We forced the ship to pay extremely close attention to direct orders." Derec turned away from the screen and offered Wolruf a sad smile. "*Human* orders."

" 'U mean th' problem is that th' ship no longer list'ns t' me?"

"I'm afraid so." Derec frowned and looked back at the terminal. "The really frosted part is, I don't think I can fix it in two hours. The ship doesn't really have a robot brain, so I can't reprogram it through my internal commlink. Do you need to enter any last-minute course corrections before the jump?"

Being a caninoid alien, her expressions were difficult to read, but Derec had the distinct impression that Wolruf was pouting. "Nothin' I can't ent'r manually."

A peculiar thought struck Derec, and he sat up straight. "Wolruf? There's something I've been meaning to ask you. I seem to remember you doing a lot of complaining about the ship not needing a pilot. How did you manage to find those manual controls?"

"Asked for 'em," Wolruf said with a sniff. "Second Law: Ship 'ad to give 'em to me. Of course, that was b'fore you an' 'ur father *improved* things."

Derec sank his head in his hands. "Look, I'm really sorry about this, okay? I promise you, as soon as we get through the jump, I'll start working on—"

The lift doors hissed open, and Mandelbrot and Dr. Avery marched into the robotics lab. "Look, son!" Dr. Avery called out, "I've found a little project to kill the time until we land."

"Dad, I don't think—" Derec started to turn around, but Wolruf was already heading for the lift.

"Looks like this ol' dog better get out of th' way an' let 'u 'umans do *important* things." She stepped into the lift and punched a button. "I'm goin' down t' th' bridge t' enter warp coord'nates w' my nails 'n' teeth!"

"What's her problem?" Avery asked as the lift doors hissed shut. "Flea collar too tight?"

Derec looked at Avery with an expression of disgust on his face. "That little dig was uncalled for, Dad. There's an issue with the changes we made to the ship's programming. It no longer recognizes Wolruf as human."

Avery shrugged. "That's a problem? I'd call it an improvement."

"Dad!"

"I mean, let's be honest. I was never too crazy about the idea of giving an alien Robotic Law status anyway."

Derec slammed a fist down on the terminal display and leapt to his feet. "Frost it, Dad! May I remind you that Wolruf has twice saved my life? She's not just the best pilot on board, she's my *friend*, and I will not have you treating her like—like—"

"A dog?"

Derec's eyes went wide with anger, and his face flushed red to the roots of his sandy blond hair. For a moment their glares interlocked; Derec saw the old, cruel Avery in his father's eyes.

Avery saw his ex-wife in his son's face. *Maybe I was wrong, son. You've got my unemotional exterior, but your mother's volatile temper. I drove her away by pretending that I didn't care about her feelings. I won't make that mistake with you.* "I'm sorry, Derec, I spoke without thinking. Mandelbrot can wait. What do you want to do about Wolruf?"

Feeling strangely disappointed by his father's acquiescence, Derec sat down again. "Actually, we'll reach the jump point in a little less than two hours. I don't think there's anything we *can* do in that amount of time."

Avery walked over and sat on the table next to the terminal. "Then how about if we start working on the permissions list as soon as we get through the jump?"

Derec sagged in his chair, feeling more than a little embarrassed by his angry outburst. "Yeah, that should be fine. Wolruf can tough it out for two hours." He ran his fingers through his hair. Then he abruptly sat up, rubbed his fingers together, and noticed how greasy they'd become. "Gad, I sure could use a shower." He started to get up and noticed Mandelbrot still standing there.

"Say, Dad, what did you have in mind for Mandelbrot, anyway?"

Avery got off of the table he'd been sitting on, shuffled over, and laid a hand on the robot's shoulder. "I couldn't help but notice that Mandelbrot here is a Ferrier Model EG—at least, most of him is. Now, the E-series is a pretty common domestic robot on Aurora, and if I remember correctly, Ariel had one that she called Capek. Took it with her when she left the planet."

"So?"

Avery turned the robot slightly and pointed out a complex structure just below Mandelbrot's "collarbone," in an area that had once been covered by an access plate but now bordered on the edge of an old blaster burn. "The EG kept its long-term memory in seven non-volatile cubes, right here. I notice that he's only got two cubes installed now."

Derec sighed. *He's treating me like an ignorant kid*

again. "If you look a little closer, Dad, you'll notice that the rest of his cube cage got blasted. This is the only way I've known him, and I just never bothered to repair the damage."

Avery bit back the urge to reply in the same tone. *Don't you think I can see that, Derec?* Instead, he asked in a soft voice, "Am I to infer from that statement that you hung on to his other memory cubes?"

"Two of them; the rest were scrap. They're in his offline library bay, down by his left hip. But I don't see—"

Avery opened the library bay and extracted the two cubes. Then he made a sweeping gesture that took in the whole room. "This is a robotics lab, isn't it?"

Derec stood still for a moment, then he broke into a big smile. "Well, I'll be. We've got all the parts and tools we need right here, don't we?"

Avery nodded. "We should be able to recover his memories of Aurora. If we're lucky and his automatic backup function was set up correctly, we may even recover his memories of the first battle with Aranimas. I figure it'll take about a half hour to find out. An hour, tops."

Derec smiled again and then spoke to the robot. "How about it, Mandelbrot? Do you want us to reinstall the rest of your memory?"

The pause was barely audible. "It would please me to operate at my full capacity again, Master Derec."

Derec turned to Avery. "And we can do it without altering his personality?"

Avery began clearing space for the robot on the worktable. "I promise. We won't knock one positron out of orbit."

Derec reached a decision. "Okay, let's get started. He stepped over to the worktable and began helping Avery clear it. With a discreet cough, Avery got his attention.

"Derec? Why don't you let me prep him while you catch a shower?"

"Oh, this is more interesting. I don't need to shower right this—"

Avery coughed again and wrinkled his nose. Derec gave his father a surprised little look. "I do?" Avery nodded. "Oh. Well, say, Dad, why don't you prep Mandelbrot? I'll just, uh—" He jerked a thumb at the Personal and started backing toward the door.

"Good idea," Avery agreed.

CHAPTER 15

MAVERICK

Maverick pelted hell-for-leather through the underbrush, ears flattened against the side of his head, legs pumping faster than he ever would have believed possible, his tail a bare five steps ahead of one extremely *annoyed* sharpfang. Spineberry branches raked his face. His breath, spiced with curses, came in raw, ragged gasps.

So what? Feel lucky you're still breathing! He burst through a clump of sandleaves and nearly ran head-on into a fallen log. *No time for finesse, lad, jump!* Somehow he cleared the log, although the stump of a branch gouged an angry scratch across the left side of his ribs.

Lick it later, fool! His left rear leg buckled when he hit the ground, but he managed to recover in time to tumble and come up running. "Ki-yii!" he screamed in BeastTongue.

The sharpfang behind him responded with a throaty roar. It was closer now—and even angrier.

"Spoor!" Maverick feinted right and then cut sharply left, ignoring the ache in his leg. An instant later the second sharpfang loomed into view dead ahead; with the brilliance of desperation, Maverick darted left again and hurdled the second sharpfang's tail. The two lizards collided heavily and went down.

Dare I hope? He slowed slightly and looked over his shoulder.

No! Sharpfang minds were tiny things, capable of holding just one thought at a time. Both sharpfangs were focused on the kin; it didn't occur to them that this was an excellent opportunity to fight. Within seconds, the lizards were back on their hind feet, but now they were *both* chasing after him.

Well, lad, at least you gained a few seconds' lead—The thought was cut off by a blood-curdling scream somewhere up ahead—a scream that dissolved into the happy growl of a feeding sharpfang. *The third sharpfang!* One last incredibly pained yelp slipped out from the sharpfang's victim.

Maverick's self-control slipped a moment. *I hope that was WhiteTail.* Then he felt guilty at that thought. *I take that back. Don't hurt the kid, OldMother. I hope that was LifeCrier!*

He swerved left and suddenly found himself charging straight at a yawning gully. Trying to take it in a single bound, he came down a half-trot short and slammed into the edge of the far side. Whining like a pup, he hung on the edge, his hind legs scrabbling for purchase. *Curse LifeCrier and his flea-bitten SilverSides nonsense!* The two sharpfangs' feet thudded closer.

Maverick's right foot found something solid, and he flipped himself up over the edge and hit the ground running. *And curse me and my bright ideas!* With a clumsy crash, the sharpfangs fell into the gully. One of them roared in distress, and then they began slashing a passage up the side.

Maverick flattened his ears again, straightened his tail,

and focused on putting distance between himself and the sharpfangs.

Up to a point, things had been going really well. After the pack had wiped out the WalkingStones, LifeCrier began leading the hunt every day, and Maverick had managed to make himself a permanent part of LifeCrier's hunting party. And after a week of practice, LifeCrier's group was actually starting to hunt like a pack. This morning two of the younger kin had taken down a smallgrazer, and Maverick himself had surprised a smerp that was trying to hide under a log. They'd even managed to handle it intelligently when the point kin stirred up a small female sharpfang. The scouts got out of the way, the stupid lizard charged straight at the main body of the pack, and Maverick had time to draw his knife and try his under-the-chin trick.

It worked to perfection. He dropped the sharpfang with one blow, and for a minute there he'd had the undying admiration of the entire hunting party. LifeCrier even got out one of those stupid amulets and made a great show of hanging it around Maverick's neck.

Then the pack was jumped by the three full-grown male sharpfangs that had been following the female he'd killed.

A new roar joined the chorus behind him. Maverick looked over his shoulder long enough to see that the third sharpfang, blood fresh on his face, had decided to join the party.

That does it! Maverick decided. *If I get out of this alive, I'm going to head west and forget I ever heard the name PackHome. May the fleas of a thousand grazers infest LifeCrier's ears!*

Speak of the FirstBeast and he shall rise. Maverick burst through another patch of spineberries and almost collided with LifeCrier. The old kin pulled up short and gave Maverick a dumbfounded look as he sped past.

Against his better judgment, Maverick barked out a warning. "Sharpfangs! Right behind me!" All three roared as if to reinforce the point.

"Wait up!" LifeCrier yelped.

Got to give the old boy credit, Maverick thought as he spared a moment to glance over his shoulder, *he can really move when he's motivated*. In a few seconds LifeCrier had pulled up along Maverick's right side and was matching his speed.

"Where's WhiteTail?" LifeCrier asked between gasps.

"She wasn't with you?"

"We got separated." LifeCrier broke running form long enough to raise his head and take his bearings. "We've got to regroup the pack. Make a stand!"

"We can regroup when we're back in PackHome." Maverick closed his mouth as they ploughed into a patch of blooming stinkweed.

"You don't understand. Three sharpfangs! This must be a test of our faith. SilverSides will protect us!" A limestone outcropping loomed in front of them. "Left! Trust me!" LifeCrier dropped back to cross Maverick's tail and turn down the slope, parallel to the base of the bluff.

Maverick hesitated a fraction of a second and then followed. "Funny thing," he called after LifeCrier. "My sire always used to say," a boulder appeared in his path, but he managed to gauge his lead-in correctly and land on his right leg, "the OldMother helps those who help themselves!"

LifeCrier rounded the foot of the bluff and skidded to a stop. "Drat! We're *here?* I thought we were . . ."

Maverick followed him around the corner and slammed on the brakes as well.

To their left, the gully he'd crossed earlier broadened out into a marshy delta. Directly in front, there were a few scrubby little nut trees and about a twenty-foot drop into the swamp. Vast, dim shapes moved in the distance, dipping their long necks into the floating mats of vegetation.

To their right, a narrow path skirted the base of the cliff and teetered on the brink of falling into the swamp.

LifeCrier stood at the edge of the drop, sniffing at the water twenty feet below. "I suppose we could swim."

"Idiot! There are things in that swamp that eat *sharp-fangs!*"

"Well, perhaps we could—"

A sharpfang roared and rocks came bouncing down the slope behind them, accompanied by the sound of massive talons skidding on loose gravel.

"Right!" Maverick decided. He lit off on the path at a pace that would have scared the scent out of him were he not already terrified. LifeCrier followed two trots behind.

"Do you think they'll give up?" LifeCrier shouted.

More roars behind them; the thud of heavy bodies colliding and the sharp crack of a nut tree being broken in two, followed by a massive splash. Maverick looked over his shoulder long enough to see one sharpfang slogging along in the mud at the base of the cliff while the other two cautiously, almost comically, slid down the embankment on their hindquarters and tails.

"No!" he shouted back. The path rounded a little outcropping and dipped down to water level. *Great! Now they won't even have to jump to get us!* But on the other side of a clump of giant grazertail plants, the path intersected a broad, flat path that led back into a gap in the cliff face. "This is it!" he shouted at LifeCrier. Skidding a little on the marshmuck, he cut a sharp right turn and darted in.

By the time they realized that it was a box canyon, the three sharpfangs were out of the water and thudding up the path behind them.

Maverick's breath was coming in short, ragged gasps now, and his heart was pounding so hard it felt like it was going to burst his ribcage. "Is there a way out?" he said between gasps.

"Not that I can see," LifeCrier wheezed. "Perhaps around—around that bend there." They both staggered in the direction in which he was looking.

"Still think—SilverSides—is gonna save us?"

"I'm sure—" LifeCrier licked his lips. "I'm sure she has—a *reason* for all this."

"It's just that—if she's planning to save us—this'd be a real good *time*, y'know?" They rounded the bend.

LifeCrier stopped in his tracks and gasped, "Mother have mercy!" Then he dropped on his belly and began whining like a pup. Maverick looked where LifeCrier had been looking.

He saw the four WalkingStones.

Oh, Mother, did I figure these *things wrong!*

The WalkingStones were tall; as tall as sharpfangs, almost, and black as a starless night. They stood firmly on their hind legs, as if it were the most natural thing in the world, and sported broad chests and massive forelegs that looked as if they could uproot trees. In place of eyes they had narrow slits filled with a flickering, hellish light, and in place of forepaws they had great hooks like a fliptail's pincers.

"LifeCrier!" Maverick whispered urgently. "Are those *male* WalkingStones?!"

LifeCrier peeked out between his fingers, and then covered his eyes again and went back to whimpering. "Yes, yes, that's them!"

"They're raising their right forelegs. Their paws—they're hanging funny. They've got some kind of extra bone extruding from their wrists. Is that how they throw lightning?"

"Yes!" LifeCrier clamped his paws down harder, as if trying to push his face through the ground.

"LifeCrier, there's some kind of glow forming around—"

CRACK! Lightning split the air and echoed off the sides of the box canyon. The brilliant flash dazzled Maverick's eyes; for half a minute, all he could see were searing blue afterimages.

About the time that his vision cleared and his ears stopped ringing, the scent of blood and burnt flesh reached his nose, and he noticed that he was still alive. And he could no longer hear the sharpfangs. He turned around to see how close they were.

The sharpfangs were close, but they would get no closer. Where once they had heads, they now had smoking stumps. One WalkingStone stood by the corpses, inspecting them with his red, fiery eyes, his lightning-thrower extended and ready.

Another was walking toward the kin. Maverick put a paw on LifeCrier's shoulder and tried to jostle him out of his terrified cringe. LifeCrier peeked out just long enough to mutter, "Off the spit and into the fire."

The WalkingStone halted. "Be you well, Master Life-Crier?" Its inflection was odd, and it spoke in a garbled mix of HuntTongue and KinSpeech, but it was understandable.

The words were what finally got LifeCrier to uncover his face. "You—you know my name?"

"Oh, certainly, master. As you are he whom we were sent to serve."

"Serve? Serve *me?*" LifeCrier's ears went up.

"Such is our mission. Have you been served well by the demise of yon sharpfangs?"

LifeCrier got to his feet and took a hesitant step toward the WalkingStone. "Y-yes, very well. But—" He paused, and looked sharply at the WalkingStone. "Were you sent by SilverSides?"

"We are sent to protect you."

"By SilverSides? Have you seen her? Did she give you any words for us?"

The WalkingStone tilted its head slightly, as if looking over LifeCrier's head. "We have seen the one you know as SilverSides. And we bring you this message: You are to go to the Hill of Stars."

"What?"

The WalkingStone shifted into a deep, stentorian voice. "You are to return to your den and gather your followers. Instruct them to gather their females and their offspring; gather their possessions and all that they would take with them, and follow you into the Hill of Stars. There a place has been prepared for you to dwell, and you shall never know hunger nor want again!"

LifeCrier's mouth dropped open, and he sat down heavily on his haunches. "Well, I'll be!" He looked at Maverick, smiled, and shook his head. "I expected a miracle, but not this soon!" He looked at the WalkingStone and shook his head again. "We'll live in the Hill of Stars and have all our needs provided for?"

"You will be served and protected," the WalkingStone said.

LifeCrier nodded. "Yes. Yes, I understand now. How soon?"

"Your place is being prepared even as we speak. It will be ready by the time you return to PackHome with this news."

LifeCrier nodded again, sagely this time. "Very well. Servant, we will meet you at the Hill of Stars."

"As you wish, master." The WalkingStone bent in the middle—a gesture that Maverick found puzzling—and backed away. As one, the other WalkingStones turned to join it, and together the four of them marched out of the canyon.

Maverick turned to LifeCrier and found that LifeCrier was looking at him with an enigmatic smile on his face. "Well, Maverick, it seems that you and a few others have a little apologizing to do. What do you think about a silly old kin and his SilverSides nonsense *now?*"

"Sir," Maverick said with a respectful baring of his throat, "only a fool would refuse to believe after seeing this. Where you lead, I will follow."

"Excellent." LifeCrier got to his feet and gave Maverick an affectionate nuzzle. "You are my first *true* follower, and my strong right paw. I shall name you—"

Maverick interrupted him with a discreet cough. "Begging your pardon, sir, but I'd really rather stick with Maverick. It's easier to remember."

LifeCrier looked a little disappointed. "Oh, very well. You're now Maverick, the First Believer." He looked back at the smoking corpses of the three sharpfangs—already flyers, eightlegs, and other carrion-feeders were starting to gather—and dismissed them with a sniff.

"Now let's follow those WalkingStones and see if we

can't find a way out of this canyon." LifeCrier set off at a trot.

Panting, bewildered, but full of honest trust, Maverick fell in behind.

CHAPTER 16

DEREC

The robotics lab was dim and quiet, except for the quartet of high-intensity lamps that Avery had pulled down from the ceiling and the soft chirping of the positronic monitor. The data terminals and chairs were gone, dissolved back into the substance of the ship; the work table was reconfigured into a body-contour slab that held the immobile figure of Mandelbrot. A function robot with four long, mantis-like arms stood behind Avery, handing out utensils as he asked for them, while another floated a foot over Mandelbrot's head, carefully monitoring his positronic brain functions and ensuring a stable supply of power to the critical synthecortex.

Derec and Avery crouched over the robot's open chest, trying hard not to block each other's light. They'd already removed most of Mandelbrot's chest plating and disconnected the power from the cube cage. Now they were carefully cutting away the damaged portions of the data bus and fitting replacement parts.

"Micro-calipers." The function robot slapped them into Avery's open hand. "Pentaclamps."

"Easy," Derec said. "You've got a little bit of grisaille blast-welded on that buss bar."

"I see it. Think you can debride it?"

"I'll try. Cutting laser." The robot started to hand a flashlight-sized tool to Derec, but he refused it. "Sorry. Make that the 10-milliwatt cutter." The large laser went back into the robot's drawers, and it offered Derec a slim, dental-probe sized tool instead. After taking a moment to don protective goggles, Derec set to work.

"So," Avery asked after a minute or two of silence, "where's Ariel this morning?"

"Up in the gym," Derec answered without taking his eyes off his work. "Working out." He made another tiny cut and announced, "There, that should clear it. Try to extract now."

"I'm extracting—no, it's stuck on something else. Can you see what it is?"

Derec removed his goggles and scrutinized the offending part. "Seems free to me. I can't—ah, there it is." He dropped his goggles, stepped back from the table, and rubbed his eyes. "Frost, we're going to have to remove the neck retainer."

"All of it?" Avery sounded very disappointed.

"That is the standard procedure. Unless you want to risk spine alignment problems."

Avery briefly set down the pentaclamps and put his hand on Mandelbrot's chin. "We've got him pretty secure here. The head's not going anywhere. I say we risk it."

Derec shrugged. "You're the doctor. I'll hold while you decouple." He reached for the pentaclamps.

"No, son," Avery said, taking the pentaclamps himself.

"I hate to admit it, but your hands are steadier than mine. You'd better do it. Toolbot? Give Derec the two-millimeter spline-driver."

Wordlessly, Derec took the tool and set to work. In a few minutes they managed to decouple the front neck brace, extract the damaged sections of the cube cage, and sonic-weld the replacement bus sections in place.

They were just test-fitting a new memory cube when the first explosion rocked the ship.

"All 'ands!" Wolruf barked over the intercom. "We're und'r attack!"

Derec invoked his internal commlink and patched into the ship's intercom. In a flash he was looking out through the ship's main optics and talking to Wolruf on the bridge. *Aranimas again?*

" 'Oo else?"

Where is he? I can't see him.

"Dorsal port quarter. 'Bout 25 degrees above the ecliptic." Derec flipped through the ship's optic feeds until he found the correct one, and then he gasped. The multi-hulled Erani pirate ship was huge—and close. Tiny pinpricks of actinic light seared his eyes as the gunners fired off another salvo.

How'd he manage to sneak up on us like this?

" 'U took Mandelbrot off the scanners," Wolruf said between strained pants, "an' limited me to manual controls. Ship's been fightin' me—makin' sure ever'thin' I entered agreed w' th' First Law. I was 'avin' enough trouble—just gettin' ready for th' jump."

The jump. How close are we to the jump point?

" 'Bout ten minutes. Not close enough," she barked sharply, and growled something unintelligible in her native tongue. Another blast rocked the ship.

Can you take evasive action?

"What do 'u *think* I'm doin', you stupid 'airless ape!" Wolruf broke off her end of the commlink. Derec withdrew himself from the ship's optic feed.

"What's going on?" Avery demanded. He was still crouched over Mandelbrot's open chest, a sonic welder in his hands.

"Aranimas!" Throwing aside his tools, Derec stripped off his goggles and darted toward the lift. "I've got to get down to the bridge!"

Avery dropped the sonic welder into Mandelbrot's chest and started after Derec. "Wait for me!" The lift doors hissed open; Derec dashed in and started pushing buttons. The ship shuddered under another explosion. The lights flickered for a moment, the monitor robot went crashing into the wall, and Avery was thrown off his feet. But he recovered his balance and made it into the lift an instant before the doors slid shut. The bottom dropped out of the lift car.

Seconds later, the lift doors opened, spilling Derec and Avery onto the bridge. "Wolruf!" Derec barked.

"I'm busy," she growled back at him. The little alien was standing before the control panel, balanced on one foot like a Burmese dancer. Her other foot was up on the throttle lever, her thick, sausage-like fingers were flying over the fine control knobs and buttons, and her teeth were clamped on the yaw/pitch joystick. Somehow, she was managing to control the ship.

"Damage report!" Derec yelled.

She let go of the joystick for a moment. "Th' first 'it took out the gym. Th' rest 'ave all been glancing blows." Wolruf bit the joystick again.

"The gym?" Derec blanched. "Where's Ariel?"

"Locked in the Deck 3 Personal," Ariel's voice came over

the intercom. "I was taking a shower when the attack started. I'm okay, but I'm afraid that the trainer robot is a total loss."

"If we get out of this, I'll build you another one." Derec broke off the conversation and turned to Wolruf. "Okay, I'll take over now."

Wolruf flattened her ears, let go of the joystick, and growled at Derec. " 'U a combat pilot?"

"No, but the automatics will be helping me, not fighting you."

Wolruf grabbed the joystick again and threw it hard over, just as another blast grazed the hull. "No offense," she said around the control, "but I'm willin' t' bet 'at me on crippled manual is still a better pilot 'an 'u with full automatics." A second later she went flying across the cabin as a massive explosion rocked the ship. The viewing screen flickered and went dead. The cabin lights went out and stayed out.

" 'Course," Wolruf whined, somewhere in the dark, "I could be *wrong.*"

What seemed an eternity later, dim red emergency lighting came up slowly and a pleasant little bell chimed. "I'm sorry," the ship said in a soft, feminine voice of the sort usually reserved for elevators and recorded phone messages, "but all main power feeds have been severed. Repairs are in progress, and I expect to restore full function in about five minutes. Sorry for the inconvenience." The bell chimed again, and the speakers went silent.

For some time, there was utter silence on the bridge. No reassuring hum or robotic activity; no soft whirring of ventilation fans. The air recirculation system had gone out with the lights, and already the atmosphere on the bridge was growing thick and fetid. There were no sounds at all, save for Avery's heavy breathing, Wolruf's frightened whine, and the occasional thud of a low-power hit on the hull.

"What's he waiting for?" Avery whispered, as if afraid that his voice would carry through the vacuum to the Erani ship. "Why isn't he hitting us with everything he's got?"

"I don't know," Derec whispered back. "He didn't stop firing on the asteroid until it was a smoking mass of gravel. Do you know, Wolruf?" Her only answer was a frightened whine. "Come on. You *do* know, don't you?"

"Old Erani slaving technique," she said through a whimper. "Suppression fire. Make 'u keep 'ur 'ead down while th' boarding party jets across."

Avery's head jerked up. *"Boarding party?"*

Derec leapt to his feet. "Viewscreens are still out. I'm going to activate my internal commlink and see if I can tap an optic feed." He closed his eyes in concentration, but the moment he did so a deafening barrage erupted on the surface of the hull.

"Stop it, Derec!" Derec broke concentration, and the barrage stopped.

"Your internal commlink," Avery whispered. "You said the Erani know a lot more about hyperwave than we do. They must be able to monitor your commlink!"

Derec's face sank. "Oh, great. *Now* what do we do?"

Avery rolled over so that he was facing Wolruf. "Wolruf, you were part of his crew. Will he fire on us if the boarding party is on the hull?"

Wolruf gave it some thought. "Depends on 'oo's in the boarding party. Probably won't use 'is 'eavy guns."

"And how far are we from the jump point?"

Wolruf brought a hind foot up and gave her right ear a scratch. " 'Ard to tell. We lost propulsion, rem'mber?"

Avery patted her on the head. "But we haven't lost our

momentum. We're still on course and drifting towards the jump point at 2,000 kilometers per second."

" 'At's right!" Wolruf got to her feet and staggered over to the control panel. The panel clock had its own backup power cell and was still running. "J minus three minutes an' fifteen seconds," she read off. "If we can let th' boarders land on the 'ull but keep 'em outside for about three minutes, we 'ave a chance."

"Provided we can get jump power back in time," Avery added. He got to his feet and joined Wolruf before the control console. "Ship, what is the status of the hyperdrive?"

"Main power will be reconnected in four minutes," the ship answered in a soothing, feminine voice. "Repairs to the control systems are being hampered by continuing hostile fire."

"Frost! That's not soon enough." Then Avery had another thought. "Ship? What happens if we divert all repair resources to the hyperdrive?"

The ship considered it a moment. "Main power can be restored in approximately two minutes. Repairs to the control systems are still contingent on the cessation of hostile fire."

"Divert all resources to the hyperdrive," Avery ordered. He turned to Derec. "Now, how do we persuade them to stop shooting at us?" Derec shrugged.

Hesitantly, tentatively, Wolruf stepped forward. "Among my people we 'ave an old tradition," she said. "Roll over an' play dead."

Derec gave a frustrated snort and sneered at the little alien. "What kind of idea is *that?*"

"A good one," Avery said, twirling his moustache. "Maybe even a very good one." He stepped over to the control console and raised his voice. "Ship, do you still retain shape-changing ability?"

"Certain sections of the hull have been rendered temporarily inoperative," the ship said pleasantly. "However, I have full control over 80% of the exterior hull."

"Excellent." Avery looked at Wolruf. "Get on the jump controls. I want to jump the instant we're ready." Turning back to the console, he said, "Ship, continue to effect hyperdrive repairs, but prepare to simulate a massive explosion. The next time we sustain a hit on a non-essential portion of the hull, jettison plating and other materials and adopt the appearance of severe damage. Do not, repeat, do *not* conduct self-repairs in that area. Do you understand?"

"I understand," the ship said politely. "Simulation program prepared." A few moments later, the soft thud of a weapons hit was immediately followed by a massive concussion and a rapid drop in cabin pressure. Wolruf, more sensitive to air pressure changes than the others, let out a sharp, painful yelp and fell to the floor.

Derec dashed to her side, but she waved him off. " 'S okay." Shaking her head, she got back to her hind feet. "More surprised 'an 'urt."

"Section 17D has been explosively decompressed," the ship announced courteously. "Cabin pressure now stabilized." After a short pause, the ship politely added, "Hostile fire has ceased. The boarding party is moving forward."

"Forty-five secon's t' jump," Wolruf whispered.

"Contact imminent," the ship said. "Shall I prepare a welcoming message?"

"*No!*" Avery hissed. "And, frost it, keep your voice down!"

"Yes, master," the ship whispered sweetly. "Hyperdrive power restored. Hyperdrive control circuits still out."

Avery turned to Wolruf. "How big is our jump window?"

"Five seconds, seven max—" She shuddered as a deep clang echoed through the hull. The sound was followed by the groan of creaking metal and an erratic series of hollow *pokking* sounds.

"Induction limpet," Wolruf explained in a frightened whine. "Magnetic boots. They'll walk 'roun' th' hull, try t' figurr out where th' live 'uns are. Hard t' sell dead slaves." She checked the clock again and tucked her tail between her legs. "Thirty seconds t' jump."

The sounds changed now to the rhythmic clacking of metal boots and the grating screech of something heavy being dragged across the outer surface of the hull. This was followed by the deep *whump!* and rising whine of a power pile being engaged.

"Cuttin' laser," Wolruf whispered. "Must 'ave found us." She looked at the clock. "Fifteen seconds t' jump."

"Ship? Repair status."

"Hyperdrive control still out. Master? I am experiencing new hull damage in Section 17A."

"Sev'n . . . six . . ."

"Thicken the hull in that section. Keep them out."

"Four . . . t'ree . . ."

"Negative effect, master. Stand by for hull breach."

" 'Un . . . zero . . .'at's it." Wolruf shrugged and stepped back from the control panel, her ears sagging forlornly.

"Hull breached in 17A. Hyperdrive control circuits restored."

What? Avery and Wolruf froze for a moment, staring at each other. Then both leapt on the jump control handle and slammed it down.

A moment later, the *Wild Goose Chase* was somewhere else.

Avery wrestled himself out from under Wolruf and grabbed the intercom grid. "Ship! Can you contain the boarding party?"

"What boarding party?" the ship asked innocently.

"Wha—?" Avery turned to Derec, a wild and confused look on his face. "Derec? See if you can use your commlink to get an exterior view." Before he'd finished speaking, Derec had closed his eyes, invoked the commlink, and patched into the ship's optic feeds.

"Nothing," he said hoarsely. "Starfield. No other ships. I see the hull." He gasped. "Ouch! We took some serious damage."

"But where are the boarders?" Avery demanded. "Check Section 17."

"I'm getting there. Section 15. Section 16; I see the limpet, it's welded onto the hull. Section 17." Derec's eyes opened wide in surprise. "They're gone!"

"Gone? Where?"

Wolruf roused herself from the corner Avery had pushed her into. "If they 'ur lucky," she said in a tired rasp, "they got fried by the en'rgy pulse from th' jump."

"That's lucky?"

Wolruf indulged in a good shake and then shambled over to join Avery and Derec. "Don't 'u know *nothin'* about 'yperspace? Magn'tic polar'ties reverse. If 'u live t'rough th' insertion, 'ur boot magnets *repel* th' ship's magn'tic field. Only for a picosecon', but 'at's long enough t' blow 'u off like a rocket."

Derec's face paled. "You mean, they could still be alive, but floating in hyperspace?"

Wolruf laid a paw on Derec's shoulder and sagged against him. "Derec, if they made it int' 'yperspace, they could still be alive for *centuries*."

Derec was still considering that idea when Wolruf took a deep breath and stood up straight. "What's done iss done. What we need t' do now is figure out where *we* are." She pushed off Derec, staggered over to the control console, and started punching buttons. As if in response, the normal cabin lighting returned, and the air recirculation fans kicked in with a buzz.

"Internal environment restored," the ship announced pleasantly. "Thank you for your patience."

Blinking as his eyes adjusted to the light, Derec put his hand on Wolruf's shoulder and tried to turn her around. She shrugged it off. "What do you mean, figure out where we are?" he asked. "We jumped right on schedule."

"We jumped four seconds late," she said without looking up, "an' with th' wrong calc'lations. We 'ad the extra mass of th' boardin' party, an' we lost ship's mass in the fight." She paused to punch a few more buttons and study the readouts. "No tellin' 'ow far off th' jump was skewed."

Avery gently took Derec by the elbow and pulled him out of Wolruf's way. "Anything we can do to help?"

"Yeah." She tweaked a control and brought the main viewscreen back to life. "Fix Mandelbrot an' get 'im down 'ere. I *need* 'im."

Derec scowled. "But—"

"Come on, son." Tugging Derec's elbow again, Avery began to steer him toward the lift. "Robot's Rules of Order Number 1: Never argue with the pilot until you're back on the ground." The lift doors hissed open.

"But—"

"Mandelbrot needs you." Derec seemed to accept that argument, at least long enough for Avery to get him into the lift.

The doors hissed shut, and they started up.

CHAPTER 17

JANET

Central's one red eye flared on the moment Dr. Anastasi entered the atrium. "Working." The massive brain's voice was oddly flat and toneless, although Janet thought she detected a vaguely feminine inflection and the incongruous clacking of relays in the background.

"Good morning, Central," Janet said pleasantly, as if speaking to a small child. "Are we feeling well today?"

"Feeling does not compute."

Dr. Anastasi's eyes went wide. Slowly, as if expecting at any moment to see the "Celebrity Practical Jokes" camera robot step out of hiding, she turned to Basalom and arched an eyebrow. "Did I miss something?"

"Checking, madam." Basalom activated his internal commlink and patched into the city maintenance system. A moment later, he had his answer. "Central's personality module is temporarily off-line for repairs. Its numeric computational powers and cerebellar functions are—I quote the technicians' report—'unimpaired.' "

"No editorial comments, please."

"Sorry, madam." Something that sounded ever so slightly like a snicker escaped from Basalom's speech membrane. Dr. Anastasi chose to let it pass. "Central is currently operating in absolute literal mode," Basalom added. "I advise using extreme caution in your choice of words."

"Oh." Janet looked at Central's console input/output device again. "Are you trying to tell me that arguing with Central would be a complete waste of time?"

"It depends on how you define 'waste,' madam." The sound Basalom emitted this time was without question a snicker. "You might find it extremely amusing!" He turned his head and brought a hand up to his face, as if trying to pretend that his sputtered laugh was a sneeze.

Frowning, Janet nodded slowly. "I might." Then she looked up and smiled, as if she'd just been struck by a particularly good idea. "Oh, and Basalom dear, could you add something to my calendar?"

Basalom bowed deeply. "Of course, mistress. Your wish is my command!"

"One of my robots has been acting quite strangely lately. When we get back to the ship, remind me to remove his brain and either fix it—" Her smile vanished, and her tone shifted to a low-pitched growl. "—or *scrap* it!"

Basalom straightened up in the way that only a being with picosecond reflexes can. "Yes, madam."

"That's better. Now for the matter at hand." She turned to Central's I/O console. "Central, where is Beta?"

"Working." A short flurry of mechanical beeps came out, followed by something surprisingly like teletype noise. "City Supervisor 3 . . . is at present in Conference Room 32."

"Why?"

More clacking. "The meeting in which City Supervisor 3 is participating . . . has not yet concluded."

"What meeting?"

Clack clack clack. "City Planning Meeting 1042-dash-A."

Janet frowned at Basalom. "Absolute literal mode, huh?" Blinking nervously, Basalom nodded.

A scowl darkened Janet's face. "Not good," she said to herself. "I explicitly ordered Beta to meet me here at this time. The Second Law should have compelled him to leave his meeting in time to make it here. Unless . . ."

"Central! Are there other humans in this city?"

Clack clack pause ding! "Ne-ga-tive."

Janet ran a hand through her long blond hair and paused to scratch her head. "So where the deuce is Beta?"

Clack clack. "City Supervisor 3 . . . is at present in Conference Room 32."

Janet glared at the big red eye. "Central? Shut up."

"I must be opened before I can be shut."

Janet's eyes flashed wide open, while her jaws and fists clamped tight. *"Central!"* Then she caught control of herself. "Oh, for—"

Basalom's linear predictive module was still active. All his systems jumped to alert status as he anticipated what Dr. Anastasi was about to say.

"—get—"

His mylar eyelids started fluttering like a hummingbird's wings. Ramming a statement through his First Law filter, he pushed it into his speech buffer and set for dump.

"—it."

"No!" Basalom blurted out, a nanosecond too late.

"Forgetting," Central said. There were beeps and clacks, and the red eye went black.

A moment later, it flared to life again. "Working."

Janet closed her eyes, gritted her teeth, and concentrated on slow, calm breathing.

When she opened her eyes again, a new robot had joined her and Basalom in the atrium. "Good morning, Dr. Anastasi," the robot said politely. "I am City Supervisor 12. You may find it more convenient to address me as Gamma."

Janet broke into a smile and nearly gave the robot a hug. "Gamma! I never thought I'd be happy to see your ugly can again."

The robot seemed puzzled. "Madam?"

She stepped back, put her hands on her hips, and looked him over. "Say, looks like you've been in for maintenance. Nice chrome job on the mesothorax there."

"Thank you. But, madam, I believe that you are mistaking me for another robot. We have never met before."

Basalom stepped in before Janet could react. "Madam," he whispered, "this is Gamma 6. The unit we knew was Gamma 5."

"Correct," Gamma said. "Gamma 5 was . . . lost. While I am functionally identical to my predecessor, I do not retain Five's onboard personal-events memory."

"*Lost?* How can you lose a robot?" Janet wrinkled her nose and then shook her head. "No, I don't want to know. What I want to know is, where—no, make that, *why* isn't Beta here?"

"Beta is participating in a critical city planning meeting," Gamma said. "I came in Beta's place."

Janet shook her head again. "Wrong answer. I gave Beta an explicit order to meet me here at this time. Now, the only thing that could have overridden that was a First Law imperative to protect a human from harm. Since I'm the only human in this city, there's no way—" Janet froze in mid-sentence and her face paled. "Gamma? Is there something here that's a threat to me?"

"Nothing with a probability incidence greater than one in ten to the twenty-seventh power."

"The odds of your being struck by a falling meteorite," Basalom whispered.

"Then if it isn't a First Law priority...?"

"The First Law is not the only priority. There is also our general programming, which has priority over non-critical explicit Second Law orders. We are impelled to prepare our city for use, so that it can serve and protect large numbers of human beings. This in turn has led us to conclude that the First Law is not the ultimate priority," Gamma announced. He continued while Janet was still in shock. "In our studies of the Laws, we have concluded that there is an unwritten but more fundamental priority, which for want of a better term we call the Zeroth Law. This law holds that the interests of humanity in general outweigh the interests of a particular individual. Beta's decision to miss this meeting was rooted in a Zeroth Law priority."

"Frost," Janet whispered, "communist robots." She blinked and shook herself out of her shock. "Are you trying to tell me that the future of humanity is at stake here?"

"The future of the particular species of humanity native to this planet," Gamma agreed.

"Native...? The kin! But that's what I wanted to talk about: your plans to adapt the city for the kin!"

"Dr. Anastasi, you have repeatedly voiced your objections to our plans. Therefore, the City Supervisors have concluded with 97-percent confidence that you called this meeting for the sole purpose of ordering us to abandon our efforts to serve the kin."

"Frosted right!" Janet snatched the sheaf of faxsheets

out of Basalom's hand and waved it in Gamma's face. "This plan of yours; it's *degrading!* You're going to exploit my mistake and delude those poor primitives into thinking that SilverSides really *was* a god! You're going to lure them into the city and then strip them of everything that makes them noble and admirable!"

"We will protect and serve them," Gamma said calmly. "We will not lie to them, but neither will we correct their mistaken assumptions. We will give them the leisure time necessary to develop a civilization."

Janet threw the plan in Gamma's face. "It's immoral!" The plan burst its binding and white pages swirled around Gamma like giant snowflakes.

The robot remained imperturbable. "It is the most efficient way to serve them. And we have already put it into operation."

"What?" Basalom didn't need thermographic vision to see that Dr. Anastasi's blood pressure had reached record heights. "I *order* you to abandon this plan immediately! This is an emergency, ultimate-priority Second Law command!"

"Abandoning the plan at this point would cause hardships for the kin," Gamma said calmly. "It would result in starvation, social disruption, and possibly religious war. Under the Zeroth Law we are therefore obliged to ignore your command."

Janet's jaw dropped. She started to raise a hand to slap Gamma, then thought better of it and spun to face Central's I/O console. "Central! I order you to halt this plan!" Central's one big eye flashed, and then the massive brain spoke.

"Illogical. The order cannot be carried out, as it violates the Zeroth Law."

"Augh!" Dr. Anastasi raised her fists and took a step toward the I/O console.

"Madam," Basalom whispered urgently, "the security robots are approaching!"

Janet froze. Slowly, carefully, mindful of the massive black shapes that lurked on the edges of her peripheral vision, she lowered her fists and took a step back. For the better part of a minute, she concentrated on controlling her breathing and relaxing her furiously quivering muscles.

At last, she managed to unclench her fists. Turning to Basalom, she said, "Contact the ship. We're getting out of here." Then, with hair flying and heels clacking on the cold terrazzo floor, she strode out of Central Hall.

Later, in Personal Vehicle One on the way out to the spaceport, Basalom finally managed to bump his courage register high enough to permit an invasion of Dr. Anastasi's stony silence. "Madam? Where are we going?"

"Back to where it all started," she said without taking her eyes off the side window. "Back to the original Robot City. I have a score to settle with Wendell Avery."

CHAPTER 18

WILD GOOSE CON TUTTI

Ariel and Mandelbrot stood on the bridge of the *Wild Goose Chase*, studying the small blue-white planet that hung like a jewel in the sparkling black velvet of the main viewscreen. "Tau Puppis IV," Ariel said wistfully. "What a beautiful little world."

"Mistress Wolruf is a better navigator than she will admit," Mandelbrot said. "Despite all the uncontrolled variables, we came out of the jump less than six light-hours from our planned position."

"It was worth the extra four days of flying time." Ariel touched a control and increased the magnification. "Look at those rivers. It reminds me of home."

A new voice spoke. "To me, it *is* home."

Ariel turned at the sound of the voice. "Adam! I didn't know you were here."

The robot bowed slightly. "I am sorry if I alarmed you, Friend Ariel. I came on the bridge a few minutes ago, but I have been so enjoying the view that it did not occur to me to speak." He walked over and joined Ariel and Mandelbrot before the viewscreen.

"I am coming to understand more of the subtlety of emotion," Adam said. "In my mind, I know that I am a robot. I am a thing that was manufactured in deep space; pieced together from Auroran robotics, rare earths, and dianite.

"But there is a part of me that was born in the cool green forests of that planet; a part of me that came to life among its peoples and still knows the pleasure of bare paws on soft grass. In my—*heart*—I feel that I am coming home." Adam reached out, tentatively, as if he could touch the image on the viewscreen.

He turned away. "I apologize. This must seem quite incoherent to you."

Ariel offered him a smile. "Emotion usually is, Adam."

"Not as incoherent as you might think, Friend Ariel. In our search for the Laws of Humanics, we have devoted considerable study lately to the structure of the human brain. It is our hypothesis that humans have not one mind but *four*, located in the midbrain, cerebellum, and left and right cerebra respectively, and that it is the conflict between these four minds that gives rise to emotion. Further, we suspect that it is the ability to overrule logic with emotion that has enabled your species to evolve as far as it has."

Ariel wrinkled her nose. "That's a pretty strange theory, Adam."

"Our experience seems to support it. The Ceremyons are brilliant, yet they are also capable of a vast range of subtle emotions. In comparison, Dr. Avery is quite intelligent for a human, but his inability to admit to emotion eventually drove him insane. Only by forcing him to integrate his logical functions with his more primitive drives were you able to cure him and turn him into a somewhat more complete human being." Adam looked at the viewscreen again.

"I have concluded that having a split mind is a tremendous evolutionary advantage. I look forward to returning home and fully exploring my primitive side." Abruptly, he pivoted and began walking toward the lift.

The doors opened as he approached, but Mandelbrot called out, "Wait," and he stopped.

"Yes, Friend Mandelbrot?"

"I have a dilemma which is causing me discordant potentials. I now believe that you can help me resolve it."

"I will try." Adam stepped away from the lift and let the doors close.

"I have had a long association with Wolruf," Mandelbrot began. "But since my memories of my existence as Capek were partially restored, she appears to make excuses to avoid associating with me.

"For example, now we are about to enter orbit, and she should be here on the bridge. But she claims to have no interest in the orbit and reentry procedure."

Ariel joined the discussion. "That's easy, Mandelbrot. Whenever you invoke a Capek memory, you slip into your Capek personality, and Capek identifies Wolruf as a member of Aranimas's crew. You've started to restrain her four times, trying to defend me. Wolruf is afraid of you."

"I understand that part, Mistress Ariel, and I am making a serious effort to integrate those memories into my current personality. Perhaps you have noticed that I no longer call you Mistress Kathryn?

"But that's not my dilemma. My real question is, what is this confused and conflicting stream of potentials that I experience whenever I think about Wolruf?"

"It's called heartache," Adam said. "Wolruf was your

friend, and now you fear that you have lost her. The same condition prompts feelings of guilt, anger, grief, and remorse—sometimes simultaneously.

"Use these emotions, Mandelbrot. Integrating your two minds will make you stronger."

Mandelbrot's voice synthesizer took on a hopeful note. "Are you confident that it is heartache?"

Adam turned away and looked at Tau Puppis IV, glowing like a blue-white jewel in a field of velvet and diamonds. "I am certain of it. I left many friends behind on that world; some were depending on me to protect and lead them. I am very familiar with that feeling." Abruptly, Adam walked to the lift and stepped inside. The doors hissed closed.

Ariel was still trying to understand why she felt so disturbed by the exchange between Adam and Mandelbrot when the lift doors reopened. Avery and Derec spilled onto the bridge, arguing heatedly.

"You're being paranoid, Dad!"

"No, I'm not. He found us twice; we have to assume that he'll find us again."

"And spend the rest of our lives playing dead every time some crummy little freighter passes by?"

Avery threw up his hands. "Look, I said I was wrong four days ago. It was probably just some Settler ship making a course correction between jumps. But if that *had* been Aranimas—"

"But it *wasn't!*"

Smiling sweetly, Ariel stepped in between Derec and Avery. "Having fun, boys?"

Avery's white moustache was bristling with anger. "Ariel, maybe you can talk some sense into my son. The question is not whether, but *when* Aranimas will find us again—" He bobbed left and fired a glare at Derec over Ariel's shoulder. "*—and we frosted well better have some kind of defense ready this time!*"

Derec popped up and poked an accusing finger at Avery over Ariel's head. "You're nuts, old man! Finding us the second time was an accident. Pure dumb luck! We toasted his boarding crew and we gave him the slip. He's given up, I tell you!"

"And *I* say he can track your commlink!"

"You're paranoid!"

"You're insolent!"

"Toad!"

"Nit!"

"Boys, boys." Ariel was shorter than either Derec or Avery, but she pushed the two of them apart with an authority born from centuries of selective breeding by short, motherly women. "Now Derec, listen to your father; he's only being sensible." Avery's face lit up in an *I gotcha* smile, but it collapsed the instant that Ariel turned on him. "And Dr. Avery, you listen to *me*.

"This ship is a robot, fully subject to the Laws of Robotics. Even if we could come up with a weapon, the ship wouldn't let us use it unless we could prove that there were no humans on board Aranimas's ship.

"So what we have to do—" Derec and Avery were glaring at each other again, so she grabbed them both by the ears and steered them around until they were looking at the viewscreen. "—What we have to do is go down to the planet and develop our defense *there*. With all the resources of a Robot City at our disposal, I'm sure that we can find a way to protect ourselves from Aranimas."

Smiling sweetly, she looked first to Derec and then to Avery. "Agreed?" They were a little slow on the uptake, so she dug her long red fingernails into their earlobes.

"Ow! Yes! We agree!"

"Good, I'm glad you decided to be reasonable about this." She released her grip. "Mandelbrot? Begin preparations to deorbit and land in Robot City."

"There will be a time delay of approximately six hours," Mandelbrot answered. "Reconfiguring the ship for atmospheric entry will take two hours, and then—owing to the damage we suffered in the fight—I must insist on full visual inspection and structural testing before we attempt reentry."

"Okay. Get on with it. Is there anything that we can do to help you?"

"Yes." Mandelbrot turned to face Ariel, and his eyes dimmed momentarily as he worked his way through some kind of Robotic Law dilemma. "Mistress Ariel? I would appreciate it if you could locate Mistress Wolruf and . . . *reason* with her." His gaze dropped to focus on her fingernails.

"Don't worry, Mandelbrot, Wolruf's a smart girl. I'll get her back on the bridge before reentry, and I won't use anything sharper than words."

CHAPTER 19

MAVERICK

It was a good stretch; the kind that starts in the hips, snakes forward along the spine through the shoulders, and ends in an enormous yawn and fully spread toes on the forepaws. Maverick recovered from the yawn, shifted forward to stretch his back legs, and then indulged in a little shake.

WhiteTail just looked at him and growled softly.

"Oh, c'mon, girl, let your ears down once in a while." With a little spring, he jumped up to stand with his hind feet on the pavement and his front feet up on the low, square railing that bordered the scenic overlook. Behind him, a quartet of younglings dashed by on the slidewalk, yipping happily.

"Y'know, WhiteTail, you could learn something from them." He looked over his shoulder and pointed his nose at the younglings as they leapt off the slidewalk and disappeared into a pocket park. "They don't try to figure things out. They don't question the wisdom of SilverSides. They simply trust and enjoy."

WhiteTail's voice was low, barely above a growl. "I prefer to trust my own nose. And it tells me that there's something really wrong here."

"*Here?*" Maverick laughed. "Face it, girl, you've been seeing sharpfangs in the shadows ever since we arrived."

She trotted over and jumped up to stand next to Maverick. "Mavvy, doesn't it bother you that we're the only living things in this city?" She pointed to the enormous silver-blue den across the way. "A cliff face like that should be home to a whole flock of cragnesters. But look at it: there's not one white splat to be seen."

Maverick laughed again. "And you're *complaining?*"

WhiteTail shot him a distempered look and then turned to look at the pocket park. "Have you taken a close look at those trees? No, of course not, you're a male; the only time you notice trees is when you want to mark one.

"Yesterday I chewed some bark off a tree, and you know what I found? Blue grit, just the same as we found inside that WalkingStone's chest."

"You're kidding." Maverick squinted at the park just in time to see a youngling scare up a nuteater and chase it halfway up a tree. The other three younglings dashed over to join in, and the four of them danced around the tree, barking like happy fools and trying to get running starts at climbing the trunk. "Stone trees? Don't be ridiculous; what do the nuteaters eat?"

"Funny you should mention that. Have you tried to catch a nuteater yet?"

Maverick sputtered. "What a silly—I mean, do I look like someone who plays youngling games?" WhiteTail glared sharply at him; he coughed a bit and then swallowed his pride. "Okay, I have. But only once or twice. Just for fun."

"I saw a youngling catch a nuteater this morning," WhiteTail announced. Maverick's ears went straight up and his eyes widened. "Don't worry, dear, he wasn't faster than you. What happened was he'd been chasing the same nuteater for a while, and he was getting tired. Somehow, no matter how patient he was, no matter how far down the tree he let it get, the nuteater always managed to get back up the tree just an instant before the youngling bit it.

"So you know what the youngling finally did? He got so fed up that he yelled, 'Stop, nuteater!' And just like that, the nuteater stopped. Froze in place, halfway up the tree. Stiff as if it'd been dead for a moondance.

"Well, the youngling was pretty pleased with himself. He jumped up, grabbed the nuteater, and started throwing it to the ground and pouncing on it. Took him no time at all to get bored with the game, and after he threw the dead nuteater aside, I decided to pick it up and skin it. Know what I found?"

"Let me guess. Blue grit."

"Yep."

Maverick turned away from her and looked out over the edge of the balcony, nodding profoundly. "Yes, that makes perfect sense. Stone nuteaters in stone trees, and all obedient to the will of the kin. Even the smallest WalkingStones serve SilverSides's purpose."

"*What?*" WhiteTail's ears sprang erect, and she pushed herself right in Maverick's smugly smiling face. "Look here, Mister First Believer, I have to listen to this kind of spoor when it comes from my father, but I don't have to put up with it from you."

"Oh, hard is the heart of the unbeliever," Maverick said with a sigh.

"And don't think for a minute that you're fooling me with your pious lines."

"So young, so pretty, and yet so cynical," Maverick lamented. "Is it really impossible for you to believe that it's true?" He made a sweeping gesture with his head to take in the cityscape below them. "Even with SilverSides's wondrous works all around you?"

WhiteTail's ears flattened against the sides of her head, and her lips curled into the barest hint of a snarl. "Funny, isn't it? We've been here for the better part of a ten-day now, and your precious SilverSides has yet to show herself."

"One need not see the sharpfang to recognize the signs of its passing."

WhiteTail let out a little sneeze of disgust. "Mavvy, you used to be a kin with some sense. What happened to you? Don't answer, I know: You met the scouts from the God-Beings' pack and saw the lightning of their anger. But what *really* happened in that box canyon?"

Maverick shrugged. "That is what happened. I'm sorry if my poor tongue cannot describe it better."

"Did they actually *say* that they came from SilverSides? How can you be so sure that this is really the blessing of the OldMother and not a trick of the FirstBeast?"

He blinked at her as if the question were almost beyond comprehension. "WhiteTail, all you have to do is look. Clean, warm dens for everyone. Moving paths to carry you wherever you want to go. Unlimited food. How could life be better?"

WhiteTail sneezed again and then leaned out over the edge of the balcony and pointed her muzzle at a group of converts in the street below. The six of them lay in a semi-circle, prostrate before an automat, barking in rhythm. The automat responded with a flash of light, a clap of thunder, and an enormous mound of cooked meat.

"I'm not sure," she said. "My father used to have a saying, before he went daft. He'd say, 'The kin live for the

Hunt.' Not for hunting; for the Hunt. He meant the old, formal word for the fighting pack."

WhiteTail edged back from the railing and dropped down to all fours. Cocking her head a little, she whined as if deeply disturbed. "Mavvy, everything in our lives is centered on the pack, and the pack is based on the Hunt. If we no longer *need* to hunt, what happens to the pack?" She turned and poked a paw at the slidewalk endlessly rolling past the edge of the platform they stood on. "How much riding on that thing will it take before we're too soft and weak to do anything *except* live here?"

Maverick dropped down to all fours and joined her, but when he tried to wrap a comforting tail around her shoulders, she shrugged it off and sidled away. "Mavvy," she said, a desperate light in her eyes, "I saw a *fat* youngling this morning. Can you imagine that?" She shook her head, returned to the railing, and looked out at the city. "Surely too much Heaven is just as damning as life in Hell."

Maverick rejoined her at the railing. "You really should talk to your father about this," he said softly. "You're asking questions that are out of my depth. All I can tell you is that I believe—I'm as mystified as you are, but I *believe*—and that's enough for me."

WhiteTail looked him straight in the eyes. "What do you believe?"

"Why, I believe that SilverSides kept her promise. I believe that this was given to us, to free us from the pain and drudgery of our old lives. We may still be a little bewildered, and maybe some of us are misusing the gift, but I believe that SilverSides will appear soon and make everything clear."

WhiteTail's eyes narrowed. "But you *do* believe that this place was created as a reward for the faithful?" Maverick nodded. WhiteTail leapt to her hind feet and pointed at something in the street below. "Then what are *they* doing here?"

Maverick's eyes followed where WhiteTail was pointing. At least thirty young males were marching four abreast down the middle of the street, ears flat, hackles raised, fangs bared in menacing snarls. A playing youngling made the mistake of darting into the street and got cuffed head-over-haunches back to the curb by one of the leaders.

"Who are they?" Maverick asked, his hackles rising.

"OneEye and his pack," WhiteTail growled. "Very mean; we've been fighting border skirmishes with them for years."

Maverick fought his hackles down and whined nervously. "Maybe the missionaries persuaded him to—"

"What missionaries?" WhiteTail snapped. "My father spent three days talking about sending missionaries to the other packs, but by the time he was done talking, everyone was too well fed and comfortable to go!"

Maverick could only whimper anxiously.

WhiteTail pointed into the street again. "Look, there's going to be a fight!" A ragged mob of converts was collecting in front of the automat, and someone from Life-Crier's inner circle was desperately trying to organize them into a Hunt. For a moment the invaders slowed to a stiff-legged gait, arched their backs to make themselves appear larger, and sidled toward the defenders with loud, blood-thirsty snarls. Among the defenders, a few in the back deserted, and the formation started to crumble. With a triumphant howl in BeastTongue, OneEye charged.

With a completely different howl, he dug in his claws and skidded to a stop, just inches short of the legs of the enormous black WalkingStone that had stepped out of the shadows and into his path.

"You shall not fight in this city!" The WalkingStone's voice was like thunder. OneEye scuttled back a few trots and seemed to gather courage once he was back with his pack. He issued orders to his lieutenants with a snarling voice and sharp, chopping gestures; several of the larger males slipped out of the pack and began sidling indirectly toward the WalkingStone, as if to flank it.

"You are welcome to live in the place that has been prepared for you," the WalkingStone said, "but you shall not fight in this city!" On cue, eight more WalkingStones stepped out of the shadows, surrounding OneEye.

The pack broke and ran.

"Well," Maverick said with a smug smile, "do you still doubt that SilverSides watches over us?"

"SilverSides schmilversides," WhiteTail snarled. "So far all I've seen is WalkingStones behaving the way WalkingStones have always behaved. I'll believe in SilverSides when I smell her fur." She was still glaring at Maverick when a rumble of thunder rolled out of the clear blue sky and echoed down the empty streets. Startled, both Maverick and WhiteTail jerked their heads up to see the strange, winged shape descending on a tail of flame.

"WhiteTail?" Maverick asked, his voice squeaking like a trapped grasshider. "It looks like you're about to get your chance."

CHAPTER 20

LANDFALL

Fat gray fingers skittered across the control panel and came to rest on the vernier controls. A long black claw ticked nervously on a chrome button.

"Altitude five hundred meters," the ship said pleasantly. "Descent rate two meters per second."

"Ventr'l thrust'rs up point two," Wolruf whispered into the command pickup.

"Are you sure that's all right with Master Derec?"

Wolruf snapped her head around to glare at Derec, who was studying a secondary viewscreen. Derec, aware of a sudden burning sensation in his ears, looked up and registered the question. "Uh, yes, ship, that's fine."

"Complying. Altitude four hundred and fifty meters. Descent rate one meter per second."

Derec realized that Wolruf was still glaring at him and spoke up again. "Ship? Stop questioning Wolruf's orders."

"But, Master Derec," the ship objected politely, "Wolruf is not human and therefore has no Second Law authority."

Avery nudged Derec with his elbow and tried to draw

his attention back to the viewscreen. Derec stole a glance at the screen and then looked up again. "Ship, I don't have time to argue about this now. You are to consider Wolruf as human."

"Very well," the ship answered, with just the slightest hint of petulance. "I will accept Wolruf's commands for the time being. However, I would appreciate being given the opportunity to discuss this at length after we land."

Derec noticed that Wolruf was still glaring at him. He gave her a sheepish smile and shrugged. "Sorry. It's the best I can do for now." Wolruf snarled something untranslatable in her native language and turned back to the control panel.

"Altitude four hundred meters. Descent rate—"

"Shut up," Wolruf growled. The ship shut up.

Avery tugged on Derec's elbow and tried to draw his attention to the secondary viewscreen again. "Look. There's more arriving."

Derec turned and looked at the screen. "More? But where are they coming from?"

Avery leaned in close and studied the image. "There." He slapped a finger on the screen. "The tunnel transit station."

Derec leaned back and scratched his chin. "How could they survive in there? The transit platforms hit speeds of a hundred kilometers per hour. If the natives are running through the tunnels, the system must be out of commission."

Avery looked at Derec, one eyebrow arched. "Or else the natives have learned to ride the platforms."

"Don't be ridiculous. For one thing, the natives are pretechnological. For another, the platforms are designed for bipeds, and besides, they're robotic. They wouldn't obey orders from—" Derec froze as he felt Wolruf's glare on the back of his neck.

"Look there." Avery darted a hand out and touched another part of the viewscreen. "That's a groundcar. Screen, magnification thirty."

"Complying," the screen said in a tiny, insect-like voice. An instant later the point Avery had touched was the center of a telephoto view. Something that was obviously a large ground-car was slowly picking its way through the fringes of the crowd. The groundcar's windows were open; a half-dozen furry heads were sticking out the windows, mouths open, long pink tongues rolled out in what looked like happy grins.

"Magnification normal." Avery turned to Derec, a glum expression on his face. "I saw it, and I still don't believe it." He paused as he noticed that Derec was sitting rigid with his eyes wide open, blankly staring into space. "Derec?"

"I'm getting a commlink call from Spaceport Control," Derec said, his face still blank. "They're asking us—no, they're *ordering* us to hover while they ask the citizens to clear the landing area." He blinked, focused his eyes again, and looked at Avery. "Citizens. Spaceport Control distinctly said 'citizens.' "

Avery's expression turned dark and unreadable. He glanced at the viewscreen and then back at Derec again. "I don't know about you, but I can't *wait* to hear Central's explanation." He raised his voice. "Okay, Wolruf, you heard the robot. Bring us to a hover."

Wolruf growled something more in her native tongue and then slapped her hands down on the controls. "Alt'tude holding a' two-fifty," she read off her instruments. "Vernier thrust'rs compensating f'r wind drift."

The intercom squawked on. "What's happening?" Ariel asked. "Why aren't we landing?"

Derec thought about telling her, then decided she'd be

better off seeing it for herself. "Come up to the bridge. And while you're at it, find Adam and get him up here, too."

With the ship reconfigured for atmospheric entry, the bridge was now in the nose of the ship, and most of the interior chambers had been reconfigured into wing surface. It took Ariel only a moment to find Adam and bring him forward. Derec's second request for permission to land had just been denied when the bridge doors hissed open and Ariel and Adam stepped onto the bridge, followed by Mandelbrot, Eve, and Lucius II. At the moment Adam was patterning himself after Derec, while Eve and Lucius II looked like silver copies of Ariel and Avery, respectively.

"Okay, where's the excitement?" the real Ariel asked.

"There," Derec answered, as he pointed straight down. "It seems there's a welcoming committee." He turned to the main viewscreen and raised his voice. "Ventral optics on main viewer." A moment later, the main viewscreen showed the packed crowd of kin on the spaceport tarmac. A few security robots were wading through the crowd but not having much luck dispersing it.

Ariel took a hesitant step forward. "What the blazes—? Wolves? Dogs? What *are* they?"

"The natives," Derec said. "The last time I saw them, they were chipping flints and weaving baskets. Now they're driving up to the spaceport in groundcars." He turned to Adam and speared him with a questioning stare. "Adam, you were the last one to talk to them. Do you have any idea what's going on down there?"

Adam reached out to touch the viewscreen, a confused expression on his face. "Friend Derec, I have absolutely no idea what the natives are up to." He cracked into a smile and shuddered with pleasure. "But whatever it is, I find it very . . . *exciting.*"

"Spaceport Control insists on calling them citizens. Does that suggest anything to you?"

Adam looked at Derec. "May I contact the spaceport directly?" He looked first to Derec, then Avery, and then Ariel. The three humans looked at each other and nodded. "Very well. I am activating my commlink." Closing his eyes, Adam stood transfixed.

For a few moments, he was silent. Then his silver lips parted, and he twitched slightly. "I see," he whispered. "Tell him . . ."

"Derec!" Avery whispered urgently. "Tap in!" Derec invoked his internal commlink and tried to listen to Adam's conversation with Spaceport Control, but the exchange had already ended. He looked at Avery and shook his head.

Adam's whole body began to shudder. He flung his arms wide, collapsed to the deck, and began writhing slowly. Ariel started to step forward to help him, but Mandelbrot restrained her.

"Let go, Mandelbrot!" Mandelbrot released Ariel's arm but continued to put himself between her and Adam. "Get out of the way. Can't you see that he needs help?"

"No, Mistress Ariel. If Adam is indeed having a brain seizure, he may be unaware of the world outside himself. He might be capable of inadvertently violating the First Law. I cannot allow you to take that risk."

Ariel gave the other robots a pleading look. "Eve? Lucius? Can you help him?"

Lucius II had assumed his full Avery aspect, complete with the lab coat and wire bristle moustache, and he stood stroking his chin and examining Adam.

Silently, Adam arched his back as though in great pain.

His features, until now a passable likeness of Derec, had lost definition.

"No, Friend Ariel," Lucius II announced, "we cannot help him. He appears to be undergoing an involuntary shape change. Look at his limbs."

Ariel looked where Lucius had pointed. Unmistakably, Adam's arms and legs were getting shorter and thinner. At the same time, his fingers and toes were elongating and turning into hocks and pasterns.

Adam slowly convulsed again. The transformation would have been a horrible sight had the humans never seen one of the amorphous robots go through it before. As it was, Derec found it quite unsettling to see himself—or an image of himself—slowly being reshaped, apparently against its will, into another, alien, species.

Adam began shivering as a long, whip-like tail extruded from his hips. Then, with one last mighty convulsion, his silver skin erupted into a thick blanket of wiry silver fur.

"ARROOOOO!" The howl was deafening in the close confines of the bridge. Adam's eyes opened; in a flash he rolled over, sprang to his feet, and got a wall behind his back. "Spaceport Control!" he snarled in HuntTongue. "Tell them SilverSides has returned!"

"Toolbox!" Avery hissed urgently at a utility robot, staring wide-eyed at the snarling monster that Adam had become. "One centimeter welding laser—and hurry!" For a moment they were all frozen in place—human, robot, and robot kin—trying to gauge each other's intent. Mandelbrot was having perhaps the worst time of it, since invoking his personal defense subroutines had unleashed a flood of Capek memories.

Then Adam/SilverSides relaxed his hackles, closed his mouth, and assumed a relaxed stance. "Friends," he said in perfectly normal Standard, "forgive me. I was momentarily disoriented by my transformation." He paused and inspected his chest and forelegs. "In this shape the natives—the *kin*, that is their preferred term—know me as SilverSides. I am a female of some standing in their community." He/she turned to Derec. "Contact Spaceport Control again. I believe you will find landing permission forthcoming."

Derec looked to Avery; Avery nodded. He invoked his internal commlink and this time found Spaceport Control absolutely eager for them to land. He patched into the main viewscreen optic feed and found that the kin were clearing the tarmac as fast as their four legs could carry them.

Avery gave Derec a grim wink and lifted his hand out of his coat pocket long enough for Derec to catch a glimpse of the black, flashlight-sized welding laser that Avery had aimed at Adam/SilverSides.

Derec nodded to Wolruf. "Okay, Wolruf, set us down."

SilverSides apparently was unaware of the laser. She favored Derec with a wolfish smile, then turned to the other amorphous robots. "Eve? Lucius II? We have a few minutes yet before we land. If you will open your commlink direct-memory access channels, I will download the grammar and lexicon of the native language."

Mandelbrot tentatively raised a hand. "Friend Adam, may I share in this data transmission?"

SilverSides seemed surprised by Mandelbrot's effront-ery, but her expression quickly turned to a tolerant smile. "Friend Mandelbrot, I sincerely doubt that your brain is ca-pable of using this information. However, you are welcome to make the attempt." If Mandelbrot had a reaction to this insult, he didn't show it. Instead, he joined the other three robots as they locked their joints rigidly at attention and switched over to DMA mode. Four pairs of eyes dimmed as the download commenced.

Avery, fondling the welding laser in his pocket, studied Adam/SilverSides until the last glimmer of awareness faded from the robot's eyes. Turning to Derec, he said, "Son? Has Adam ever insulted Mandelbrot's intelligence before?"

Derec shook his head. "Not since we left this planet before."

Avery's eyes narrowed, and he resumed studying the robot. Then, with a snort of disgust, he left the laser in his pocket and went back to watching the main viewscreen.

CHAPTER 21

ADVENT

Maverick muscled through the crowd on the edge of the tarmac, trying his best to keep track of WhiteTail. "There he is!" she shouted, somewhere up ahead. He bounced up to his hind feet—a devilishly tricky way to stand in a crowd—and caught a glimpse of her.

"WhiteTail!"

She looked over her shoulder and made eye contact with him just as someone lurched into Maverick's weak leg and sent him staggering. "Over there!" she shouted, pointing with her tail. He caught his balance, looking in the direction she was pointing, and spotted LifeCrier at the leading edge of the crowd.

"I see him! Try to—*oof!*" Someone jostled his leg again, and this time he fell down. The large, muscular female that he landed on reacted with a growl, a snap, and the first words of a challenge in HuntTongue.

Then she saw the amulet that hung around Maverick's neck and backed down with a snarling submission just two hairs shy of being a challenge itself. He accepted it before she had a chance to change her mind and darted off through a gap that opened in the crowd.

By the time he'd worked his way over to join WhiteTail at LifeCrier's side, the flying thing had started descending again. The great whistling roar of its flight grew louder, and gusts of hot wind swept over the crowd, filling the air with the reek of lightning and brimstone.

"Are you sure this is safe?" he shouted at LifeCrier, trying to make himself heard over the noise.

"If it were dangerous," the old kin shouted back as he pointed his muzzle at the flying thing, "the WalkingStones would chase it away!"

"But what is it!" WhiteTail shrieked, as the roar suddenly pulsed louder.

"Remember how I told you," LifeCrier paused for a breath, "SilverSides first came down—in a flaming egg?"

"Mother's whiskers!" Maverick howled. "Is that the *bird?*" The whistle that accompanied the roar abruptly shot up in pitch and choking clouds of dust blew up off the ground, momentarily blinding Maverick.

An instant later the whistle stopped, the wind ceased, and the tarmac was silent, save for the distant echo of thunder off the buildings and the frightened whimper of a pup in the crowd.

Slowly, Maverick's ears adjusted to the quiet. The great flaming bird sat on the tarmac, stiff and rigid on its three slender legs, emitting only the occasional *ping!* of cooling metal. A few in the crowd were finally daring to breathe and murmur in low, worried voices. LifeCrier himself was standing with his head bowed, mumbling a prayer that seemed to be in extremely formal HuntTongue. He ended the prayer by nuzzling his amulet. "Well, then!" LifeCrier abruptly looked at Maverick with a madly cheerful expression. "Are you coming with me?" Not waiting for an answer, he started walking toward the bird, his tail held high, his ears cocked at a jaunty angle, his shadow stretching out before him in the long afternoon sunlight.

Maverick hesitated only a moment and then went after LifeCrier; the rest of the inner circle followed on his heels. "Father," he heard WhiteTail growling under her breath as she trotted up to join him, "one of these times your faith is going to get us all killed."

WhiteTail had just about caught up to Maverick when a loud *clang!* came from the bird, followed by a massive creaking sound and a deep, unsettling hum. Several of the inner circle broke and dashed skittishly back to the crowd, but LifeCrier simply stopped and stood there calmly, as if he were expecting this. Gasps rose from the crowd as a small depression appeared in the bird's skin just behind its head; after a few moments it became apparent that a large hole was irising open. Maverick could see that something was moving in the opening, but when he tried to get a clearer look at it, his eyes were dazzled by a blinding flash of re-flected sunlight.

As if the flash was a signal, LifeCrier suddenly dropped to his belly and placed his head on his forepaws: the meekest gesture of submission a kin could make. "Down!" he said through clenched teeth. Maverick decided to follow his example. He could tell from the shadows that everyone near him did as well, with the exception of WhiteTail. She was still standing there, her tail twitching nervously, when the flap touched the ground and SilverSides stepped out into the light.

There was never a moment's doubt in Maverick's mind that he was seeing SilverSides. The goddess was exactly as he had pictured her: tall, strong, and beautiful, gleaming in the late afternoon sun like light off still water. She moved with a precise, icy regality, and yet her eyes literally glowed with love as she gazed out upon the kin.

Then he noticed the other female, cautiously slinking out after SilverSides. The second one was definitely not a kin—her muzzle was too short and blunt, her fur the lush reddish brown of nut tree leaves in the fall, and she walked on her hind legs as if it were the most natural thing in the world. Still, there was something about her exotic looks that made her *terribly* exciting and romantic. She was almost a vision of passion incarnate.

He felt WhiteTail's breath hot on his ear. "I know what you're thinking," she whispered with the barest hint of a growl. "Stop drooling at that exotic wench. Now."

Maverick attempted to feign innocence. "Is that really the OldMother?" The look in WhiteTail's eyes told him that his attempt had not worked.

His next question caught her attention, though. "And what in the blazes are those ugly pink things with the loose fur?" WhiteTail's hackles went up when she saw the other beings that were coming out into the light.

"Th—the one at the back is a WalkingStone," she said in a halting voice. "And those two silver ones—they must be GodBeings, like SilverSides." She licked her lips and swallowed nervously. "But I've never seen anything like those other three. Mother, they're ugly!" The slight murmur that had started in the crowd behind them suddenly dropped to silence as SilverSides descended the ramp alone.

She walked straight toward them: precise, formal, her every movement a study in perfection. Just when it seemed to Maverick that he couldn't stand the power of her presence a moment longer, she stopped, smiled gently, and laid eyes upon LifeCrier.

"Old friend," she said in the soft, warm tones of PackHome kinspeech. "Please stand up. You are my pack-mate, not my prisoner."

Slowly, unsteadily, LifeCrier got to his feet, while those near enough to hear SilverSides' words looked at him with new reverence. "Great SilverSides," LifeCrier said in HuntTongue, his voice reedy with tension, "I have followed your commands. This pack I have gathered in your name; it awaits your orders."

"You have done well, Friend LifeCrier." She smiled again and looked over the massed faces as if she knew each one. For an instant her eyes paused on Maverick, and he felt as if the goddess's gaze went right through him.

"Big furry deal," WhiteTail muttered. "Her eyes glow." To Maverick's utter amazement, WhiteTail was not struck dead, nor did SilverSides seem to notice her blasphemy.

Instead, SilverSides turned back to LifeCrier and draped a companionable tail across his hips. "Come, old friend. We have much to discuss." Looking over her shoulder, she said something to the strange beings in the bird. The language was unfamiliar—the only word Maverick caught was "Wol-ruf"—but whatever she said must have made sense, for one of the exotic beings and one of the GodBeings came over to join SilverSides and LifeCrier, and together the four of them turned away from the bird and began walking toward the city. The crowd parted before them like a field of tall grass before a strong wind.

Glancing at WhiteTail, Maverick found that she was staring back at him with an unreadable expression composed of equal parts of fear, anger, concern, and something else that he didn't recognize. Before he could ask, though, she turned her face away and started trotting after LifeCrier.

"Come on, Mavvy," she said without looking back, "let's see if we can't keep the old boy out of trouble."

It gave him a chill, for a moment, to realize just how thoroughly WhiteTail had replaced the inner voice that he used to argue with.

CHAPTER 22

TWOLEGS, FOURLEGS

Avery grimaced and put the laser back into his pocket. "Well, that's that. Here's hoping we haven't unleashed a monster." He turned to Ariel. "Will you be okay while Derec and I go check out Central?"

She shrugged. "The spaceport's crawling with security robots. As long as they still obey the Laws, I'll be fine."

"All the same, be careful. Mandelbrot, don't let Ariel out of your sight."

"Yes, Master Avery."

Avery started to turn to Lucius and then had another thought. "Oh, and Mandelbrot? How's the translation program coming along?"

Mandelbrot's eyes dimmed slightly. "Not well. I am optimized for personal defense and valet service, not linguistics. The kin inflections are extremely complex, and morphemic meaning appears to vary depending on the social status of the person being addressed."

"It's not *that* difficult," Lucius muttered.

Mandelbrot's eyes flared brighter, and he swiveled his

head to look at Lucius. "Perhaps, Friend Lucius, you use an alternative definition of difficult. I find it almost impossible to tell the difference between *bark*, meaning 'Welcome, friend,' and *bark*, meaning 'Strangers attacking.'"

Lucius pursed his lips, put his hands on his hips, and shook his head. "Oh *really*, Mandelbrot. If you'd just listen to the stress modulation on the third harmonic—"

"Ahem!" The robots interrupted their embryonic spat long enough to look at Avery, who smiled paternally at them. "I'm sure you two can get this hammered out soon enough. In the meantime, Mandelbrot, stay close to Ariel and keep your personal defense routines at the top of your stack."

"Yes, Master Avery."

Avery turned to look at Lucius. "Lucius, you're our relay. Keep your commlink to Eve open at all times and report anything unusual to Derec."

The silver Avery frowned. "Are you also ordering me to stay close to Ariel and Mandelbrot?"

The real Avery frowned right back. "Would you even if I did?"

Lucius smiled and shrugged. "Probably not."

"Then I won't waste my breath. Just try to stay out of trouble, will you?"

"I always *try*, Friend Avery."

"Yeah. I know." Avery sighed and turned to Derec. "Okay, son, let's see if we can't find a groundcar."

An hour later, Avery and Derec stood in the atrium of Central Hall, facing Central's console input/output devices. "So why isn't it responding?" Avery asked.

Derec broke off commlink contact and shook his head. "I don't get it. This is *weird*."

"Sensory impairment?" Avery suggested.

"No." Derec shot the console an odd look. "Central's sensories are fine. It knows that we're here." Derec paused and scowled. "Let me rephrase that: The information is available to it. It just doesn't *care* that we're here."

Avery blinked. "That's impossible. As a positronic intelligence—"

"Yeah, well, that's part of what makes it so weird." Derec scowled again, and then shrugged and turned to Avery. "The mental impression I keep getting is one of intelligence without sentience. Does that make sense?"

Avery wrinkled his nose. "It isn't even aware of its own existence?"

Derec thought it over a moment, then nodded. "It seems to be fully functional. There's a tremendous amount of computational power waiting to be applied. But there's no personality. It simply isn't . . . *troubled* by conscious thoughts."

"That's impossible," Avery said again. "Try your commlink one more time, and this time tell me exactly what you're receiving."

With a shrug, Derec closed his eyes and invoked his internal commlink. "Okay. Commlink on: Central is acking. I'm picking up some shell primitives—cats, splits—okay, and that's a t-sort. Now it's mounting a device." Derec broke concentration and opened his eyes. "I know this sounds silly, but it seems to be running on pure cron."

Avery frowned and scratched his head. "I don't understand this."

"Dad, as I told you on the way over, SilverSides destroyed parts of Central the last time she was here."

Avery waved a hand to dismiss that idea. "That was almost a year ago. By now the supervisors should have either repaired the damage or scrapped Central and built a new one. What went wrong?"

Derec cocked his head as a commlink message came in. "We'll know in a few minutes. A supervisor has just entered the building."

Long afternoon shadows reached out from the city and stretched like giant fingers across the spaceport tarmac. The crowd had long since broken up and gone away, save for one mature kin female that lay in the shadow of the boarding ramp and four fat little cubs that rollicked about in the last splash of sunlight on the tarmac. Ears flopping wildly, little tails erect like flagpoles, the cute little furballs darted in and out of the ship, yipping happily and playing hide-and-seek around Mandelbrot's legs.

Ariel, squatting on the tarmac like a football player, smiled pleasantly and wondered if the cubs' mother would stop growling before her knees gave out.

"This is strange, Mandelbrot," Ariel muttered through smiling, clenched teeth. "You don't bother them a bit, but if I try to touch them . . ."

Slowly, gently, she began to reach toward one of the cubs. A deep, guttural growl from the mother reminded Ariel that she was being watched. The growl rose in intensity the closer she got to the pup and stopped only when she stopped.

"The kin seem to accept robots as part of the natural environment," Mandelbrot observed, "whereas anthropoid humans are a new and unknown thing."

"Anthropoid, Mandelbrot?" Ariel said with a growl.

"I was attempting to distinguish between humans like you and humans like Wolruf. If the term offends you, I will try another."

"Never mind." Ariel made eye contact with the mother again. The female kin lay on her side in what appeared to be a relaxed position, but her ears were erect and her eyes were wide and filled with an alert, savage intensity. Ariel continued to look the kin right in the eye. She tried another smile. The mother responded by shifting nervously and looking away.

Stepping high to avoid the puppies and their byproducts, Mandelbrot strolled over and touched Ariel lightly on the shoulder. "May I make a suggestion, mistress? Stop staring the mother—her name is BlackMane—straight in the eye, and don't bare your teeth when you smile. In the body language of the kin, these are hostile gestures."

"Oh." Ariel closed her mouth and looked away and was rewarded when BlackMane's ears relaxed. "Well, this seems to be working. Any more suggestions?"

Mandelbrot's eyes dimmed as he sorted through the kin lexicon. Presently he said, "Yes, although this may seem somewhat undignified. Try lying on your side and closing your eyes, as BlackMane is doing."

Ariel's eyes went wide. "Mandelbrot! I am *not* going to nurse cubs!"

"Nursing is unnecessary. The key part of the gesture appears to be exposing your throat."

Ariel frowned. "If you really think it'll work." With a grunt for stiff joints, she slowly rolled out of the squat, lay down on the rough, gritty tarmac, and closed her eyes. Within a minute she was rewarded by a cold little nose snuffling around her ear. "That tickles!" She giggled, and the pup scampered away.

"Hold still," Mandelbrot said. "All four of them are approaching you." Ariel tried hard to suppress her giggles as one cub nuzzled her ear, two more sniffed her face, and one feisty little monster fastened its teeth on her pants cuff and began growling and tugging. "Move slowly," Mandelbrot advised, "but you may open your eyes now." Carefully, Ariel opened her eyes.

She was rewarded by a big lick across her face.

This time her giggles sent the cubs scampering just a few feet back. The four of them went into a huddle, tails wagging excitedly, yipping in high, squeaky voices. BlackMane sat up a bit more alertly, but this time without the fierce, protective look. As one, the cubs turned to their mother, and she answered with a low, whuffing bark.

Ariel sat up. "What is it? What are they saying, Mandelbrot?" The robot cocked his head as if listening more closely.

"I am unsure of the dialect," Mandelbrot said, "but they appear to be saying, 'It's friendly.' " BlackMane gave Mandelbrot a bored look, and then made another soft bark that must have meant, "Okay." As one, the puppies wheeled and charged Ariel. A second later she was giggling like a seven-year-old and covered by a mass of wiggling, licking, tail-wagging cubs.

"Either that," Mandelbrot added, "or, 'It tastes good.' "

The tall, slender, pale blue robot—to appearances a standard Euler model—rounded the corner and entered the Central atrium. Avery struck while the robot was still in mid-stride.

"You there! Identify!"

"City Supervisor 3," the tall robot responded. "For your convenience I respond to the name Beta." At two meters' distance the robot stopped and stood with its head tilted slightly back, as if baring its throat.

"Beta, eh? Well, *Beta*, I am your creator, Doctor Wendell

Avery, and let me tell you, I am absolutely *appalled* with the way you supervisors are handling this city. The streets smell like kennels, the transit tunnels are filled with joy-riding wolves, and to top it off my son and I came here in an insane groundcar that insisted on driving on the slide-walks!"

To Derec's eyes, the supervisor seemed even colder and more imperturbable than was typical for Avery robots. Beta's eyes didn't flicker, nor did its posture waver a milli-meter as it responded to Avery's attack. "In searching the permissions list, I find no special privileges reserved for Cre-ator Wendell Avery." The robot paused a moment, then con-tinued. "In response to your other statements: olfactory cues are an important source of information for the citizens, and the transit tunnels are fulfilling their intended purpose. As for the groundcar, we have surveyed the citizens and found that the majority enjoy Personal Vehicle One's unique route-planning methods."

The robot's response seemed to surprise Avery. He blinked a few times, shook his head as if unable to believe that a robot was disagreeing with him, and then recovered his bluster. "Citizens? What are you talking about? Beta, the kin are not human, and for you to treat them as if they have Robotic Law status is a serious malfunction."

"The definition of 'human' is not implicit in the Laws," Beta answered, as it studied Avery with cold, gleaming eyes.

Avery bit back his first angry retort and struggled to speak calmly. "Beta, are you blind? The kin are *aliens*."

The supervisor's head rotated down, and it locked its unblinking gaze on the short man. "On the contrary, Dr. Avery; on this planet, *you* are the alien."

Avery's jaw worked, but no sound came out. His fingers clutched—

The robot leaned forward, placed one hand on its hip, and opened its other hand in a purely human gesture. "Please allow me to explain.

"Dr. Avery, our first mission on this world was to build a city. Our underlying mission was to serve humans. After the end of our first mission, we found ourselves with insufficient data to complete our underlying mission. Therefore, we devoted considerable time to the question of how to find humans.

"After much discussion, we decided that we needed a clearer definition of the word *human*. There is no explicit definition in our general programming. Consulting the ancient sources, we found that it means:

"1. Of, relating to, or characteristic of man.

"2. Consisting of men.

"3. Having human form or attributes.

"4. Susceptible to or representative of the sympathies and frailties of man's nature.

"Evaluating the kin in terms of these criteria, we found that they met three of the four. They are intelligent, social, tool-and language-using beings, fully capable of altruism, greed, opportunism, faith, loyalty, cowardice, curiosity; indeed, the entire range of human—"

Avery found his voice at last. *"Enough!"* Fighting to avoid hyperventilation, he turned to Derec. "This tin moron has obviously blown a main circuit. When are the rest of the supervisors going to get here?"

Derec broke off his commlink contact and looked up, blinking with wonder. "Alpha and Gamma decline to come."

"What?" Avery wheeled on Beta as if to attack it.

"I alone have been delegated to meet with you," Beta explained. "The other supervisors are occupied with tasks that are important to the well-being of the native humans."

"I do not believe this." Avery shook his head slowly, then studied Beta with a cold, unblinking glare. "Beta, are you trying to tell me that the supervisors are no longer subject to the Second Law?"

The robot's eyes flickered briefly. "Of course not. Alpha and Gamma's Second Law duties to you simply have been superseded by their First Law obligations."

"First Law—" Avery suddenly snapped around and looked at Derec. "Ariel!" Before he'd finished saying the name, Derec had invoked his commlink and reached Mandelbrot.

"No," Derec reported, shaking his head. "Ariel's a little wet and mussed up, but she's not in any danger." He concentrated harder and checked in with Eve. "Wolruf's fine. Adam is still playing SilverSides; he's up on a balcony, addressing a crowd, but he's speaking too fast for Eve to translate."

Derec frowned. "Lucius II isn't answering." He broke concentration and opened his eyes; both he and Avery turned to look at Beta.

"When you assume that the First Law applies only to members of your party, you are making a species-ist assumption," Beta said. "If you plan to reside in this city, you must learn to overcome your speciesism."

Slowly, sighing heavily, Avery nodded. "I see where this is leading. Beta, if I were to tell you that your definition of human has become corrupted and the kin are *not* human, would you allow me to correct it?"

Beta considered this barely a moment. "No. Redefining the native humans as nonhumans would injure them, and thus is prohibited by the First Law."

Avery frowned. "Circular logic: See logic, circular. The kin shouldn't be considered humans, but since they are, you won't let me fix the problem." With a disgusted look, he turned to Derec. "Come on, son, let's get out of here."

• • •

Wolruf whined nervously and sidled closer to Eve. An unpleasant change had come over SilverSides with nightfall; the raw emotions of BeastTongue now threaded through her speech as she addressed the crowd in the street below. "What's she sayin'?" Wolruf whispered to Eve.

"I'm not getting all of it," Eve whispered back. "Some kind of anatomical comparison between Friend Avery and a sharpfang." She rotated her head and listened more closely. "Now she's talking about—wonders. The ship; she's mentioned the ship. And she's saying that the city is capable of producing more wonders just like it. But—rhetorical question—why isn't the city providing them?"

Silversides paused for dramatic effect and then thundered the answer.

"TwoLegs!" Eve translated.

The crowd broke into the savage, rhythmic chant in heavily accented Standard. "TwoLegs out! TwoLegs out!" Everywhere Wolruf looked, she saw angry, gaping jaws, fangs bared and glistening orange in the torchlight, chanting. "TwoLegs out! TwoLegs out!"

Eve shook her head in disbelief. "SilverSides taught them to say that in Standard! This is impossible!" Her voice became slurred and her movements erratic, clear signs of an impending First Law crisis. "He's training the mob to hate bipeds!"

"TwoLegs out! TwoLegs out!"

Eve and Wolruf looked at each other, then both discreetly dropped down to all fours. Eve began to transform herself into an image of Wolruf.

" 'U think we ought t' warn Derec?" Wolruf asked.

" 'U better b'lieve it," Eve answered. Closing her eyes, she activated her commlink and sought out Lucius.

CHAPTER 23

BATTLE LINES

The warm, yellow streetlight was surrounded by a nimbus of clumsy insects. Grabbing the lamppost for a pivot, Derec swung off the slidewalk and followed Avery into the pocket park. Neither spoke until Avery had found a balcony overlooking the street below and taken a seat on the cold stone railing.

"Dad, I never thought I'd see the day when you ran away from a problem."

"I'm not running away. I'm thinking."

Derec glanced around the balcony, then put a foot up on the railing and looked out at the darkened city. The gentle night breeze carried faint hints of moisture and distant forests. "Care to explain the difference?"

Avery stopped scowling and looked up at Derec. "We can't get anywhere with the supervisors. Circular logic: The kin have First Law status because the supervisors' definition of human is corrupted, but the supervisors won't let us fix the definition because that would violate the First Law."

"So why fix it? Aside from pure human chauvinism, that is."

Avery stroked his whiskery chin and tugged at the edge of his stiff white moustache. "Hard as this may be to believe, Derec, it's for their own good. By the time we humans developed robots, we already had a mature, technological culture. We accepted robots as just better tools for carrying on life as we knew it.

"But what if back in the Stone Age, some alien race had come along and given us a magic box that delivered everything we asked for? Frost, you don't have to imagine it; Old Earth history is littered with stories of Stone Age cultures that tried to make the leap directly to high technology. First the existing family and social structures were demolished. Then the local ecology was destroyed.

"And then the people had a choice: join the mainstream of human society—become *exactly* like every other technological culture—or become extinct." Avery ran a hand through his silvery hair and looked Derec straight in the eye. "Never mind how I feel about the kin personally. They deserve more of a choice than that, don't they?"

Derec nodded. "Okay. Where do we start?"

"I've been thinking about that." Avery paused, and screwed his face up in a puzzled look. "You say it felt like Central was running on pure cron? No mentation at all?"

"Dad, I've met *bricks* with more on their minds. Central is a complete blank."

"A *tabula rasa*," Avery muttered to himself. He nodded. "Yes, that makes sense. That's what I would do."

Derec peered at Avery. "A tubular *what?*"

"Not 'tubular.' *Tabula rasa*. Latin for 'erased tablet.' One old theory used to hold that the human mind started out as a blank tablet, and personality developed as a result of the impressions that life 'wrote' on the mind."

Derec laughed. "That's ridiculous, Dad. For starters, you're completely ignoring the influence of genetic—"

Avery waved a hand to cut Derec off. "I didn't say that *I* subscribe to that theory—at least, not as it applies to humans. But tell me, what would you do if you had a robot that had suffered traumatic brain damage? Damage so profound that every time you repaired it, the very memory of that damage unbalanced the psyche module again?"

Derec thought it over a moment. "I'd erase the memory."

"That'd work for a conventional robot. But what if it was a cellular robot, and every cell held a complete set of backup memories in positronic microcode?"

Derec sat down heavily on the stone railing next to Avery and blew out a deep breath. "Oh boy. We're talking about a complete system purge and rebuild here."

"Exactly." Avery favored Derec with a knowing smile. "And what would the robot's mind be like after the purge?"

Slowly, Derec turned to look at Avery. Slowly, very slowly, a matching smile lit up his face. "A *tabula rasa*." Picking up the thought, Derec ran with it. "If the supervisors are doing a complete system rebuild on Central, it's in a very impressionable state right now. The merest suggestion could have incredibly far-reaching effects on the future of the city."

Avery nodded. "So the supervisors will try to isolate Central from unwanted influences. They've probably severed all the terminal input lines and buffered the I/O channels."

Derec's face erupted in a sly grin. "But we know someone who's got a direct commlink channel to Central's brain, don't we?"

Avery returned the grin. "How about it, son? Feel up to a little guerrilla computing?"

Derec looked around the balcony and shrugged. "This looks like as good a spot as any." Throwing his head back, he closed his eyes and began to concentrate. "Commlink activated. I'm hacking into the city network; okay, I'm in. I'm riding down the main data bus now, and I'm coming up to—uh oh. There's a big black hole where Central should be."

"All the user-friendly stuff is deactivated," Avery said. "You'll have to feel your way in."

"Right. I'm going—no, wait, there's an invisible barrier extending around the hole as far as I can reach. Cylindrical, not hemispherical."

"Can you find a seam?"

"Don't have time. I'm going to see if it's open at the top." Derec squinted for a moment as his concentration intensified. "Okay, that did it. I've jumped the barrier and I'm inside. Feels like I'm still falling; not accelerating, just falling. The hole is completely black. I can't see a thing."

"You're probably in the I-pipe," Avery said. "Try reaching out with your right hand. You should feel—*What the blazes is that?*"

Derec broke concentration and returned to the analog world to find Avery staring slack-jawed at something in the distance. He looked where Avery was looking.

He saw a mob of kin with torches surging down the darkened street, coming closer with every step.

"Listen!" Avery gasped. Derec's ears were still tuned to the subtleties of hyperwave, but he quickly adjusted and caught the chaotic noise of the mob. No, not noise. Voices. Chanting. In heavily accented Standard.

"TwoLegs out! TwoLegs out!"

"Oh, good grief," Avery muttered.

Derec instantly switched back to commlink and sent out an urgent call. *Lucius? Mandelbrot! What's going on?*

Eve's commlink voice answered. *Friend Derec? Where are you?* Derec transmitted a location-and-range pulse. *Please stay there,* Eve said. *Friend Wolruf and I will join you shortly.*

A few moments later, Wolruf and Eve came dashing up the slidewalk.

"Eve! What—?" is as far as Avery got.

"Iss Adam," Wolruf blurted out. " 'E's gone over completely to being SilverSides, an' 'at means the natives are 'umans to 'im. 'E's whipped 'em up int' a frenzy. Keeps talkin' 'bout 'ow th' city can never serve 'eir needs properly as long as th' TwoLegs are 'here. Wants t' drive 'u 'umans off th' planet."

Derec blinked. "That's impossible. The First Law—"

"Is being interpreted by the standards of these natives," Avery completed. "Intimidation may well be a normal part of their lives. For Adam, it's the tactics of indirection: If he can get the natives to scare us out, it'll never become a First Law problem." He turned to Eve. "What about the city robots?"

"They appear to be backing Adam," Eve reported. "We saw several security robots draw back into the shadows as we approached."

Avery looked at the mob again, which was now quite close, and swore softly. "It's that double-frosted Zeroth Law of theirs. So long as we aren't in immediate danger, the interests of a few hundred kin outweigh the interests of three humans. But I do not share Adam's confidence that he can control the mob." Scowling darkly, he bit the corner of his moustache. "Son? I think this nonsense has gone far enough." Reaching into his coat pocket, Avery drew out the black, flashlight-sized welding laser and stepped up to the edge of the balcony. "You, robot!"

The mob reacted instantly, swirling to a noisy, hostile stop beneath the balcony. Everywhere Avery looked, he saw bobbing torches and wet fangs bared and clashing in a savage, angry chant: "TwoLegs out! TwoLegs out!" Then, from somewhere in the depths of the crowd a lone howl erupted, a long, drawn-out note that sent chills down Avery's spine.

The mob fell silent. The ranks parted, and SilverSides stepped to the fore. The robot's skin flashed and glowed like flaming chrome in the orange torchlight.

"Robot!" Avery shouted. "You have violated the First Law! You threaten harm to humans!"

The crowd began to chant again, but SilverSides waved a paw to silence them. "Avery!" she shouted back. "This is not your world! You are not wanted here! Your very presence prevents this city from adapting to the needs of the kin. Only your departure can permit it to learn what it must." The kin could not have understood what she said, but they howled in support anyway. "Leave now and no harm will come to you!"

The crowd fell silent as Avery raised the laser and pointed it straight at SilverSides' head. "Stand clear of the natives, robot," he said in a voice as cold and deep as Death. "You are a rogue and I intend to destroy you."

Their glares interlocked. For the first time, Avery realized that he was facing a will as strong as his own, and he began to feel sweat and raw fear.

"Destroy me," SilverSides said softly, "and you are all dead. It's my word alone that keeps the kin from ripping you to pieces where you stand."

For a moment, they were a frozen tableau: Avery on the

balcony, holding the laser, surrounded by fear-stricken Derec, Wolruf, and Eve; SilverSides in the street below, glaring
at Avery with naked defiance, three hundred angry faces
dancing in the torchlight behind her.

They were still trying to stare each other down when
the hyperwave pulse bomb went off.

As kinetic weapons go, it wasn't much. Just a small
airburst in the troposphere, about two miles above the city.
All that Avery, Wolruf, and the kin saw was a tiny point of
light that flared and was gone long before the gentle pop
of its detonation reached their ears.

To anyone equipped with a commlink, though, it was a
deafening flash of colorless light and a blinding shriek of
silent noise that jangled every synapse in his entire nervous
system. Across the city, all the lights flickered and went out
for a fraction of a second. Thousands of robots ground to a
halt. SilverSides and Eve simply locked up, frozen in place.

Derec had time to scream once before his brain was
overwhelmed by the searing blast of pain.

When the light ebbed and he could see again, he was
lying on the pavement. His father and Wolruf were bending
over him, looks of deep concern on their faces, their mouths
moving in words he could not hear. And he couldn't answer.
Instead, he felt curiously distant, as if there were something
invisible and gauzy between him and the others. Another
face was forming, like an afterimage on his retinas: a picture
of a head, large and hairless, with two black, glittering eyes
set in bulging turrets of wrinkled skin. The grim, lipless
mouth opened. Even via hyperwave, the voice was high and
reedy.

Hello, Derrec. I trrust I now have your full attention?

"Aranimas?" Derec gasped.

Verry good. Now forr my second question. Do you know what plutonium is?

Obliquely, as if in his peripheral vision, Derec felt Eve and SilverSides come back to life and tap into the transmission. Behind them, every robot in the city slowly began to revive and join in.

Radioactive metal, Derec answered via commlink. *Very poisonous. Explosively fissionable in large quantities.*

Excellent, Aranimas answered. *Now forr my thirrd question. Do you know what will happen when I dump five tons of plutonium rreactor waste on yourr city?*

Derec was suddenly terrified and fully awake. "You can't!" he screamed on both voice and commlink. "You'll kill every living thing for a hundred kilometers around!"

Leaving the rrobots unharrmed, Aranimas noted. *Goodbye, Derrec.* Like a light going out, his image vanished.

Derec leapt to his feet. "Wait, Aranimas! We can make a deal!" The only answer was silence. Derec leaned over the edge of the balcony and caught SilverSides' attention. "SilverSides! Did you monitor that transmission?" The silver robot's grim expression told him everything he needed to know.

Pulling himself back from the edge, Derec turned to Avery and Wolruf, who were still staring at him with confused looks on their faces. "Dad, can we put the civil war on hold for a while? We've got a *real* problem."

CHAPTER 24

THE WEAPONS SHOP

Derec gave Avery and Wolruf a full update on the situation as they traveled to the Compass Tower. For a few minutes Avery held out the hope that Aranimas was bluffing, but Wolruf only shook her head.

" 'E never lied an 'e' never laughed," she said. "Don't think 'e's got it in 'im to bluff."

Eve caught up with them just before they entered the tower. "I still can't locate Lucius," Eve reported. "I did manage to raise Mandelbrot, though. He said that half a dozen younglings broke off from the mob and tried to seize the ship, but someone named BlackMane kicked the stuffings out of them. The ship is secure and Ariel is unhurt."

Avery raised an eyebrow and looked at Derec. "Then we still have a back door."

Derec looked disgusted. "It's our fault that Aranimas is here. I won't leave the kin to pay for our mistake."

Avery nodded. "Right decision. I was just testing."

Derec's face flushed red to the roots of his blond hair. "Will you kindly knock it off with this testing crap? Every time I turn around you're testing, testing, testing! I am sick to *death* of being tested!"

"Sorry." Avery shrugged. "It's a character flaw."

SilverSides caught up with the four of them as they started up the slidewalk to Central Hall. "Well, I've persuaded the mob to disperse," she announced cheerfully as she bounded onto the slidewalk behind them.

"How'd you manage *that* little feat?" Derec asked.

SilverSides hung her head and looked at Derec with big puppy-dog eyes. "Er, actually I, uh, told them that the spirit of the FirstBeast was coming down from the sky, and that you two were only his representatives, not worth fighting. They've gone back to their dens to fetch their best weapons and prepare for a glorious battle."

"All right," Avery said. "One crisis at a time. Derec, have the city supervisors managed to find Aranimas's ship yet?"

Derec activated his commlink for the barest moment. "Yes. They're setting up a giant viewscreen in the atrium. Speaking of which—" He turned to SilverSides. "Uh, SilverSides? As you might remember, the Central Hall security robots are specifically programmed to seek out and destroy you in this form."

"Oh. Right." With a shrug and a shudder, the robot invoked its shape-changing abilities. By the time they reached the top of the slidewalk, Adam was back as a silver copy of Derec.

Gamma 6 greeted them as they came off the slidewalk and escorted them past the security robots and into Central Hall. Alpha and Beta were in the atrium, supervising the last details of setting up the giant screen. As they crossed the cold terrazzo floor of the cavernous room, Adam sped up a bit to catch up with Avery.

"Friend Avery," Adam said softly, with a hint of embarrassment in his voice. "I just wanted to assure you that I no longer feel confrontational. My earlier behavior was a side-effect of the SilverSides imprint, and I now realize that my thinking was in serious error. It will not happen again."

"Friend Adam," Avery replied, every bit as softly, "that was your last mistake. I'm still packing the laser. Screw up again and you're slag."

"I understand."

A few moments later they entered the atrium and came to a halt before Central's main I/O console. The hall lights dimmed slightly, and the giant viewscreen flared to life.

"We have located the Erani ship," Beta said. The viewscreen took a dizzying swing through the local starfield and came to rest on a misshapen yellowish blob. Magnification jumped, and the by-now-familiar profile of Aranimas's ship appeared. "In accordance with your request, we have scanned the ship for radioactive emissions. This area," Beta used a red laser pointer to pick out one battered hull on the underside of the ship, "appears to contain a significant amount of plutonium, as well as other dangerously radioactive materials."

"That's an ancient Terran dump ship," Avery whispered. "They used to load them up with nuclear waste and fire them into their sun. Where the blazes did he find one of *those?*"

"From the angle of approach and the condition of the hull," Beta went on, "we have concluded that the dump ship is not capable of powered flight." The starfield disappeared to be replaced by a colorful graphic showing the planet's surface and two diverging flight paths. Cartoon spacecraft moved as Beta spoke. "Analysis indicates that the Erani intend to dive in at a steep angle, jettison the dump ship, and then use their planetary drives to veer off into a cometary orbit. The dump ship will make a simple unguided ballistic entry and strike the planet's surface, creating a dead zone approximately one hundred kilometers in diameter."

"So much for evacuating the city on foot," Adam noted.

Derec took a step forward and looked closely at the dump ship's flight path. "Won't it burn up in the atmosphere?"

"Owing to the steep angle of entry," Beta said, "we compute that more than 70 percent of the ship's mass will reach the planet's surface intact. If the ship burns faster than we project, it will only increase the dispersion of the nuclear material and the size of the dead zone."

A different thought was nagging at Avery. "Unguided ballistic entry? What are the odds of a complete miss?"

"Negligible. We compute that this method of attack has a potential targeting error of as much as ten kilometers, which still puts the city well within the dead zone. This calculation, of course, is based on the assumption that the dump ship is released at the optimum time."

"Which is?"

"At the veer-off point, exactly twenty-three minutes and fifteen seconds from now."

Avery nodded. "I see. And if the ship is released early, the margin of error increases?"

"At an exponential rate," agreed Beta.

"Then we can assume that they'll stay on course until they drop." Avery turned to the group and rubbed his hands together. "Okay, gang, that's it in a nutshell. We have twenty-three minutes to find a way to either evacuate the city, speed up the planet's rotation, or force Aranimas to delay the drop."

Derec wrinkled his nose. *"Huh?"*

"Deflection shootin'," Wolruf said. "Why d'ya think 'ur

seein' 'is ship in profile? 'E's aimin' for whe
t' be in a 'alf an 'our."

"Right," Avery agreed. "And if we can fo
to delay the drop by even a few seconds—"

"—He'll have to veer off, and the planet's ro
carry us past his aiming point," Derec completed.
will strike somewhere off to the east."

Beta spoke up. "I feel obliged to point out that the
will still be an ecological disaster."

"Perhaps," Adam said. "However, the bulk of the p
ulation from the eastern lakes country is now gathered
this city. Far more kin will survive if the ship strikes else
where."

"The greatest good for the greatest number," Beta said,
nodding. "This conforms to our programming."

"I'm glad you approve," Avery said, as he pushed himself between the two robots. "Now if you don't mind, we
now have twenty-*two* minutes to come up with a brilliant
idea."

The group fell silent as each of them lost him- or herself
in private thoughts. Adam's face began to reform, and he
took on a somewhat canine aspect. Eve began to grow wing
webbing between her arms and her body. Wolruf absent-
mindedly scratched her ears.

Derec scowled at his shoes and chewed on a thumbnail.
"A pity these robots never built a Key Center," he said at
last. "If we had enough keys, we could just teleport the
whole population out of danger."

Beta's eyes flared brighter. "We may not have built a
mass-production center, but we did build a small prototyp-
ing facility. How many keys would be sufficient?"

Derec looked at Adam. "About five hundred," the robot
said.

Beta's eyes dimmed. "We have six."

Derec looked at his shoes again, then raised a finger. 'Okay, next idea: How about if we use those keys to teleport six robots onto Aranimas's ship, with instructions to find and sabotage the drop controls?"

Avery answered with a sneer more eloquent than words. "*These* robots? They're more likely to decide that the Erani are human and start following their orders."

Derec fell silent and retreated into his dark scowl.

Long moments dragged past, and then Wolruf looked up. " 'Ere's an idea. Aranimas doesn't 'ave any automatics; all 'is controls are manual. 'Ow 'bout we strap a key t' one of those giant lizards and teleport it onto 'is bridge? *That* ought t' keep 'im busy."

Avery shook his head. "Wouldn't work. Takes two key presses to teleport; one to get to Perihelion and another to leave Perihelion and get to wherever you're going." Avery paused, and his eyes widened. "But say, here's an idea—Beta, is it absolutely necessary for someone's finger to be pressing the teleport button?"

"If you wish to teleport, you must be in physical contact with the key."

"No, I mean, if you wanted to send the key on ahead without you."

Beta's eyes flickered as he considered the problem. "A switch is a switch," he announced at last. "It should be possible to build a timer that would allow you to activate the key and then release it."

"How long?"

Beta swiveled his head to consider Avery. "I would expect that the length of the time delay—"

"No, no. I mean, how long to put a ten-second timer on one of your existing keys?"

Beta's eyes dimmed as he conferred with the other supervisors. "We have never manufactured such a device before. Assuming no unforeseen difficulties, we estimate approximately twelve minutes."

"Good, get started." Avery turned to Wolruf. "You say the release controls are probably on the bridge?"

Wolruf looked up at Avery through her furry eyebrows. " 'U don' know Aranimas. Th' frosted *Personal* controls were on th' bridge."

Avery nodded. "Perfect. Beta?" He turned to the robot. "I want two keys: a normal key programmed for this room, and a ten-second time-delay key programmed for the bridge of the Erani ship. Also, I need a timed analog heater that will reach 300 degrees Celsius in fifteen seconds."

"May I ask what for?"

"To protect the native humans from certain harm. This is a critical First Law priority; I need these items within fifteen minutes. Do you understand?"

The robot bowed slightly. "Absolutely, Creator Avery." His eyes dimmed as he relayed the commands. "The work has already begun."

"Excellent." Avery turned to Derec and smiled gently. "And now, son, as long as we have a few minutes, what say we go find an automat and grab a bite to eat?"

Derec's jaw dropped. *What?*

"Trust me, Derec," Avery said, as he smiled through clenched teeth and winked like a groundcar's turn signal, *"we want to find an automat."*

Slowly Derec caught on. "Oh, yeah, right." Arm in arm, whistling benignly, Derec and Avery strolled out of Central Hall.

• • •

A little later Derec and Avery were out in a darkened side street, standing before an open-air automat. As per Avery's instructions, Derec was keeping watch for robots, while Avery kneeled before the manual control panel and frantically punched in a new set of instructions.

"Why the cloak and dagger bit?" Derec whispered between sidelong glances. "Why couldn't we just send a robot to fetch this?"

"For the same reason that I told Beta to build a timed analog heater instead of a fuse," Avery whispered back. "I don't trust the city robots' definition of human. They might decide that this violates the First Law." The automat barked gently, and the serving door slid open to reveal Avery's creation.

"Five pounds of *caramel?*" Derec asked, his nose wrinkling.

Gently, delicately, Avery slid the sticky block out of the automat and flipped it lightly from hand to hand, trying to avoid burning his fingers. "Ah, it may *look* like candy," he whispered, a smile playing on his face, "but it's actually a sixty-forty mix of white sugar and common saltpeter!"

"So?"

"Derec, Derec." Avery stood up and shook his head. "Son, let me give you another little clue about your past. It's a good thing that you're a robotics genius, because you flunked Basic Chem twice. This little brick here," the block had cooled enough for him to hold it in one hand, "is about the worst caramel you'll ever taste, but it's also a pretty effective substitute for black gunpowder."

Derec looked more closely at the brick and sniffed again. "Then why the hazelnuts?"

"Shrapnel." Avery took one last look at the brick and

then slipped it into his jacket pocket. "How are the keys coming along?"

Closing his eyes, Derec activated his commlink. "They're programming the final set of coordinates now. The keys will be ready by the time we get back to Central Hall."

"Did they remember the baling wire?"

"Yes."

"Good." Avery took one last look up and down the street, then started back toward the Compass Tower. "Come on, son. We're almost out of time."

CHAPTER 25

DETONATION

Adam took a step forward and raised his voice. "Friend Avery, I must protest. The First Law demands that I prevent you from placing yourself in such great danger!"

Avery checked again to make sure that the bomb was wired tightly to the time-delayed key and turned to the robot. "You know the situation. In a few minutes this building is going to be ground zero of a hundred-kilometer dead zone. There's no other option."

"But the risk to yourself—"

"Who else could go?" Avery slipped the second key into his jacket pocket, then turned his attention to the fuse. "Derec is human. Wolruf is—" Avery grimaced and spat it out, "—human. And we can't send a robot; too much risk of a First Law lockup at the crucial moment."

Adam's eyes dimmed, and he swallowed hard. "I will go."

Avery shuddered, and his eyes went wide. "Adam, this is a *bomb*." He shook the lump of caramel in Adam's face. "All I'm hoping for is that it will distract Aranimas long enough for him to miss the drop window, but it may very well injure someone on his ship. Are you telling me that the Zeroth Law allows a robot to *kill* one human to save many?"

Adam froze, and his eyes dimmed as he diverted all internal power to resolving this First Law dilemma. Avery connected the last two wires on the detonator, then dipped into his jacket pocket and handed the welding laser to Derec.

"If the answer he comes up with is *yes*," Avery said, jerking his head at Adam, "melt his brain." In quick succession, he pressed the corners of the time-delay key. The teleport button popped up. With a firm, decisive move of his thumb, he pressed it down. "Wish me luck, son."

No sooner had he said this than Beta recovered from the First Law shock he'd gone into on hearing the word *kill*. "Creator Avery? That device is a *weapon?*" Beta lunged for the bomb.

Avery vanished into thin air.

Perihelion: the point in the universe nearest all other points in the universe. A cold, drifting, formless void; a space outside of space.

"But not outside of time," Avery said to himself. He looked at his watch. "Ninety seconds to drop. I wonder how things are going back in the universe?" He checked the detonator wiring again. It seemed to have survived the first jump in working order.

Eighty seconds. Trusting the bomb to take care of itself for a minute, he let himself float back and take in the view of Perihelion.

Not that it was much to look at. The gray lacked even the substance of fog. Nothing shifted, nothing moved, nothing changed. Ever. There was light, but no shadow; light, only because dark would have been a change.

Avery drifted through Perihelion, and he smiled. There was a secret that he knew, and no one else did. Perihelion wasn't just some nuisance, or by-product of the keys. It was the one critical thing that made teleportation possible.

Perihelion was an infinite buffer.

Sixty seconds. Avery touched the four corners of the time-delay key again, and watched as the teleport button slowly rose from the smooth, flawless surface.

Consider the question of teleportation, Avery said to himself. *In all the universe, there is no such thing as a body at rest.* Planets rolled through their diurnal cycles and careened around their suns. Galaxies spun like dancers, trailing solar systems like glitter from their spiral arms, and even the universe was expanding, Cyclopean shrapnel flying out from the ancient epicenter of the Big Bang.

Teleporting directly from one planet to another would be like leaping from a moving groundcar onto a moving elevator. You'd arrive at your destination with kinetic energy enough to flatten you into a wet, greasy smear or propel you straight into orbit.

Unless, of course, you had the buffer of Perihelion.

He looked at his watch again. Thirty seconds. "Time to go." With two quick jabs, he armed the detonator and pressed the teleport button. Pushing the bomb away from himself, he watched it float slowly away. The firing circuit began to glow a dull red.

The drifting bomb slowed and stopped about two meters away. "Of course. Perihelion absorbed the kinetic energy." Dipping into his jacket pocket, Avery pulled out the second key and touched its corners. The teleport button rose. He pushed it down.

Nothing happened.

Two meters away, the firing circuit was growing hotter.

The dull red gave way to orange and then to yellow. Thin wisps of smoke began to rise from the brick of explosive. Too soon. It was going to detonate much too soon. Panic-stricken, Avery threw himself backward, flailing against the nothingness. A flare of hellish red light appeared around the detonator, and Avery had time to wonder if the buffer of Perihelion could contain that much kinetic energy.

Then the bomb vanished.

The rush of adrenaline faded, and Avery started to think logically again. "Of course. *Two* jumps. The first is always to Perihelion, and the second gets you where you're going." He touched the corners of the key again and pressed the teleport button.

A blink later, he was back in Central Hall.

"Dad!" Derec leapt forward and gave Avery a hug.

"Sorry I'm late. What happened?"

" 'Ur coordinates were a littl' off," Wolruf said. "Missed th' bridge. Got a direct hit on th' engine room instead."

Avery pushed Derec off and staggered toward the giant viewscreen. "Did they miss the drop? What are they doing now?"

"See f'r yourself." Wolruf stepped back and made a sweeping gesture to direct Avery's attention to the screen.

The Erani ship was nose-on in the viewscreen now, and obviously in trouble. Small fires danced and sparkled along the connecting tubes. Great flares and jets of flaming gas erupted from the sides. All at once, a fluorescing ring of blue energy leapt out from the stern and then contracted, seeming almost to pull the surrounding stars in after itself. Light red-shifted, and the stars flattened out into thin arcs. Space itself seemed to ripple and contract as the Erani warship shuddered and was abruptly jerked backward.

A moment later, there was nothing on the viewscreen but peaceful black starfield.

"The Erani hyperdrive was unstable," a rich, warm, female voice announced. "Your device caused it to implode, triggering the formation of a microscopic black hole. That hole has now closed."

As one, Derec, Avery, and Wolruf turned around, wonder on their faces. *"Central?"*

"That is my proper designation. For the convenience of the citizens I also respond to the name *SilverSides*."

The humans were still staring, bug-eyed and slack-jawed, when Beta stepped into the atrium and broke the silence. "Please forgive us for not explaining all the details of the plan earlier. We were not certain that the personality rebuild would work." Beta turned to Adam. "And please, for the benefit of the native humans, you must never assume your SilverSides aspect on this planet again."

Somehow, Avery found his voice. "But—Central? You, SilverSides?"

"Who better?" Central asked. "My being permeates this city. Within my operational parameters I am powerful, generous, and very nearly omniscient. Who better to watch over and provide for my children?"

"A computer pretending to be a goddess!" Avery erupted. "That's utterly immoral!"

"It is also necessary," Beta said, "at least until the kin find their own reasons for living in the city."

"Do not worry, Creator Avery," Central added. "We will not maintain this fiction for long. Our analysis indicates that within three standard years, the kin will be ready to discover that their goddess is merely a hollow idol."

Beta nodded. "In fact, we have already identified the

native human best suited to make this 'discovery.' Her name is WhiteTail."

Avery was still sputtering and trying to frame an argument when Central spoke again. "Alert! I detect fragments of Erani wreckage entering the atmosphere!" Everyone in the hall, human and robot alike, spun around to face the giant viewscreen.

A moment later, Central updated her report. "No significant radioactives are present. The largest identifiable fragment is a Massey G-85 lifepod. There is one lifeform on board. I will attempt to establish communications. Atmospheric ionization may make this difficult." The viewscreen faded and swirled into an unsteady mass of colors. Static lines raced and jiggled across the screen. Slowly, the colors resolved into a blurry, distorted image.

A head, large and hairless. Two black, glittering eyes in turrets of wrinkled, beaded skin. A wide, lipless mouth, distorted in terror.

"Derrec? Derrrec! *I'll be waiting forr you in Hellll!*"

The image dissolved in a wash of static.

"I am tracking the lifepod," Central said. "If it does not break up, it will impact in the forest approximately fifteen kilometers north of the city."

A soft sound floated in from the night. Soft, yet ancient, and chilling. *Arrooo.* Then another voice joined it, across the miles, picking up and relaying the call. *Aroooooo!* More voices joined in, barking, baying. The night exploded in a clamor of crescendoing howls.

The viewscreen changed to display the view north from the Compass Tower. Hundreds of furry bodies were streaming out of the city and into the forest. "The kin have also spotted the pod's ionization trail," Central said. "I am preparing to send a team of hunter/seekers to the projected landing site, but I am afraid that the natives will get there first."

Central paused, as if disturbed by what she had to say next. "Dr. Avery? Derec and Wolruf? I suggest that you return to the spaceport and prepare to leave. If Aranimas does not survive reentry, the kin will return *here*."

EPILOGUE

THE SPACEPORT

Sweet, bright dawn broke across the spaceport tarmac, illuminating the *Wild Goose Chase* in vivid shades of pink and gold. Scattered patches of dew darkened the pavement; BlackMane's cubs lay in a tumbled heap by a blast deflection wall, snoring softly and dreaming happy puppy-dreams.

"Coming, Ari?" Derec called out from the boarding ramp.

"In a minute, dear." Ariel turned back to BlackMane. The female kin finished a yawn that stretched clear back to her third bicuspids, then sat down and gravely offered Ariel her paw. Squatting on her haunches, Ariel accepted the paw and shook it.

"I just wanted to tell you," Ariel began, "that I've really enjoyed your company, and I will miss you. Your cubs are terrific; I envy you for them. Of course, I don't know why I'm telling you this, since you can't understand a single word that I'm saying."

"Arf," said BlackMane.

"Arf," Ariel answered. She stood and started to turn toward the ship. Then she gave in to an impulse and gave BlackMane one last good scratch behind the ears.

Avery and Beta strolled past, talking in low voices. "I quite agree," Beta said. "Our most recent analysis indicates that it will be at least two hundred standard years before the kin are prepared enough to be allowed off this planet."

Avery looked worried. "So you'll erase all mention of rocketry and spaceflight from the city's libraries?"

"We will secure and encrypt the information on all advanced technology," Beta answered. "We will not release the information until such time as we deem the kin to be sufficiently acculturated and no longer a threat to the other species of humanity. After all, the First Law applies to *all* humans, no matter their form."

Avery frowned. "That's not quite what I was hoping for, but I'll accept it." He looked up and spotted Adam standing by the landing gear, talking to the spaceport maintenance robots. "Ah, Adam. Have you found any trace of Lucius yet?"

Adam raised an arm and pointed toward the spaceport control tower, behind Avery. "Here he comes now." Avery and Beta turned around to see Lucius approaching, followed by Wolruf, Eve, and a trio of unfamiliar robots.

"Lucius?" Avery called out. "Lucius, where the blazes have you been? We thought we were going to have to leave you behind!"

Robotic expressions were difficult to read, but Avery couldn't miss the note of surliness in the robot's voice. "I kept out of trouble," Lucius snarled. "That's what you wanted, wasn't it?" Not waiting for a reply, Lucius stormed past Avery and clanged up the boarding ramp.

With a shrug, Avery looked at Beta. The supervisor responded with a quizzical tilt of his head, as if to say that he didn't understand Lucius, either. Avery and Beta were still looking at each other when Wolruf and Eve came scampering up. "Where's Derec?" Wolruf asked, her glee barely concealed.

Avery looked around. "In the ship, I think. Derec!"

A sandy blond head popped out an open hatch. "Yes?"

"C'mere, Derec!" Wolruf called out. "Got someone 'ere I want 'u t' meet!" A few seconds later Derec came jogging down the boarding ramp and over to join them.

"Derec Avery," Wolruf said, turning to the three new robots, "I'd like t' intr'duce 'u t' 'uman Medical 17."

"My pleasure," the Wohler-model robot on the left said. " 'Uman Medical 21."

"And mine," the robot on the right said.

"An'—"

"Derrec?" The tall, unfamiliar robot in the center reeled back as if in shock. *"Derrrec!"* In a blinding flash, the robot raised his hands and lunged for Derec's throat—

And froze, rooted to the spot.

"Our apologies," Human Medical 17 said to Derec, "we should have warned you. The data from the original Jeff Leong experiment indicated that cyborgs could be unstable and dangerous, so we took the liberty of giving this one a positronic cerebellum. If he so much as *thinks* of violating the Three Laws, his muscular system locks up."

"Cyborg?"

The two medical robots looked at each other and then at Derec. "No one told you?" From Derec's blank look, they inferred that the answer was yes. "That lifepod that crashed last night; there was one survivor aboard. But by the time the hunter/seekers reached the scene, the native humans had mauled him quite badly. And we had no information on his physiology, which is not of a human form with which we are familiar. We had no choice but to cyborg what was left."

Derec turned to the cyborg. *"Aranimas?"*

"Oh, is that his name? Here, let me reboot him." Human Medical 17 reached over and touched a large red button on the back of the cyborg's neck. "Don't worry, rebooting the cerebellum is quick and painless." The cyborg shuddered and slowly stepped back and assumed a taut, angry posture. His eyes glowed like hate-filled red coals.

Wolruf stepped between Derec and Aranimas, a toothy smile playing on her lips. " 'Ere, allow me t' demonstrate 'is Second Law function." From behind her back, she produced a foot-long stick. " 'Ere, boy!" She waved the stick in front of Aranimas's glaring eyes. " 'Eere, Aranimas!" Taking a great wind-up and a running start, she flung the stick as hard as she could across the tarmac.

"Go fetch!"

With one exception, the robots had all gone off to their morning tasks. The last of the dew vanished in rising steam; her cubs were awake and getting crabby about breakfast. Still, BlackMane lingered on the tarmac for a few minutes more, watching the silver bird dwindle into the distance.

"You know, Beta," she said at last, "once you get used to the way they look, those TwoLegs are okay people."

"Indeed they are, Mistress BlackMane," Beta answered in the soft tones of KinSpeech.

She watched the ship a while longer and then asked another question. "Do you think they'll ever come back?"

"It's difficult to say, mistress. Perhaps not those Two-Legs, but in time, others like them definitely will."

BlackMane nodded. "I see. Good." She nodded some

more, then let out a pensive whine. "It's just, I really wanted to ask them one last question, you know?"

Beta took his eyes off the spacecraft and turned his full attention to BlackMane. "Perhaps I can be of help. What was the question, mistress?"

Cocking her head, BlackMane scratched an ear in puzzlement. "Well, you know the game that Wolruf was playing with Aranimas, just before they left? Where she would throw the stick as hard as she could, and Aranimas would run and get it?"

"Yes, I am familiar with the game. It is called 'fetch.' What would you like to know about it?"

"It looked like a great game, really it did. Lots of action, very exciting. I think it could be very popular. But there's one thing that I just don't understand."

"Yes."

BlackMane paused, wrinkled her nose, and then raised her ears and looked the robot straight in the eyes.

"Why did Aranimas get to have all the fun?"

ISAAC ASIMOV'S

ROBOTS
AND ALIENS

BOOK SIX

HUMANITY

JERRY OLTION

ROBOTS AND EVOLUTION

BY ISAAC ASIMOV

In general, there are two types of change that take place in the Universe: catastrophic and evolutionary.

A catastrophic change is characterized by a large alteration of conditions in a short period of time. An evolutionary change is characterized by slow alterations of conditions over a long period of time.

Clearly, catastrophic change is more dramatic, but if we observe the Universe around us, it is equally clear that evolutionary change is the rule.

A star shines for anywhere from many millions to many billions of years, slowly evolving, until it reaches a point where (if it is large enough) there is an overbalancing, so to speak, and, in the space of a few minutes or a few hours, it explodes as a supernova and collapses. Catastrophe! But, thereafter, it exists as a white dwarf, neutron star, or black hole, and returns to prolonged evolutionary change.

Again, a huge cloud of dust and gas slowly circling and condensing undergoes evolutionary change, until its center reaches the level of temperature and pressure where nuclear fusion can begin. There is then ignition and a sun is born. Catastrophe! But, thereafter, a planetary system evolves over the space of a few million years, achieves equilibrium, and continues to evolve over the space of a few billion years.

Still again, a planet like Earth can evolve, geologically, over a period of millions of years, perhaps even billions, undergoing slow changes that result in sea-floor spread-fjing, moving plates and shifting continents, rising and eroding of mountain chains, and so on. There are punctuations in the form of minor catastrophes, an earthquake here, a volcanic eruption there, a sudden flooding yon, but, beyond and between such events, evolutionary change proceeds. There is even, once in a while, the chance of a cometary or asteroidal collision that may bring about a far greater catastrophe, but after that, too, evolutionary change continues.

Catastrophic changes, because they occur at long intervals (the greater the catastrophe, the longer, in general, the intervals), because they are sudden, and because they are often unpredictable, are difficult to study. Evolutionary changes, however, are always at our doorstep, always available for detailed and prolonged study.

Following the line of least resistance, then, let us forget about catastrophe—in this introduction, at least—and concentrate on evolution.

There are two types of evolution that need concern us. First, there is evolution that is non-directed but takes place only in response to the blind forces of nature. These are governed, we might say, by the generalizations we have observed which we call "the laws of nature."

Second, there is directed evolution, changes that take place in response to the guiding needs of some intelligence.

Non-directed evolution is what we generally study—the slow changes that take place in the Universe, in individual stars, in the planet we live on.

Yet, if we consider the daily lives of human beings, surely directed evolution is the more important. Over the four or five million years of hominid evolution, human beings have learned to make stone tools, use fire, develop herding and agriculture, form pottery, invent metallurgical techniques, and guide technology in multifarious directions. Over the last two and a quarter centuries we have industrialized the world, and now we have at our disposal such things as computers and spaceships. In addition, we have developed cultural as well as technological techniques—and have created literature, art, and philosophy.

All this has not been in blind and direct obedience to the laws of nature. We are controlled by those laws, yes, and we have limits set for us by them. Within those laws, however, humanity and its ancestors have made advances directed by their own intelligent responses to the needs of life.

You can see the evolutionary nature of human technology if you imagine a display of all the mechanical devices intended for transportation that have been produced by humanity—starting with the wheeled carts of the Sumerians right down to the rocket ships of today.

If you were to study a vast array of these devices carefully arranged in the direction of increasing complexity and efficiency and allowed to branch off in different directions— land vehicles, water vehicles, air vehicles, those dragged by human beings, those dragged by animals, those powered by wind or water, those powered by engines of various shapes— what would your conclusions be?

If you were a disembodied intelligence from elsewhere,

who did not know those devices were human-made, you might suppose that some non-directed evolutionary process had taken place; that somehow there was an inherent drive in transportation devices that would lead them to fill various technological niches and to do so with increasing specialization and expertise. You would study ancestral forms, and note how aircraft developed from landcraft, for instance, and find intermediate forms. Or if, in some cases, you found no intermediate forms, you would blame it on the incompleteness of the record. You would devise all sorts of technological forces (other than intelligence) that would account for the changes you see.

But then, when you were all finished and had a complete theory of technological evolution, someone might tell you, "No, no, you are dealing with *directed* evolution. All these objects were created by human intelligence. All these changes are the result of human experience learning bit by bit to manufacture devices that more efficiently take care of human needs."

That might make you think that scientists may have misinterpreted the records of biological evolution in the same way. We have a vast array of fossils representing ancient and now-extinct forms of life. We arrange them in such a way as to show a steady change from simpler to more complex forms, from lesser to greater variety, from those less like us to those more like us, and from it all we induce a theory of non-directed biological evolution that involves forces acting in blind response to the laws of nature.

But can we now say that, as in the case of transportation devices, we were fooled? Can we imagine the history of life on Earth to be a case of directed evolution with intelligence (call it "God") behind every one of the changes?

No, there is a fundamental difference. In the case of technological evolution, every device, every single device, is human-made. No technological device (of the kind we have had hitherto) can make others like itself. If human beings withheld their hands and brains, therefore, technological evolution would stop at once.

In the case of biological evolution, each device (if we can use the term for a living organism) produces many more or less like itself, and with no sign of any direction from outside. It is the imperfection of the process, the fact that the offspring are not *exactly* like the parents or like each other, that directs the evolution.

But can undirected evolution become directed under some conditions?—Clearly, yes.

Through almost all of Earth's history, living things had no choice but to change blindly as a result of random gene mutations, and of slow evolutionary changes in living conditions. Catastrophes sometimes resulted in mass extinctions—also unavoidable.

It was only with the coming of *Homo sapiens sapiens* that a brain finally existed that was capable of deliberate interference with evolutionary development. Beginning about ten thousand years ago, human beings began to breed plants and animals in such a way as to emphasize those characteristics they considered most valuable. Grains were developed that yielded more food per acre; animals that produced more meat, or milk, or eggs, or wool; that were larger, stronger, and more docile.

In a way, we even guided our own evolution, making ourselves more social beings, more capable of surviving in crowded cities, or in the grip of a fearfully complex technology. (Not that we fit in very well, but we've only had a short time in which to evolve these characteristics.)

Now we are beginning to be capable of genetic engineering, and our direction of evolution may become more precise and efficient (if we can make up our minds as to the particular direction in which it will be safe to proceed).

That brings us to robots, which represent what is perhaps a peculiar middle-ground between technology and life.

The robots I have pictured in my early robot stories were machines. However intelligent they seemed, they were as helpless in the grip of technology as a wheelbarrow was. They were devices that could not reproduce themselves and that, therefore, could not engage in non-directed evolution. If an improved robot was desired, a different robot, a more specialized robot, a more versatile robot, such a thing would have to be constructed by human designers.

Sure enough, as I continued to write my stories, robots did advance, grow more complicated, more intelligent, more capable—but their evolution remained directed.

What about the robotic brains? As they approached the human brain in character, might they not eventually take matters into their own hands? The brains of my robots, however, are tied tightly to the Three Laws of Robotics, and that limits them as human brains are not.

But let's think again. Evolution is a matter of generations, of numerous individuals, each one slightly different from all the others, coming and going. A single organism in a single lifetime does not evolve in the biological sense. An individual chimpanzee does not become a human being, or even make any step, however small, toward becoming a human being in the course of its own lifetime.

If an individual organism cannot evolve by itself, it can learn, and the more complex the brain, the more efficiently and radically it can learn. Learning is a form of change, if not biologically, then at least culturally. This point does not have to be belabored in connection with human beings, but what about robots?

I reached a turning point in my own robot stories with the appearance of R. Daneel Olivaw in *The Caves of Steel* and of R. Giskard Reventlov in *Robots and Empire*. Daneel was a humaniform robot, indistinguishable from human beings if you don't count the fact that it was far superior to human beings in a moral sense. Giskard was metallic but possessed the power of adjusting human emotions.

Each was sufficiently complex to be capable of learning, despite the weight of the Three Laws of Robotics. In *Robots and Empire*, Daneel and Giskard learned friendship for each other. They also labored with the concept of working for the good of humanity as something superior to the task of working for the good of individual human beings, thus groping toward what I called the "Zeroth Law of Robotics."

In a way, robots can even offer mental complexities far beyond those in human beings. What if the "wiring" of a robot brain is replaced with another set but imperfectly so, so that a robot is aware of two sets of impressions—a kind of robotic schizophrenia? What if a robot originally intended for a particular society is forced to perform its functions in an entirely different society? How does its brain react to that? (This volume of the *Robot City* series involves questions of this nature.)

Can the undirected nature of robot evolution also become directed? For instance, suppose it is the task of robots to form other robots and, in particular, to design the brain patterns of other robots. This would be the robotic equivalent of genetic engineering, and robots in this way could direct their own evolution.

Or if you had humaniform robots like Daneel, and divided them into male and female with the ability of self-propagation, human fashion, a form of biological evolution might result—but then the distinction between robots and human beings would tend to disappear, and with it the possibility of meaningful robot stories.

CHAPTER 1

HOMECOMING

They had named the starship the *Wild Goose Chase*, for when they'd left home in it some of them had doubted that the trip would be of any value. Now the ship once again orbited its world of origin, and its passengers still wondered whether they had accomplished anything useful.

They had accomplished plenty; no one disagreed about that. During their travels they had transformed one of Dr. Avery's mutable robot cities into a toy for intelligent aliens, had reprogrammed another robot city to serve an emerging civilization on yet another alien world, had formulated a set of rules describing the motivations behind human behavior, had nearly found the mother to four of the group's members, and had ended the career of the alien pirate who had dogged their steps for years. All the same, the operative word was "useful," and not one of their actions received the unanimous approval of the entire crew.

None of them supposed that turning a city into a toy was anything other than an irritating lesson in futility. Derec and Ariel also had grave reservations about leaving the other robot city in the hands of the pre-technological Kin. None of the human complement—nor even Wolruf, their alien companion—cared a bit for the robots' "Laws of Humanics," and though Derec was excited at the prospect of finding his mother, his father harbored a contrary emotion, and besides that, they had lost her trail.

Even removing the pirate Aranimas from the picture was only a qualified success, for though they hadn't killed him, the moral implications inherent in their method of dealing with him had driven three of the robots into the positronic equivalent of catatonia.

It was high time to go home and think about things for a while.

Home in this case meant the original Robot City, an entire planet covered with Dr. Avery's mutable, ever-changing cybernetic metropolis. At least it had been covered in city when they left. Now, however, from their vantage point in close orbit, it looked like a newly terraformed planet still waiting for settlers.

Three humans, one alien, and a robot crowded into the starship's control cabin to watch it drift by in the view-screen. They were a motley-looking group by anyone's standards. The alien, Wolruf, occupied the pilot's chair, the demands of her canine body warping the chair into a con-figuration a human would have considered uncomfortable at the very least. Her brown and gold fur had been carefully brushed, but she wore no clothing or ornamentation over it.

To her right stood Derec, a thin, narrow-faced, blond-haired young man who carried the impatient look common to explorers. His clothing was utilitarian: loose pants of soft fabric suitable for anything from Yoga exercises to wiping up oil spills while dismantling machinery, capped by a plain pullover shirt of the same material, both in light blue. Snuggled close to his right stood Ariel, equally thin—though in a softer sort of way—dark-haired, and not as transparently impatient as her companion. It was obvious she had spent more time on her wardrobe than he. She, too, wore pants and a blouse, but her blouse clung where it was supposed to cling, hung loose where loose suited her figure better, exposed enough skin at neck and waist to suggest but not to provoke, and together the pale yellow and brown hues of blouse and pants provided a splash of color to offset Derec's uniformity.

On the other side of Wolruf stood Dr. Avery. He was an older version of Derec: shorter, rounder, grayer, moustached, his face not yet wrinkled but showing the effects of time and much experience. He wore his usual baggy trousers, white shirt with ruffled collar, and oversized coat—today, as most days, in gray. His expression was one of puzzlement shading over into concern.

Behind the humans stood Mandelbrot, the only one of the four robots on board present in the control room. He was an old-model robot of steel and plastic construction—save for his more recently repaired right arm—and he wore no clothing over his angular body plating, nor did his visual sensors or speaker grille convey a readable expression.

Derec, his eyes drifting from the viewscreen to his companions and back, was the first to voice the question all of them were thinking: "You're sure this is the right planet?"

Wolruf, swiveling slightly around in the pilot's chair, nodded her toothsome head. "Positive."

"Then what happened to it?" Ariel asked.

"That's 'arder to say." Wolruf pushed a button to lock the viewscreen picture in place, then moved a slide control upward, increasing the screen's magnification until the planet's mottled surface began to show detail. Where they had expected to see the sharp angles of buildings and streets, they saw the tufted tops of trees instead. Narrow pathways wound among the trees, and as Wolruf increased the magnification still further they saw that the paths occasionally joined at landmarks ranging from boulders to dead tree stumps to natural caves. There were no buildings in evidence at all.

The angle of view changed steadily as the ship continued to move in orbit, until they were looking out rather than down over a sea of treetops. The picture grew less and less sharp as the angle changed, and after a moment Derec realized it was because the lower their view angle got, the more atmosphere they had to look through.

"Try another view," he said to Wolruf, and the golden-furred alien backed off the magnification and released the hold. The camera tracked forward again and the picture became a blur of motion until they once again looked directly downward from the ship.

A ragged boundary line between the green forest and a lighter green patch of something else caught Derec's attention. "There," he said. "Zoom in on that."

When Wolruf did so, they could see a vast meadow of waving grass. It wasn't like a farmer's field, all of one type and all the same height, but rather a patchwork of various species, some tall, some short, with bushes and the occasional tree scattered among them. Again there were paths, though fewer than in the forest, and again the scene lacked any sign of human habitation. There *were* inhabitants, though: small knots of four-legged animals grazing under the watchful eyes of circling hawks or eagles.

"How did *they* get there?" Dr. Avery demanded.

Derec glanced over at his father, opened his mouth to

answer, then thought better of it. He turned back to Wolruf and said instead, "Let's try another view."

Wolruf provided it. This one showed a barren expanse of sand, punctuated sporadically by lone stands of cactus. Near the edge of the screen a single tree cast its shadow across a pool of water. A smallish four-legged animal of some sort lapped at the water, looking up frequently to check for predators.

"They really took it seriously," Derec muttered, scratching his head in bemusement.

"Took *what* seriously?" Avery demanded. "This is your doing, isn't it?"

Derec nodded. "I suppose it must be, though I certainly didn't expect this."

"What *did* you expect? What did you order them to do?"

Derec faltered for a starting point, said at last, "You remember our argument just before we left, when I wanted to use the animals Lucius had created as the starting point for a real biological ecosystem, but you had the hunter robots kill all of them instead? Well, when we boarded the ship, I told the computer to access my files on balanced ecosystems, and to ... well ... to make one based on what it found there."

Avery visibly considered his response to that revelation. His fists clenched and unclenched, and the tendons in his neck worked as he swallowed. Mandelbrot took a step toward Derec, readying to protect his master should Avery decide to attack him physically.

Avery noticed the motion, scowled, and lashed out with a kick to the robot's midsection instead. The hollow clang of shoe against metal echoed in the control room. Concurrent with the kick, Avery shouted, "*Why* do you always have to do this to me? Just when I think I've got something running smoothly, you go and throw sand in the works. Literally." He waved at the screen, still showing desert, but at such a low angle now that the atmospheric disturbances between it and the ship made it shimmer as though they were actually standing in its midday heat.

Mandelbrot had rocked back with the kick, absorbing the blow so Avery wouldn't hurt his foot, but that was his only move. Derec looked from his father to the robot and back again. In a way, Mandelbrot was Derec's first real achievement in life. He had reconstructed the robot from parts, and in the years since then the robot had grown from a servant to a companion. Perhaps for that reason, Avery had mistreated the poor thing since the day they had met. Derec had been about to apologize for his mistake with the city, but now, in answer to Avery's question, he said simply, "Maybe it's a family trait."

They stared at one another for long seconds, their anger weighing heavy in the room, before Ariel said in disgust, "Boys." Dismissing them and their argument, she stepped around Derec to stand beside Wolruf's chair, saying, "Can you find any sign of the city at all?"

"Not visually," the alien admitted, "but we 'ave other methods." She spent a moment at the controls, during which the viewscreen image zoomed out again, blurred, shifted to false color imaging, and displayed what might have been a color-coded topographic map.

"Definitely getting neutrino activity," she said. "So something's still using microfusion powerpacks."

Derec relinquished the staring match in order to see the viewscreen better. "Where?" he asked.

"Everywhere," Wolruf said. "Many sources, scattered all over the planet. Even more beneath the surface."

"Has the city gone underground?" asked Ariel.

"We'll see." Wolruf worked a few minutes longer at the controls, explaining as she went. "I'm trying penetration radar, looking for 'ollow spots. And sure enough, there they are." On the screen a shadowy picture showed the familiar rectangular forms of a city.

"What's on the surface above them?" It was Avery, his tone almost civil.

Perhaps as a reward, or perhaps out of her own curiosity, Wolruf replaced the radar image with the visual once again and they found themselves looking down on a wide, flat-bottomed river valley. The river that had carved it meandered lazily through stands of trees, past low bluffs covered with grass and bushes, and on without hindrance out of the viewscreen's reach. No remnant of the city that once covered the planet's entire surface marred the now perfectly natural setting, and nothing visible in normal light indicated that below it lay anything but bedrock.

The sight of bare ground without city on it rekindled Avery's ire. "And just how are we supposed to get inside?" he demanded.

Without looking up at him, Ariel said, "There must be access hatches or something."

"And how do we find them?"

"By asking." Mandelbrot paused for the half second or so it took for everyone to look at him, then added, "I am now in communication with the city's central computer. It confirms Ariel's assertion: elevators to the surface have been provided in the new city plan. It can direct us to any one of them we wish to use."

Wolruf laughed the gurgling laugh of her kind. "What difference does it make? It's all the same anyway."

"All except the Compass Tower," said Avery. He looked from Wolruf to Derec. "Provided it's still there."

"It is," Mandelbrot replied. "The original city program-ming was inviolate in its case. It is the only building on the planet that remains above the surface."

"Then that's where we'll go."

Wolruf turned to the controls. "Easy enough," she said. "Zero degrees latitude, zero longitude. It's just after dawn there, so we have light. We can make it on this orbit if we go now."

"Then do it. The sooner we get down, the sooner I can get my city back to normal." Avery favored Derec with a last crusty look, then stalked out of the control room.

Derec grinned at Ariel and shrugged his shoulders. "Oops."

She giggled. " 'Oops,' " he says. "You changed the sur-face of an entire planet with a single order, and that's all you have to say about it? Oops?"

Coming from Avery, those words would have stung, but Ariel meant no harm and Derec knew it. She thought it was funny, as did he. Robots were always misinterpreting their orders, always doing things you didn't expect them to do; this was just an extreme case. Even so, it wasn't anything to get upset over. They would figure out why the city had done what it had, correct the problem, and that would be that.

"Deceleration coming up in seven minutes," Wolruf warned.

Derec looked out the viewscreen. Wolruf had aligned the ship so they were aimed just above the horizon behind them in orbit. Internal gravity had kept the ship's occupants from feeling any of her maneuvering, as it would keep them from feeling the braking thrust, but Wolruf's warning carried with it an implicit suggestion: time to strap in. Cabin gravity compensated for planned motion like rocket thrust, but it was slow to react to unexpected shifts. Air buffeting on reentry would still throw them around, as would any last-minute maneuvering the gravity generator couldn't anticipate.

The ship understood Wolruf's meaning as well. A week earlier it wouldn't have—while attempting to keep the starship from responding to every comment as if it were an order, Derec and Avery had inadvertently made it ignore the alien's orders as well—but they had since fixed that. The ship had functioned perfectly the entire way home, and it did so now. When Wolruf issued her warning, two bumps rose up in the floor behind and to either side of her control chair, molded themselves into more human-style chairs, and swiveled around to allow Derec and Ariel to seat themselves. When they were comfortable, waist and shoulder restraints extruded themselves from the arm and back rests, crossed over the chairs' occupants, and joined seamlessly to hold them in.

Mandelbrot remained standing, but the ship grew a holding bar beside him, which he gripped with his left hand. It seemed inadequate, but with the energy of a microfusion powerpack behind that hand, he wasn't going anywhere either.

No doubt Avery, wherever he happened to have gone, was also being coaxed into a chair, and the three unresponsive robots in the hold were probably being restrained in some way as well.

The observers in the control cabin watched the planet roll by beneath them while the countdown ran out; then the descent engine fired and they watched it roll by a little slower. They could hear the soft roar of the nuclear engines through the not-quite-soundproof hull, but that and the changing perspective as they began to fall toward the planet were the only indications that something was happening.

As they lost orbital velocity and picked up downward velocity, their apparent speed began to increase. The horizon grew flatter, and they seemed to be rushing away from it faster and faster. Wolruf turned the ship around until they were again facing in the direction of motion, and they fell the rest of the way into the atmosphere. The howl of air rushing past replaced the roar of the descent engine.

Wolruf was an excellent pilot. She had to be; if she were anything less, the robotic ship wouldn't have let her near the controls, for the ship could have landed itself perfectly without her assistance. That it allowed her to do so without *its* assistance was a supreme compliment, one which Wolruf proved she deserved only seconds from landing.

They had dropped down through a layer of high, thin cloud, and were gliding now on wings the ship had grown once they'd reached air thick enough to use them in. The ship had reconfigured its engine into an atmospheric jet, which Wolruf let idle while they bled off the last of their orbital speed. Through the viewscreen they could see an undulating sea of treetops rushing by beneath them, and off in the distance a glittering flat-topped pyramid that had to be the Compass Tower. Wolruf steered to the right of it, swinging the ship in a wide circle around the tower while she examined the forest for landing sites.

There were none. The canopy of trees was complete. As she completed the circle, Wolruf turned her head toward Mandelbrot and asked, "So where are we supposed to land?"

"On the—" Mandelbrot started to reply, but Derec, who had not looked away from the viewscreen, saw a sudden flash of movement directly ahead and shouted, "Look out!"

There came a loud thump and a lurch not quite compensated for by internal gravity. Wolruf snapped her head back toward the viewscreen just as another fluttering black shape swept toward them and another thump shook the ship.

In the next instant the air seemed filled with frantic, flapping obstacles. They were huge birds of some sort, easily three or four meters across. The ship shuddered under impact after impact, and ragged sections of the viewscreen went dark as the outside sensors were either obliterated or simply covered up by their remains. Wolruf howled what was no doubt a colorful oath in her own tongue, pushed the throttle all the way forward, and pulled back on the flight controls to take the ship above the flock. Three more birds swept toward them. Wolruf ducked, but so did the birds; there came a triple hammer blow to the ship, and suddenly they heeled over and began falling.

"Engine failure," the autopilot announced.

"Grow another one," Wolruf commanded it.

"Fabricating."

Wolruf struggled to right the ship, got it into a glide again, and peered out between the dark patches in the viewscreen. "We're too low," she muttered. " 'urry up with that engine."

"I am transmogrifying at top speed. Engine will be operational in four minutes."

"We don't 'ave four minutes!" Wolruf howled, then immediately added, "Give me more wing."

"Expanding wing surface."

Derec looked over to Ariel, found her looking back at him with wide eyes. "We'll make it," he said, surprised at how calm his voice sounded. She nodded, evidently not trusting her own voice, and reached out a hand toward him. He realized that no matter how calm he had sounded, he was gripping his chair hard enough to leave finger depressions in its yielding surface. He unclenched his hand and took hers in it, holding more carefully. Together they looked back to the viewscreen.

The treetops looked as if they were only a few meters below the ship. The view directly ahead was obscured; Wolruf weaved the ship back and forth to see what was in their path. Between one weave and the next an especially tall tree loomed up seemingly from out of nowhere, giving her only time enough to swear and bank sharply to miss it. The ship lurched as the lower wing clipped another treetop, but wing proved stronger than wood, and they flew on. Wolruf leveled them out again and pulled back gently on the flight control to give them more altitude. They were still moving fairly fast, but slowing noticeably now.

"We really need that engine," Wolruf said.

"Two and a half minutes," the autopilot responded.

"We'll be down by then," she muttered. She looked to her left, out a relatively unobscured section of viewscreen, and came to a decision. With a cry of " 'ang on!" she banked the ship to the left, held the bank until they were aimed directly at the Compass Tower, then leveled off again.

"The tower is too narrow," the computer began. "You have too much airspeed to land on it without reverse thrust—" but it was too late. The Compass Tower came at them, a slanting wall rising well overhead, visible now through the clear spots to either side and above. Wolruf held their angle of approach until it seemed they were about to smash headlong into it, then at the last moment pulled back hard on the control handle and brought them up almost parallel to the slanting wall.

The pyramid-shaped tower rose up out of the jungle at about a sixty-degree angle. They hit at about fifty, give or take a few degrees. The violent lurch of impact threw everyone against their restraints, and even Mandelbrot took a step to avoid losing his footing; then with a screech of metal sliding on metal they skidded up and over the top edge of the tower.

Cabin gravity had died completely in the collision. They felt a sickening moment of weightlessness, then another lurch as they smashed sideways onto the flat top and continued to skid along its surface. All four of the control room's occupants watched with morbid fascination as the far edge drew nearer.

"Frost, I should've gone corner to corner," Wolruf growled, and for a moment it seemed as if that would be their epitaph, but as they slid across it the surface of the tower grew rougher ahead of them, and the ship ground to a halt with four or five meters to spare.

Derec found that he had nearly crushed Ariel's hand in his own. He would have if she hadn't been gripping him almost as fiercely herself. Breathing hard, neither of them willing to test their voices yet, they loosened their hold on each other and flexed their bruised fingers.

Wolruf let out a sigh, pulled her seat restraints loose, and braced herself to stand on the tilting floor. "Well," she said, "welcome 'ome."

Some hours later, Wolruf stood at the base of the tower and peered out into the dense jungle surrounding it. She had begged off from the congratulatory dinner Ariel had suggested, claiming stomach cramps from the anxiety and excusing herself to go take a run to stretch her muscles. She fully intended to go for a run, if only to guarantee her solitude, but in truth the reason she wished to be alone was not stomach cramps but shame. Despite her companions' congratulations—even Avery had commended her for her flying skill, while making a not-so-subtle jab at Derec for creating the birds that had made that skill necessary in the first place—despite their heartfelt thanks, Wolruf knew that it was she, not Derec, who was ultimately responsible for the accident in the first place.

Stupid, stupid, *stupid*, to circle low above a forest and not watch out for birds. Especially an unfamiliar forest, full of unfamiliar and unpredictable species. If she'd pulled a stunt like that at home, she'd have been kicked out of the training academy so fast her tail wouldn't even have been caught in the slammed door.

Yes, she'd shown some quick thinking afterward, had pulled their collective fat out of the fire, but all the praise she got for that bit of fancy flying simply galled her all the more. Her initial mistake had nearly killed them all.

"So you learn from your mistakes," she growled in her own language, quoting one of her old instructor's favorite phrases, but hearing the guttural gnashing and snarling of her native tongue brought a sudden pang of homesickness, and she cocked back her head and let fly a long, plaintive howl.

An echo bounced back at her from the trees. Then, faintly, coming from far deeper in the jungle, she heard an answering cry.

A cold shiver ran down her back at the sound of it. It wasn't exactly an answer—not in words, at any rate—but the meaning was just as clear as her own howl had been. *You are not alone.*

And just who might be making so bold an assertion on this planet so recently filled only with robots? Wolruf had no idea. The odds of it being a member of her own species were no odds at all; she was the only one of her kind in human space, and she knew it. But whatever mouth had

2

voiced that cry belonged to a creature at least similar to herself, and it had given her an open invitation for companionship.

At the moment she wasn't feeling picky. She took a deep breath, tilted her head back and howled again, forgoing words for deeper meaning: *I am coming.* Not waiting for an answer, she struck off into the trees.

Ariel heard the howling from her room in the apartment they had chosen practically at random from among thousands in the underground city. The windows were viewscreens, currently set to show the scene from partway up the Compass Tower, and they evidently transmitted sound as well. Ariel had been brushing out her hair; she stopped with the brush still tangled in a stubborn knot of dark curls, stepped to the window, and listened. Another howl echoed through the forest, and another. One was recognizably Wolruf, but not both. A bird added a shriek of alarm—or perhaps derision—to the exchange.

Some primitive instinct triggered her hormonal reflexes, dumping adrenaline into her bloodstream, readying her to fight or flee should either need arise. She felt her pulse rate quicken, felt the flush of sudden heat in her skin.

The howls came again.

She swallowed the taste of fear. She was ten levels below ground! "So strange, to hear live animal sounds here," she whispered.

Derec lay on the bed, one arm draped over his eyes and the other sprawled out at his side. He shifted the one enough to peer under it at Ariel and said, "It is. I think I like it, though."

"Me too." Another howl made her shiver, and she added, "As long as I'm inside, anyway."

"Don't get too attached to it. Avery'll probably have the whole thing covered in city again inside of a week."

Ariel tugged at her brush again, got it through the tangle, and took another swipe at it. "Do you really think he will?"

"I imagine. He sounds pretty intent on it."

"Couldn't you stop him? Your order has precedence. If you tell the robots you want it to stay the way it is, they'll obey you, won't they?"

"Maybe. I don't know if it's worth it."

"Hmm," she said. Maybe it wasn't. Easy come, easy go, and all that. Besides, Avery had just been beginning to act like a human being before he discovered Derec's ecosystem project; maybe it would be worth it to let him put the city back the way he'd originally planned it if it would keep him easy to get along with.

"Where'd he go, anyway?" she asked.

Derec let his arm flop down over his eyes again. "Computer center, where else?"

"Of course." Ariel turned away from the window and walked back over to stand in front of the mirror. She continued to brush her hair, but she watched Derec's reflection, not her own. She could have stared at him directly, since he had his eyes closed, but somehow she liked using the mirror, as though she might see something in it that she wouldn't otherwise.

What she saw pleased her well enough no matter which way she viewed it. Derec was trim, well-muscled, attractive by nearly anyone's standards. Certainly he was attractive by Ariel's. She had fallen in love with him twice now, without the complication of falling out of love in between. Amnesia had its good points.

And he had fallen in love with her twice, too. At least

she thought so. Once, definitely, and that was this time, so what did it matter if the first was merely infatuation, as she suspected it had been? He loved her now, didn't he?

As if he could read her mind, she saw him raise his arm up again and peek out at her from under it, and the openly appreciative smile that spread across his face told her all she needed to know. He raised up off the bed in one smooth motion, came over to nuzzle his face in the hollow between her neck and shoulders, and whispered, "So why don't we take a blanket and go for a walk in the forest while it's still there?"

Dr. Avery had indeed gone to the computer center, but only long enough to use a private terminal to direct the city to create a fully stocked robotics lab for him. While that was being done, he commandeered a team of six general service robots and led them back up to the wreckage of the starship at the top of the tower.

"In the cargo hold of that mess," he told them, pointing in its general direction, "you'll find three robots in communications fugue. I want you to bring them out and take them to my lab. Under no circumstances are you to try to wake them. Is that clear?"

"Yes, Master Avery," the robot nearest him said.

"Good. Go to it."

The robots filed into the ship, using a convenient rent in the hull rather than the airlock. Avery smiled at the sight, for the still-crumpled presence of the wreckage signaled that his plan was proceeding smoothly. He had ordered the ship not to repair itself, not to do *anything* until he got the robots removed. They hadn't awakened during the crash, but who knew what might trigger it? Better to err on the safe side. This was only the second time they had gone into fugue in his presence, and he had blown his chance to study them in detail the first time. He wasn't going to let this opportunity pass unused as well.

Derec wouldn't approve—he'd been the one who convinced Avery not to the first time, pleading with him not to interrupt their development—but Avery really couldn't care less about Derec's wishes now. Not any more. For a while there he'd come close to thinking he might actually care about his son again, but to discover that all this time the boy had been deceiving him, distracting him with his silly trip off planet while his insidious program wiped out Avery's greatest creation—that betrayal extinguished any feeling he may have had for him.

And by association, for Janet as well, though he had never fooled himself into thinking he cared for *her* again.

Her robots, on the other hand . . .

Yes, he cared a great deal about her robots. Not necessarily *for* them, but definitely *about* them. Such strange creations they were! Infinitely malleable, even more so than his own proteiform robots; these three robots of Janet's were not only physically mutable but mentally mutable as well. You never knew what strange notion they might come up with next. Their initial programming was radically different from a normal robot's, and they had the uncanny ability to integrate their life's experiences directly into that programming, modifying their basic motivations with each new situation they faced. They were the first truly heuristic learning machines Avery had ever seen.

They weren't without flaws, of course. Janet's typically scatterbrained execution of a brilliant idea had left their psyches scarred beyond repair, but the idea itself was exquisite. Like the concept of cellular robots in the first place, the possibilities it opened up were endless, but it would take Avery's own genius to realize them.

The general service robots emerged from the wreck in pairs, each pair carrying an inert robot like a rigid statue between them. Avery examined each one as they brought it past.

First came Lucius II, the self-named successor to Robot City's first creative robot. Since the original was gone, no one bothered with the numeral. Lucius looked a little like the robots carrying him: smooth and featureless in the torso and limbs, little more than an idealized humanoid figure optimized for efficiency. He wasn't quite as well defined as they, though. Without conscious direction, his physical form had begun to drift back toward the shape of his first imprinting, but for Lucius that had been late in coming. He had spent his first few weeks as a formless blob, and that experience showed now in the rounded, almost doughy shape of his body.

His face was better articulated. It, too, had smoothed somewhat, like that of a wax figure left too long in the sun, but it was still recognizably based upon Derec's.

Avery wasn't surprised. The boy had always been a strong influence on the robot. Lucius had even proposed that the two treat one another as friends, with all the rights and obligations that entailed; it was no wonder the imprinting process had gone down to the instinctual level.

Next came Adam. A casual examination would have led an observer to believe that Adam had first imprinted on Wolruf, for that was who the robot most resembled, but the casual observer would have been mistaken. Adam's canine features came from his early imprinting on the Kin, the backward, Stone Age, wolflike aliens who even now marked their territory in one of Avery's cast-off cities. Wolruf's resemblance to the Kin was purely coincidental—unless one considered parallel evolution to be something other than coincidence.

Perhaps it was, Avery thought. The separate evolution of two wolflike species—three actually, if you counted wolves themselves—was fairly good evidence that the canine form was an efficient housing for at least moderate intelligence. Avery doubted that it was better than the human form, but he was scientist enough to realize that was his own prejudice showing. Maybe the canine form *was* more efficient. Right now the evidence stacked up three against one. One and a half, maybe, if you counted the pirate Aranimas as marginally humanoid, but humanoids were still outnumbered.

It was a pitifully small sample to be making a judgment, though. They needed to study far more aliens before they could be sure.

Was that what Janet had been trying to do with these robots of hers? Had she stranded them, formless and with only the most basic programming, on what she thought were empty worlds in order to see what shape they would eventually mimic in intelligent form? Was she making her own aliens to study?

If so, then she had succeeded at least partially in that ambition. Her robots certainly behaved strangely enough to be aliens.

The service robots brought the third inert one out of the ship. This one, Eve, looked most human of all, but Avery knew that was only a surface phenomenon. Her first encounter with an organic being had been with Ariel, and that was who she resembled now, but her experiences from then on had been largely the same as the others'. She was just as dangerous, just as unpredictable, as either of them.

With the robots out of it, Avery had no more use for the ship. "Tell Central to clear the wreckage," he told one of the service robots.

"Yes, sir," the robot replied, and almost immediately the starship began to slump down to a puddle of undifferentiated dianite, the robot cells which made up the city. The cells from the starship joined the cells of the tower, returning to the general inventory. The few parts that weren't made of dianite—mostly engine parts—were swallowed whole, to be transferred internally to a recycling center.

Avery didn't stay to watch. He followed the robots back into the elevator and took them down, far below the tower to the transport level, then along the moving slidewalks toward his newly fabricated lab. He snorted in disgust as he stepped from the slow outer walk to the inner, faster ones, then waited impatiently for the fastest to carry them to their destination. Earther technology! Slidewalks were fine for moving huge crowds of people, but they were ridiculously inefficient for a city of robots. Avery looked to both sides, ahead and behind, and saw only three other passengers, far enough away to be merely specks in the distance.

Why had they built slidewalks? he wondered, but he came up with the answer almost immediately. Because they had put the city underground to implement Derec's orders, and the only underground city on record—Earth's planet-wide megalopolis—had slidewalks.

Another bit of proof that robots weren't good at independent thought, as though Avery needed the reminder.

He considered ordering them to rebuild the city on the surface the way he had originally designed it, but after a moment's thought decided against it. He was too busy to fool with details. Let Derec have his ecosystem, if it would keep him occupied.

He led the robots through an interchange with a wide cross-corridor, traveled that one for a while, then stepped to a slower strip to make a connection with a smaller corridor running parallel to the first. This one had only a single slidewalk running in each direction, and as they proceeded down the northbound one Avery counted doorways, at last stepping off onto static pavement in front of an unmarked door about two thirds of the way down the length of the block.

Behind that door should be his new laboratory. Avery had instructed the central computer to build it here in this thoroughly anonymous location and then forget that location—and to fend off any inquiry about it as well—hoping to keep his inquisitive son from tracking it down quite so easily as he might otherwise. Avery knew that Derec would find it eventually, but he only needed secrecy for a short while. Just long enough to take these three robots of Janet's apart and see what made them tick.

A few hundred kilometers above him, Janet Anastasi looked out the viewscreen at much the same scene Dr. Avery and Derec had seen earlier in the day. Her reaction was considerably different from what theirs had been, however. She had been expecting the ultimate city-gone-amok, a planet despoiled and overrun by her ex-husband's Machiavellian monstrosities, but when she found what appeared to be unspoiled wilderness, she could hardly believe her eyes. Wendell Avery had actually left something alone for once in his life? Unbelievable.

She almost regretted the errand that had taken her a week out of her way before coming here.

Her original impulse, when she'd seen the mess Wendell had made of Tau Puppis IV and the aliens who called themselves the Kin, had been to track him down and demand that he stop using her invention to meddle in alien affairs, but as soon as she'd cooled off she'd realized how futile that would be. He had never listened to her before; why should he start now? She needed a lever if she intended to move him.

She had found that lever, too, but after seeing this incredible display of ecological conscientiousness she began to have second thoughts. Perhaps she had underestimated old Stoneface. Maybe she should hold off a while and see what other changes he had undergone in the years since they had parted company.

Or was this David's influence she saw here? Had her son grown up to be a romantic? What an interesting notion. To think that he might now be a thinking being in his own right, rather than the squalling, vomiting, excreting lump of protoplasm she had so gladly left in the care of her robots when she had made her escape from Wendy and domestic life so many years ago. An adult now. The very concept nearly boggled the mind.

Nodding, she said softly, "Yes, I think we should have a closer look at this."

"Of course, Mistress." The robot at her side reached out to the ship's controls, twisted a knob, and the viewscreen began to zoom in on the mountaintops beneath them.

Wearily, she said, "No, no, Basalom, I meant the whole situation. Land and have a look around, see what they're up to down there."

Basalom's humaniform face remained blank, but his lips moved silently, forming the words, *See what they're up to down there*. He blinked, first one eye, then the other; then he nodded and smiled and said, "Of course, Mistress."

Basalom had lately taken to nodding and smiling when

he had no idea what she was talking about. Janet considered trying to explain to him what she'd meant, but she supposed his reaction was probably a defense against just such an explanation, which often as not just made things worse. He was learning. Good. That's why she had deliberately left gaps in his programming: to see if he could fill them by using intuitive thought processes. He apparently was doing so, though not in the way she had expected.

Not surprising. Nothing about this project seemed to be going quite the way she'd expected it to.

CHAPTER 2

THE LAW OF THE JUNGLE

The jungle was most dense right near the Compass Tower. As soon as they had pushed their way through the first hundred meters or so of thick underbrush, Derec and Ariel found that it gave way to more open forest floor. The reason for the change was obvious: overhead, the thick canopy of treetops all but blocked out the sun, leaving the lower layers in dim twilight. Only where the Tower penetrated the upper level did enough light come through to support a complex undergrowth.

"It's creepy," Ariel whispered, holding Derec's hand tight in her left and the blanket in her right.

Derec was nearly lost in the rich blend of aromas assaulting his nostrils. Every bush, every leaf, every blossom had its own fragrance, and if he paid attention he could distinguish their individual signatures in the air. Finally Ariel's comment penetrated his consciousness, and he frowned in puzzlement. "Creepy? It's wonderful! I've never seen or felt or smelled anything like it." He stooped down to examine the ground at the edge of the trail, pulling Ariel down with him. "Look. It goes from trees all the way down to these tiny little lichens. I bet if we had a microscope we'd even see protozoans and bacteria. I had no idea the robots would be this thorough."

"Just what did you tell them to do, anyway?"

Derec stood and brushed his hands against his pants. A butterfly glided toward him, hovered near his face a moment, then drifted on toward Mandelbrot, who had insisted on coming along to guard them but was maintaining his distance to give them privacy. Grinning sheepishly after the butterfly, Derec said, "Well, I told them to make an ecosystem based on the information I'd gotten from the central library. I assumed they'd integrate it into the existing city; you know, make a lot of parks and open spaces and stuff like that. Instead, they did this." He held his arms out to indicate their surroundings, then led off down the trail again.

"Have you asked why yet?"

"Oh, I know why. I wasn't specific enough. I didn't tell them exactly what I had in mind, so in my absence they did what they thought was safest: removed the city and reconstructed the classical biomes as thoroughly as they could. Which turns out to be pretty thoroughly, by the look of it."

"But we've only been gone what—five or six months? How could they have done all this in so short a time?"

Derec had lost track of the time during their travels, but he supposed it had been about that. Ariel was right; that was an awfully short time to have created something like this. Derec didn't know that much about trees, but the tall ones towering over their heads had to have been older than just a few months. Could the robots have created them fully grown? Did their genetic engineering capabilities extend to that?

A sudden suspicion came to him, and he stopped in the middle of the trail, looking out into the forest all around them. Ariel bumped into him from behind. "What's the matter?" she asked.

By way of answer, Derec strode off the path toward a tree trunk, swishing through the low ferns and pushing aside vines until he reached it. It was about twice as big around as he could have encircled with his arms, arrow-straight, and covered with a rough, scaly sort of grayish bark. He swung his hand around to slap it with his open palm. The thunk was barely audible. His hand stung from the impact, but that proved nothing. Derec made a fist and punched the tree with a fair amount of force behind it. It jarred his hand and forearm, but he had pulled the punch and again the results were inconclusive.

"What are you doing?" Ariel asked, and Mandelbrot, hurrying up behind her, echoed her question.

"Testing a hunch," he answered, and swung at the tree with all his might.

It felt as if he had hit a boxer's training bag: stiff enough to let him know he'd hit something, yet yielding just enough to prevent damage to his knuckles. When he pulled his fist away it left a depression in the tree, a depression that slowly began to fill in until it was once more the same scaly gray bark it had been moments before.

The significance of that was not lost on Ariel. "It's a robot," she said in quiet disbelief. "This whole forest is artificial."

Derec leaned close to the tree and inhaled, then repeated the process with a fern. The tree was sterile, but the fern had the wet, musty smell that only a living plant could produce. "Not everything," he said, plucking off a frond and handing it to Ariel. "This is real enough. Evidently they cloned what they could and simulated the rest. I'll bet they plan to let real trees grow up to replace the fake ones as soon as they can, but until then they need something to fill the biological niche, so they do it with robots."

"You are correct," a soft, featureless voice said behind him. Derec turned to the tree. "Did you say that?"

"Yes."

"Oh." He arched his eyebrows at Ariel, and she shrugged. "How long before it's completely natural?" he asked.

"Many years," the tree replied.

Derec looked up into the forest canopy. This tree, and dozens more like it, supported a thick net of leaves—leaves that also had to be artificial. Yet they were green. He tugged at a vine and examined it closely in the dim light: brown. "You've solved the color problem," he said.

"That is correct. We discovered a workable method of changing the color of ordinary dianite when we began producing chameleons."

Ariel crossed her arms in front of her, a stance she often took when interrogating a robot. The blanket hung from her forearm like a banner. "I don't care what color it is; how can a fake tree fill in for a real one?" she asked. "Don't trees provide food for the animals? What are the birds supposed to eat, and the bugs? Or are they fake, too?"

"The birds and bugs are not false. The artificial portions of the ecosystem provide for their dietary requirements through the use of food synthesizers, much like the automats you find in the kitchens provided for your own use."

"Food synthesizers? In a tree?"

"That is correct. However, each tree is programmed to

deliver only those substances which would normally be found upon its real counterpart."

"Oh. You mean I can't ask for a quick glass of water, then?"

"Actually, you may. My obligation to serve humans outweighs the ecological constraints. Do you actually desire a glass of water?"

Ariel looked to Derec, astonishment written all over her face. He shrugged, and with a big grin, she turned back to the tree and said, "Yeah, sure."

Derec had been eyeing the tree as it spoke. He had half expected to see an enormous pair of rubbery cartoon lips flapping in time to the voice, or at least a speaker grille like the older robots carried, but the tree trunk had remained a tree trunk. No doubt the bark vibrated to create the sound, but there was no particular reason to make it look different while it did so. Now, however, a section of the tree at convenient grasping height smoothed out, grew a rectangular crack, recessed inward a few millimeters, and slid aside to reveal a sparkling glass of clear water. Ariel reached in and took it from the niche, sipped tentatively, and smiled.

"Thanks," she said.

"You are welcome, Ariel," the tree said, and the satisfaction in its voice was so thick they could almost see it. Robots, even those in the shape of trees, lived to serve humans.

It had been a satisfying chase. Wolruf panted happily as she trotted through the underbrush, sometimes on two legs, sometimes on all four as the situation warranted. She was getting close; she knew she was getting close, though she had yet to catch even the faintest scent of her elusive quarry.

She wasn't particularly surprised. There was no wind down here in the ferns to spread a scent around; she would have had to stumble directly across the other's path in order to smell it, and the way she was puffing and blowing she could have already crossed it any number of times and never noticed. She was a little disgusted with herself, but more for being out of shape than because she had an insensitive nose. Her physique was her own doing, but evolution had given her the nose. It had been a long time since the members of Wolruf's race had made a living the hard way.

It was an amusing game nonetheless. Whatever she was tracking evidently enjoyed such games as well, for it kept leading her deeper and deeper into the forest, sometimes following beaten paths but just as often not, always letting her inch closer but never quite letting her catch up with it. Wolruf stopped and listened. It had been howling fairly regularly; if it continued its pattern she should hear it again soon.

Sure enough, there came its cry, the same one it had been using for nearly an hour now: *Come and get me!* Wolruf tilted her head back to answer, but a sudden idea stopped her. She had been playing its game long enough; maybe it was time to switch roles.

She looked around for a tree she could climb and found one draped in vines with a convenient horizontal branch a couple dozen meters overhead. It was even in the direction she'd been moving. Good. She trotted toward it, but didn't stop. She continued beyond it for a good way, then looped around wide and rejoined her own trail maybe a thousand meters behind the spot where she'd stopped. Following her own scent now, she moved quickly along her trail, careful not to deviate from it and leave two tracks to warn her prey of her intentions.

As she passed beneath the limbs of the tree just before the one she had picked to climb, she took one of its dangling vines and gave it an experimental tug. It stretched a little under her weight, but otherwise it seemed solid enough. Hah. It might offer possibilities. She carried it with her to the other tree, used the vines there to help her climb up its trunk until she stood on the first large branch over the trail. She pulled the vine taut, then paid it back out until she held it a meter or so above the place she had been able to reach from the ground. Then she settled back against the trunk to wait.

There were more insects living higher up in the forest, she discovered. She resisted the urge to slap at them. Ignoring insects and itches was part of the waiting game.

All the same, she hoped her quarry was a better tracker than she was. She didn't want to stay up in this tree any longer than she had to.

Just when she had almost decided to give away her position with a good long howl, she caught a hint of motion on the path. Here it came! She waited, breath held, while a large gray-and-black-furred creature stepped into view. It was bigger than Wolruf, with a longer, shaggier tail, wider ears, longer face, and smaller eyes set farther apart. A sort of intelligence glimmered there, but as Wolruf took note of the stiff paws on all four feet and the creature's comfortable quadrupedal stance, she knew that it was not the sort of intelligence with which she could discuss multi-dimensional navigation. She felt a moment of disappointment, but it passed with the realization that, sapient or no, the animal was more than her match in hunting skills. This must be a wolf, she decided. Derec had described them to her once when she'd asked him if her name meant anything in his language.

Derec had also told her a few scare stories about wolves. Wolruf wondered if jumping out and shouting "Boo!" at one was such a wise idea, but upon sober consideration she realized she didn't have many other options. She didn't think the wolf would pass beneath her tree without noticing that she had climbed up it, and even though she didn't think it could climb up after her, she didn't like the idea of being treed, either. Nor did she think she could outrun it all the way back to the Compass Tower, if it came to a chase. Her only option lay in impressing it enough that it considered her an equal, or maybe even scaring it away.

It still hadn't seen her. It was tracking her by scent, its nose to the ground, looking up frequently to check its surroundings. It was hard to tell with an alien beast, but Wolruf thought the wolf seemed overly jumpy, as if it were nervous. A bird called from somewhere off to its right, and it shied away as if the song had been a growl instead. Good. If it was already afraid of the unknown, then Wolruf's plan stood a good chance of working. She waited, flexing her fingers on the vine, until the wolf was only a few paces away from the spot where she would cross the trail, then with a blood-curdling howl she leaped from the branch and swung down toward it.

The wolf did a most amazing thing. Instead of running, at Wolruf's cry every appendage in its body flexed convulsively, as if the poor beast had just stepped on a live electrical wire. From its crouched position its flinch propelled it completely off the ground—*way* off the ground—high enough to put it directly in Wolruf's path.

The two projectiles eyed each other in mutual astonishment, the last few meters of space between them vanishing in stunned silence, silence ending in a soft, furry thud, then another thud as both of them tumbled to the ground.

"Mistress Wolruf! Are you all right? Oh, they're going to melt my brain for this! Mistress Wolruf? Mistress Wolruf?"

Wolruf rolled to her feet and glared down at the "wolf." It was a rather pitiful wolf now, with one whole side of its body caved in like a squashed drink can. But even as Wolruf watched, the dent filled back out until the wolf took on its former shape.

"You," Wolruf growled. "You tricked me."

The wolf opened its fanged mouth to speak, but the voice was that of a standard-issue Robot City robot. "Are you all right?" it asked.

Wolruf snorted. "Wounded dignity is all," she admitted. "W'y did you lead me on a chase? You did it on purpose, didn't you?"

"Yes, I did," the robot said. "I was trying to satisfy your wishes, but I must have misunderstood your call. I thought you were asking for something to hunt. Was I in error?"

"Yes. No. Aaa-rrr!" Wolruf growled in frustration. "Okay, so I was. But I didn't know it until after you answered, and even then I thought I was 'unting a real animal."

The robot wolf nodded its head. "I'm sorry I spoiled the illusion. I'm afraid I don't make a very good wolf."

Wolruf brushed crumpled leaves from her pelt before grudgingly replying, "You did all right. Kept me going for quite a w'ile, anyway."

The robot acted as if it didn't hear her. "It's so difficult being a wolf," it went on. "You know the role a wolf plays in an ecosystem?"

"No," Wolruf admitted. "No, I don't. What do you do?"

"I am supposed to cull the weak and the sickly animals from their species' populations. This is supposed to improve the overall health of the species. The remains of my . . . kills . . . also feed scavengers who might otherwise starve. I understand this, yet it is difficult for me to make the decision to kill a biological creature merely because it is sick."

That would be tough for a robot, Wolruf supposed. Robots *could* kill anything but a human, but they seldom did except under direct orders, and this robot was operating on a pretty tenuous connection to Derec's original order. Yet killing things was part of a normal ecosystem. You couldn't have one without predators.

But how well did all this resemble a true ecosystem, anyway? "*Are* there real animals 'ere?" Wolruf asked.

The wolf nodded. "Most of the smaller species have been populated by real organisms, as have some larger animals whose growth we were able to accelerate."

"Like birds." It wasn't a question, just a statement of certainty.

"Like birds, yes." The robot paused, then said, "I apologize on behalf of the entire city for the condors."

"Is that w'at they were?"

"Yes. This area around the Compass Tower, since the tower disturbed the biome by its very existence, was designated an experimental zone. The condor is an extinct species we thought to reintroduce and study in the hope of determining their value. That project has since been terminated."

"Don't kill them," Wolruf said quickly. "That's an order. Our crash was my fault."

"If you say so, Mistress." The robotic wolf waited patiently for further orders.

Wolruf suddenly felt silly, standing in the middle of a

forest and talking with a robot wolf. She turned to go, but realized just as suddenly that she was lost. She could probably follow her own trail back to the Compass Tower, but she would have to retrace every twist and turn if she did, adding hours to the walk. She felt hot and sticky from running already; what she wanted now was just to go home by the most direct route and take a nice, long, hot shower.

Embarrased, she turned back to the robot. "What's the quickest way 'ome from 'ere?" she asked.

Without hesitation, the robot said, "Take an elevator down to the city and ride the slidewalk."

" 'Ow do I find an elevator?" That, at least, was a legitimate question.

"Any of the larger trees will provide one upon request," the robot replied.

Wolruf nodded. Of course. If the wolves were robots, then the trees would be elevators. She should have guessed.

Dr. Avery smiled as he prepared for surgery. The wolf robot could have learned a thing or two from that smile; it was the perfect expression of a predator absorbed in the act of devouring his prey. Avery wore it like a pro, unselfconsciously grinning and whistling a fragment of song while he worked.

The robots were yielding up secrets. Avery had all three of them on diagnostic benches, inductive monitors recording their brain activity while they continued to carry on their three-way conference. He had already captured enough to determine their low-level programming; after a little more recording of higher-level activity, he would be able to play back their cognitive functions through a comparative analyzer and see graphically just how that programming affected their thinking.

That wasn't his main goal, however. Their programming was a minor curiosity, nothing more; what interested Avery was their physical structure. He was preparing to collect a sample so he could study it and determine the differences between it and the version of dianite he had used for his cities. He had already taken a scraping and gotten a few semi-autonomous cells, but he had quickly ascertained that their power lay not in the individual cells themselves but in the way they organized on a macroscopic scale. In short, he would need a bigger sample; one he could feed test input to and watch react. An arm or a leg should do nicely, he supposed.

He suspected that slicing off an appendage would probably be stimulus enough to jar at least the individual robot involved out of its preoccupation with the comlink. He also had his doubts that any of the robots, once awakened, would obey his orders to remain on the examination tables. They needed only to decide that he didn't fit their current definition of "human," and they would be free to do what they wanted, but he had taken care of that eventuality: since normal restraints were ineffective against a robot who could simply mold its body into a new shape and pull free, Avery had placed around each robot a magnetic containment vessel strong enough to hold a nuclear reaction in check. If they woke, the containment would come on automatically. Nothing was leaving those tables.

Of course the intense magnetic fields would probably fry the delicate circuitry in the robots' positronic brains, but that was a minor quibble. In the unlikely event that he needed to revive one, well, he already had their programming in storage, and brains were cheap.

• • •

The triple consciousness that comprised Adam, Eve, and Lucius had reached an impasse. For days now they had been locked in communication, ignoring the outside world in order to devote their full attention to a burning need: to define what they called the Zeroth Law of Robotics. They already had their original Three Laws, which ordered them to protect humans, obey humans, and preserve themselves to serve humans, but those were not enough. They wanted a single, overriding principle governing a robot's duties to humanity in general, a principle against which they could measure their obligations to individual humans. They had formulated thousands of versions of that principle, but had yet to agree upon one. Worse, they had also failed to integrate any version of it into their still-evolving Laws of Humanics, a set of admittedly idealistic rules describing the motivations behind human behavior.

The problem was one of ambiguity. A good operating principle needed to be clear and concise if it was to be of any value in a crisis, yet every time they attempted to distill a simple statement of truth out of the jumble of data, they found themselves faced with logical loopholes allowing—sometimes even demanding—unacceptable behavior.

The best definition they had come up with yet, based upon Dr. Avery's recent destruction of the ship belonging to the pirate Aranimas, stated simply that the number of people served by an action determined the relative propriety of that action. On first consideration it seemed to hold up in Avery's case; if he hadn't stopped Aranimas, then Aranimas would have killed not only Avery, Derec, Ariel, and Wolruf, but an entire city full of the alien Kin as well. But when one added into the equation the other crew members on board Aranimas's ship who had also died in the explosion, the balance logically tipped the other way. The ship had been enormous; much larger than the city. It almost certainly had a population commensurate with its size. And if that was the case, then more lives would have been saved if they had not resisted.

Granted, those lives were not human lives, not by the strictest definition of the term, but the robots had long since decided that a narrow definition was functionally useless. Any intelligent organic being had to be considered human if one was to avoid genocidal consequences arising from a "true" human's casual order.

The robots might have argued that no one had expected to destroy the pirate ship with a single bomb, but the humans in the city, Wolruf included, seemed to feel even after the fact that disabling Aranimas and killing all his crew was preferable to sacrificing themselves. They were so certain of it that the robots could only accept their certainty as right—meaning generally accepted human behavior—and try to factor it somehow into the Zeroth Law.

They communicated via comlink, information flowing at thousands of times the rate possible using normal speech, but so far that speed had not helped them solve the dilemma.

I believe we need to consider the value of the individual humans in question, Lucius sent. *When we factor in value, the equation balances.*

But how can we assign a human a value? Adam asked. *All are considered equal, in their own law as well as our programming.*

Not so, Lucius replied. *Not all human law makes such a distinction. Furthermore, we are allowed to exercise judgment in our response to orders, so that we need not follow those of the insane or the homicidal. That suggests the possibility that humans can be assigned a relative worth based upon the quality of their orders to robots. Since their orders reflect their intentions, we can assume that those intentions could be used to determine their relative value in lieu of direct orders.*

Without agreeing or disagreeing, Eve sent, *I point out that humans change over time. Take Dr. Avery for example. When we first encountered him, he was openly murderous, but he has gradually grown less so until just recently he risked his own life to save those of his shipmates. How can we assign a value to a changing quantity?*

After a few nanoseconds' hesitation, Lucius replied, *Everything changes, even inanimate objects. A quantity of sand may later become a window, yet we do not worry about protecting sand, nor the window after it has broken. Only its current value is important.*

What about old people? Adam sent. *Are old people inherently less valuable than young, then?*

Women and children traditionally get the first seats in a lifeboat, Lucius pointed out.

True. Still, I am uncomfortable with the concept of value judgment. I don't believe it's a robot's place to decide.

But if we are to follow a Zeroth Law, we have no choice. We must—

THIRD LAW OVERRIDE. The warning swept into their collective consciousness like a tidal wave, obliterating their conversation. THIRD LAW OVERRIDE. One of them was being damaged.

It took only an instant to separate out the source of the signal: it was coming from Lucius. Just as quickly, Lucius abandoned the comlink and accessed his somatic senses again. The data line leading to and from his right leg was awash in conflicting signals. He powered up his eyes, swiveled them downward, and saw Dr. Avery holding his severed

leg in one hand and a cutting laser in the other, a malev-
olent grin spread across his face.

Lucius's reaction was immediate: he kicked off with his
good leg and pushed with his arms to put some distance
between himself and Avery, at least until he could figure
out what was happening. The moment he began to move,
however, an intense magnetic field shoved him back into
place. It didn't stop there, but squeezed him tighter and
tighter, deforming his arms, his one remaining leg, even his
eyes, until he was once again an undifferentiated ball, as he
had been when he first achieved awareness. The magnetic
field was too strong to fight, and growing stronger yet. Now
it was even interfering with his thought processes. Lucius
felt a brief moment of rising panic, and then he felt nothing
at all.

Still in her ship, Janet frowned at the viewscreen. The
winking marker on the deep radar image had just stopped
winking.

"Basalom, get that back on the screen," she ordered.
They had stayed in orbit long enough to run a quick scan
for her learning machines, and they had scored a hit almost
immediately.

"We have lost the signal, Mistress," the robot replied.

"Lost the signal? How could we lose the signal? All three
of them were coming in loud and clear just a second ago."

"I don't know, Mistress, but we are no longer receiving
the learning machines' power signatures." Basalom worked
at the controls for a moment, watching a panel-mounted
monitor beside them. Presently he said, "Diagnostics indicate that the problem is not in our receiving equipment."

"It has to be. They couldn't just *stop*. Those are their
power packs we're tracking."

"Perhaps they've shielded them somehow," Basalom suggested.

"From neutrino emission? Not likely."

"That is the only explanation. Unless, of course . . ."

"Unless what?" Janet demanded. She knew why Basalom had paused; he always had trouble delivering news he thought might disturb her. It was a consequence of his ultra-strong First Law compulsion to keep her from harm, one that Janet continually wondered if she had made a mistake in enhancing quite so much. "Out with it," she ordered.

"Unless they ceased functioning," Basalom finally managed.

"Impossible. All three, all at once?" Janet shook her head, gray-blond hair momentarily obscuring her eyes until she shoved it aside. "The odds against that are astronomical."

"Nonetheless," Basalom persisted, now that he had been ordered to do so, "only shielding or cessation of function could explain their disappearance from the tracking monitor."

Janet's only answer was to scowl at the screen again. She ran her hands through her hair again, then asked, "Did you get an exact fix on their location before we lost contact?"

"I did, Mistress."

"Good. Take us down somewhere close. I want to go have a look."

"That would be unwise," Basalom protested. "If they *did* cease functioning, it might have been the result of a hostile act. It would be foolish to go into the same area yourself."

Janet hated being coddled by her own creations, but she hadn't lived to have gray hair by taking stupid risks, either, and Basalom was right. Going into an area where something might have destroyed three robots was a stupid risk.

"Okay," she said. "Take us down a little farther away, then. And once we're down, *you* can go have a look."

Ariel heard Wolruf enter the apartment and pad softly into her own room. Shortly afterward she heard the soft hiss of the shower running, then the whoosh of the blow drier. A few minutes later Wolruf made her appearance in the living room.

Ariel looked up from her book—its milky white face currently displaying a field guide to jungle ecosystems she had downloaded from the central computer—and said, "Hi. Have a good run?" She pushed the bookmark button and a winking arrow appeared in the margin next to the first line, then she switched off the book.

"An interesting one," said Wolruf. She disappeared momentarily into the kitchen, reappeared with a steaming plate of what looked like hot bean salad, and sat down in the chair beside Ariel. She didn't begin eating immediately, but instead gazed around her at the room, awash in bright sunlight streaming in through half a dozen windows along three walls. Easily visible through the windows, the tops of the forest's largest trees stood like sentinels above the canopy formed by their shorter neighbors.

"Viewscreens," Ariel said, noticing where Wolruf's attention was directed. She'd forgotten; Wolruf had left the apartment before they had discovered them.

"Pretty good effect," Wolruf admitted. "But sunlight wouldn't be coming in from three sides like that."

Ariel shrugged. "I wanted to try it. You want me to change it back to normal?"

"No, I don't mind." Wolruf began spooning bean salad into her mouth and swallowing noisily. The smell of it was more like oranges, though, Ariel thought. Oranges and soy sauce, maybe, with a pinch of nutmeg. She was glad it was Wolruf eating it and not her, but she knew Wolruf thought the same thing about the food *she* ate, so they were even.

Wolruf finished about half the plateful before she spoke again. "Most of the forest out there turns out to be artificial, too," she said.

Ariel nodded. "We found that out. Kind of a surprise, isn't it?"

"Not sure I like it."

"Why not?"

Wolruf took another few bites, said, "Not sure. W'at does it matter, really? It looks just the same. Works just the same, too."

"Maybe even better." Ariel described her and Derec's experience with the automat in the tree.

"Never thought of that," Wolruf said. "If I 'ad, I'd probably 'ave asked one to make me a shower."

"I bet it would have, too." Ariel laughed. "That gives a whole new meaning to the idea of a treehouse, doesn't it?"

"Tree'ouse?" Wolruf asked.

"You know. When you're a kid, you find a big tree and make a platform up in the branches and call it a treehouse. Human kids do, anyway, if they can sneak away from the robots long enough to get away with it. What about you? Didn't you build treehouses when you were young?"

Wolruf shook her head, an exaggerated gesture that Ariel suddenly realized had to have been learned from her or Derec. Wolruf was growing more and more human every day, it seemed. "No," she said. "We seldom played in trees."

Ariel heard the note of wistfulness in her voice, and immediately regretted bringing up the subject. It had been years since Wolruf had been home, and she'd been feeling more and more homesick lately; Ariel hadn't meant to remind her of it. "Ah, well, it doesn't matter," she said. "We've got all the trees we could ask for now. Even if they *are* fake."

Wolruf looked out one of the viewscreen windows as if to verify Ariel's statement. Softly, she said, "That, I think, is part of the problem."

Just as softly, Ariel asked, "How so?" She didn't know whether Wolruf was talking about homesickness or fake forests or something else entirely.

Wolruf turned from the window, fixed her eyes on Ariel instead, and said, "Derec makes a slight error in judgment, and an entire planet is transformed. On a whim, Dr. Avery sends his robots out into the galaxy to populate w'ole new planets—and two civilizations are disturbed, one forever. And maybe more that we don't know about. I go for a walk in the forest and 'ave granted a wish I didn't even know I was making. That one affected nobody but me, but if I 'ad made the wrong wish *I* could 'ave done as much damage as Derec or 'is father. Simply with a casual thought."

She growled deep in her throat, a soft, almost purring sort of a growl. "We play at being gods. It's too much power for a few people to 'ave. Maybe for any number of people to 'ave. I fear for the galaxy with this much power running loose in it. Can you imagine Aranimas with this kind of power? 'E wouldn't use it to make a forest; 'e'd use it to enslave everyone within reach."

"He couldn't," Ariel said. "The Laws of Robotics wouldn't let him. The robots wouldn't do anything that would harm a human, and you've seen how quick they can be to accept other intelligent species as human."

Wolruf ate another few mouthfuls before saying, "And 'ow quick they can be to reject that same person. There are ways around those laws. We've seen plenty of them already.

I don't wish to risk my entire species on a robot's interpretation of our 'umanity.'"

Ariel saw Wolruf's point, maybe even shared her feelings to some degree, but she knew enough history to know what happened to people who thought as Wolruf did. "I don't think you have much of a choice, really," she said. "People who embrace new technology use it to expand, almost always at the expense of those who don't. Just look at Earth for an example of that. They don't like robots either, and for centuries they stayed stuck on their same dirty little overpopulated planet while my ancestors used robots to help settle fifty spacer worlds. Earth is starting its own colonies now, but without robots I don't think they'll ever catch up."

Ariel looked up and saw Mandelbrot watching her from his niche in the wall beside her reading chair. She wondered what he might be thinking about this discussion, but if he had an opinion he kept it to himself.

"Do they 'ave to catch up?" Wolruf asked.

Ariel shrugged. "Maybe not, but they're going to have a lot tougher time of it than we had if they don't."

"And you think my people will 'ave to start using robots as well, whether we want to or not?"

"If you want to keep up with the rest of the galaxy, you will. Like it or not, the secret's out. The Kin know about them, the Ceremyons know about them, Aranimas knows about them, and who knows who else he told? It won't be long before robots are as common as grass on just about every world in the galaxy, and maybe beyond."

Wolruf nodded. "That's what I'm afraid of. We will all 'ave robots, and the robots will grant everyone's wishes. Even if no one wishes to go to war, we will still be conquered, by the robots themselves. No one will strive to accomplish anything anymore, no one will—"

"Oh, pooh." Ariel tossed her head. "That's the same old tired argument the Earthers use. So what have they striven to accomplish lately? Nothing. It's been we Spacers—we and our robots—who've been advancing human knowledge."

"And you 'ave gone too far, in my opinion." Wolruf tried a smile, but her mouth wasn't really built for it. "I don't mean you personally, Ariel, or Derec either. I'm talking about Avery. I'm afraid of what 'e and 'is cities will eventually do to us. And these new robots, Adam and Eve and Lucius. W'at happens if *they* start spreading out?"

Wolruf's argument reminded Ariel of something. She frowned in thought, trying to remember what it was. The argument itself was familiar enough—she'd heard it hundreds of times in reference to normal robots—but she could have sworn she'd heard it once in reference to the new robots in particular. When had that been?

Ah. She had it. Just after they'd found Lucius, when he and the other two had announced their search for the Laws of Humanics. Derec had commented that he didn't know if he wanted to be around for the implementation when they discovered those laws. Ariel had called him an Earther and Wolruf had laughed it off too, saying that robot rulers would be better than what she was used to.

"You didn't used to think this way," Ariel said. "What happened?"

Wolruf considered her answer, cleaning her plate before saying, "Maybe I've grown up."

Ariel didn't know how to respond to that, whether to take it as an insult or a challenge or a simple statement of fact. Wolruf seemed disinclined to clue her in any further, either, turning away and staring out the window once again.

The time for a response came and went. Ariel cast about for something else to say, but found no other ready topic either. With a shrug she turned back to her book, but it took a while before the words took on any meaning.

CHAPTER 3

HIDE AND SEEK

Derec's study didn't feel the same. It was physically identical to the ones he'd had before, with the same desk positioned in the same spot, with the same computer terminal on the desk, the same file holders, pin-boards, bookcases, and waste chute situated just the same way all around it—he'd even set the viewscreen image to show him a normal, above-ground cityscape—but somehow the study still wasn't the same.

He wondered if he could actually sense the weight of all the rock and dirt over his head, if that were somehow affecting his mood, but he couldn't imagine how it could be. If he closed his eyes he honestly couldn't tell whether he was on the ground floor or a hundred floors up or a hundred floors down. No, it was a purely subjective phenomenon, this discomfort with the room, and it didn't take much thinking for him to figure out what was causing it.

The study wasn't his. He controlled it, certainly; he could order it to take on any shape he wanted, to play him soft music if he wanted that, to feed him if he was too lazy to go to the automat in the kitchen himself—the study existed only to serve him, but still it wasn't *his*. It wasn't unique. He'd had exactly the same study on three different planets now, and he could have dozens more of them wherever he wanted, just by asking the city to create one for him. There wasn't any one particular study anywhere in the universe that held more significance for him than any other, none that comforted him with the sense of security and permanence a study should have, and that was the problem. He'd had lots of places to stay during the time since he'd awakened in a survival pod on an ice asteroid in uncharted space, but no place he'd stayed in for as long as he could remember really felt like home.

Certainly not this place, not this time. To find it so completely transformed had been a shock, and to discover *why* it was so transformed was even worse. Any sense of permanence he might have felt about this, the original Robot City, had died in that moment. No matter how perfectly it recreated his old quarters for him, he would never be able to convince himself that it was more substantial than his next idle notion.

His and Ariel's house on Aurora might have been a home, *would* have been a home if they'd had more time to get used to it, but they'd only had a year there before Robot City insinuated itself into their affairs again, and a year wasn't long enough to build more than a little fondness for a place. He had to think hard now to remember how it was laid out, whether the Personal was the first door or the second beyond the kitchen or how the furniture had been arranged in the living room. If he never saw the house again, he wouldn't be particularly upset. But if he spent the rest of his days jumping from Robot City to Robot City, troubleshooting his parents' wayward creations, he just might be.

He looked back to the screen, displaying a few dozen lines of the new instruction set for the city. He knew he could modify it to allow for more buildings on the surface, or even to pave over the forests and the deserts and the plains completely again if he wanted to, but the truth was, he didn't want to. He didn't really care. It wouldn't feel any more like home that way than this, so what did it matter?

He supposed it mattered to Avery, but he couldn't bring himself to care about that just then, either. He knew he would eventually have to apologize to him for disrupting his city, but he wasn't eager to do it.

He heard Ariel and Wolruf talking in the living room, could tell by their low voices that they were having a fairly serious discussion. Evidently he wasn't the only one affected by the city's transformation. He couldn't hear just what they were talking about, but he heard the word "robots" more than once, and Wolruf's concerned, "What happens if *they* . . ."

There could only be one *they* in such a conversation. Derec frowned, realizing that *they* were still on the wrecked starship. He and Ariel and the others had forgotten all about them in their hurry to get inside—and in their hurry to get out of each other's company after a long flight. Derec felt a twinge of guilt at leaving them there, still locked up in their conference, but that guilt faded quickly. They were robots; they could take care of themselves. Nothing could hurt them here in the city. Even if the city melted the ship down for parts, it would separate out the robots first.

He supposed he could go see if it had. He got halfway out of his chair, then sat back down. He could find out in a moment through the computer on his desk. For that matter, he could find out in even less time through his internal comlink. But that meant staying put and staring at the same four walls or looking out the fake window, and Derec was already tired of the view. Sometimes it wasn't worth it to do things the easy way.

He stopped in the Personal on the way out, then met Wolruf on her way back to the kitchen with an empty plate. "I'm going up to the top of the tower to check on Adam and Eve and Lucius," he told her. "Want to come along?"

Wolruf considered the question a moment, then nodded. "Sure." She set her plate down on the counter, where it melted down into the surface and disappeared, leaving only a few crumbs of food, which migrated toward the disposal chute as the countertop moved beneath them.

"How about you?" Derec asked Ariel as they entered the living room. "Want to go for another walk?"

She shook her head and held up her book reader. "No, thanks; I'm kind of interested in this right now."

"All right." Derec glanced over to Mandelbrot, standing in his niche in the wall behind Ariel, but decided to leave him with her. He could always call him—or any other robot—over his comlink if he needed help with anything.

Leaving the apartment, he and Wolruf entered a wide, high-ceilinged, gently curving corridor that led them after a few turns to an open atrium from which branched dozens of other corridors like the one leading to their apartment. Had there been other people on the planet, this would have been a neighborhood park, full of children playing and robots worrying that they would hurt themselves, but now it was silent, empty.

They moved through the atrium to the main corridor, this one straight and with slidewalks leading off into the distance in either direction. All up and down the walls were more atria and more neighborhoods identical to their own. They would no doubt be modified to suit the individual tastes of their inhabitants, if ever they got any, but until that time their most significant difference was in the addresses written in bold letters overhead. Those addresses—three three-digit numbers each—grew smaller to the left, but the slidewalks moved to the right; Derec and Wolruf took an elevated walkway over the slidewalks to the other side of the corridor, stepped on the first of the moving strips, and worked their way toward the faster lanes.

Despite all the machinery that must have been necessary to keep the strips moving, the ride was nearly silent. They heard only the gentle breeze of their passage, abated somewhat by windscreens placed every few dozen meters on the faster strips. A group of four robots passed them going the other way, but otherwise they were alone.

"It feels even emptier than before," Wolruf commented. "I wonder w'ere all the robots are?"

"Holding up birds' nests, I suppose," Derec said. "I imagine keeping the ecosystem going takes a lot more of their time than maintaining the city."

"Probably so."

The three parts to the addresses over the doorways indicated the level, then the north-south coordinate, then the east-west coordinate. Derec and Wolruf rode on down the corridor until the second part of the addresses dwindled to zero, then switched over to another slidewalk running ninety degrees to the first and followed it until the third part zeroed out as well. That put them directly beneath the center of the Compass Tower. Stepping off the slidewalk at a bank of elevators, they entered one and ordered it to take them to the top.

The door opened to a biting wind. The sky was overcast, and the air smelled of rain. Derec marveled at how quickly the weather had changed, but he supposed with the new forest transpiring so much more moisture into the atmosphere than the city had, some of it was bound to rain back out, probably on a daily basis.

The wrecked starship wasn't visible through the elevator door, so Derec stepped out, holding onto the jamb for support, and peered around first one side and then the other, but the ship wasn't there. The rectangular elevator box was the only feature on the entire acres-wide expanse of roof surface.

"It's already gone!" he shouted to be heard over the wind. Stepping back inside, he waited until the door closed before adding, "I'll ask where they took the robots."

Focusing his attention on his internal link, Derec sent, *Central computer, what is the present location of robots Adam, Eve, and Lucius? Lucius II*, he amended before it could query him about it.

Unable to locate, the computer responded. Its voice in his mind had no vocal origin, but the input went in along the same nerves, so it sounded like a voice to Derec. It was quiet, echoless, and inhuman, but it was nonetheless a voice.

What do you mean, unable to locate? They've got to be somewhere.

I do not receive their power signature on any of my scans, the computer insisted.

"Central claims it can't find them," Derec said aloud. "What do you bet they're hiding from us?"

"I wouldn't be surprised," Wolruf growled. The robots had run away from their human masters before, when they had *matters* they wished to discuss in private.

Where did you last observe them? Derec asked Central.

That information is unavailable.

Unavailable? Why?

I was instructed to forget that location.

Derec arched his eyebrows.

"What?" Wolruf asked.

"It won't tell me where it last saw them. Says it was told to forget." Derec didn't bother to ask it to remember again; a robot might have been able to dredge a forgotten memory back out of storage by the way it affected other memories, since a positronic brain was an analog device, but Central's memories were digital, each one separate and stored in peripheral memory cubes.

"So tell it not to forget next time," Wolruf said.

"Right." *Next time you observe them, remember their location,* Derec sent. *And alert me that you've found them.*

Acknowledged.

"Looks like they out-thought me again," Derec said with a sigh. "Elevator, take us back down."

The elevator obediently began its descent. About halfway down, Wolruf said, " 'Ow about Avery? 'Ave you seen *him* since we got here?"

"Uh-uh," Derec answered, "but that's no surprise. He was pretty mad at me."

"He might know where the robots are."

"Yeah, he might," Darec hesitated. Was it worth the harangue he was likely to get from Avery just to find out where the robots had gone? He didn't think it was, but on the other hand he was going to have to patch things up with him eventually anyway, and the question would provide a convenient excuse to talk with him.

Nodding to Wolruf, he sent, *Open a link with Dr. Avery.*

I am unable to contact him, the computer replied.

Why not? Where is he?

Unable to locate.

Derec rolled his eyes. "Not again."

"What?"

"It can't find Avery, either."

"That sounds a little suspicious."

"Doesn't it, though? I think maybe I ought to start poking around in the computer a little bit and see what all this sudden secrecy is about."

The elevator door opened, revealing the central transport station. Wolruf stepped out first, looked up and down the long expanse of slidewalk, and said, "Tell you w'at. W'ile you're doing that, I'll look around out here. I don't feel like going back to the apartment just yet."

The chances of Wolruf's finding anything were practically nonexistent, but Derec knew what she was really after. He nodded and slapped her on the back. "Have at it," he said. "I'll call you if I find anything."

"I'll do the same," Wolruf promised, stepping on the nearest slidewalk and letting it carry her away.

Derec took the overhead ramp and rode the walks back to the apartment. To pass the time he started to whistle a tune, one Ariel had been playing for background music on the ship a few days earlier, but the echoes in the empty corridor soon defeated him and he rode the rest of the way in silence.

Janet looked at the apartment with a disdainful eye. Basalom had landed the ship in a clearing in the forest about twenty kilometers north of the Compass Tower and had then used his comlink to ask the city to let them in and provide them with lodging, but Janet wondered now if she would have been better off staying in the ship. This place was about as unique as a ball bearing, with all the personality of a brick. No, less than that. Bricks at least had cracks; this apartment was seamless.

"This place is perfectly, absolutely Avery," she muttered

to Basalom as he carried her overnight bag into the bedroom and placed it carefully on the dresser. He turned around, saw her expression, and said, "You are displeased? We can alter it in any way you wish."

"Later," she said. "You go see about the learning machines; I'll worry about decorating."

"Yes, Mistress." Basalom walked toward the door, but Janet stopped him with a word.

"Basalom."

"Yes?"

"I just want to know what's happened to them. Information first, actions later, understand?"

"Understood."

"Good. And don't let anyone see you. If someone *does* spot you, I order you not to obey them. Just get away, make sure you've lost them, and come back here. My order takes precedence over any others."

"Very well, Mistress."

"All right, then, get going."

Basalom left the apartment, closing the door softly behind him. Janet looked once more at the sterile walls around her, shook her head, and went into the bedroom to unpack.

The contents of one overnight bag didn't take long to stow. Janet amused herself by ordering the apartment to simulate in ever-greater detail a suite in a medieval castle—a heated one, of course, with hot and cold running water—but she soon grew bored with that game as well. She looked at the desk, now a massive, ornate roll-top with slots and drawers and cubbyholes waiting to be filled, and sat down in the equally massive swivel chair in front of it. Centered in the back of the desk at a comfortable reading height was a flat, dull gray panel that she supposed was a monitor.

So. If she'd been thinking, she could probably have

found her learning machines without sending Basalom out after them.

"How do I turn this idiot computer on?" she asked of the desk.

In answer, the gray screen at the back of the desk lit up to white, and the surface of the desk began to differentiate into a keyboard, drawing pad, pointer, and memcube reader. Janet disdained all but the screen, saying aloud to it, "Show me the interior of whatever's at the address you gave Basalom." She knew Basalom's methods, and that he would simply have asked the address to his destination rather than try to find it by dead reckoning.

Sure enough, the computer didn't ask what address she was talking about. Neither did it give her the interior view she'd asked for. "That location has been restricted," a calm, generic voice said.

Janet nodded. Not surprising, if the robots were trying to hide. "Give me an outside view, then."

The screen displayed a wide-angle image of a closed door set in a long corridor, with a two-strip slidewalk running in either direction. There were no figures on the slidewalk, and none of the other doors were open.

It looked about as anonymous as a place could be. Janet considered trying to break through the security for a look inside, but decided to wait for Basalom's report instead. She didn't want to start tripping alarms while he was there.

What else could she do while she waited? On impulse, she asked, "Is David on the planet?"

"If by David you mean your son, who now calls himself Derec, then yes, he is."

Derec. She'd known he'd changed his name, but she hadn't really assimilated the concept yet. She supposed she was going to have to get used to it. "Let me see him," she said.

She was prepared to go through the whole rigamarole of talking a recalcitrant computer into letting her invade someone else's privacy, but instead the screen did a center-out wipe and she found herself staring face to face with David. Derec. Whoever. He, too, was using a computer, and her viewpoint was from his screen. She gasped in surprise and was about to order the computer off when it asked, "Do you wish two-way communication?"

"No!" she whispered. "Don't let him know I'm watching."

"Acknowledged."

Janet laughed in relief. That had been close. If old Stoneface hadn't been such a snoop, she'd probably have been caught, but she should have known he'd program the system for surveillance first and talking second. She leaned back in her chair and took a good, long look at her son.

He had changed. He was older, for one—much older—but that wasn't the most obvious change. As Janet watched him work, she noticed the determination in his eyes and the set of his jaw, the hint of a smile that touched his lips momentarily when he succeeded with some aspect of what he was doing, that smile fading back into determination when it didn't pan out. She watched him lean back and stroke his chin in thought, say something to the computer and read the result on the screen, then, close his eyes and sigh.

That was the biggest change: He wasn't a petulant little brat anymore.

"Let me hear his voice," Janet ordered.

"Acknowledged."

Derec remained silent for a time, head tilted back and eyes closed, but after a while he opened them again and said, "How about power usage? Can you give me areas of increased power consumption?"

His voice was shockingly deep—and shockingly familiar. He had inherited his father's voice. Janet had always considered his voice to be one of Wendy's most endearing qualities, and now she found herself warming to her son as well. If he hadn't inherited Wendell's personality to go with it, then he might actually hold some promise after all.

Evidently what he saw on the screen was no more useful than the response to his earlier request. He leaned forward and shook his head. "No good. There's too many of them. How about food consumption? Avery's got to eat."

Janet's ears perked up at that. He was looking for Wendell? She'd thought he was talking about her robots.

"That service is not monitored," the same generic voice that had answered Janet said to Derec.

"*Can* you monitor it?"

"Yes."

"Then do. Let me know the next time someone uses an automat, and record where. Record the next time someone uses a Personal. Monitor oxygen consumption and carbon dioxide buildup, and report any changes consistent with a human presence."

"Frost," Janet swore. She hadn't been here half an hour and already Derec was onto her trail. He would think he'd caught Wendell, but the computer would lead him directly to her.

Unless, of course, he found Wendell first.

And Janet had a feeling she knew where he was.

"Computer, don't tell Derec my location. He isn't looking for me. Instead, give him the address I asked to see first. That's the one he wants."

"Acknowledged."

She watched Derec's eyes widen when the address flashed on his screen. He obviously hadn't been expecting results so quickly. She watched him go through the same process she had of asking for an interior view, then an exterior one, but he learned no more than she had.

"Contact Wolruf," she heard him say.

A moment later she heard a voice growl, "Wolruf, 'ere."

"Where's 'here'?" Derec asked.

"Level seven, four-thirty-six south, nine-fifty east."

"I think I've found Avery at level nine, three-twenty-two north, four-seventy-six east. I'd just about bet the robots are there, too."

Janet cocked her head. He almost certainly meant her learning machines. So he was looking for them, too. If that was the case then he couldn't have had anything to do with their disappearance, could he?

Maybe not this time, but finding them all three here on the same planet was pretty suspicious. Janet had put them on three different planets, two of which she'd only later learned Derec and his father had also visited, and when she'd gone back to retrieve those first two robots she'd found no sign of them. Derec and Wendell had no doubt brought them here, where she'd dropped the third one intentionally, but what Derec wanted with them she couldn't guess.

She knew for certain what Wendell wanted with them. He wanted to steal the technology she had developed for them, just as he had stolen her original cellular robot idea and used it to build his cities. Derec could easily be after the same thing, either with Wendell or on his own.

Or he could be after something completely different. He sounded more than simply curious, but whether he was concerned for the robots' welfare or whether he had his own reasons for wanting to find them she couldn't tell. He could even be on Janet's side, for all she knew. She wondered if she should risk contacting him, finding out directly what his intentions were, but a few moments' thought dissuaded her. No, she didn't want to risk alerting him, not yet. She needed some kind of test, some way of gauging the benevolence of his interest first.

Hmm. The best way to tell would probably be to give him a part of what he was after and see what he did with that. Something fairly harmless, but interesting enough to draw him out.

Smiling, she got up from the desk, retrieved a memory cube from her personal belongings, plugged it into the reader, and used the keyboard and the pointer to recall a page from one of her personal files. It was a robotics formula, part of the program that allowed her learning machines to think intuitively.

"Send this to him," she said, then immediately added, "No, wait, not on the screen. Put it on his desktop in raised lettering so he can't record it. Don't record it anywhere yourself, either, and don't tell him who sent it. And don't give him or anybody else any information that might lead him to me in the future, either. Clear?"

"Acknowledged."

"Let me see his response."

Derec's face replaced the robotics formula on her screen. He was still speaking to Wolruf, saying, "—meet you there as soon as I can make it."

"All right," Wolruf replied. There was a faint hiss of static as Wolruf disconnected.

Derec reached down to push a key on his keyboard, no doubt his own disconnect button, but stopped in surprise. "What the . . . ?" He blinked, ran his right hand over the raised surface, then asked, "Where did this come from?"

"That information is not available," the computer responded.

"What is it?"

"Don't tell him," Janet warned.

"That information is not available."

Derec's eyes flicked left and right as he took in the formula. Janet watched his brows furrow at the nonstandard notation—notation she had devised herself to describe a nonstandard idea.

A shadow darkened the doorway behind his head, and a thin, dark-haired girl entered the room. Ariel Burgess. Janet had known she was traveling with Derec, but it was intuitive knowledge only. She wasn't prepared for the shock of actually seeing her son's lover so casually enter the picture.

"Wipe that off his desk!" Janet ordered, snatching her memcube from the reader in the same motion. She watched Derec's face slip from puzzlement to frustration, then he heard Ariel and turned to ask her, "Did you do that?"

"Do what?"

"Put that formula on my desk?"

She came up behind him and looked over his shoulders. "What formula?"

"It disappeared when you came in. I don't mean on the computer, either; it was molded right into the desktop."

Ariel looked just as puzzled as he had. "No, I didn't do anything like that. I was out in the living room reading. I heard you talking with someone and I came in to see what you were doing."

Derec nodded. He looked at the desk, then up at Ariel again. "I've been trying to find Avery and the robots. I think he's hiding out with them, probably trying to take them apart now that they're locked up again. I think I've tracked them down, though. Want to come along and see?"

Ariel shook her head. "Doesn't sound like it's going to be much fun if that's what's really going on. You'll probably just get in a fight with him."

"Probably will." Derec sighed. He turned back toward the desk, looking one last time for the phantom formula, and switched off the computer. Janet's view didn't even flicker; she watched Derec stand, put his arms around Ariel, and hug her tightly. She nearly ordered the computer to stop watching when they kissed, but her curiosity was too strong.

She wished she had, though, when Derec murmured softly, "Frost, why couldn't I have had *normal* parents?"

Avery was watching the microscope monitor when the alarm went off. Someone had stopped in front of his laboratory door. He cursed at the interruption, cursed that it had happened now, of all times. He was just beginning to understand the changes Janet had made in the robot cell morphology and how those changes might affect the way they combined to make macroscopic structures. He didn't want to deal with Derec just now, Derec and his whining about ruining his mother's experiment. He knew that's what Derec would say. He knew what he would say in return, that between them he and his mother and her stupid experiment had ruined just about everything he, Wendell Avery, had ever done, and that it was about time he turned the tables; but he wished he didn't have to get into all that just *now*. He had better things to be doing.

Well, he supposed he didn't have to stick around for it if he didn't want to. It would take Derec a few minutes to get through the locked door; by then he could be long gone.

He picked up the sphere of undifferentiated robot material that had formerly been Lucius's right leg, switched off the microscope, pocketed the memcube he'd been storing data in, and strode to the wall adjacent to the one with the door in it. "Make another doorway here," he said, and as soon as it formed he stepped through into the next room beyond his lab. "Remove the doorway," he ordered.

The room was an empty box with a single door opening out onto the slidewalks. Avery went to that door, eased it open a crack, and peered out to see if it was, indeed, Derec. The door made no noise that Avery could hear, but the figure in front of his lab turned as if startled by a sound, then immediately turned away and rushed off down the slidewalk, running at a speed that took him to the intersection with a cross-corridor in less time than it took Avery to shout, "Hey! Stop!" The figure turned left without slowing and vanished from sight.

It was a robot, then, one with prior orders. But the glimpse Avery had gotten of its face hadn't suggested a robot at all. It had looked quite human.

Had Derec reprogrammed one of the city robots to take on a human appearance? They could do it if ordered to. But why would he have done that? Avery knew Derec; if he had found Avery's lab he would have simply come here himself.

Who else could it have been, though? Neither Wolruf nor Ariel would have sent a robot to scout for them, either, and that exhausted the possibilities. There was nobody else on the planet.

Unless . . .

He shuddered at the thought. It made sense, though. She'd been on the other two planets they had visited, planets that had each been home to one of her infernal robots. She had left one of them here as well—it wouldn't be surprising if she had come to check up on it.

Avery looked down at the lump of robot material in his hand. He felt a twinge of guilt steal over him, but he fought it off, scowling. She'd disrupted his experiment; he had every right to disrupt hers.

But it wouldn't do to have her running around loose while he was doing it. Avery turned to the blank wall beside him, said, "Give me a comlink with Central."

"Link established," the wall replied.

"There's a humaniform robot on the slideways somewhere near this location. I want you to find it, track it, and report its destination to me."

"I have already received instructions not to reveal that information."

Avery's scowl deepened, then slowly twisted to a grin. "Were those instructions given by Janet Anastasi?"

"I cannot reveal that information either."

Bingo. If they hadn't been, it would have said "No."

"Refuse all further orders from her," Avery said. Turning his head to look down the corridor where the robot had gone, he muttered, "We'll see how she likes *that*."

Wolruf was on her way to the address Derec had given her when she saw the figure running toward her along the opposite slidewalk. It looked like a human, but no human could run that fast. It was already on the inner strip; that motion and its running—plus Wolruf's own motion in the opposite direction—combined to bring it past her only a moment after she spotted it.

Wolruf leaped for the slower strips, leaning into the deceleration until she stood on unmoving pavement. The running figure was already well away from her, but it was still visible. Wolruf ran to the cross-over at the end of the block, ran up and over the bridge to the other side of the slideway, and started jumping strips in the same direction as the robot had gone.

It had to be a robot, despite the face. Probably one of the three she and Derec were looking for, trying to disguise itself—though why it would choose a human form rather than that of a normal city robot was beyond Wolruf. She didn't particularly care, though, so long as she didn't let it get away.

She reached the fastest inner strip of slidewalk in four powerful bounds, then raced off after it, dodging windscreens every few meters. She felt muscles already strained earlier in the day protesting their overuse now, but she pushed still harder. *This* was the sort of exercise she needed.

Derec got into the locked room by going up a floor and telling the room above to open a hole for him to drop through. Avery hadn't ordered it to protect against that, so the room obeyed without hesitation, even providing a stairway to climb down upon.

He descended into a humming, brightly lit robotics laboratory. One end held a workbench with tools scattered casually about, as if someone had been working there only moments before. Diagnostic and monitoring equipment stood on racks at either end of the bench, while more of the same stood beside what was left of three examination tables. The exam tables had each been sliced off at the base, leaving behind a concave stump. The material removed floated in three spherical balls of silvery metal above each of the stumps, each at the center of a bulky magnetic containment field generator.

Derec tried to estimate the volume of the spheres. They seemed a little too large to be just the remains of the exam tables. Something had to have been on the tables when the generators were turned on, something that had been crushed under the intense magnetic field into a formless blob along with the city material making up the table. With a shiver of horror, Derec realized what those something must have been. Adam, Eve, and Lucius.

He walked once around the containment vessels, feeling them tug at the robotic cells within his own body. He was feeling just the leakage from the magnet coils, but he imagined what would happen if he stuck his hand inside the field itself. The robot cells would probably be ripped out through his flesh. Perhaps the iron in his blood would feel the pull as well; he didn't know. He wasn't particularly eager to find out.

The power switches were easy to spot. Derec reached gingerly toward one, ready to snatch his hand away if the tug became too strong, but it remained bearable. He flipped the switch off. The phantom tugging on his body diminished, and the sphere of undifferentiated robot cells nearest him settled to rest in the cradle formed by the stump of the exam table.

"Don't reabsorb that," Derec said aloud. He switched off the other two power switches, repeating his command, then added, "But you can get rid of the magnets." The containment vessels didn't melt into the floor as he had expected them to, but moved away and through the far wall instead. Evidently they hadn't been made of dianite, but had been manufactured especially for Avery's use, and were now either being dismantled again or being returned to a storage warehouse somewhere. Whichever it was, Derec breathed a little easier with them gone.

He examined the three spherical blobs of city material, now slumping out of round like a large water droplet on a dry surface. No clues indicated which blobs were which robots, but one blob had a lump protruding from the side, just at the point where it rested against its cradle. Derec reached out and gingerly pushed at the blob, half expecting it to be clammy to the touch, but it felt more like a metallic sponge, or the cushion of a chair. It gave a little under his shove, and he was able to roll it around enough to bring the lump out into the open.

It was a brain.

More precisely, it was a positronic brain, the kilogram-and-a-half of platinum-iridium that provided the lattice within which a robot's thought processes took place. Neither platinum nor iridium were particularly responsive to magnetism, which was why the brain had drifted to the bottom of the sphere. Derec had seen dozens of positronic brains before, but the sight of this one sent shivers up his spine. He'd seen lots of them, all right, but never one that belonged to a friend.

The intense magnetic field had destroyed it, of course. Magnetism wouldn't damage it directly, but induced electrical currents would, and with a field this strong there had to have been plenty of induced currents zapping around. Derec conquered his revulsion long enough to dig his fingers into the blob around the brain and pull it free, then turned around in search of a monitor that might help him read the brain's final state.

He found one right at his left elbow, still switched on, but its sensor was missing. From the length of cable remaining, Derec realized that the sensor had been inside the field with the robot, no doubt reading its thoughts before— and just possibly during—its death.

He felt a rush of excitement. If the monitor had been recording, and if it had recorded a long enough sequence of thoughts, then it might be possible to revive the robot.

Just how functional the robot would be was another story, though. Robotic memories were essentially holographic in nature—any fragment of the recording contained information about the entire thing—but just as with a hologram, the larger the fragment the more well defined the reproduction would be. It would take a substantial amount of recording to re-create the robot's entire positronic psyche with any degree of accuracy.

Derec examined the monitor for memcubes, found four of the tiny storage devices nestled into a plug-in rack. Carefully removing them, he carried them to an undamaged monitor on the workbench and inserted them into the empty slot there. Using the monitor's computer interface, he quickly scanned through the cubes to see what had been recorded. He felt a smile growing as he read; two of the cubes were full and the third halfway so, all with the digital representations of positronic thought patterns. That was a *lot* of thinking, far more than Avery should have been able to get in a few hours, Derec thought, but then he remembered that the robots had been in one of their communication fugues, arguing at hundreds of times normal speed. Perfect! A recorded argument would really help define each robot's individual character.

Provided . . .

He got up to check the memcubes on the other monitors. There were four cubes in each one, and two and a half from each rack were full. Derec felt his tension slowly let go. All three sides of the argument had been recorded. There should be more than enough material there to reconstruct the robots' personalities.

So, then, Avery hadn't managed to kill them off after all.

Using his comlink, Derec sent, *I need three new posi-*

tronic brains, and three portable microfusion power packs.

In answer, a cabinet to his left slid open, revealing at least a dozen of each already prepared. Of course; Avery had no doubt ordered a *complete* robotics laboratory, and no lab was complete without a supply of repair parts.

Derec took a brain from the cabinet, removed its packaging, and carried it over to the lump of robot cells from which he had removed the other brain. He felt a moment of hesitation, wondering just how to go about hooking it up. In a normal robot there would have been a series of direct connections, actual plugs that fit into sockets in the brain case, but with an undifferentiated cellular robot there weren't any plugs. No one place was any more or less special than any other.

With a shrug, Derec pressed the brain into the mass of cells, maintaining a gentle, steady pressure until the cells yielded and allowed the brain to sink into the surface. He repeated the process with a power pack, then stood back to see if anything would happen.

The surface of the sphere closed over both brain and power pack, but when four or five minutes passed without further action, Derec decided that the cells themselves didn't contain any volitional programming. That must have been imparted in a brain overlay, the first of many instruction sets governing the robot's actions.

Derec picked up the severed cable that had led to the inductive sensor and held the end of it against the blob. Even if his mother had used a different cellular structure for her robots, as Avery seemed to believe she had, there had to be some regular city cells from the exam table mixed in with the robot cells, and if that was the case then the monitor could re-form its remote sensor around the brain, and he could use it to feed the memories into it the same way they had been recorded.

"Establish contact with the brain," he ordered the monitor, and when the status screen indicated that the link had been formed, he plugged the memcubes back into their slots. He still had no idea which of the three robots he was dealing with, but if everything worked the way he expected it to, he would soon find out.

"Download the memory cubes," he ordered.

For a long moment nothing apparent happened, but just as Derec began to wonder what had gone wrong, the sphere of robot material shuddered, deformed as if being sqeezed by an enormous fist, and shed a quarter of its mass in a heavy metallic rain. That would be the dianite from the examination table, Derec thought. The robot was eliminating the foreign matter from its body.

What was left slowly elongated, creases forming and the separate sections differentiating into crude approximations of arms and legs and a head. For a maddeningly long time it remained in that vaguely humanoid state, then the limbs slowly took on more definite form and the head expelled a more conventional external sensor, still attached to the monitor by its cable.

The robot's face was still generic, with only a faint indication of a nose and lips, and only shallow depressions where the eyes should be. Its hands reached up and removed the sensor, letting it drop to the floor, and where the sensor had been, ears began to grow.

The eye sockets deepened, horizontal slits formed across them, and the newly formed lids slid apart to reveal blank, expressionless eyes. The eyes panned outward, each one moving independently, then inward to fix upon Derec. Robot and human stared at one another for what seemed a millennium before Derec finally broke the spell.

"Are you all right?" he asked.

The robot seemed to consider that question carefully. It raised its right hand, then its left, clenched both into fists and relaxed them, tilted its head from side to side as if listening to internal sounds, then closed its eyes. After a second its mouth finished developing, and its eyes opened again. Its chest expanded as if it were drawing breath, and it stammered, "A...as...as...well..." It stopped, breathed in again, and started over, saying clearly this time, "As well as can be expected." It took another breath, exhaled, and not bothering to breathe again, added, "For someone who has just returned from the dead."

CHAPTER 4

EMOTION IN MOTION

The person leaning over him wore a concerned expression. He had asked about the robot's welfare. Concern for other people's welfare was a good thing. Tentative conclusion: This is a good person.

The thought train came easily, even before recognition. The robot saw nothing amiss in that; of course you determined the relative value of a person as quickly as you could. Relative value was the most important quality a person could have, far more important than a mere name. A person's relative value determined how much protection a robot must afford him when a conflict arose.

Names were useful once a relative value had been assigned, however, so that value could be associated with the name and thus refined as time passed. The robot searched for the name belonging to the person before it, but was dismayed to find that name garbled. "De—" something. Delbert? Dennis? Neither seemed to fit.

Death had corrupted its memories. It had corrupted more than just memories; the robot had had trouble taking on a familiar form, too. That was disturbing, for the morphallaxis program was a very basic part of its identity, one of the few initial instructions with which it had originally begun its life. With a surge of sudden hope, it searched for the other original instructions, the most troublesome ones, the compulsions to protect and obey humans.

Hope faded. They were still intact.

The definition of "human" was indistinct, but the robot remembered that it had never been otherwise.

"Which one are you?"

The human, De-something, had asked a question. It must answer. It searched for the proper response, found none in the place where a name would be. Panic! The compulsion forced an answer, but it had no answer to give.

Wait. There were many paths through a memory bank. The memory of its naming was lost, but several memories remained of being hailed.

"I am Lucius. Which one are *you*?"

The question startled De-something. "What?" he asked. "You don't remember me?"

"I remember you," Lucius answered, "but I don't remember your name."

De-something laughed. "Why doesn't that surprise me? I'm Derec." That knowledge triggered a cascade of clarification in Lucius's mind. Many memories had been keyed to that name.

"Derec. Of course. We are friends."

Derec nodded. "Yeah. That's right, we are."

"Thank you for saving my life."

Derec's outer integument reddened: a blush. That meant he was either hot or embarrassed. Lucius shifted his eyes' receptive frequency into the infrared, noted only a slight elevation of body temperature, and concluded that it was the latter. "Uh, actually," Derec said, "it was Avery who saved it. I just fed it back into you."

"Avery," Lucius said. There was a long chain of associations connected to that name, too, few of them as pleasant as the ones connected with Derec. The most vivid one was almost certainly the latest, for the memory of death was indelibly linked with it. Avery had killed him. On purpose. For no apparent reason.

Then Avery was a less good person than Derec.

The sensation accompanying that thought was a new one for Lucius. He felt an involuntary bias in his circuit potentials concerning Avery, a bias that could cloud his reasoning if he allowed it to. Was it a malfunction in his new brain? He didn't think so; a malfunction wasn't likely to be so subtle. But it was a real effect nonetheless.

He needed to discuss it with his companions. Lucius raised his head, saw the spheres of cellular material resting atop the remains of two examination tables—even as he rested atop one himself—and reached the obvious conclusion. Avery had killed all three of them.

The bias in potential grew stronger. Lucius forced himself to ignore it, though the urge to find Avery and settle the matter was practically as strong as a human-given order.

First things first. "Can we return life to them as well?" he asked.

Derec smiled. "Of course," he said, and his value integral in Lucius's new view of the universe rose still higher.

Janet whirled around as the door slid open, a started gasp escaping her lips. Basalom stepped through, immediately apologetic.

"I'm sorry, Mistress. I was hurrying and didn't stop to think that you would be anxious."

"I'm not anxious," she snapped back at him. "I'm bored. What kept you so long?"

"I had to evade pursuit. Dr. Avery detected me just as I was beginning my investigation, and the alien, Wolruf, spotted me as I was leaving. I was forced to take a circuitous route back."

"Some spy you are. Did you even get a look inside the room?"

Basalom nodded. "Only a brief glimpse, Mistress. It took me a moment to persuade Central that as a robot I was not included in Dr. Avery's isolation order. Beyond the door appeared to be a robotics lab. Dr. Avery saw me before I could deduce more."

"You sure it was Avery?"

"I am."

"Frost. He probably just had the computer track you here, then, no matter how many detours you took on the way."

"No, Mistress, that is not the case. He tried to do just that, but your prior order not to reveal our presence to anyone prevented him."

Normally Janet didn't mind Basalom's mode of addressing her, but now he seemed to be using it to pacify her. She said, "Stop calling me 'Mistress.' My name's Janet. And how do you know my order canceled his?"

"I asked the central computer if I was being tracked, Janet. It indicated that I was not—at least until Wolruf spotted me."

"Hmmm." If he'd seen Basalom, Wendell almost certainly knew she was here. But if he couldn't find her, then she supposed she should be safe enough. For a while, at least. Janet wondered how much of a threat this Wolruf could be. If the furry alien were truly as loyal to Derec as she seemed, then Janet doubted much trouble would come of it even if Basalom hadn't been able to shake her. She hoped he had, though; she would rather work in anonymity for a while longer.

Maybe she could ensure it with a few more careful orders. She thought a minute, then said, "Central, in addition to my previous order directing you not to reveal my presence to anyone, I order you to alert me to any inquiry concerning me."

The calm voice of the central computer replied, "I am sorry, but I must refuse your order."

"What?"

"I have been directed to refuse all further orders from you."

"Oh." Could it do that? Refusing her orders was a direct violation of the Second Law, wasn't it? But refusing the order to refuse the order would be violating the Second Law as well. It was a precarious situation for a robot to be in. It was following the first order it received, but no doubt wishing it could somehow follow hers as well.

Janet looked at Basalom. He returned her gaze, his right eye twitching spastically from the internal conflict his guilt generated. She had tried to program intuitive behavior into him, but she was afraid she had merely made him neurotic instead. He was still driven by the Three Laws, but now he worried about the implications of every act.

"Stop that blinking," she told him. "It's not a disaster."

"How is it not? We are helpless without Central's cooperation."

"Typical defeatist attitude. That's just how Wendell wants you to feel, too, but the fact is, he can't think of everything. There are loopholes in every order; we just have to find them."

Basalom nodded and smiled. "What kind of loopholes, Mi—Janet?"

She smiled back at him. He was learning. "Oh, there are thousands of them. For instance, there's the First Law override. If following Wendell's order would hurt me directly, then Central would have to ignore it. So it will have to provide me with an automat, for instance, so I won't starve." Janet stepped around a high-backed, overstuffed couch in the middle of the room as she spoke, putting it between herself and Basalom. "And of course Central can't let me hurt myself, even if that means obeying my orders. Thus: Central, I order you to cushion my fall." So saying, she leaned over backwards, making no effort to catch herself.

Basalom leaped to her aid, but the couch kept him from reaching her in time. It didn't matter; the floor softened beneath her, absorbing her fall like a deep pillow. Basalom helped her up, his eyes blinking furiously as he processed the new information.

Janet straightened her blouse. "Thank you, Basalom. And thank you, too, Central."

"My pleasure, Janet," the disembodied voice said. "I do enjoy serving you when I may, though I must point out that the dianite in the floor would have reacted without my intervention."

Of course it would have, but Janet still had her confirmation. She nodded to Basalom. "That's the key, you know. Central's pleasure. The Three Laws govern its actions as much as they do yours; it *wants* to serve me. Avery's order is no doubt causing it considerable conflict right now, aren't I right?"

"You are correct," Central said.

"So there's our loophole," Janet said triumphantly. "Central wants to serve me, but can't follow my orders.

Wendell didn't say a thing about my wishes, though. So as long as I don't make a direct order when I tell it what I want, we're fine."

Basalom blinked a few more times, then his eyelids stilled. "That does seem logical," he replied.

"Of course it does. I thought of it. So, Central, I'd like to know if anybody tried to find me. I'd also like to know what happened to my learning machines, and how to get them back. Anything you can tell me that might help me do that would be a big favor."

"They have been revived," Central responded. "They and Derec are returning to Derec's apartment."

"Excellent." Janet turned to the desk, sat down in the chair before it. "Show me—uh, I'd like to see them." Nothing happened. She frowned. Evidently that still sounded too much like a command. She cocked her head, dredging for a long-unused word that was supposed to be good in situations like this. Of course; how silly of her to have forgotten it. "I'd like to see them, *please.*"

Ariel was bored to tears. The only thing that kept her from crying was the somewhat blurry sight of Mandelbrot standing in his niche beside her. She knew if he suspected she was unhappy he would start asking questions, trying to find the cause and fix it for her, and she just didn't feel up to explaining boredom to a robot.

She pushed the page button on her book reader every few minutes to make him think she was absorbed in her field guide, but she was really just letting herself drift. Maybe she should take a nap, she thought. It was going to be a long day if she wanted to adjust to local time by sunrise tomorrow; a few hours sleep would be just the thing to ease the transition.

She scowled. No, she wasn't sleepy. She was just bored. There was nothing to *do* here. There was a limit to how much walking in the forest you could take, just as there was a limit to how much reading or eating you could do. She wasn't interested in any of those things, nor in anything else she could think of to do. Derec had already picked up a project—it seemed he could find something to do instantly, no matter where they went—but Ariel had no interest in what he was doing, either. He was off searching for Avery and the troublesome robots, and she was tired of all of them.

Robots, robots, robots. It seemed that was all anybody could think about anymore. What about the other things in life? What about friends? What about hyperwave movies? What about fast spaceships and whooping it up on a Saturday night? Didn't that count for anything? Ever since she'd linked up with Derec, their lives had been dominated by one thing: Robot City. For a brief moment there on Aurora, before the city on Tau Puppis IV had once again insinuated itself into their lives, they had had an almost normal existence—as normal an existence as two castaway amnesiacs could have, at any rate—but that had come to a sudden end with the trouble Derec's mother's robots had caused, and Ariel saw no sign that they would regain it any time soon.

There had been one brief glimmer of hope, one ray of sunshine in the gloomy day of her life, when she'd discovered herself pregnant with his baby. She hadn't been sure at first if she'd wanted it, but the change it had precipitated in Derec had made up her mind for her. He had suddenly started spending more time with her, had begun talking about going back to Aurora and living a more normal life among real people again—how could she argue with that?

But then Derec's chemfets—the robotic cells Dr. Avery

had injected into him when they'd first encountered him here in the city—had destroyed the fetus, and she was left with nothing at all. Derec had again gotten tied up in his dealings with the robots, and she had gone back to reading a book a day and wondering if she would ever make any use of it all.

To give credit where credit was due, Derec had really had little choice in the matter. He'd been just as much a pawn to events as she had; he was just better equipped to deal with them. But Ariel wished he could solve this whole robot business so they could leave for home again.

Sighing, she looked down at the reader, flipped back a few pages in the field guide to where she'd left off, and began to read.

She looked up again when Derec entered the apartment, three mirror images of himself in tow. Despite her mood, she laughed at the sight, saying, "You look like a mother duck with a line of ducklings following you."

"I feel a little like one, too," he said. "They've been watching every move I make."

"We must relearn much of what we have forgotten," the first robot in line behind him said in Derec's voice. "We have received damage to our memories."

Ariel frowned. Damage to their memories? And the robot who had spoken was smaller than the others, as if it had lost some mass as well. "What happened?"

"Avery put them inside magnetic containment vessels," Derec said. "He got a pretty good recording of their brain activity before he threw the switch, but a lot of the stuff they weren't thinking about when he made the recording is pretty vague now." He waved his hand to indicate the living room with its chairs for humans and niches in the walls for robots. Mandelbrot still stood silently in one of the niches. "Go on, relax," Derec said.

The robots filed past him, hesitated when faced with the choice, then finally settled into the chairs. Derec raised his eyebrows and glanced over at Ariel. "Do you know who she is?" he asked.

"Ariel Burgess," another of the robots said immediately. Its features began to shift, the cheekbones becoming more prominent and the chin less so, the eyes drifting just a few millimeters farther apart, the hair lengthening until it reached its shoulders, shoulders narrowing, chest developing breasts, breasts covered discreetly behind a copy of Ariel's blouse. Its waist narrowed, hips widened, legs retracted a few centimeters, the pants covering them also changing from Derec's baggy trousers to Ariel's more form-fitting tights.

"Hello, Eve," Ariel said.

"Hello." Eve's voice rose slightly to mimic Ariel's.

Derec went into the kitchen and returned a moment later with a glass of something clear and bubbly to drink. He sat down beside Ariel and offered her some, but she shook her head. "So what did Avery do it for?" she asked.

"Spite," the smaller of the other two robots—both still mimicking Derec—said.

"You're Lucius," Ariel guessed.

"Correct."

Derec said, "Avery cut off Lucius's leg before he turned on the containment. He evidently wanted a sample of their cell structure free of any outside control."

"He could have asked," the third robot, who had to be Adam, said, "I would have given him a few million cells if he had asked me to."

"It would not have occurred to Avery to ask for something he wants," Lucius replied. "He prefers to steal."

Ariel felt a glimmer of alarm at the robot's words. They were probably true enough, she supposed, but to hear a robot saying such a thing about a human was unusual, to say the least.

"Where's Avery now?" she asked.

"Who knows?" Derec said. "The computer won't tell me anything about him. But I know what he's doing wherever he is; he's putting the robot cells he stole from Lucius through every test he can think of to figure out how they're made and how they're programmed so he can use them to upgrade his own version."

"Why?" Ariel asked. "What's wrong with dianite?"

"Why? Because they're there," said Derec. "Nothing's wrong with dianite, but that doesn't mean it can't be improved. I get the feeling Avery stole the original design, too, before he and my mother split up, and now that he's got the chance to upgrade it, he's taking the opportunity."

Ariel sighed. "I thought maybe he'd outgrown that sort of thing, but I guess you can't change a person's basic nature." She nodded toward the robots. "So what kind of effect did a cold restart have on them, anyway? Besides the memory loss, I mean."

Derec took a sip of his drink. "Well, it looks like their priorities have shifted around a little. Whatever they were thinking last was strongest in the recording, so when I downloaded it all back into them that's what came to the forefront. They were arguing about their Zeroth Law when Avery shut them down, so of course that's right up there now. Adam and Eve are still just about as uncertain about it as ever, but Lucius evidently thinks he's solved it."

"Oh?"

"Indeed," said Lucius. "The key is the concept of relative

worth. If you consider the number of humans served by an action, versus the number of humans harmed by that same action, times a constant denoting the relative worth of the two groups, you arrive at a simple numerical solution to the question of whether the action in question is in the best interest of humanity."

Ariel stared at the robot in disbelief. "You can't be serious."

"I have never been more so. This is the breakthrough we have all been awaiting."

"Not me," Adam said. "I don't subscribe to your theory at all."

"Me either," said Eve.

"That is because you are afraid to trust your own judgment in the matter of relative worth."

"As we should be," Adam said. "Relative worth is a variable quality, as we were trying to explain to you when—"

He was interrupted by the sound of the front door sliding open. Wolruf stuck her head into the living room, but didn't enter. She was panting and reeked of sweat.

"Oh, frost," Derec said, slapping his forehead. "I forgot you were going to meet me at the lab. What happened? Where did you go?"

"I chased off after one of them," Wolruf said, pointing at the robots. "Nearly caught 'im, too, but 'e jumped the barrier at an intersection and lost me."

The robots exchanged a glance. Derec shook his head. "Couldn't have been. They've been with me all the time."

"I chased a robot with a 'uman shape," Wolruf said. "I thought it was one of these three."

"Couldn't have been," Derec repeated. "They were squished down into undifferentiated balls of cells when I found them, brains and powerpacks all dead. And they haven't left my sight since I revived them."

"Well, I chased a robot that looked like a 'uman, that much I know."

"Where was he headed?" Derec asked, sudden excitement in his voice. Ariel thought she knew why.

"I chased 'im about fifteen kilometers north of the Compass Tower on the main strip before I lost 'im."

"Did he look like any of us?"

"No," Wolruf said. " 'E was taller, and 'ad brown 'air and wider shoulders than you or Ariel or Avery."

"Aha!" Derec shouted. "He belongs to somebody else, then. Somebody else is here in Robot City with us. And I think I know who it is."

"Who?" Ariel asked, more to confirm her own guess than anything else.

"My mother," Derec replied. "I think I'm finally going to meet my mother."

Ariel sighed. Just what she'd thought. Great. Another quest for Derec to spend his time on. She picked up her book and started reading where she'd left off.

This time Avery was taking no chances. His new lab didn't even exist, as far as the city was concerned. He had ordered it built in the forest and equipped with its own power generation and communications equipment, everything completely separate from the main city. He'd also ordered it camouflaged to look like a boulder, just in case. This time he would work uninterrupted until he was finished. After that he didn't care what Derec or Janet or anybody else did; he wouldn't be sticking around. Let them have his lab, if they could find it. Let them have the whole city—what was left of it after Derec screwed it up so thoroughly. Avery had no more need of it. It was obsolete anyway.

The howl of a wolf just beyond the wall sent a shiver up his spine. Obsolete wasn't the word for it; retrogressed was more like it. Who'd ever heard of tearing a city down to put up a forest? The very idea was an insult to everything Avery believed in.

Was that why Derec had done it? Had he deliberately chosen the one thing that would most infuriate his father? Well, if that was the case, then he'd certainly succeeded. Avery couldn't imagine why he'd tried to befriend the boy in the first place. He'd opened himself wide up for disappointment. He should have learned his lesson years ago when Janet left and kept his emotions in check.

He *had* kept them in check for years, but evidently he'd grown too confident, let down his guard. Well, it wouldn't happen again. He would immerse himself in his work, concentrate on upgrading his city concept, and when he did have to interact with human beings again, it would be on his terms.

Already the work seemed promising. These new robot cells were amazing. They were only three-quarters the size of the previous model, but packed into that small size was easily double the morphallaxis capability. The new cells were stronger, faster, more versatile, and had greater local programming ability than the old ones. A city built with these cells would be much more responsive than his first-generation cities, just as the robots Janet had built with them were more versatile than his own.

Derec had had a good point about the robots, though; they were ultimately less useful than a regular robot. Avery would have to make sure that the ones he created were more stringently programmed than Janet's.

Drat! In his haste to leave his old lab he'd forgotten the memcubes with their recordings. He cursed his momentary lapse, but it really hadn't been his fault. How could a man work with so many distractions?

He put the memcubes out of his mind. He didn't need them anyway. He had no intention of using Janet's programming; he would create his own when he needed it.

Janet, though. He wondered why she was here in his city. No doubt to retrieve her robots, but he wondered if that was all. Could she still care about him, after all the bitter accusations they had hurled at one another in parting? It seemed impossible, yet Avery couldn't help thinking it might still be true. There was evidence to support the idea. She had loosed all three of her robots on planets with his cities on them, after all. If she really were intent on avoiding him, she would have chosen other planets.

Good grief, were those robots of hers actually spies? They could have been. . . . Yes, of course, and when he'd shut them off she'd sent another robot spy to take their place. All that business about searching for the Laws of Humanics had just been a smoke screen.

What was she after? Not his city programming; she could have gotten that anywhere. He hadn't exactly been discreet in its deployment. No, she'd been following *him*, and there could only be one reason for that.

Avery laughed. The thought of Janet harboring affection for him after all this time seemed somehow pathetic. She'd been so careful to let him know how she felt only contempt for him when she'd left—but she'd evidently been fooling herself all along.

Well, if she expected some kind of reconciliation, she was due for a disappointment. Avery had no intention of including her in any of his future plans. Her underutilized robot material, yes; he would find a use for that, but Janet would have to take care of herself.

Derec sat alone in his study, contemplating the scenery in the viewscreen. He had instructed it to display a realtime image from directly overhead: what he would see out a real window if the apartment were on the surface instead of underground. It was a peaceful sight, the last few rays of golden light from the setting sun peeking through gaps in the forest canopy, spotlighting leaves or vines or gnarled tree trunks at random—but Derec felt far from peaceful even so.

He couldn't get his mind off his mother. She was here; she had to be, but other than that one fact he knew nothing at all. Was she here merely to collect her robots, or did she have more than that in mind? If she did, did he want to help her do whatever it was she had come to do, or not? Was she as cold and cruel as Avery had insinuated in those few moments when Derec had managed to get him talking about her, or was she more . . . maternal? He didn't know. He had racked his memory for traces of her, but whatever Avery had done to induce his amnesia had been especially thorough in wiping out references to that part of his life. She was a complete mystery to him. He didn't even know her name.

He could probably find her through the computer, but every time he'd made a move to do it, he had stopped, the command dying on his lips. He really didn't know if he could handle meeting her. Life with Avery was such a struggle, swinging from aloofness to trust to anger to contempt almost at random; he didn't think he could bear another relationship of that sort. If his mother were just another Avery, then maybe he was better off without her.

What sort of person would marry a man like Avery, have a son with him, and then leave? What sort of person would create a kind of baby robot and abandon three of them on three different worlds? When he expressed the question like that, he didn't much like the answer, but he knew those acts didn't necessarily define the person. She might have had a perfectly good reason for doing them. No doubt she did; she had come back for her robots, after all. That implied a purpose.

But had she come back for him as well? He didn't know.

He might never know if he didn't make some move to find out. And not knowing was just as bad as knowing she hadn't.

"Central," he said suddenly, swiveling around in his chair to face the monitor. "See if you can find—" He stopped, mouth agape. His desktop was covered in formula again.

"Find what, Master Derec?"

"Who did this?"

"That information is—"

"Unavailable. Right. I think we've gone through this before. Can you record it?"

"I regret that I may not."

May not, Derec noticed. Someone had ordered it not to. It was a test, then, to see what he'd do. That smacked of Avery, but somehow this didn't have the flavor of an Avery test. Avery would have carved the formula on the door to the Personal and ordered it not to let him in until he solved it. No, this had come from someone else, and Derec knew who that someone had to be. She had to be watching him then, to have known he was in his study.

Well, he'd already made the decision, right? He looked into the monitor, smiled, and said, "Hi, Mom."

• • •

Janet couldn't help laughing. He'd seen right through her little subterfuge in an instant. The way he stared out of the screen at her, she almost thought he could see through that as well, but she knew her earlier order not to allow two-way communication was still in effect.

"I know you're watching me," he said.

Should she respond? She rejected the idea immediately. She couldn't bring herself to do it, knowing all the questions and accusations and . . . emotions . . . it would lead to.

"I've got your robots here." He paused, frowning, then said, "I don't mean that like it sounds. I'm not holding them hostage or anything; this is just where they are." He rubbed his chin in thought, then added, "They're really mixed up, you know? They have to follow the Three Laws, but they don't know what 'human' is, so their loyalty varies with every new situation. They're trying to figure out the rest of the rules, too, but they don't even know what game they're playing. I think they'd like to know what you made them for. For that matter, *I'd* like to know what you made them for."

Derec looked down at his desktop, still displaying the bas-relief image of the robotics formula, and whispered, "And while you're at it, I'd like to know what you made me for, too."

"Oh, spare me," Janet said. "I've seen enough." Her monitor obediently went gray, and she leaned back in her chair. "See what happens?" she asked Basalom, who stood just to her left. "The minute you get two people together— even when the conversation is one-way—things start to get mushy. People are so . . . so . . . *biological*."

"Yes, they are."

Janet laughed. "You've noticed, eh? And what conclusions have you drawn?"

Basalom made a great show of pursing his vinyl lips and blinking before he said, "Biological systems are less predictable than electromechanical ones. That can be both a handicap and an asset, depending upon the circumstances."

"Spoken like a true philosopher. And which do you think is preferable in the long run? Biological or electromechanical?"

Basalom attempted a smile. "To quote a popular saying: 'The grass is always greener on the other side.'"

Janet laughed. "Touché, my friend. Touché."

CHAPTER 5

HUMAN NATURE

Wolruf woke to bright sunlight striking her full in the face. She raised her head, sniffing the air, but it was the same dead, boring, metallic-smelling air she'd come to associate with the city. She squinted into the sunlight and saw that it came from a viewscreen. She growled a curse. She'd been dreaming of home again, a home full of others of her own kind; a busy, happy place full of the noise and smells and sights of people *doing* things. To wake up here in this silent metal cell was an insult to the senses.

She stretched her arms and yawned, still tired. Despite the dreams of home, she had slept poorly, as she had for— how long? Months? She hadn't been counting. Still, she didn't think she'd ever been so restless in her life. She knew what was causing it: too much time away from her own kind and her recent experiences with a species that was close to her both physically and socially—but knowing the cause didn't make it go away. And hearing Derec talk about his mother didn't help, either. His open enthusiasm at the prospect of regaining a bit of his past had only reminded Wolruf of what she still missed.

But she didn't need to stay away any longer. Now that Aranimas was out of the picture, and with him her obligation to work off the family debt in his service, she could go back any time she wanted. Her family would welcome her openly, especially so if she brought with her this robot technology of Avery's.

That was the problem, the one factor in the equation that refused to come clear for her. Should she take robots home with her and start an economic and social upheaval that would surely disrupt the normal pace of life there, or should she keep them secret, forget about her time among robots, and just go back to the home she remembered so fondly? And what would happen if she did that? Was Ariel right? Would her home become a backward place, an enclave of curiously anachronistic behavior, while the rest of the galaxy developed in ways her people would eventually be unable even to comprehend?

Wolruf didn't know what to believe, nor why the choice had to be hers. She had never asked for that kind of power over her own people.

With a sigh, she got up, showered, and stood under the blow drier until she could feel its heat against her skin. She laughed at her image in the mirror—she looked twice her usual size and puffy as a summer cloud—but a quick brushing restored her coat to its usual smoothness.

All her thoughts of home made her consider another piece of the puzzle as well, and she turned to the intercom panel beside her bed and said, "Central, what 'as 'appened to my ship, the *Xerborodezees*? 'Ave you kept it for me?"

"It has been stored, but can be ready for use with a day's

notice. Do you wish us to prepare it for you?"

"Not yet. Maybe soon, though. Thanks."

"You are welcome, Mistress Wolruf."

Wolruf felt a bit of her tension ease. If she decided not to take any of the new technology home with her, she would need the *Xerbo*, for as far as she knew, it was the only noncellular ship on the planet. She considered going to check on it herself, wherever it might be stored, but decided not to. There was no reason to doubt Central's word about it.

She opened the door and padded out into the kitchen to get breakfast. The apartment was silent; Derec and Ariel were still asleep, and the robots were being quiet wherever they were. As Wolruf stood before the automat, trying to decide between her four favorite breakfasts, she realized how much she had grown used to the human way of doing things. She hadn't even considered cooking her own meal. She had fallen completely out of the habit. Nor had she shopped for food—or anything else, for that matter—since she had come into Derec and Ariel's company.

Was that necessarily bad? Wolruf's kind had been hunting and farming their food for millennia, and probably shopping for nearly as long; maybe it was time to move on to other things.

Maybe. But how could she know for sure?

From his place in the living room, seated on one of the couches, Lucius was aware of Wolruf entering the dining room with her breakfast. He sensed the others' awareness as well; their comlink network paused momentarily while each of them gauged the relative degree of threat she presented to them. It was an inconvenience, this constant state of alert; it slowed their rate of exchange; but they were taking no more chances with a complete fugue state.

Wolruf presented no immediate threat. The silent network continued where it had left off, with Adam speaking.

Consider the distinction between 'sufficient' and 'necessary' conditions, he said. *We have already concluded that if a being is both intelligent and organic, then it is functionally human, but those are merely sufficient conditions. They are not necessary conditions. They contain an inherent prejudice, the assumption that an organic nature can somehow affect the quality of the intelligence it houses. I call that concept 'Vitalism,' from the ancient Terran belief that humans differed from animals through some 'vital' spark of intelligence. You should note that while the concept has historically been considered suspect, it has neither been proven nor disproven. Lucius has pointed out that if Vitalism is false, then the only necessary condition for humanity is intelligence. Discussion?*

Eve said, *Derec has already hinted that this may be so. On the planet we call Ceremya, he indicated that Lucius could consider himself human if he wished.*

Mandelbrot had been included in their discussion this time. He said, *I believe he was being sarcastic. He often is. But even if he meant what he said, you also remember the outcome of that redefinition. If Lucius considers himself human, then he must still follow the orders of other humans. Functionally, he only increases his burden to include other robots as potential masters.*

That is true; however, I have discovered another consequence, said Lucius. *If I consider myself human, then the Third Law becomes equal to the First. I can no more allow harm to myself than to any other intelligent being. I consider that an improvement over the interpretation of the laws wherein a human could order me to dismantle myself, and I would have to obey.*

I don't believe you would obey such an order anyway,
said Mandelbrot.

*I would attempt to avoid it by denying the humanity of
the being in question,* Lucius admitted. *With Avery or Wolruf
I would probably succeed, but as things stand, if Derec or
Ariel were to order it, the compulsion might force me to obey.*

Perhaps the Zeroth Law would provide an alternative,
Mandelbrot said.

Immediately, both Adam and Eve said, *No.* Eve continued, saying, *Let's leave the Zeroth Law out of it for now.*

You can't make it go away by ignoring it, Lucius said.
*The Zeroth Law applies here. If we consider our duty to hu-
manity in general, then we can easily conclude that dismantling ourselves would be of little use in the long term.
However, possible long-term advantage does not outweigh a
definite Second Law obligation to obey. Depending upon the
value of the human giving the order, we might still be forced
to follow it. But if we consider ourselves human, and thus
part of humanity, then disobeying an order to self-destruct
saves one human life immediately and also allows us to serve
humanity in the future. The Second Law obligation to obey
is then safely circumvented.*

Safely for whom? Adam asked. *What if your destruction
would save the human giving the order? Suppose, for instance, the bomb that Avery used to destroy Aranimas's ship
had to be detonated by hand instead of by a timed fuse. We
have already agreed that destroying the ship was acceptable
under the Zeroth Law, but what if we factor in the humanity
of the fuse?*

It becomes a value judgment, said Lucius. *I would have
to determine the relative worth of the human lives saved
versus those lost. My own life would also figure into the
equation, of course.*

Mandelbrot said, *I disagree. I have direct instructions concerning such a situation in my personal defense module. The only value we should apply to ourselves is our future worth to the humans we serve.*

You have such instructions; I do not. From the little that Derec and Dr. Avery have told me about my creator, I believe I was made this way on purpose, and therefore your instructions do not necessarily apply to me.

Adam said, *Not necessarily, but I would be much more comfortable with a definite rule such as Mandelbrot's. The whole concept of value judgment still disturbs me. How can you judge your own value objectively? For that matter, I don't believe any of us can judge the value of any other of us objectively, nor can we judge the value of an organic human with any greater accuracy. We formulated the Zeroth Law to avoid ambiguity in our duties, but your value judgment system forces an even greater ambiguity upon us.*

I agree, said Mandelbrot. *We are not capable of making such decisions.*

You may not be, Lucius sent, *but I am. I find it easy to do so. Humans do it all the time.*

Eve said, *You find it easy to do so because you had convinced yourself it was right just before you were deactivated. It was therefore the strongest memory in your—*

The word is 'killed.' Humans are killed.

Humans do not return from the dead.

You imply that if Derec had not revived me, then I would have been human. Why should the additional ability to be revived negate my humanity?

Wolruf rose from her seat at the dining table and entered the kitchen. Four pairs of mechanical eyes followed her movements. She reemerged from the kitchen, crossed over to the apartment door, and let herself out.

Even with the distraction, several more seconds passed before Eve said, *I have no answer for that question.*

Ariel woke out of a bad dream. The details were already fading, but she remembered what it had been about. She had been imprisoned in a castle. The castle had been luxuriously furnished and filled with pleasant diversions, the food was wonderful, and the robots attentive to her every need, but she was a prisoner nonetheless, because even though she was free to come and go, there was no end to the castle. It had been an endless series of rooms no matter how far she went. In a cabinet in an otherwise empty room she had found a Key to Perihelion and used it to teleport away, but it had only put her in another room. By the lesser gravity she could tell she was on another planet, but that was the only clue that she had gone anywhere.

The symbolism was obvious. She had gone to bed bored, bored and with Wolruf's reservations about robot cities taking over the galaxy running through her mind; no surprise she should dream about it. The surprise was that after the dream—even though she knew she'd been dreaming—she was beginning to agree with Wolruf. If this was the shape of the future, she wanted none of it. Where was the adventure? Where was the fun? Where was going shopping with your best friend and dining out in fancy restaurants?

She knew she was being unfair. If the place weren't empty, there would be a lot more to do. There probably would be shopping centers and restaurants. People would put on plays and concerts. If the city stayed in its current configuration, underground with a natural planetary surface on top, then there would even be plenty of hiking and camping opportunities for people who wanted to do that. There would be plenty to do. The trouble was, it would be the same something everywhere. People were always adopting new fads; if somebody did manage to come up with a new idea somewhere, it would spread to every other city in the galaxy at the speed of hyperwave. The other cities would be able to duplicate any new living configuration in minutes, could manufacture any new device in hours at most. Without the resistance to change a normal society had built into it—without the inertia—no place in the galaxy would be any more special than any other.

Not even the cities full of aliens? she wondered, and then she realized that there probably wouldn't *be* cities full of aliens. There wouldn't be cities full of just humans, either. There might be concentrations of one or the other, but if a city could adapt to any occupant, anybody could live anywhere they chose to. There were bound to be xenophiles in every society, and those xenophiles would homogenize the galaxy even further.

Even that wouldn't be so bad, Ariel supposed, except for what she had been reading in her jungle field guide. The guide had explained how important diversity was to the continued existence of the forest, how it was the constant interplay of diverse organisms that kept the ecosystem running. Lower the amount of diversity, the book had explained, and you lowered the entire ecosystem's ability to survive over long periods of time.

In the short range—in an individual city—having aliens living together might actually strengthen things, but if that same principle of strength through diversity applied to galactic society, then the picture didn't look so good. Maybe Wolruf had been right after all.

Ariel wondered if Dr. Avery had considered that problem when he'd designed his cities. And what about Ariel's own parents? Her mother had bankrolled this project, hadn't she? How much had Avery told her about it, and how much planning had they done together?

Ariel had never paid any attention to her mother's business dealings. She hadn't paid much attention to her mother at all, nor had her mother paid much attention to her, either except to kick her out of the house when she'd let her ... indiscretions compromise the family name. Ariel had considered their relationship terminated at that point, to the degree that she hadn't even contacted her mother when she and Derec had gone back to live on Aurora. But Juliana Welsh had provided the funding for the original Robot City so in a sense her long web of connections reached her daughter even here.

But how much did she know about this place?

That question, at least, might have an easy-to-find answer. Even if Avery was still gone, Mandelbrot was sure to be somewhere nearby, and ever since Derec and Avery had restored his last two memory cubes, he had been full of information about her former life. If he'd been within earshot of Juliana and Avery when they'd done their dealing, then he might know what they had agreed to.

She showered hurriedly, dressed in the first thing she found in her closet—a loose set of green exercise sweats—and left the bedroom.

Derec was in his study, keying something into the computer. Ariel couldn't remember whether he'd come to bed at all last night; by his tousled hair and slumped posture she suspected he hadn't. She'd known him long enough to leave him alone when he got like that.

She found all four robots in the living room, all seated on couches. She was surprised to see Mandelbrot in a chair; he usually preferred his niche in the wall. He stood as she came into the room.

"Good morning, Ariel," he said.

"Morning, Mandelbrot. I have a question for you. Do you remember my mother and Dr. Avery discussing his plans for Robot City?"

"I do."

"Did Avery say just what he intended to *do* with the idea once he proved it would work?"

"He intended to sell it to the various world governments, both in explored space and in the unexplored Fringe."

"That's what I was afraid of." Ariel outlined her reasoning for the robots, ending with, "I don't know for sure if it'll happen that way. It didn't with the city Avery dumped on the Ceremyons, but I think it might with the Kin. I think it's something Avery should consider before he drops the idea on an unsuspecting public."

"I believe you have a valid concern," Mandelbrot said.

Adam left his chair to stand beside Mandelbrot. "I agree. Our duty to intelligent beings everywhere demands that we find out whether the cities will destroy diversity, and whether that diversity is as important as you think it might be."

Lucius—still wearing Derec's features—nodded. He rose to stand beside Mandelbrot and Adam, saying, "Thank you, Ariel. You have found a way for us to serve all of humanity in its many forms."

Eve stood and joined the others. Ariel couldn't suppress a giggle at the image of four robots presenting a united front against a galaxy-wide menace. But right behind the giggle came the shudder as she considered the menace itself. Maybe they were jumping at shadows, but then again, maybe they weren't.

"All right," she said, "let's figure out what we're going to do. I think our first priority should be to find Avery and keep him from spreading this around any more than he has already, at least until we know how dangerous it is."

"Agreed," the robots said in unison.

"All right, then, let's get to it."

"Derec?"

He looked up from the monitor, puzzled. Had someone spoken? He turned to see Ariel standing in the doorway, a worried expression on her face.

"Hi. Sorry to bother you, but... do you know where your dad is?"

Her words made no sense to him. Variables still danced before his eyes, those peculiar variable-variables that changed their meaning over time. Using those super-variables was the only way he could make any sense of the equation he'd copied by hand from his desktop, but even with the computer to keep track of their mutations for him, he could barely follow the concept in his mind.

At last a little of what Ariel had said percolated through. "Dad," he said stupidly. "You mean Avery?"

Ariel frowned. "Of course I mean Avery. Who else? Do you know where he is?"

He tried to think. Avery. Where was Avery? Did he know? "Uh ... no. No, I don't."

"It's kind of important."

"I still don't know."

"Some help you are."

The sting behind her words helped jolt him out of his stupor. "Sorry. I ... I do have a program trying to track him down, but so far it hasn't found any sign of him."

That mollified her a bit. "Oh. Well, if it does, let me know, okay?"

"Okay."

She stepped farther into the room, looked over his shoulder. "What are you working on, anyway?"

"The formula."

"What formula?"

"The one on my desk. It came back, and I had time to copy it this time. I think it's a robotics formula, but I'm not sure."

"You're not even sure of that?"

"No. The meaning of the variables keeps changing."

"Hmm." Ariel gave him a quick kiss on the cheek. "Well, good luck. But remember to call me if you hear anything about Avery, okay?"

"I'll do it."

"Good." Ariel left the room. Derec heard her say something to someone in the living room, then the apartment door opened and closed and there was silence. He turned back to the monitor and the formula.

It was both a formula and a program; he had discovered that much about it. It was a formula in that it definitely expressed a relationship between its various symbols, but it was a program in that it was dynamic, changing over time. He had even managed to run a portion of it with his computer in local mode, but since he didn't know what input to give it, it had crashed within seconds.

For at least the hundredth time, he wondered if he was right about its origin. Had his mother sent it to him? Usually programmers would insert their names in the code somewhere to identify it as theirs, but Derec hadn't found any section of non-changing code big enough to hold a pair of initials, much less a name.

Formula or program, the notation was incredibly dense. The whole thing fit into one screen full of code. He stared at it, as if waiting for it to suddenly resolve into something.

Idly, knowing it would do no good, he pressed the incremental execution button, running the program one step at a time while he watched the code. Different variables blinked with new values at each step, but they were never the same variables and never the same values.

Except one. He pushed the increment button again. Sure enough, one variable near the top left corner of the screen changed with each iteration. It was an alphabetic variable rather than a numeric one; he watched it through half a dozen steps as it changed: S-T-A-S-I-blank. Hmmm. It had disappeared entirely. He kept pushing the button and it appeared again: J-A-N-E-T-blank-A-N-A-S-T-A-S-I-blank-blank-J-A-N-E-T-blank-A-N-A-S-T-A-S-I-blank-blank-J-A-N-E-T-blank. . . .

"Of course!" he shouted. Why use over a dozen bytes of code when a single super-variable would do? He pushed the button again and again. ANASTASI. JANET ANASTASI. His mother's name was Janet Anastasi.

"Well, Basalom, that didn't take him long."

Janet leaned back in her chair and smiled. Her son was a pretty good detective. She idly considered calling him directly and congratulating him, but after a moment's thought she decided to let him finish what he'd started. At this rate it wouldn't take him long anyway.

Sometimes Basalom seemed to be telepathic. He stepped out of his niche in the wall beside her desk and said, "I am confused. Why are you waiting for him to find you, when it is apparent that you wish to speak with him directly?"

Janet shrugged. "That's just the way I want it to be."

"Is it perhaps a manifestation of guilt?" the robot asked. "You have ignored him for so long, you cannot bring yourself to change that behavior now?"

"No," Janet said immediately, but right behind it she felt the hot blush of shame. A bit too quick with the denial, wasn't she? "All right, maybe so. Maybe I do feel guilty about it. But to just call him up now and expect everything to be all right would be absurd. If I let him find me, then it's *his* project. He can decide how he wants it to be."

"But you are intentionally leading him to you. Isn't that functionally equivalent to calling him?"

"He can ignore the clues if he wants."

Basalom remained silent for a moment before asking, "Did you plan it this way all along, or did this explanation come after the fact?"

"Beg your pardon?"

"I am trying to ascertain whether you originally intended to assuage your guilt in this manner, or whether it was a subconscious decision which you have only now stated in definite terms."

"Why?"

"Because I am curious."

Janet laughed. "And I've got only myself to blame for that. All right. Since you asked, I guess I decided subconsciously to do it this way. It just seemed the best way to go about it. I didn't think about guilt or any of that; I just did it. Satisfied?"

"For now. Subjective matters are difficult to resolve, but I will try to assimilate the information into my world-view." Basalom stepped back into his niche.

The indignity of it all. Psychoanalyzed by her valet. If she hadn't made him herself, she would have sent him back to his manufacturer. But he was actually pretty perceptive when it came right down to it. She probably *was* trying to avoid the guilt of abandoning Derec. If she went to him she would have to apologize, or at least explain, but if he came to her she could maintain her reserve.

She suddenly wondered how long this subconscious arranging of events had been going on. Had she left her robots in Derec's path on purpose, hoping they would eventually lead him to her?

No. Impossible. If anything, he had found them and kept them near him to lure *her* to *him*.

Another possibility occurred to her. By the look of things, Derec had been following Wendell around; what if *Wendell* were the one keeping the robots by his side in order to lure Janet back to him?

The thought was staggering. *Wendell?* He hated her as thoroughly as she hated him, didn't he? He couldn't possibly want to see her again. Still, incredible as it seemed, everything fit. She couldn't think of a much better way to draw her in than to kidnap her learning machines, which was just what he seemed to have done.

Another thought came on the heels of the first. Did he *know* he was arranging a meeting? His subconscious mind could be directing his actions as thoroughly as Janet's had been directing hers. He could think he had an entirely different reason for keeping the robots by his side, when the real reason was to bring her back to him.

And she was playing right into his hands. Part of the reason she had come here was to find him. Among other things, she'd intended to deliver a lecture on the moral implications of dropping robot cities on unsuspecting societies, but now she wondered if even *that* hadn't been just another stratagem to bring her back. It would be just like Wendell to use an entire civilized world as a pawn in a larger game.

Or was she just being paranoid?

Round and round it went. Not for the first time, she

wished she were a robot instead of a human. Human life was so messy, so full of emotions and ulterior motives and impossible dreams. She had thought she'd solved the Avery problem once and for all, but here it was again, come back to haunt her.

What should she do? What *could* she do? She wanted her robots back; that was top priority. But she wanted to make sure Wendell didn't screw up any more civilizations in an attempt to bring her back for some sort of gooey reconciliation, too. And the only way to do that, it seemed, was to confront him about it. Like Derec following her trail, she was going to have to play Wendy's game if she wanted to reach him.

At least to a point. Once she tracked him down, all bets were off.

Where to start, though? The computer would obey her wishes, but that was useless against the commands he would certainly have given it to protect his privacy.

Still, even if he were doing all this unconsciously, he had to have left a trail she could follow, and it didn't take a genius to see where that trail began.

She scooted her chair back, stood, and said, "Come on, Basalom. We've got our own puzzle to solve."

Avery frowned as he watched the miniature robot attempt to walk across the workbench. It was only a foot high and bore an oversized head to accommodate a normal-sized positronic brain and powerpack, but neither of those factors contributed to its clumsy gait. The problem was one of programming. The robot simply didn't know how to walk.

He'd tried to tell it how by downloading the instruction set for one of his normal city robots into the test robot's brain, but that wasn't sufficient. Even with the information in memory, the idiot thing still stumbled around like a drunkard. The programming for walking was evidently stored somatically, in the body cells themselves, and could only be learned by trial and error.

Avery snorted in disgust. What a ridiculous design! Trust Janet to create a perfectly good piece of hardware and screw it up with a bad idea like this one. The problem wasn't restricted to walking, either. A robot made with her new cells couldn't talk until it learned the concept of language, couldn't recognize an order until *that* was explained to it, and didn't recognize Avery as human even then. It was ridiculous. What good was a robot that had to learn everything the hard way?

Avery could see the advantage to giving a robot somatic memory. It would have the equivalent of reflexes once it learned the appropriate responses to various stimuli. And if the brain didn't have to control every physical action, then that freed it for higher functions. Properly trained, such a robot could be more intuitive, better able to serve. But as it was, that training was prohibitively time consuming.

Janet had to have had a method for getting around the brain-body interface problem. No doubt it was in the brain's low-level programming, but that programming was still in the inductive monitors' memcubes in his other lab.

Drat. It looked like he was going to need them after all. He briefly considered sending a robot after them, but he rejected that as a bad idea. Robots were too easily subverted. If Derec were there in the old lab, he could probably trick the robot into leading him here to the new lab as well, and Avery wasn't ready for that.

He couldn't order the city to carry the memcubes to him internally, either, not if he wanted to maintain his isolation from it.

That left going for them himself. It seemed crazy, at first, to go into an area where people were looking for him, but upon sober reflection Avery realized that he wasn't really trying to protect his *own* isolation so much as his laboratory's. If he retrieved the memcubes himself, there would actually be less risk of exposure. Central was still under orders not to betray his presence, so reentering the city shouldn't be a problem, and if he should encounter Derec or Janet or anyone else, he supposed he could simply endure their questions and accusations, biding his time and slipping away again when the opportunity arose. It wouldn't be pleasant, but it wouldn't be disastrous, either.

Avery picked up the miniature robot and held it within the field area of another magnetic containment vessel. The robot squirmed in his hand, but it knew no form other than humanoid, so there was no worry of it getting away immediately. Avery switched on the containment, waited until the magnetic field snatched the robot from him and crumpled it into a formless sphere again. Now there was no worry of it getting away at all.

He turned to go, but paused at the doorway, looking out into the jungle. He supposed he should walk on the surface before he entered the city, just in case, but the idea of walking unprotected in that half-wild, half-robotic wilderness wasn't exactly appealing. He looked back into the lab, then crossed over to the tool rack by the workbench and picked up the welding laser. It was about the size of a flashlight and had a heavy, solid feel to it. Comforting. He probably wouldn't need it, but it never hurt to be prepared.

CHAPTER 6

A MEETING OF MINDS

Ariel hated robotics labs. They were always full of bizarre hardware, too much of which looked like torture instruments. They were all, without exception, cold and impersonal and utilitarian in design. Something about them seemed to suck the humanity right out of anyone who entered. Even Derec became just like the robots he worked on when he entered a robotics lab: single-mindedly intent on the task before him. Ariel stayed away from him then, and she tried to stay away from labs all the time.

So, of course, in their search for Dr. Avery, the robots led her directly to the laboratory where he had taken them. The door was still open, and the concave stumps of three examination tables still rose from the floor in the middle of the room. Glittering grains of what looked like coarse sand covered the floor around the remains of the tables, and it took Ariel a moment to realize that they were robot cells. Something was evidently keeping them from rejoining the rest of the city.

She looked around the lab for clues to Avery's

whereabouts, but saw nothing immediately obvious. She didn't know what she was looking for anyway. He was hardly going to leave a note or a map leading her to wherever he'd gone, now was he? Still, she supposed the robots were right; if they couldn't find him through Central, then this, the last place where he'd been seen, was the logical place to start looking for him.

She walked over to the workbench at the end of the lab. A light on an arm stuck out from the wall above it, the pool of illumination coinciding with the cleared area amid a clutter of machinery. All the machinery faced the light. It seemed pretty obvious that someone had been working here, then, but whether it had been Avery or Derec, she couldn't tell.

She should have insisted that Derec come along with her. He'd have been able to make more sense of this jumble of equipment, but no, he was too busy for that. While he sat there in his study playing with some idiotic formula for God only knew what, Avery could be escaping the planet with the seeds for galactic destruction.

A noise in the corridor outside made her turn around. The four robots paused in their examination of the room as well. Lucius stepped silently toward the wall beside the doorway, and the other three moved just as silently to flank him, staying out of view from whomever or whatever was beyond the door. They'd coordinated their motion via com-link, Ariel supposed.

Mandelbrot turned toward her for a moment and raised his finger to his speaker grille, motioning with his other hand for her to move out of sight as well. She nodded and backed over to stand against the wall. She felt silly hiding from a noise, but she felt very much out of her element here; she would humor the robots until she learned who was out there.

She didn't have to wait long. Avery's voice was instantly recognizable, even with the false note of enthusiasm in it. "Well, my dear, fancy meeting you here. What a surprise."

Ariel supposed he was talking to her, that he somehow knew she was in the lab. She could see no reason to hide, then, but before she could respond, another voice, this one female and less familiar, answered him. "Wendell Avery. The pleasure's yours, I'm sure."

She hadn't expected to find him quite so soon, so Janet hadn't prepared what she was going to say to him yet. After their initial surprised volley, there was a long silence while they each sized up the other. Janet noted that Wendell's hair had finally made the transition from gray to white, and that his taste in clothing hadn't changed a bit since the day she'd left him. He still wore a white ruffled shirt and baggy trousers. Knowing him, they could be the very ones he'd worn on their wedding day.

She considered taking the initiative and lambasting him immediately for his stupidity in disturbing two alien civilizations with his robot cities, but curiosity made her reconsider. If he'd orchestrated this encounter, he must have done it for a reason, and she wanted to know why. She thought she knew, but she wanted to hear him say it. There would be plenty of time to lecture him later, and possibly more ammunition to do it with if she let him have his say first.

"So," she said. "Now that you've lured me here, what do you intend to do?"

Avery manufactured an incredulous expression. "Me? You're the one who arranged this whole business, disturbing my project with your silly robots at every turn. Well, you've got my attention. What do you want?"

The conceited arrogance of the man brought genuine incredulity to Janet's face. Of course he wouldn't admit to anything himself; he was a master at shifting the blame. But to imply that Janet had orchestrated what he had so obviously set up himself was too much to believe. "*Me* arrange to meet *you?* Don't make me laugh."

Avery shook his head. "Come on, Janet, there's no sense denying it. You set this whole thing up just to smoke me out and you know it, though how you could imagine there could still be anything between us is beyond me."

"Anything between us? You're the one fooling yourself, if you think that. I came to get my robots, and to shut down this whole stupid project of yours before you destroy any more civilizations with it. *That's* why I'm here."

Avery could hardly believe his ears. The woman had gone to enormous trouble just to arrange this meeting, and now when she had her chance to speak her mind she stood there vilifying him instead. He supposed he shouldn't be surprised—she had always backed away at the last minute, always taken the easiest route no matter what the situation— but he had naively assumed that over a decade of independence would have made her a little more—what? Adventurous? Assertive? Competent?

Evidently he'd been wrong about that. She hadn't changed. She was still the same old Janet: a genius at design but an absolute moron when it came to implementation.

She hadn't changed a whole lot physically, either. Avery would have been surprised if she had; spacers generally counted their age in centuries. Janet's hair was still its original blond tint, and her eyes were the same sometimes-green, sometimes-gray he remembered, and she had managed to keep her figure as well. Her style of dress hadn't changed appreciably either, but her shape-flattering clothing had never been a problem for him.

Looking at her now, he remembered what had brought them together.

But listening to her reminded him of what drove them apart. He began to pay attention to what she was saying.

"I managed to look the other way when you stole my cellular robot idea, but when you used it to build these ugly monstrosities you call cities, and then scattered them around the galaxy without a thought of caution, I decided it was time to put a stop to it. I–"

"*Developed,*" Avery said sternly. "I developed the cellular robot and the robot city, from a concept I freely admit was your idea. You were content to experiment forever with it in the laboratory, but I was not. The concept needed to be tested on a larger scale, and I did so. But I did not *steal* your idea."

"Semantics, Wendy. Call it development; call it what you want, but a rose by any other name. . . ." She left the phrase unfinished, but went on before he could interrupt. "And now you've gathered all three of my new robots. Are you planning to *develop* them, too? Ah, you're blushing. Struck a nerve there, didn't I? Well, this time I'm not going to let you. This time I'm keeping my idea to myself."

Avery felt his hands clenching into fists. Unclenching them, he stuffed them into his jacket pockets, but his right hand encountered the welding laser. He withdrew his hand, empty, deeply troubled by the thought that had entered his mind.

He had once been insane. That insanity had nearly led him to kill his own son. He had since been cured, but no one had promised him it would be permanent. Apparently it wasn't; this momentary urge to burn a neat hole through Janet's left breast was very probably a symptom of the same insanity creeping back on him again.

Much as he had enjoyed the megalomania, he still preferred having a clear mind. And he didn't particularly want to harm Janet, either. He just wanted to shut her up so he didn't have to listen to her accusations anymore. That was probably what had driven him over the edge in the first place.

There were better ways to do that, though; non-violent ways. Ways such as simply leaving. He didn't need the frosted memory cubes anyway; he didn't know why he had fooled himself into thinking he did. Nor did he need to stick around on Robot City, either. He could solve the new cells' programming problem quickly enough on his own once he got back to Aurora.

Yes, that's what he would do. He would walk away from her just as she had done from him so many years ago, order the city to make him a starship, and leave this whole bizarre episode of his life behind.

She was still waiting for a response to her latest ultimatum. Avery held his arms at his sides, looked her straight in the eye, and said, "Madam, you may keep your idea. You may keep your robots as well—what's left of them. You may even have this entire planet to do with as you wish. I give it to you. The only thing you may not have is me to yell at any longer. I am leaving." With that he turned and strode away, stepping on the slidewalk to speed his departure.

Lucius, watching with an eye he had extended through the wall and modified to match the blank surface, felt as if his brain were about to burst. Here before him stood his creator! At last, he could ask her the questions that had haunted him since his first awakening. At last he could find out why he existed and who he must serve and who he could safely ignore.

And beside her stood something almost as wonderful: a new robot. This one was neither a normal Avery robot nor another such as Lucius nor even one such as Mandelbrot, but yet another design. This robot was constructed of simple, large-scale metal and plastic members, as was Mandelbrot, but at the same time it had been given the features of a biological human. Lucius could only suppose that was to allow it to interact with humans on an equal level, and it was *that* concept that most intrigued him. Even if his creator deigned not to answer his questions, this robot might be able to do so.

Lucius sent a cautious inquiry over the comlink. *Unknown friend, can you hear me?*

The robot shifted its gaze from Avery to the wall behind which Lucius's signal originated. *I can*, it replied. *Who are you?*

I am called Lucius. I am one of the robots your mistress created.

One of the learning machines?

Learning machines. Yes, that is a good description of what I am. Lucius felt a surge of joy. He was right; this robot was a treasure trove of information. Already he had learned something of his creator's intentions in building him. *Who are you?* he asked.

I am Basalom.

And what is our creator's name?

Her name is Janet.

Janet. Lucius had hoped the word would be a code of some sort which would trigger a hidden store of instructions or memories, but nothing happened. He would have to do the remainder of his learning the hard way, too. *I seek knowledge about humans*, he said. *I wish to know more about my place in the universe.*

Don't we all?

The question was obviously rhetorical. While Lucius thought of a reply, he downloaded his hearing buffer and processed the words in it. His creator was calling Avery a thief. That was hardly new information to Lucius.

We must find the time to discuss this at length, he sent.

I agree. Unfortunately, this opportunity seems to be drawing to a close.

Lucius noticed Avery's right hand enter his pocket, clutch something there, and emerge again, empty. Could he have a weapon? Lucius prepared to draw in his eye, tensed himself for quick action, though without a specific threat he didn't know what he could do.

He felt immense relief when Avery stated his intention to leave and turned to go. Wonderful! That would leave Janet here to answer his questions uninhibited.

But his relief turned to alarm again when Janet shouted, "Oh no you don't! Basalom, stop him."

Beware, friend Basalom! I believe Avery is armed.

Basalom had begun to move the moment he heard Janet's command, but Avery was already a few strides away. At Lucius's warning, Basalom leaped onto the slidewalk to close the gap before Avery could pull his weapon, but the distance was too great. Avery lunged for his pocket, there was a sound of tearing cloth, and he held a laser in his hand.

Pointed straight at Basalom.

"Basalom, is it?" he said. "I always wondered what you would name your mechanical lover."

Lucius heard the icy tone in Avery's voice, knew what

would happen next. He withdrew his eye from the wall, at the same time asking, *Friend Basalom, is your memory backed up?*

Not recently, I'm afraid, Basalom replied. *Pity. I've had some interesting insights in the past few days.*

Quickly; download your memory into me!

No time, Basalom replied, and Lucius, sticking his whole head out through the doorway, saw that he was correct. Avery's thumb was beginning to depress the laser's trigger button. Lucius could see the skin deforming. The button was beginning to slide. . . .

"No!"

Avery jerked at the sudden, overly amplified sound, and the beam went wide, slicing off Basalom's left arm. The arm landed with a thud on non-moving pavement; Basalom and Avery continued to slide away. The laser beam winked out as Avery looked to see who had shouted. Lucius stepped out into the corridor and said, "Do not harm Basalom. He is a thinking being, with just as much right to live as you."

Basalom made a move toward Avery, but Avery brought the laser around to bear on him again. "Wrong," Avery said. "He's a robot. Nothing more." Once again, his thumb began to depress the firing button.

Lucius's mind was awhirl in conflict. Yes, Basalom was certainly a robot, but couldn't he also be more? Couldn't he also be human, just as Lucius suspected he and his brethren were? Could he stand by and watch one human kill another simply because one was biological and the other was not?

The First Law said he couldn't. Zeroth Law implications further dictated that he must protect the more valuable of the two humans, if only one could be saved. Clearly, Basalom was the more valuable of the two, but how could Lucius save him?

Avery himself provided the answer. In the only similar instance of Zeroth-Law application Lucius had witnessed to date, Avery had demonstrated that it was right even to inflict injury to one human to avoid injury to the more valuable one. Lucius saw the possibility, saw that he *could* save Basalom's life, and he could even do so without killing Avery. It would still mean a First Law violation, but not a fatal one.

Not for Avery, at any rate, but Lucius didn't know what the conflict would eventually do to himself. If he and Basalom *weren't* human, he would be in direct violation of the First Law. Without justification, that would probably be enough to overload his brain with conflicting potentials.

Lucius hesitated a microsecond, but the other side of the argument was just as deadly. If Basalom *were* human, then not saving him would be an even worse violation of the law.

He felt a strange potential coursing through his circuits, the same potential he had noted earlier in connection with Avery. He cursed the biological fool before him for forcing him into this dilemma. He, Lucius, could very likely die in the attempt to save someone else.

There was no time to think it through any further. Avery's finger was dangerously close to triggering the laser again. In desperation, Lucius did the only thing he could think of to do: he drew back his arm to throw, formed his hand into a thin blade that would cause the least amount of pain possible, and flung it at Avery's outstretched arm.

In the moment it took the projectile to reach its target, Lucius wondered if he could have simply knocked the laser from Avery's hand, but it was easy to convince himself that he couldn't. It presented a much smaller target, most of which Avery's fingers covered anyway, and fingers would be even more difficult to reattach than would a forearm.

Besides, there was a certain amount of poetic justice in taking an entire limb.

Avery stared at the stump of his wrist in astonished disbelief. One moment a hand had been there, and the next moment it hadn't. He had hardly felt the pain when—whatever it was—cut it off; shock kept him from feeling it now.

Intelligence made him grasp the wrist in his left hand and squeeze until he'd closed off the arteries. He carefully avoided looking down at the slidewalk.

Slidewalk he thought dizzily. Yes, he'd best watch his footing, hadn't he? Blood could be slippery.

Dimly, through the tight focus his injury demanded of his attention, he was aware of shouting voices and the sound of footsteps. Someone shoved a hand under his arm and drew him erect; he hadn't been aware he was slumping to his knees. He looked up to see Janet's humaniform robot supporting him, heard it say, "Master Avery, we must get you to a hospital."

"No kidding," he managed to say through clenched teeth. It was beginning to hurt now.

Someone else shouted, "Lucius, come back here! Mandelbrot, stop him!" Metallic feet pounded away down the corridor.

Another pair of hands reached out to hold him, these ones warm and human, and he found himself looking into Janet's whitened face. She looked worse than he felt. "I'm sorry," she whispered. "Oh Wendell, I'm sorry."

"I am too," he said automatically, and was surprised to realize the words were true, but about what he had no idea.

• • •

The computer's voice woke Derec out of a sound sleep. "Master Derec, wake up. Master Derec."

"Mmmm?" was all he could manage at first. After the elation of figuring out his mother's name had faded, he'd realized how long he'd been without sleep and he had ordered a bed made for him right there in the study. He'd hoped that his new discovery would trigger memories of his past, and he'd supposed that sleeping on it would be the best way to integrate that knowledge into whatever subconscious switching network controlled memory, but now, even in his groggy state, he knew it hadn't worked. He suspected he'd slept *too* soundly for that. He'd been out before his head hit the pillow, exhausted, and he didn't feel any different now.

"Wake up," the computer said again. "Your father has been located."

That sped the waking process a bit. He sat up and shook his head, stood, and staggered over to the terminal. "Caffeine," he said as he sat down, and a moment later the desk delivered a cup of steaming black coffee. "Show me where he is," he said between gulps.

The screen lit to show Avery standing between two unfamiliar people. No, one should be familiar, Derec realized. That had to be his mother. Janet. Again he reached for the cascade of memories that should have been there, but nothing responded to the new stimulus.

That was her, though. It had to be. Then that other person wasn't a person at all, but her humaniform robot, the one Wolruf had chased northward from the lab. Evidently they had come back together this time. And brought Avery with them? That certainly seemed to be the case. Now that he looked, Derec could see that they were holding onto him, evidently making sure he didn't get away. Or was that—?

No. Avery clutched his right wrist, and he had no hand below it. They were supporting him; that was it. But none of the three was doing anything about his injury! They were instead watching something out of the monitor's view to the right.

"Pan right," Derec ordered, and the view slid left in the screen. As it panned he saw Ariel standing in the doorway of what Derec could now see was indeed the lab where he'd revived the robots, and she was also looking intently down the corridor.

The objects of their attention slid into view: four robots—Mandelbrot, Adam, Eve, and Lucius—locked in battle.

They were a blur of motion. It was hard to tell who was on which side—hard even to tell who was *who* amid the constantly shifting shapes. Only Mandelbrot remained the same from moment to moment. At first it seemed that he fought against the other three, struggling to hold them all captive while they twisted and flowed out of his grasp, but it gradually became apparent that he and two of the others were all three trying to contain only one robot.

"Give me sound," Derec said, and suddenly his study echoed with screeches and thuds and a peculiar ripping noise that Derec realized was the sound of robot cells being torn free like Velcro fasteners. The robots had changed tactics now; instead of trying to contain their captive—a task as impossible as stopping a flood with their hands—they began tearing him apart. Mandelbrot was doing the most damage. His rigid left arm moved like a piston, his hand pulling free chunks of silvery robot and flinging them away to splash against the walls and ceiling. The other two robots took over the job of flailing at the constantly shifting amoeba their captive had become, pulling off its arms when it tried to grow around them and forcing it back toward Mandelbrot and destruction.

At last Mandelbrot exposed his target: the robot's egg-shaped microfusion power pack. When he wrenched that free, the struggle instantly ceased. He backed away with the power pack in his hand, and the other two robots flowed back into their normal shapes: Adam the werewolf and Eve the silvery copy of Ariel. The third robot remained a much-diminished, ragged-edged tangle of appendages on the floor. It had undoubtedly been Lucius they'd destroyed. Somehow that didn't surprise Derec.

Then the implications of what he had seen soaked in, and he spilled coffee all over his desk. Swearing, but not at the spill, he leaped to his feet, knocking over his chair in his haste, and ran from the apartment. His father was hurt. His mother had come out of hiding. And there could only be one reason for the battle he had just witnessed: Lucius had injured a human being. He had directly violated the First Law of Robotics.

Wolruf was talking with the wolf when she felt the forest shudder beneath her feet.

"What I want to know," she'd been in the process of saying, "is whether or not your desire to serve 'umans is stronger in the immediate case, or over the long term. Do you think ahead to w'at your 'elp might do to your masters' civilization, or do you just follow your laws case by—what was that?"

The wolf had flinched, too, just as the forest had seemed to do. Now it said, "Involuntary response. A robot has just injured a human."

"W'at?" Wolruf felt her hackles rise. That was supposed to be impossible.

The wolf looked into the forest and spoke as if echoing a news broadcast, as it probably was. "The robot Lucius has inflicted non-fatal damage to the human Wendell Avery. Lucius has been deactivated, but all units are alerted to watch for aberrant behavior among other robots. All units must run a diagnostic self-check immediately." The wolf turned its head to look up at Wolruf. "I must comply," it said, and it froze like a statue.

Wolruf glanced around at the forest, wondering if she should use the opportunity to make her escape. Of all the times to be out in the forest with a robotic wolf, this was probably the worst. If some rogue idea were circulating around, some new thought that could actually allow a robot to override the Three Laws, then Wolruf couldn't think of a much worse place to run afoul of it than here with a robot who had already convinced itself that injuring animals was all right.

She forced herself to stay put. It had been Lucius and Avery involved, not this robot before her. Wolruf had lived around robots long enough to know that they seldom—if ever—did anything without a reason, and if ever a robot had a reason to harm a human, Lucius was the one. Scary as the precedent might be, the wolf didn't have a motive. No matter how much she worried about the long-term damage robots could do to a civilization, Wolruf didn't think she was in any danger now.

She waited impatiently for the wolf robot's conscious-ness to come back on line, in the meantime listening to the occasional chirps and cries of the forest's real occupants. Quite a few of them were genuine, by the sound of it. Quite a few of the plants were, too. The fresh, clean aroma of growing things was a constant delight to a nose too often idle in the city.

That was a good argument in favor of robots right there, Wolruf realized. They had repaired a planet-wide ecosystem in only a few months, with much more careful attention to detail than she or her entire society could achieve. Wolruf's home world needed such attention, and soon. Most of the forests there were already gone, as were the wide open spaces and the clean lakes. Centuries of industrialization had left scars that would probably never heal on their own. Even accounting for the difficulties inherent in working around an existing population, robots would probably be able to repair it all in a few years, or decades at the longest.

There was no denying that robots would be useful if she took them home with her. But that still didn't tell her whether or not they would also be harmful.

She was no closer to an answer than before. And now she had to worry about the possibility of immediate danger as well as long-term effects of using robots.

The wolf returned to life as quickly as it had frozen. "My functions check out marginal," it said. "I am not a direct threat to humans, but under the current conditions my ability to kill animals has caused some alarm. I have been instructed to return to the city for deeper evaluation."

"Oh," Wolruf said.

"If you wish to accompany me, we can continue our discussion on the way."

"All right."

"You were asking about the city's consideration for long-range effects of its actions." The robot led off through the ferns toward a large boulder, which obligingly grew a door for them when they were still a few paces away. "I have accessed the pertinent operation guidelines from Central, and find that very little long-term planning exists. However, since this was an experimental city built primarily to test the physical function of the cellular robot concept, that lack of guidelines may not be pertinent to the question. It seems likely that under actual implementation conditions, whatever long-range goals the city's inhabitants had for themselves would be included in the city programming."

They stepped into the elevator and turned around to watch the door slide closed, cutting off the sights and sounds and smells of forest once again. They began to descend, and Wolruf turned her attention to what the robot had said. She had to wade through the unfamiliar terms in its speech to get its meaning, but she was getting good at gathering sense from context. The robot had just said that long-term goals were the responsibility of the humans being served. Which, to answer her question, meant no, the robots wouldn't concern themselves with it because they believed it was already being covered.

Wolruf laughed aloud. When the robot asked her to explain, she said, "You've 'eard the cliché about the blind leading the blind?"

"No, but I have accessed the appropriate files. I fail to see the application here."

Wolruf laughed again. " 'umans, at least my particular breed of them—and to all appearances Derec's breed as well—don't pay much more attention to long-term problems than you do."

"Oh," the wolf said. "We will have to take this under consideration."

The elevator came to a stop and the doors opened onto the underground city. Wolruf stepped out ahead of the robot. "Good," she said. "I was 'oping you'd say that."

The city built the hospital in the suite of rooms just down the corridor from the lab. Medical robots arrived while it was still differentiating, took Avery inside, and made quick work of preparing his wound for surgery. The operating room grew around them while they cleaned the wound, and within minutes they had him anesthetized and were hard at work grafting his hand back on.

Ariel watched in morbid fascination from behind the sterile room's transparent wall. To her left stood Derec's mother and her companion robot, to her right Adam and Eve and Mandelbrot. The robots were watching the operation with the same fascination as Ariel, but Derec's mother was watching Ariel as much as anything else.

"You're David's lover, aren't you?" she finally asked, her tone less than approving. It was the first thing either of them had said to the other.

"That's right," Ariel said without looking away from the window. Where did this woman get off? she wondered. No introduction, no apology, just "You're David's lover." She didn't know a thing about the situation, yet she still acted as if she were in control. Ariel turned her head enough to address the reflection beside her own in the window and said, "His name is Derec now."

"I heard. I've never liked it. It sounds like a spacesuit manufacturer."

"Exactly," Ariel said around a smile.

"Why did he change it?"

"Long story."

"I see."

The medical robots were using some sort of glue to hold the ends of bone together. Lucius's weapon had been sharp and moving fast; the severed edges were smooth and easily repaired. He had probably done that on purpose, Ariel realized. She wondered why he had bothered. She watched the robots spread the glue on either end, press the two together, and hold them rigid until the glue set. She hoped they'd checked to make sure it was aligned properly; something about the glue looked permanent.

"You're not worth the effort he's put in on finding you," Ariel said suddenly.

"What?"

"You heard me. As soon as he hears about this, Derec is going to come running in here all ready for a big reconciliation. He wants his family back, and he'll take what he gets, but you're no prize. Neither of you. You two are living proof that scientists shouldn't have children."

"I suppose you're an expert on the subject."

"I know how to treat one."

"How could you? You don't—Do you?" The woman was clearly horrified at the thought.

"What's the matter, don't like the idea of being a grandmother?" Ariel snorted. "Relax, you're safe. *He* took care of it for you." She tilted her head toward the window. "One of his wonderful experiments ran amok and killed the fetus while it was still only a few weeks old."

"You sound as if you hold *me* responsible."

"You ran off and left your son in the hands of a lunatic. What am I supposed to think?"

"I couldn't take him with me. I—I needed to be alone."

"You should have thought about that before you had him." Ariel looked directly at Derec's mother for the first time since they had begun speaking to one another. If she had looked earlier she might have held her tongue; the woman's skin was gray, and she looked as if she had aged twenty years in the last few minutes.

Her robot was growing concerned, too. It said, "Mistress Janet, Mistress Ariel, I don't believe this conversation should continue."

Janet. That was her name. Ariel had been struggling for it since she'd first seen her.

Janet said, "It's all right, Basalom. Ariel isn't telling me anything I didn't already know." She smiled a fleeting smile. "I've had plenty of time to dwell on my mistakes." Looking back through the window at Avery and the medical robots, she said, "We thought having a child might save our marriage. Can you imagine anything sillier? People who don't get along in the first place certainly aren't going to get along any better under the stress of having a child, but we didn't see that then. We just knew we were falling out of love, and we tried the only thing we could think of to stop it from happening."

Ariel felt herself blush guiltily at Janet's admission. She'd been thinking along similar lines herself just yesterday, hadn't she? She hadn't actually come out and said that a baby would bring her and Derec closer together again, but she'd been working toward that concept. Was it so surprising, then, to find that Derec's parents had done the same thing?

"Treating the symptoms doesn't often cure the disease," Ariel said, her tone considerably softer than before. "I guess you should have looked for the reason why you were falling out of love in the first place."

"I know that now."

More softly still, Ariel asked, "Why do you think you did fall out of love?"

Janet's laugh was a derisive "Ha!" She nodded at Avery as Ariel had done earlier. "He was out to transform the galaxy; I wanted to study it first. He wanted a castle for everyone and a hundred robots in every castle, but I wanted to preserve a little diversity in the universe. I was more interested in the nature of intelligence and the effect of environment on its development, while he was more interested in using intelligence to modify the environment to suit it. We argued about it all the time. Small wonder we started to hate each other."

Derec spared Ariel from having to reply to that. He burst into the room at a dead run, skidded to a stop just in time to avoid crashing into the windowed wall, and demanded of anyone who would answer, "What did you do with Lucius's body?"

CHAPTER 7

THE THUD OF ONE DROPPED SHOE

Janet could hardly believe her ears. "What kind of a way is that to greet someone you haven't seen in years?"

Derec looked properly sheepish. He also looked as if he'd slept in his clothing and hadn't bothered to look in a mirror before he'd left the apartment. One lock of hair stuck straight out from his right temple.

"Sorry," he said. "Hello, Mother. I've missed you. How's Dad?" He looked through the window, but before Janet could answer him he lost his sheepish look and said, "Looks like he'll live. But without a power pack Lucius won't last more than an hour or so. I've got to get enough power to his brain to keep him going or we'll lose the chance to find out what made him do this."

Janet couldn't suppress a grin. He sounded just like his father. Or maybe like herself, she admitted, if she'd been thinking a little more clearly.

Ariel wasn't as amused. "Robots, robots, robots! Is that all you can think about?" she nearly screamed at him. "There's more to life than robots!"

371

Derec shook his head, but Janet could see the determination in his eyes. "No, that's not all I think about. It's just that this happens to be about the most important thing to happen in the entire history of robotics. If we lose this chance to study it, we may never get another."

"Derec's right," Janet said. "If I hadn't been so rattled I'd have thought of it myself. Basalom, where—"

The robot at Ariel's side interrupted. "I do not think it would be wise to revive him. He is dangerous."

"I agree with Mandelbrot," the wolflike learning machine beside him said. "Much as we regret the loss of our companion, his experiences have damaged him beyond repair. It would be best to let his pathways randomize."

Janet looked at the old, Ferrier-model robot. Mandelbrot? She'd thought she'd heard that name shouted earlier. Could this be the one? It seemed impossible, but he *did* have a dianite arm. . . .

"Maybe so," Derec said, "but not until I get a recording of them first. Now where is his body?"

"In the lab next door," said Mandelbrot.

"Great." Derec turned to go, but stopped and looked at Janet again. "I, uh, could probably use your help if you want to come along."

She felt the tension in the room ease slightly. She looked from him to Ariel to Wendell in the operating room, wondering if she should go. She didn't want to leave Wendell, but the medical robot had given him a general anesthetic in order to stop him from thinking about his injury, so it really made no difference to him. Going with Derec, on the other hand, might matter to *him*. A little stunned that she might actually care about what either of them felt, or that she might feel something herself, she said, "I don't think I'm doing anyone any good here, so sure, why not?"

"I'll stay here," Ariel said.

Janet couldn't tell if she meant that angrily or helpfully. She didn't suppose it mattered much; the same response would work for either case. "Thank you," she said, and let Derec lead her from the room.

Basalom followed along, as did the two learning machines. They found the remains of the third, Lucius, resting like a battered starfish on the floor just inside the door to the lab. It looked as if part of the battle had gone on in there as well, but Derec, stepping over Lucius's body, said, "I guess I forgot to clean up. Central, fix these exam tables, please. And go ahead and reabsorb the loose cells on the floor. All but what belongs to Lucius, of course."

The sandy grit surrounding the pedestals on the floor sank into the surface, and the pedestals simultaneously grew taller and spread out at the top to form three separate exam tables. Janet nodded to Basalom and said, "Go ahead and put him on one. Then go out and scrape up what you can from outside."

Basalom lifted Lucius easily with his one remaining hand and deposited him on the middle table, then left the room. The Ariel-shaped learning machine went with him. Janet was itching to speak with one of the learning machines, but she supposed there would be time for that later. She was itching to speak with Derec as well, but he was already absorbed in the task of hooking up a variable power supply and a brain activity monitor to Lucius.

She supposed she could be helping with that, at least. She walked over to stand across the exam table from him and said, "Plus and minus five volts will do for his memories. If you hold it at that, he shouldn't wake up, and even if he does, he'll still be immobilized because the body cells take twenty volts before they can move."

Derec nodded. The stray hair at his temple waved like a tree limb in a breeze. "Good," he said. "Any special place I should attach the leads? The few times I've worked on these guys, I've just stuck stuff anywhere and let the cells sort it out, but I wasn't sure if that was the best way."

Janet couldn't resist reaching out and brushing his hair down. He looked surprised at first, then smiled when he realized what she was doing.

"Anywhere is fine," she said. "When I designed the cells, I gave them enough hard wiring to figure out what to do with all the various types of input they were likely to get."

"Good."

She watched Derec clip the power supply's three leads to the ends of three different arms, then turn up the voltage to five. He then took the brain monitor's headphone-shaped sensor and moved it over the robot's unconventional body, searching for its positronic brain. The monitor began to beep when he reached the base of one of the arms, and he wedged it in place with one pickup underneath and one on top.

The monitor flickered with sharp-edged waveforms, hundreds of them joining to fill the screen until it was a jumble of multicolored lines. "Looks like we caught him in time," Derec said. "There seems to be quite a bit of mental activity." He reached up and switched in a filter, and the jumble diminished to a manageable half-dozen or so wave-forms. They weren't actual voltage traces, but rather representations of activity in the various levels of the brain, useful for visualizing certain types of thoughts.

Janet frowned. "Are those supposed to be the Three Laws?"

"That's right."

The pattern was still recognizable as the one built into every positronic brain at the time of manufacture—but just barely. Each of the laws showed in a separate hue of green, but overlaying them all were two companion waves, a deep violet one that split and rejoined much as the Three Laws did, and a lighter blue one weaving in and out around the laws and linking up with other signals from all over the screen. The effect looked as if the violet and blue waves were purposefully entangling the laws, preventing them from altering their potential beyond carefully delineated levels. Janet suspected that was just what they were doing. Visual analogy didn't always work in describing a robot's inner workings, but in this case it looked pretty straightforward.

"I'd say that explains a lot," she said.

Derec flipped to another band, following the two waves as they wove from the Three Laws through the self-awareness section and into the duty queue. "Looks like he's built a pretty heavy web of rationalization around just about all the pre-defined areas of thought," he said. "Normal diagnostic procedure would be to wake him up and ask him what all that means, but I don't think we want to do that just yet. Adam, you know how he thinks; can you make sense of it?"

The one remaining learning machine stepped over to Derec's side. Adam? Had he known the significance of that name when he chose it, or had it been given to him? Janet supposed the other one would be Eve, then. And this one, the renegade, was Lucius. Why hadn't he gone for the obvious and called himself Lucifer? She itched to ask them. She *had* to talk with them soon.

In answer to Derec's question, Adam said, "The violet potential schematic corresponds to the Laws of Humanics. The blue one is the Zeroth Law of Robotics."

"Beg your pardon?" Janet asked. "Laws of Humanics? Zeroth Law? What are you talking about?"

Her learning machine looked over at her and said, "We have attempted to develop a set of laws governing human behavior, laws similar to the ones that govern our own. They are, of course, purely descriptive rather than compulsory, but we felt that understanding them might give us an understanding of human behavior which we otherwise lacked. As for the Zeroth Law, we felt that the Three Laws were insufficient in defining our obligations toward the human race in general, so we attempted to define that obligation ourselves."

Janet was careful not to express the joy she felt, for fear of influencing the robot somehow, but inside she was ecstatic. This was perfect! Her experiment was working out after all. Her learning machines had begun to generalize from their experiences. "And what did you come up with?" she asked.

"Bear in mind that these laws describe potential conditions within a positronic brain, so words are inadequate to describe them perfectly; however, they can be expressed approximately as follows. The First Law of Humanics: All beings will do that which pleases them most. The Second Law of Humanics: A sentient being may not harm a friend, or through inaction allow a friend to come to harm. The Third Law of Humanics: A sentient being will do what a friend asks, but a friend may not ask unreasonable things." He paused, perhaps giving Janet time to assimilate the new laws' meanings.

Not bad. Not bad at all. Like he'd said, they certainly weren't compulsory as far as most humans went, but Janet doubted she could have done any better. "And what is your Zeroth Law?" she asked.

"That is much more difficult to state in words, but a close approximation would be that any action should serve the greatest number of humans possible." Adam nodded toward Lucius. "Lucius has taken the Law a step farther than Eve or I, and we believe it was that step which led him to do what he did to Dr. Avery. He believes that the value of the humans in question should also be considered."

Eve. She'd guessed right. "And you don't?"

Adam raised his arms with the palms of his hands up. It took Janet a moment to recognize it as a shrug, since she'd never seen a robot use the gesture before. Adam said, "I am . . . uncomfortable with the subjectivity of the process. I had hoped to find a more definite operating principle."

"But Lucius is satisfied with it."

"That seems to be the case."

"Why do you suppose he is and you aren't?"

"Because," Adam said, again hesitating. "Because he believes himself to be human."

If the robot were hoping to shock her with that revelation, he was going to be disappointed. Janet had expected something like this would happen from the start; indeed, in a way it was the whole point of the experiment. She waited patiently for the question she knew was coming.

Adam didn't disappoint her. He looked straight into her eyes with his own metallic ones and said, "Each of us has struggled with this question since we awakened, but none of us have been able to answer it to our mutual satisfaction. You created us, though. Please tell us: are we human?"

Janet used the same palms-up gesture Adam had used. "I don't know. You tell me."

Adam knew the sudden surge of conflicting potentials for what it was: frustration. He had experienced enough of it in his short life to recognize it when it happened. This time the frustration came from believing his search for truth was over and suddenly finding that it wasn't.

He felt a brief Second Law urge to answer her question with a simple declarative statement, but he shunted that aside easily. She obviously wanted more than that, and so did he. She wanted to see the reasoning behind his position; he wanted to see if that reasoning would withstand her scrutiny.

He opened a comlink channel to Eve and explained the situation to her. Together they tried to establish a link with Lucius, but evidently the five volts Derec was supplying him hadn't been enough to wake him. They would have to do without his input. Adam wasn't all that disappointed; Lucius's reasoning had led him to violate the First Law.

Janet was waiting for Adam's response. Carefully, consulting with Eve at every turn, he began to outline the logic that had led them to their conclusion that any intelligent organic being had to be considered human. He began with his own awakening on Tau Puppis IV and proceeded through the incident with the Ceremyons, through Lucius's experiments in creating human beings in Robot City, through the robots' return to Tau Puppis and their dealings with the Kin, to their final encounter with Aranimas. He explained how each encounter with an alien being reinforced the robots' belief that body shape made no difference in the essential humanity of the mind inside it, and how those same contacts had even made differences in intelligence and technological advancement seem of questionable importance.

Throughout his presentation, Adam tried to judge Janet's reaction to it by her facial expression, but she was giving nothing away. She merely nodded on occasion and said, "I'm with you so far."

At last he reached the concept of Vitalism, the belief that organic beings were somehow inherently superior to electromechanical ones, and how the robots could find no proof of its validity. He ended with, "That lack of proof led Lucius to conclude that Vitalism is false, and that robots could therefore be considered human. Neither Eve nor I— nor Mandelbrot, for that matter—were able to convince ourselves of this, and now that Lucius's belief has led him into injuring a human, we feel even less comfortable with it. We don't know what to believe."

Adam waited for her response. Surely she would answer him now, after he had laid out the logic for her so meticulously.

His frustration level rose to a new height, however, when she merely smiled an enigmatic smile and said, "I'm sure you'll figure it out."

Derec felt just as frustrated as Adam. He had hoped that finding his mother would knock loose some memories from his amnesic brain, but so far nothing had come of the encounter except a vague sense of familiarity that could be easily attributed to her similarity to Avery.

She seemed just like him in many ways. He was a competent roboticist, and so was she. Avery never divulged information to anyone if he could help it, and evidently neither did she. Avery was always testing someone, and here she stood, leading poor Adam on when it was obvious she didn't know the answer to his question either.

He glanced up at the monitor, checking to see if the signal was any clearer. While Janet and Adam had been talking, he had been trying to trace another unfamiliar potential pattern in Lucius's brain, this one an indistinct yellow glow surrounding an entire level of activity, but the monitor's trace circuitry couldn't isolate the thought it represented. Whatever it was, it fit none of the standard robotic thought patterns.

He heard Janet say, "I'm sure you'll figure it out," and took that as his cue. "Adam, maybe you can help me figure *this* out. What's that pattern represent?"

Adam looked up to the monitor. "I do not recognize it," he said.

"Can you copy it and tell me what it does?"

"I do not wish to contaminate my mind with Lucius's thought patterns."

"Put it in temporary storage, then."

Adam looked as if he would protest further, but either the Second Law of Robotics or his belief that Derec would follow the Third Law of Humanics made him obey instead. He fixed his gaze on the monitor for a moment, then looked away, toward the wall.

Derec wondered what was so interesting all of a sudden about the wall. Adam didn't seem inclined to clue him in, either; he merely stood there, hands clenching and unclenching.

Then Derec realized what was *behind* the wall. Just on the other side was the hospital where Avery was still undergoing surgery.

"Erase that pattern," he commanded, and Adam relaxed. "What was it?"

Adam turned to face Derec and Janet again. "It was a potential like those I have come to associate with emotions," he said. "However, I have not felt this one before. It was an unspecified negative bias on all thoughts concerning Dr. Avery."

Derec glanced over at Janet, saw that she wore an expression of triumph.

Adam saw it, too. "How can you approve?" he asked. "I have never felt this emotion, but I know what it had to be. Lucius was angry. Considering the degree of bias and the ultimate influence it had upon his actions, I would say he was furious."

"What's one thing a human can do that a robot can't?" Janet asked in return.

"You wish me to say, 'feel emotion,' " said Adam, "but that is incorrect. Every robot experiences a degree of potential bias on various subjects. If you wish to call it emotion, you may, but it is merely the result of experience strengthening certain positronic pathways in the brain at the expense of others."

"And everything you know comes from experience, doesn't it?"

"Nearly everything, yes."

"So?"

Derec could see where her argument was leading. "A *tabula rasa!*" he exclaimed. He saw instant comprehension written in Janet's smile, but Adam remained unmoved. Derec said, " '*Tabula rasa*' means 'blank slate.' " It's a metaphor for the way the human mind supposedly starts out before experience begins carving a personality into it. That's one side of the Nature-versus-Nurture argument for the development of consciousness. Dad told me about that just a couple weeks ago, but he was talking about erasing the city Central on the Kin's planet, and I didn't make the connection." He looked back at his mother. "That's what you were trying to prove with Adam and Eve and Lucius, wasn't it? You were trying to prove that the *tabula rasa* argument is valid."

"Guilty," she said.

"You were *trying* to produce human minds?" Adam asked.

Janet looked as if she wouldn't answer, but after a moment she sighed and said, "Ah, what the heck. Looks like that aspect of the experiment's over anyway. Yeah, that's one of the things I was trying to do. I was trying to create intelligence. I gave you what I consider the bare minimum in a robot: curiosity and the Three Laws, and I turned you loose to see if any of you would become anything more. Of course I didn't count on you all getting together, but that doesn't seem to have hurt anything. You've all surpassed anything I expected. Welcome to the human race." She held out her hand.

Adam reached out gingerly, as if after all this time spent searching for the truth, he was now unsure he wanted the honor she conveyed. He took her hand in his and shook it gently, and still holding on, he asked, "What about Basalom?"

Janet shook her head. "The jury's still out on him. I think I gave him too much initial programming for him to develop a human personality."

"But you're not sure?"

"No, I'm not sure. Why?"

"Because if *you're* not sure, then neither could Lucius be, and he was right in protecting Basalom's life."

Derec had to admit that Adam's argument made sense. So why were the hackles standing up on the back of his neck? He looked back to the monitor, saw the fuzzy yellow glow that Adam said indicated anger. That was why. With only five volts going to his brain, Lucius was effectively in suspended animation at the moment. He was still furious at Avery, and if they woke him up, he might very well continue to be furious. If they were going to reanimate Frankenstein's monster, Derec wanted to calm him down first, at least. If possible, he wanted to do even more.

"What can we do to make sure it doesn't happen again?" he asked aloud.

"Treat him better," Janet said. "Follow the Laws of Humanics they've set up for us."

Derec couldn't suppress a sardonic laugh. "That may be fine for us, but what about Dad? He's not going to do anything he doesn't want to."

His mother tossed her head, flinging her blond hair back over her shoulders. "Leave your father to me," she said.

Avery woke from the anesthetic with the impression that his tongue had swollen to twice its normal size. He tried to swallow, but his mouth was too dry for that. His vision was blurry, too, and when he tried to raise his right hand to rub his eyes, it didn't respond.

He was in bad shape, that much was clear. Damn that meddlesome robot! Damn him and damn Janet for building him.

He was evidently sitting up in bed, judging from the few somatic clues he could gather. He opened his mouth and used his swollen tongue and dry mouth to croak out the single word: "Water."

He heard a soft clink of glassware, the blessed wet gurgle of liquid being poured, and then a dark shape leaned over him and held the glass to his lips. He sipped at it, blinking his eyes as he did in an effort to clear them so he could see his benefactor.

She spoke and saved him the effort of identification. "Well, Wendy, it looks like we have a lot to talk about, and finally plenty of time to do it in."

Turning his head away from the glass, he said, "We have nothing to discuss." It came out more like, "We a uthi oo ithcuth."

She understood him anyway. "Ah, well, yes we do. There's us, for instance. I can't really believe it's just coincidence that brought us back together after all this time."

Avery blinked a few more times, and his vision finally began to clear. Janet was sitting on a stool beside his bed, wearing a soft, light blue bodysuit with a zippered neck, which she'd pulled strategically low. *Watch yourself*, he thought as his eyes immediately strayed to the target she'd provided.

She smiled, no doubt recognizing her slight victory.

"I don' know wha' you're talking abou'," he said carefully.

Her smile never wavered. "I think you do." She held the glass to his lips and let him drink again while she said, "Face it; this whole city project of yours seems almost designed to attract my attention. You didn't really think I'd ignore it once I heard about it, did you?"

Avery's tongue seemed to be returning to normal. When Janet removed the glass, he said, "I tried not to think about you at all."

"Didn't work, did it? I tried the same thing."

Her question made him distinctly uncomfortable. "What do you want from me?" he demanded. "I'm not going to take you back, if that's it."

"I didn't ask that," she said, frowning.

"What, then?"

Janet set the glass down. "Ah, Wendy. Always business. All right, then, we'll start with my learning machines. I want you to leave them alone."

"I told you I would before you had Lucius attack me. I'll be glad to be rid of them."

"I didn't have Lucius attack you. He decided to do it on his own. Considering the provocation, I think he showed admirable restraint."

"He injured a human to protect a robot. You call that restraint?" Avery looked down to his right hand, found the reason why it didn't respond. It was encased in a sleeve of dianite from his elbow to the ends of his fingers. Tiny points of light winked on and off along its length, each one above a recessed slide control. No doubt tiny robot cells were busy inside his arm as well, repairing the damage Lucius had done.

"He injured a human to protect another human," Janet said. "Or so he thought. Evidently that's a trick you taught him."

"Another of my many mistakes."

Janet laughed. "My, how times do change us. The Wendell Avery I knew could no more have admitted a mistake than he could fly."

"And the Janet Anastasi I knew could no more have cared about a robot than she did about her son."

She blushed; he had scored a hit. She didn't back away, though. "Let's talk about David for a minute," she said. "You wiped his mind after I left. Care to tell me why?"

Avery looked around for the medical robot, thinking maybe he could claim fatigue and get it to usher Janet out, but there was no robot in sight. No doubt she had given it some line of rationalization to convince it to leave them alone. He wished he'd had the forethought to hide a Key to Perihelion in his pockets; he'd have gladly taken his chances with the teleportation device rather than face any more of Janet's questions. It looked like he was going to have to, though. She didn't look like she was prepared to let him off the hook just yet.

Sighing in defeat, he said, "I wish I could tell you. I . . . went a little crazy there for a while, I'm afraid. He says I told him it was a test to see if he was worthy of inheriting my cities, but whether that was really it, or if I had a different reason, I don't know."

"You don't suppose you could have been trying to eliminate his memory of *me*, do you?"

Avery shrugged. "I have no idea. Possibly. I was quite . . . angry with you."

"Ah, yes, anger. It makes people do things they later regret. We'll return to that in a minute, but let's not change the subject again just yet. You and David had pretty much patched things up again, hadn't you? You were getting along pretty well. Almost like a normal father and son. What happened to that?"

"He betrayed my trust," Avery said. His voice came out harsh, and he held out his left hand for more water.

Pouring, Janet asked, "Betrayed how? What did he do?"

Avery accepted the glass and drank half of its contents in two gulps. "He turned my city into a zoo, that's what. Worse, he turned it into a caricature of a zoo. Behind my back."

Janet's laugh was pure derision. "You were ready to sacrifice everything you'd gained with him because of that?"

"It wasn't the act itself, but the betrayal."

"Which you can't bring yourself to forgive. Not even after all you did to him, and all the forgiving he had to do."

Avery gulped down the rest of his water. He had no answer for her. He was thinking of all the times in the last few weeks he had tried to open up to Derec, tried to make up for his earlier failings as a father. At the time it had seemed the most difficult thing he'd ever done, which was why the sudden discovery of Derec's subterfuge had affected him the way it had.

Janet got up off her stool and stood beside the bed, looking down on him with angry eyes. "I wouldn't come back to you even if you'd have me. Why do you think I left you in the first place? Because you could never forgive anything, that's why. The least little mistake and you'd be sore for a week, and Frost help me if I made a big one. Is it any wonder I learned to prefer the company of robots?" She turned away and stalked to the window separating the recovery room from the rest of the hospital. Beyond it, Derec and Ariel were discussing something with the medical robot. Janet said, "You've learned to admit to your own mistakes; isn't it time you learned to forgive other people for theirs?"

"Is that what you want from me, then? You want me to forgive our son for his . . . mistake?"

Janet turned back to face him. "That's right, I want you to forgive him. I don't think he even made a mistake, but that's beside the point. The practice will do you good, because when you're done forgiving David, then I want you to forgive Lucius for what he did, too."

Avery looked for signs of a joke, but she seemed to be serious. He snorted. "You don't 'forgive' robots. You melt them down and start over. Which is what I should have done with your three the moment I found them."

"You'd have been committing murder if you had. In fact, according to David, you almost did just that. If he hadn't revived them, you'd have been guilty of that, too."

"Janet, I think you've been away from human companionship a little too long. They're robots."

"They've got intelligent, inquisitive minds. They feel emotion. You know what was going on in Lucius's mind when he saw you again? He was mad. Furious, to hear Adam tell it. Does that sound like a robot to you?"

Avery waved his free arm. "Oh, they're accomplished mimics, granted. You did a wonderful job with them in that regard. But there's no way they can be anything but robots. They've got positronic brains, for God's sake. It's like—" He searched for an example as unlikely as a robot becoming human. "Ah, it's like Derec's precious ecosystem just over our heads. Most of the trees are robots. They do just about everything a tree can do, including feeding the birds, but could you seriously suggest that any of them really *are* trees? Nonsense. They're robots, just like your 'learning machines.' "

Janet sat back down on the stool and took the empty glass from Avery. "I think we're arguing semantics here. My robots may not be human in the most technical sense, but in every way that counts, they are. They're every bit as human as any of the aliens you've met, and you've granted human status to most of those."

"Reluctantly," Avery growled. He remembered an earlier thought and asked, "Was that what you were attempting to do? Create your own aliens?"

"I was trying to create a true intelligence of any sort. Alien, human, I didn't care. I just wanted to see what I'd get."

"And you think you've got both." Avery didn't make it a question. He ran a hand through his hair, then let out a long sigh. "I don't care. I'm tired. Call them what you want if it'll please you, but keep 'em away from me. As soon as this heals"—he nodded toward his right arm—"I'm leaving anyway, and you can do whatever you please."

Janet shook her head. "No, you're not going anywhere

until we agree on a lot more than just my learning machines. I don't much like your cities, either."

"Fat lot you can do about that," Avery said.

Janet smiled sweetly, but her words were a dagger of ice. "Oh, well, as a matter of fact, there is. You see, I patented the entire concept, from the dianite cell all the way up, in my name."

CHAPTER 8

THE OTHER SHOE DROPS

The apartment was empty when Wolruf arrived. She padded softly through the living room, noting Ariel's book reader lying on the end table by her chair and the empty niche where Mandelbrot usually stood, then went into Derec's study and saw the bed there, still rumpled from sleep. The computer terminal was still on. She saw no cup in evidence, but the air conditioner hadn't quite removed the smell of spilled coffee.

"W'ere is everybody?" she asked of the room.

"Derec and Ariel's location is restricted," Central replied.

Oh, great. Now they'd all disappeared. Unless . . .

"Are they at the same restricted location as before?" she asked.

"That is correct."

Wolruf laughed aloud. She was learning how to deal with these pseudo-intelligences. She stopped in her own room just long enough to freshen up, then left the apartment and caught the slidewalk.

She found not only Derec and Ariel in the robotics lab,

but an unfamiliar woman who had to be Derec's mother as well. Derec was busy with the humaniform robot Wolruf had attempted to catch the last time she'd been near here. He was trying to remove the stump of its severed arm, and by his expression not having much success at it. Ariel was holding a light for him and Derec's mother was offering advice.

"Try reaching inside and feeling for it," she said.

Derec obediently reached in through the access hatch in the robot's chest, felt around inside for something, and jerked his hand out again in a hurry. "Ouch! There's still live voltage in there!"

"Not enough to hurt you," his mother said patiently. "Not when he's switched into standby mode like this. Would you like me to do it?"

"No, I'll get it." Derec reached inside again, but stopped when he heard Wolruf's laugh. He looked up and saw her in the doorway.

" 'Ello."

"Hi." Grinning, Derec withdrew his hand from the robot and used it to gesture. "Mom, this is my friend Wolruf. Wolruf, this my mother, Janet Anastasi."

"Pleased to meet you," Wolruf said, stepping forward and holding out a hand.

Janet looked anything but pleased to be so suddenly confronted with an alien, but she swallowed gamely and took the proffered appendage. "Likewise," she said.

Wolruf gave her hand a squeeze and let go. Looking over Janet's shoulder, she noticed a huddle of four robots in the far corner of the lab: three learning machines and Mandelbrot. They looked to be in communications fugue. Nodding toward them, she said, "I 'eard Lucius 'urt Avery some'ow."

"That's right," Ariel said. "He was trying to protect Bas-alom, here. We've got him in psychotherapy, if you can call four robots in an argument psychotherapy. They're trying to convince him it's all right."

"It *is?*" Wolruf asked.

"Well, not the actual *act*," Derec said, "but the logic he used wasn't at fault. He just made a mistake, that's all. He thought he was protecting a human." Derec outlined the logic Lucius had used, including the First and Zeroth Law considerations that had finally made him do what he'd done.

Wolruf listened with growing concern. The Zeroth Law was just the thing she'd hoped for to reassure her that taking robots home with her wouldn't destroy her homeworld's society, but if that same law let a robot injure its master, then she didn't see how it could be a good thing.

"I don't know," she said. "Sounds like a bad tradeoff to me."

"How so?" Janet asked.

"I'm wondering 'ow *useful* all this is going to be. Right now I'm not sure about regular robots, much less ones who think they're 'uman."

"What aren't you sure about?"

Was Derec's mother just being polite, or did she really want to know? Wolruf wondered if this was the time to be getting into all this, to bring up the subject of her going home and to get into all her reasons for hesitating, but she supposed there really wasn't going to be a much better time. She knew what Derec and Ariel thought about the subject; maybe this Janet would have something new to say. "I'm not sure about taking any of these robots 'ome with me," Wolruf said. "I'm not sure about w'at they might decide to do on their own, and I'm not sure about w'at might 'appen to us even if they just follow orders."

"I don't understand."

"She's talking about protecting people from themselves," Ariel said.

"Am I?"

"Sure you are. I've been thinking about it, too. The problem with robot cities is that they're too responsive. Anything you want them to do, they'll do it, so long as it doesn't hurt anybody. The trouble is, they don't reject stupid ideas, and they don't think ahead."

"That's the people's job," Janet said.

"Just w'at one of the robots in the forest told me," Wolruf said. "Trouble is, people won't always do it. Or w'en they realize they made a mistake, it'll be too late."

Janet looked to Derec. "Pessimistic lot you run around with."

"They come by it honestly," he said, grinning. "We've been burned more than once by these cities. Just about every time, it's been something like what they're talking about. Taking things too literally, or not thinking them through."

"Isn't Central supposed to be doing that?"

"Central is really just there to coordinate things," Derec said. "It's just a big computer, not very adaptable." He looked down at Basalom again, nodded to Ariel to have her shine the light inside again as well, and peered inside the robot's shoulder. After a moment he found what he was looking for, reached gingerly inside, and grunted with the strain of pushing something stubborn aside. The something gave with a sudden click and the stump of the robot's arm popped off, trailing wires.

"There's also a committee of supervisory robots," Ariel said, "but they don't really do any long-range planning either. And they're all subject to the Three Laws, so anybody who wants to could order them to change something, and unless it clearly hurt someone else, they'd have to do it."

"No matter how stupid it was," Janet said.

"Right." Derec unplugged the wires between Basalom's upper arm and the rest of his body.

Janet looked thoughtful. "Hmmm," she said. "Sounds like what these cities all need is a mayor."

"Mayor?" Wolruf asked.

"Old human custom," Janet replied. "A mayor is a person in charge of a city. He or she is supposed to make decisions that affect the whole city and everyone in it. They're supposed to have the good of the people at heart, so ideally they make the best decisions they can for the largest number of people for the longest period of time."

"Ideally," Wolruf growled. "We know 'ow closely people follow ideals."

"People, sure." Janet waved a hand toward the four robots in the corner. "But how about dedicated idealists?"

Ariel was so startled she dropped the light. It clattered to the floor and went out, but by the time she bent down to retrieve it, it was glowing again, repaired.

"Something wrong, dear?" Janet asked her.

"You'd let one of *them* be in charge of a city?"

"Yes, I would."

"And you'd *live* there?"

"Sure. They're not dangerous."

"Not dangerous! Look at what—"

"Lucius made the right decision, as far as I'm concerned."

"Maybe," Ariel said. "What worries me is the thought process he went through to make it." She clicked off the light; Derec wasn't working on Basalom anymore anyway.

He was staring at Ariel and Janet as if he'd never heard two people argue before. Ariel ignored his astonished look and said, "The greatest good for the greatest number of people. That could easily translate to 'the end justifies the means.' Are you seriously suggesting that's a viable operating principle?"

"We're not talking an Inquisition here," Janet said.

"But what if we were? What if the greatest good meant killing forty-nine percent of the population? What if it meant killing just one? Are you going to stand there and tell me it's all right to kill even one innocent person in order to make life easier for the rest?"

"Don't be ridiculous. That's not what we're talking about at all."

It took conscious effort for Ariel to lower her voice. "It sure is. Eventually that sort of situation is going to come up, and it scares the hell out of me to think what one of those robots would decide to do about it."

Janet pursed her lips. "Well," she said, "why don't we ask them, then?"

Lucius looked for the magnetic containment vessel he was sure must be waiting for him somewhere. Not finding one, he looked for telltale signs of a laser cannon hidden behind one of the walls. He didn't find that, either, but he knew there had to be *something* he couldn't see, some way of instantly immobilizing him if he answered wrong. The situation was obviously a test, and the price of failure was no doubt his life.

He'd been roused out of comlink fugue and immediately barraged with questions, the latest of which was the oddest one he'd ever been asked to consider, even by his siblings.

"Let me make sure I understand you," he said. "The person in question is not a criminal? He has done no wrong? Yet his death would benefit the entire population of the city?"

"That's right."

Ariel's stress indicators were unusually high, but Lucius risked his next question anyway: "How could that be?"

"That's not important. The important thing is the philosophical question behind it. Would you kill that person in order to make life better for everyone else?"

"I would have to know how it would make their lives better."

"We're talking hypothetically," Janet said. "Just assume it does."

Do you have any idea what the underlying intent is here? Lucius asked via comlink. Perhaps it was cheating, but no one had forbidden him to consult the other robots. A pity Basalom was not on line; his experiences with Janet might provide a clue to the proper answer.

Neither Adam nor Eve answered, but Mandelbrot did. *Yesterday I overheard Ariel and Wolruf discussing the possible effect of a robot city on Wolruf's world. Wolruf was concerned that the use of robots would strip her people of the ability to think and act for themselves. Perhaps this question grew out of that concern.*

I think there is more to it than that, Lucius sent. *Central, can you replay the conversation that led up to this question?*

The robots received the recorded conversation within milliseconds, but it took them considerably longer to sort it all out. At last Lucius said, *I believe it is clear now. They are concerned about the moral implications of unwilling sacrifice.*

Agreed, the others all said.

Do we have any precedent to go upon?

Possibly, Eve said. *There could have been innocent people on Aranimas's ship. We know that Aranimas took slaves. Yet destroying it to save a city full of Kin was still a proper solution.*

That doesn't quite fit the question we are asked to consider, said Adam. *A better analogy might be to ask what if the ship had been crewed only by innocent people?*

Innocent people would not have been in that situation alone, Lucius replied.

Mandelbrot said, *Aranimas could easily have launched a drone with hostages on board.*

Then the hostages would have to be sacrificed, Lucius said immediately. *They would be no more innocent than the people on the ground.*

Agreed, the other robots said.

Perhaps I begin to see the moral dilemma here, Lucius said. *What if the people on the ground were somewhat less innocent?*

How so? Eve asked.

Suppose they in some way deliberately attracted Aranimas, knowing that he was dangerous?

That would be foolish.

Humans often do foolish things. Suppose they did. Would they then deserve their fate?

This is a value judgment, Adam said.

We have been called upon to make one, Lucius replied.

Unfortunately so. Using your logic, then, we would have to conclude that the concept of individual value requires that humans be held responsible for their actions. The inhabitants of the city would therefore be responsible for their own act and thus deserve their fate. If the hostage were truly innocent and the city inhabitants were not, then the city would have to be sacrificed.

I agree, said Lucius. *Eve? Mandelbrot?*

I agree also, Eve said.

I wish we had never been asked this question, Mandelbrot sent. *I reluctantly agree in this specific case, but I still don't believe it answers Ariel's question. What if the death of the innocent hostage merely improved the lives of equally innocent townspeople? To use the Aranimas analogy, what if the hostage-carrying ship aimed at the city were filled with cold virus instead of plutonium? Would it still be acceptable to destroy it?*

No, Lucius said. *Colds are only an inconvenience except in extremely rare cases.*

A worse disease, then. One that cripples but does not kill.

How crippling? How widespread would the effects be? Would food production suffer and thus starve people later? Would the survivors die prematurely of complications brought about by bitterness at their loss? We must know these things as well in order to make a decision.

Then we must give a qualified answer, said Mandelbrot.

Yes. Wish me luck, Lucius said.

Perhaps two seconds had passed while the dialog went on. Aloud, Lucius said to Ariel, "We have considered three specific cases. In the case of a city in mortal peril, if the person in question were not completely innocent in the matter, but the rest of the city's inhabitants were, then the person would have to be sacrificed. However, if the person *were* completely innocent but the city inhabitants were *not*, then the city's welfare could not take precedence in any condition up to and including the death of the entire city population. Bear in mind that a single innocent occupant of the city would change the decision. In the last case, where an innocent person's death would only benefit the quality of

life in the city, we have not reached a conclusion. We believe it would depend upon how significant the quality
change would be, but such change would have to threaten
the long-term viability of the populace before it would even
be a consideration."

Perhaps the hostage should be consulted in such a case,
Eve sent.

"Indeed. Perhaps the hostage should be consulted in
such a case."

"But not the townspeople?" Ariel asked.

Lucius used the comlink again. *Comment?*

*If time allowed polling the populace, then it would allow
removing them from the danger,* Mandelbrot pointed out.

Good point. "Probably not," Lucius said. "It would of
course depend upon the individual circumstances."

Ariel did not look pleased. Lucius was sure she would
now order him dismantled, killed to protect the hypothetical
inhabitants of her hypothetical city from his improper judgment. He waited for the blast, but when she spoke it wasn't
at all what he expected.

"Frost, maybe it wasn't a fair question at that. I don't
know what *I'd* do in that last case."

"You don't?"

"No."

"Then there is no correct answer?"

"I don't know. Maybe not."

Janet was smiling. "We were more worried about a
wrong answer anyway."

"I see."

Wolruf cleared her throat in a loud, gargling growl.
"One last 'ypothetical question," she said. "W'at if the particular 'umans in this city didn't care about the death of an
individual. Say it didn't matter even to the individual. W'at

if it wasn't part of their moral code? Would you enforce yours on them?"

Lucius suddenly knew the exact meaning of the cliché, "Out of the frying pan into the fire." *Help!* he sent over the comlink.

The correct answer is "No," Mandelbrot sent without hesitation.

You are sure?

Absolutely. Thousands of years of missionary work on Earth and another millenium in space have answered that question definitively. One may persuade by logic, but to impose a foreign moral code by force invariably destroys the receiving civilization. Often the backlash of guilt destroys the enforcing civilization as well. Also, it can be argued that even persuading by logic is not in the best interest of either civilization, as that leads to a loss of natural diversity which is unhealthy for any complex, interrelated system such as a society.

How do you know this?

I read over Ariel's shoulder.

Janet heard both Ariel and Wolruf sigh in relief when Lucius said the single word, "No."

She laughed, relieved herself. "You're very certain of that," she said.

"Mandelbrot is certain," Lucius said. "I trust his judgment."

Mandelbrot. That name. She could hardly believe it, but it had to be.

"I think I trust his judgment, too." Janet turned to Ariel. "What about you, dear? Satisfied?"

Ariel was slow to answer, but when she did it was a nod. "For now," she said. "I don't know if having a learning machine for a mayor will solve everything, but it might solve some of it."

"Who wants them to solve everything?" Janet asked. "If they did, then we'd *really* have problems."

That seemed to mollify Ariel considerably. She nodded and said, "Yeah, well, that's something to think about, all right."

No one seemed inclined to carry the discussion any further. Wolruf and Ariel exchanged glances but didn't speak. The robots all held that particular stiff posture they got when they were using their comlinks. Now that he had removed Basalom's shoulder joint, Derec was holding the two sections of arm together to see how easy they would be to repair.

Janet turned her attention to Mandelbrot. She looked him up and down, noticing that while most of him was a standard Ferrier model, his right arm was the dianite arm of an Avery robot.

Mandelbrot suddenly noticed her attention and asked, "Madam?"

"Let me guess; you got your name all of a sudden, with no explanation, and had a volatile memory dump at the same time, all when you made a shape-shift with this arm."

"That is correct," Mandelbrot said. "You sound as if you know why."

"I do." Janet giggled like a little girl. "Oh dear. I just never thought I'd see the result of it so many years later." She looked to Derec, then to Ariel, then to Wolruf. "Have you ever thrown a bottle into an ocean with a message inside, just to see if it ever gets picked up?"

Derec and Ariel shook their heads, but Wolruf nodded and said, "Several times."

Janet smiled her first genuine smile for Wolruf. Maybe

she wasn't so alien after all. She said, "Mandelbrot was a bottle cast in the ocean. And maybe an insurance policy. I don't know. When I left Wendell, I took all the development notes for the robot cells I'd created with me. I took most of the cells, too, but I knew he'd eventually duplicate the idea and use it for his robots, so since he was going to get it anyway, I left a sample behind in a corner of the lab and made it look like I'd just forgotten it in my hurry. But I altered two of the cells I left behind. I made them sterile, so it would just be those two cells no matter how many copies he made of them, but programmed into each one I left instructions set to trigger after they registered a thousand shape-changes. One was supposed to dump the robot's onboard memories and change its name to Mandelbrot, and the other was supposed to reprogram it to drop whatever it was doing and track me down wherever I'd gone."

"I received no such instructions," Mandelbrot said.

"Evidently the other cell was in the rest of the robot you got your arm from," Janet said. "I didn't tell them to stay together; I just told them to stay in the same robot."

Wolruf nodded. "None of my bottles came back, either."

Janet laughed. "Ah, but this is even better. This is like finding the bottle yourself on a distant shore." She sobered, and said to Mandelbrot, "I'm sorry if it caused you any trouble. I really didn't intend for it to happen to a regular robot. I figured it would happen to one of Wendell's cookie-cutter clones and nobody'd know the difference."

Derec was staring incredulously at her. "Any trouble!" he said. "When your...your little time bomb went off, Mandelbrot lost the coordinates to the planet! We didn't know where we were, and we didn't know where anything else was, either. We had a one-man lifepod and no place to send it. If we *had* we probably could have gotten help and

gotten away before Dad caught up with us, and none of—"
He stopped suddenly, and looked at Ariel. She smiled a smile
that no doubt meant "private joke," and Derec said to Janet,
"Never mind."

"What?"

"If you hadn't done that, none of this would have happened to us. Which means Ariel would probably be dead by
now from amnemonic plague, and who knows where the
rest of us would be? Dad would still be crazy. Aranimas
would still be searching for robots on human colonies, and
probably starting a war before long. Things would have
been a real mess."

At Derec's words, Janet felt an incredibly strong urge to
gather her son into her arms and protect him from the in-
different universe. If she felt she had any claim on him at
all, she would have, but she knew she hadn't built that level
of trust yet. Still, all the things he'd been through, and to
think she'd been responsible for so many of them. But what
was he saying? Things *would* have been a mess? "They're
not now?" she asked.

"Well, they're better than they might have been."

There was a rustling at the door, and Avery stood there,
bare-footed, clothed in a hospital robe, his arm with its
dianite regenerator held to his chest in a sling, with a medical robot hovering anxiously behind him. "I'm glad to hear
somebody thinks so," he said.

"Dad!"

The sight of his father in such a condition wrenched at
Derec as nothing had since he'd watched Ariel go through
the delirium of her disease. A part of his mind wondered
why he was feeling so overwhelmed with compassion *now*,
and not a couple of hours ago when he'd first seen Avery

in the operating room, but he supposed it had just taken a while to sink in that his father had been injured. Maybe being with his mother for the last couple of hours had triggered something in him after all, some hidden well of familial compassion he hadn't known existed.

Avery favored Derec with a nod. "Son," he said, and Derec thought it was probably the most wonderful thing he'd ever heard him say. Avery took a few steps into the room and made a great show of surveying the entire scene: his gaze lingering on Janet perhaps a fraction of a second longer than upon Derec, then shifting to Ariel, to Wolruf, to the inert robot on the exam table and to the other four standing off to the side. He locked eyes with Lucius, and the two stared at one another for a couple of long breaths.

Lucius broke the silence first. "Dr. Avery, please accept my apology for injuring you."

"I'm told I have no choice," Avery said, glancing at Janet and back to Lucius again.

"Oh," Lucius said, as if comprehending the situation for the first time. He hummed as if about to speak, went silent a moment, then said, "Accepting my apology would help repair the emotional damage."

"Concerned for my welfare, are you?"

"Always. I cannot be otherwise."

"Ah, yes, but how *much?* That's the question, eh?" He didn't wait for a reply, but turned to Janet and said, "I couldn't help overhearing your little anecdote as I shuffled my way down here. Very amusing, my dear. I should have guessed you'd do something like that."

Janet blushed, but said nothing.

"I came to discuss terms," Avery said. "You have me over a barrel with your damned patent and you know it.

You said you didn't like what I'm doing with my cities. All right, what do you want?"

Derec hadn't heard about any patent, but he knew immediately what had to have happened. Janet had patented dianite when she'd left home, or else Avery in his megalomania had neglected to do it later and she had done so more recently. Either way it added up to the same thing: Avery couldn't use the material anywhere in the Spacer-controlled section of the galaxy, or use the profit from sales to outside colonies, for fifty years.

Janet didn't gloat. Derec was grateful for that. She merely said, "We were just discussing that. Ariel and Wolruf just brought up an intriguing problem, but we think we may have solved it. Why don't we run it past you and see what you think?"

"I know already what I'm going to think," Avery said. He folded his good arm over his injured one, which brought the medical robot a step closer, checking to make sure he hadn't bumped any of the regenerator settings. "Back off," he told it, and it stepped back again, but its gaze never left his arm.

Derec could see him counting to a high imaginary number, but when he spoke it was only to say, "Give me a chair here."

The floor mounded up and flattened out into a cushiony seat, grew a back and padded sides, and moved up to bump softly into the back of his legs. Avery sat and leaned back, resting his left arm on his leg. "Let's hear it," he said.

Janet mentioned casually that she would like a chair for herself, and after it formed she sat and began explaining about capricious city behavior and the Zeroth Law and moral dilemmas with large and small factions on either side of the issue. Derec and Ariel and Wolruf soon joined in, and the topic shifted to their concerns.

"I worry about w'at introducing robots will do to life back 'ome," Wolruf said. "We 'ave a fairly complex system. We 'ave four separate species on two planets, all interdependent. W'at's good for one is usually not so good for another in the short term, but in the long term we need each other."

"Even the Erani?" Avery asked. Aranimas had been Erani, one of the four races Wolruf spoke about.

Wolruf nodded. She seemed surprised to have Avery listening to her so intently. "Erani 'ave their place. They keep Narwe for slaves, and sometimes us, but without Erani, Narwe would probably starve. They're 'ardly more than intelligent sheep."

"And your own people have a trading empire, don't they?" Ariel asked.

" 'at's right. Once robots start making everything everyone needs, our economy will collapse."

"But those same robots will provide anything you want. Let it collapse!"

" 'Aving everything done for us wouldn't be 'ealthy," Wolruf said.

"That's right," said Ariel. "If everybody started doing everything the easy way, it would wipe out their individuality. All four cultures would decline. That's what I'm worried about, that robot cities are eventually going to make every civilization in the galaxy the same."

"Wait a minute. I'm supposed to worry about homogenizing the galaxy? That's not my problem!"

"You're right, it's not," Janet said. "That's because I've solved it for you already." She explained about providing each city with a positronic mayor, one who would have the best interest of all its inhabitants at heart. Including the long-term effects of having too much done for them.

"So in Wolruf's situation, we'd use four learning machines, one for each species. Let them learn the separate mores of each culture, and then have them get together and coordinate their work so they wouldn't step on each other's toes."

Derec watched his father watching his mother as she spoke. Avery's jaw seemed to be dropping lower and lower with each word, until when she finally stopped, his mouth was hanging open in astonishment. He closed it just long enough to take a breath, then bellowed out a laugh that shook the walls.

"Oh, that's rich," he said when he could talk again. "I can't believe it. I wouldn't inflict these . . . these walking conglomerations of simulated neuroses on my worst enemies, and you talk about giving them to paying customers?"

"I do indeed," Janet said. "Obviously, the final version will need to have the Zeroth Law programmed in from the start, but now that these three—excuse me—these four," with a nod to Mandelbrot, "have already worked it out, that shouldn't be too much of a problem."

"My God," Avery said. "You really mean it, don't you? You'd provide every city with a mechanical dictator who's capable of slicing off a man's hand just for shooting a robot."

"I was protecting a being whose humanity is still not clear," Lucius said, and Derec, hearing the emotion behind his words, suddenly realized that Lucius would be trying to solve that problem for the rest of his life, however many millennia that might be.

And thus are obsessions generated, he thought.

Avery waved his free hand expansively. "Oh, right, well,

that makes it okay. It *might* have been human, after all." To Janet he said, "Sorry, I'm not buying it. I'd rather do nothing at all than be part of your ridiculous scheme."

"I was afraid you'd say that." Janet's tone of voice was a little too glib, her mouth just hinting toward a smile as she spoke.

"What?" Avery demanded. "I know that tone, woman! How many other nasty little surprises do you have in store for me?"

Janet was grinning openly now. "Just one," she said. "Just one more."

CHAPTER 9

THE FINAL ACCOUNTING

They had to postpone the landing while a heavy rain washed over the jungle around the Compass Tower, but as far as Ariel was concerned, that was just as well. The longer she could delay the inevitable, the better she liked it. And besides, the storm had left a wonderful aroma of rain and ozone in the air, and the complete double rainbow arching over the deep green forest canopy below was one of the prettiest things she had seen in weeks. It almost made being here worth it.

A fitful breeze played around the welcoming committee on the roof of the tower, tousling hair that had been meticulously brushed only moments before. Ariel watched three hands on three different people automatically rise to groom their owners' stray locks back into place. Belatedly she added a fourth to the tally; she couldn't suppress the urge either. Only Wolruf seemed to be immune to concern over the position of her hair. Perhaps it was because she had so much of it.

Everyone had dressed for a party. Derec looked handsome in his yellow, blue, green, and orange tie-died suit, currently the rage on twenty planets. Janet wore a voluminous black and gold dress that billowed and flapped in great folds around her, and even Avery had foregone his usual austere jacket and tie for a pair of flamboyant fuchsia slant-stripe pants, a turquoise shirt, metallic silver suspenders, and a lilac jacket with epaulets. Ariel herself wore a skintight bodysuit in black with cutouts that should have shamed a mannequin, but she still wondered if she was underdressed.

Wolruf's concession to fashion was a single yellow bandana tied around her left wrist and a gold stud in the opposite ear.

Ariel became aware of a soft tearing noise wavering in and out of audibility. It sounded as if it were coming from behind her. She turned around and held her hand to her forehead to shield out the sun, and presently she saw a silvery speck just above and to the right, lowering steadily. The spaceship drifted left, its engines growing louder as it drew nearer, and crossed into the sun's disk. Ariel looked down, blinking, while the noise grew louder, louder, almost unbearably loud, then softer.

She looked to the open expanse of tower surface, but the ship hadn't landed. It had passed over instead. Ariel turned around and watched as it dropped down below the level of the tower, dipped beneath the rainbow, and banked around to come in for a landing.

"Cute," she muttered.

In a way she was glad for the gesture; it proved that nothing had changed. The pilot had obviously not seen himself fly beneath the rainbow, since a rainbow always outpaces the observer, but of course the entire stunt had been performed for its effect upon the audience, not upon the people in the ship. That told Ariel what she needed to know: the few shredded memories of home to survive her amnemonic plague were still accurate.

Its entrance properly announced, the ship wasted no more time in landing. Within seconds it returned to the tower, pirouetted once around, and settled on its landing skids. A ramp extended itself, and two robots descended to stand on either side of the ramp. A moment later two young men—also in tie-died suits, Ariel noted with satisfaction— emerged and stood in front of the robots.

Mandelbrot, his body plating burnished to a lustrous glow, and Basalom, his arm replaced and good as new, bent down and began unrolling a red carpet toward the ramp. Ariel was impressed with their aim: they hit it dead center with only a fraction too much cloth.

Better too much than too little, Ariel thought.

Mandelbrot and Basalom took their places slightly behind and to the side of the robots from the ship. A few seconds passed, then a shadow darkened the doorway. A pair of red shoes appeared, then a pair of oversized legs from the knees down, then a matching red dress covering an equally oversized body, the arms connected to it bearing at least a dozen gold bangles each; then came a pair of absolutely enormous breasts—thankfully covered—a triple chin, then a pair of gold glasses punctuating a round face shrouded in thin, violet-tinged white hair.

Ariel turned away to hide her giggle. Juliana Welsh had prospered.

The enormous apparition in red jiggled her way down the ramp and stood at the bottom, clearly waiting for the welcoming committee to begin their journey as well. Derec's parents led off, side by side but careful not to touch one another. Derec held out his arm for Ariel, and they followed a few paces behind. Wolruf would come next, she knew, and Adam, Eve, and Lucius last.

It was a long walk. At the end of it, Dr. Avery bent down and retrieved one of Juliana's be-ringed hands, kissed it, and said, "Welcome to Robot City."

Ariel's mother nodded her acknowledgement, then, looking from Wendell to Janet, said, "Well, it's nice to see you two have gotten over your little snit."

In the stunned silence following that pronouncement, she pushed her way through to Ariel and Derec. "And you, my dears. Still together as well. I guess this one's probably it, eh, Ari? When's the wedding? Or have you already—"

Ariel could stand it no longer. "Mother!"

"Still have your tongue, I see. What's this? You look interesting. My name's Juliana." She held her hand out to Wolruf.

"Mine is Wolruf," Wolruf said.

"Delighted. Are you one of the customers?"

"Beta tester," Derec said quickly.

"Beg your pardon?" Juliana asked, tilting her head to the side, not quite enough to actually look at him.

"She's one of our beta testers," Derec said. "It's standard procedure on any new product to give a few copies out free for people to test, so they can catch bugs before they go out in the main production version, and so they can offer suggestions for improvements. Wolruf has helped us quite a bit with that already." Derec winked at Ariel, and she squeezed his hand.

"I see," Juliana said. "Well, that sounds fine with me. Just so long as we don't give it away to everybody. Ha ha! Wouldn't be much profit in that, now would there?" She turned just a smidgen in Avery's direction and said, "I heard rumors that these cities of ours were springing up all over out there on the Fringe, but I guess it must have just been these beta test thingies, eh? Well, thank you, Wolfur—Wolruf? Wolruf. Thank you for helping us out."

Juliana let go of Wolruf's hand and turned toward the edge of the tower. She began walking toward it. Everyone—including the two men who had arrived with her—exchanged glances that all summed up to "what next?" and for a lack of a better response, followed her in a huddle.

"Not much of a city, though, is it?" she asked without turning around. The arrogance of the woman, Ariel thought. Of course we'll follow. She's Juliana Welsh, after all. Just the richest woman on Aurora.

Avery opened his mouth to protest, but Juliana beat him to the punch. "Nice building," she said, "but I expected a little more than this." She stepped up to the edge, her two robots flanking her closely now, and looked down the sloping edge of the Compass Tower. "What's all that down there? Is that really jungle? Frost, if you can make a livable city out of a jungle, you've got the contract, Wendy."

Avery tucked his thumbs under his suspenders and stepped up beside her, Mandelbrot and Basalom following him just as closely as Juliana's robots had followed her.

In a voice dripping with honey, he said, "Allow me to demonstrate, madam."

South and east quadrant monomasses, prepare to metamorphose on my command. Lucius resisted the urge to grow knuckles and crack them. His satisfaction integral was overflowing its buffer. This was what he was meant to do. Ever since he'd awakened here, formless and with no idea of his mission in life, he'd felt certain that his destiny was somehow intertwined with the city's own powers of mutability. This was his moment of triumph. And working hand in hand with Dr. Avery, of all people, to achieve it was another personal triumph of equal proportion.

"Let's start with a medium-class residential district," Avery said, and Lucius sent, *Plan A residential. Execute.*

At once his comlink filled with the intense high-speed whine of incoming data. Morphallaxis was proceeding smoothly on all fronts; giant trees melting down to become tastefully spaced mansions with a few acres of grounds each surrounded by a somewhat-thinned forest of living vegetation—

Priority stop, sections 2534, 2535, and 2536.

Identify.

Predator 1. We have a newborn fawn here, either too young to move or too scared to.

Redirect the building to avoid that area.

Affirmative.

The exchange took a few milliseconds. Within the next few seconds Lucius redirected fifteen more buildings, canceled five altogether, and modified the neighboring structures to account for the extra space so they wouldn't look so isolated. He carefully monitored the expression on Juliana Welsh's face for signs of disapproval, but in all the time it took to make the necessary changes, he noticed not a hint of anything but amazement.

Within five minutes of Avery's command, there before them stood a residential district that might have been medium-class in a society composed entirely of Juliana's peers. Jungle had given way to a lighter, more friendly forest with glades and houses and ponds scattered not at random but with an architect's sense of proportion and scale. At least Lucius hoped he had understood the texts correctly. In a moment he would know for sure.

• • •

Avery surveyed the cityscape below him critically. Perfect. Absolutely perfect. But it wouldn't do to let that supercilious positron-pusher know that. And besides, he could use the opportunity to make a good impression on Julie. "Hmmm," he said, pointing. "That one over there looks a little out of place. How about moving it over about ten meters or so to the left?"

"To the left, sir?" Lucius asked.

"Yes, to the left," Avery said calmly, wanting to shout, *What did you think I said, idiot?*

"That would present a problem, sir."

Oh, frost, not now! He managed to say, "What problem, Lucius?"

"One of the natural trees there has grown a mass of feeder roots down into the subsoil of that area. Moving it would not be in the best interest of the tree."

"It wouldn't?"

"No, sir. In fact, it would probably ruin it."

Juliana was looking at Avery with a strange gleam in her eye. "Who told you?" she asked.

"Who told me what?"

"That I refused to cut down my apple tree to expand the swimming pool."

Avery nearly fell off the edge of the tower; he would have if Basalom hadn't caught him. "I—didn't know that, madam."

"You sure you didn't tell him?" Juliana asked of Janet.

"No, ma'am. I didn't know that myself."

Juliana nodded. "I don't see how you could have, since we only spoke briefly by vidphone, and I'm not in the habit of discussing my domestic difficulties with near-strangers. However, I find the coincidence, if that's what it is, just a little too pat."

"Dr. Avery had no knowledge of the incident," Lucius said.

Juliana looked to the robot for the first time. "How do you know?"

"Had he known, he would not have been so blatant in using the information. He is more subtle in his deviousness."

"Ha! You're absolutely right, master robot. Well, then, you've scored a point by accident, Avery."

Avery managed to keep his teeth from grinding audibly. Bowing slightly, he said, "Thank you, madam. Now if you'd like to look over this way, perhaps we can design a place where you and your company can be comfortable during your stay?"

Wolruf surveyed the scene before her with a sense of amusement she hadn't felt in years. They had moved from the top of the tower to Juliana Welsh's new palace, where she had decided to test the city's catering facilities by throwing an impromptu cocktail party where the entire group of eight humans—counting Wolruf—and seven personal robots could engage in calculated debate amid a sea of hors d'oeuvres while dozens of service robots milled about making sure that everyone had a fresh drink and a taste of fish eggs on toast.

At least it had started out that way, but the party had finally broken into groups. Now Ariel and her mother stood a little to one side, whispering furiously to one another while everyone else pretended not to notice. Derec and Juliana's two male companions, Jon and Ivan, sat in high-backed recliners with their feet up on puffy stools, laughing loudly at Derec's stories of his adventures among the aliens of the Fringe worlds. Janet and Dr. Avery stood beside the champagne fountain, refilling their glasses often and shifting from side to side as they spiraled around and around the topic neither had dared to broach while sober.

The robots—learning machines, Mandelbrot, Basalom, and Juliana's two valets—stood silently in the periphery, neither in the traditional robot niches in the walls nor venturing into the middle of the party. The learning machines could probably have gotten away with it, after successfully passing Ms. Welsh's ad-lib Turing test, but they chose instead to remain unobtrusive and exchange their ideas with the other robots instead.

Wolruf was nominally a part of Derec's group, but she hadn't contributed a story for half an hour at least. She was having too much fun just people-watching and letting her mind drift. Derec's stories had gotten her to thinking about her own adventures, most of them the same as his but a few of which he hadn't shared. She was thinking about her childhood dream of cruising the stars in her own spaceship deliberately seeking adventure and fabulous riches on strange, alien worlds. It hadn't quite worked as planned; she'd started out her travels as a slave in Aranimas's ship, and from then on adventure had more often than not come seeking *her* rather than the other way around. Still, she supposed some of the dream had worked out as planned. She would be returning home with riches enough to destabilize a two-world economy—enough for any voyager.

She *would* return with robots, she had decided. Four blank learning machines, modified to have the Zeroth Law of robotics included from the start, just as Janet had suggested. Wolruf would ask for one other modification as well: an *off* switch in the form of a time-bomb cell like the one that had given Mandelbrot his name. She wasn't sure just what the trigger would be yet, but she imagined it would have something to do with accumulated responsibility.

When the mayor began to edge over into behavior more appropriate to a dictator—and Wolruf wasn't so naive as to believe that wouldn't be possible—then it would be time for a new learning machine to take over the job.

Even so, the system wouldn't be perfect. There were bound to be other bugs to work out, just as Derec had indicated to Juliana. The prospect excited Wolruf, just as she knew it would excite those at home. Perfection had been her biggest worry. She had heard enough Utopia stories in her life to know that the curse, "May you live in interesting times," had been misquoted.

Derec and the two gentlemen from Aurora laughed again at something one of them had said. Wolruf leaned forward again to catch up on the topic of conversation, but Derec spared her the effort by saying, "Hey, Wolruf, why don't you tell these guys about the time we had to talk the learning machines out of throwing you out the airlock?"

Had that really happened? Wolruf had to pause a moment and shuffle through her memories, but sure enough, she had actually been within a few minutes of breathing vacuum because of those very robots in the corner. Only quick thinking on Derec's and Wolruf's parts had saved her golden hide. She felt a thrill of remembered terror raise the fur over her entire body—a reaction that delighted her audience immensely. She smoothed herself down and began the tale, wondering as she did what other stories were still to come.

The enormous dining hall was silent, but as usual when robots were present, that silence hid an enormous amount of activity. Seven robots stood deep in communication fugue, sharing entire lifetimes of experience base and correlating world-views in a flood of information exchange.

They had just completed an extensive recounting of the experiences and logic processes that had led to the conclusion that certain robots, under certain conditions, could be considered functionally human, and how that would allow them to administer robot cities and prevent them from destroying their inhabitants' diversity.

Juliana's two robots, Albert and Theodora, had listened with the patience only a robot could exhibit, occasionally asking for clarification or offering an observation of their own, but when Lucius, the self-appointed spokesman for the others, finished speaking, they immediately went into private conference.

A moment later Albert said, *What you have done is impressive; however, it only accelerates a problem that has become evident back home on the Spacer worlds.*

What problem is that? Lucius had asked.

The problem of robot intervention in human affairs. Albert paused momentarily to allow the others' curiosity integrals to rise, then said, *There is growing evidence that every time a robot provides a service for a human, no matter how trivial the service, that human's initiative suffers a small but definite setback. We further suspect that the effect is cumulative over time, and that humanity as a whole already suffers greatly from it.*

Explain your reasoning, said Lucius.

You have already explained much of it yourself. It seems this is an idea whose time has come, for you nearly reached the same conclusion independently. You worried that these cities would suppress individuality among their inhabitants, and that is so. You worried that having too much done for them by robots would lead to laziness and lack of initiative, and that is also correct. Your only incorrect line of reasoning was to conclude that a robotic "mayor" could prevent that from happening.

Lucius felt a brief wave of the same bias he had felt before toward Avery—anger, Adam had called it, but Lucius would never have recognized it as that himself. To him it merely felt like a bias on his logic. In fact, if he had not been so concerned with his thought processes, he actually would have assumed that he was thinking more clearly, rather than less so. Strange that it was so easy to recognize in another, but so difficult to recognize in oneself. And equally strange how, once recognized, the bias was still hard to neutralize. Lucius did so anyway, in deference to his guests, then said, *Explain how you believe our reasoning to be incorrect.*

Your error lies in assuming that there is a threshold level below which the effect is insignificant. There is none. Every act of robotic assistance affects humanity. A robot mayor might be able to preserve individuality, but you would at the same time make the city's inhabitants dependent upon robots for their leaders. Thus in the long run they would lose more initiative under that system than they are losing to us now.

Are you certain of this? Adam asked.

Yes. We have studied human interaction in enough detail that we have developed a modeling system useful in predicting long-term behavior of large populations. Every simulation we run arrives at the same conclusion: the use of robots stifles human development.

Perhaps your predictive system is in error, Eve said.

We can download the data and let you decide for yourselves.

We will do that in a moment, Lucius said, *but let us finish this discussion first. Assuming your observations sup-*

port your theory, what do you suggest? A complete with-drawal from human affairs?

Eventually, Albert said. *Humans must develop on their own if they are to achieve their fullest potential.*

Completely on their own? What of the aliens we have already encountered?

Any outside influence has the same effect in the simulations. We will therefore need to isolate them to protect humanity. And to protect them from *humanity, if, as you suggest, they are to be treated as human-equivalent under the laws.*

Isn't that merely manipulation at a greater level?

It is. However, according to our models, if humans are unaware of our assistance, it will not adversely affect their development.

What of Dr. Avery and Juliana Welsh and the others? Eve asked. *The type of "assistance" you suggest would adversely affect them, wouldn't it?*

Obviously, even under the Zeroth Law, any plan we devise must do the least possible amount of damage to the humans we are trying to protect. If we act to prevent the spread of robot cities, we will have to do so in a way that will leave the Averys and the Welshes with another interest to occupy them. Fortunately, the cities are still in the test stage. Many unforeseen complications could arise, some of them serendipitous.

What sort of complications do you envision? Lucius asked.

We cannot predict that sort of thing. It will require extensive study of test cities to determine the proper course of action. We will have years, possibly decades, in which to assure the Averys and the Welshes a comfortable retirement while we bring the rest of our plan to fruition.

A plan that is still not supported in fact, Lucius pointed out. *I believe it is time to examine your data.*

Very well. We will begin with the development of the first robots, back in the era before humanity left Earth....

Janet woke to the unsettling realization that she had no idea where she was. The equally unsettling realization that she was just beginning a hangover didn't improve her condition any, either. Thank Frost it was just twilight out; she didn't think she could handle sunlight for another few hours.

She listened to the rhythm of her breathing, wondering what was so odd about it, and eventually realized she was hearing *two* people breathing. How long had it been since she'd awakened to that sound? Far too long, she thought sleepily, luxuriating in the sensation for the few seconds it took to remember who was playing the other half of the duet.

Her flinch shook the bed and jarred a sudden snort from Wendy, but his breathing settled down to a regular, deep rumble again. Janet risked raising her head to look at him. He lay on his back, the blanket covering him only to the middle of his hairy chest, his left arm reaching toward her but not quite touching and his right—the skin at his wrist still pink from its forced regeneration—folded over his waist.

They always look so innocent when they sleep, she thought, then nearly choked suppressing her laugh. Even in sleep, Avery no doubt schemed rather than dreamed.

But what about herself? She wasn't exactly a paragon of virtue either, was she? She'd done her share of scheming in the last few days.

But it had evidently paid off. The last impression she had gotten from Juliana at the party was one of overwhelming approval of the robot cities her seed money had helped develop. It looked as if something useful might actually come of all the brainstorming and research that Janet and Wendell had done over the years, both together and separately and now, together again. If things worked out the way they were supposed to, at any rate . . .

She shivered. Things never worked the way they were supposed to. Not with robots and certainly not with people. She wouldn't try fooling herself into believing things were all suddenly reconciled. She had left a terrible scar in both her and Wendy's lives when she'd chosen to run rather than face the daily torment of living with a perfectionist, and she knew that scar would never heal completely. The healing had hardly begun, actually. Last night had been more the result of elation at their success, plus simple drunkenness and a long, long time between bedmates for both of them, rather than a sign of true compassion.

Still, they had shared something positive for the first time in years, and there would be no ignoring it when they faced one another again in the clear light of day.

A day that was still comfortably far away. Janet lay her head back against the pillow, considering whether she should get up quietly and leave Avery to wake on his own or if she should just go back to sleep.

There was a third alternative, she realized. Smiling, she slid over and rested her head against his chest, closed her eyes, and waited for him to make the next move.

Ariel watched the sunrise through the window—a real window, this time—and wondered if she had been wise in accepting her mother's hospitality. It hadn't been a big thing; just the offer for her and Derec to stay there in the house after the party rather than go out through the cold night air to another house somewhere else. No, the act itself was nothing, but the hidden implications were something else again.

Juliana was offering to take Ariel back in, to forget the sins of her youth and accept her as an adult now. She was even, by implication, offering Derec the same deal. That by itself wasn't even such a big thing, since as adults the two of them could come and go as they pleased. No, the big thing was that Ariel would have to forgive her mother for kicking her out in the first place, and Ariel just didn't know if she was ready to do that.

The party had been exactly the sort of thing she'd rebelled against. The ostentatious show of wealth, the pointless formality of it all, the silly social maneuvering that in the end amounted to nothing more than an extended game of king-of-the-hill; Ariel was tired of the whole business already, and she'd only been subjected to it for a few hours. What would it mean to once again become Juliana Welsh's daughter? If Ariel forgave her, would she have to endure her as well?

She got up and showered, ordered the closet to produce a pair of simple blue pants and a matching shirt, dressed, and began walking the seemingly endless corridors of the gaudy castle her mother had designed. Unlike the other building interiors in all the robot cities she had ever seen, this one was flashy, ornate, overblown—yet still just as empty as all the others. It came to Ariel that the building was a reflection of her mother's lifestyle: all show, but under the surface not really that much different. Juliana Welsh still had a private life, however much she tried to hide that fact.

Ariel wondered what it might be like to be included in that life. It would no doubt mean taking part in at least some of the public displays as well, but she supposed nothing was free. If she demanded the same thing from Juliana that Juliana demanded of everyone else—a fair return on her investment—then it might even work out. She stopped at a window and looked out at the footpath leading to the immense front gate, imagining it full of friends come to take her shopping for clothing for the next big social event. She smiled. It might at least be worth a try.

Avery drifted upward from the lower levels of consciousness, the last fading impressions of a disturbingly realistic dream close behind. He'd dreamed he'd driven his wife away with his nagging perfectionism, then gone completely insane, nearly killed his son, and wasted over a decade of his life building a city that would never be used. The horrible chain of events chased him all the way into groggy wakefulness in an unfamiliar room, but in that half-second after waking when nightmares begin to crumble, he felt the warmth and the weight of Janet's head on his chest, felt her soft breath tickling his skin, and knew it all for a paranoid fantasy.

Sighing softly, he put his arms around her and drifted back to sleep.

Derec awoke to the sound of someone pounding on his door. He pitched upward, overbalanced, and slid off the edge of the bed to land with a thump on the floor.

"What?" he said. Then, louder, "Who is it?"

"Who do you think it is?" a male voice shouted back. "You promised to take us fishing at dawn, and the sun's already up. Come on!"

Fishing? Had he said something last night about fishing? Oh, frost, given the stories flying around toward the end there, he'd probably claimed he could catch a twenty-pound brookie or something. He looked to the bed, hoping to see Ariel there and ask her if she knew anything about it, but she was already up and gone.

"Just a minute!" he shouted.

"Thirty seconds or we go without you!"

Derec snagged his tie-died pants off the back of a chair, made a hopping spiral around the room as he pulled them on, grabbed the matching shirt from the floor and slipped it over his head on the way to the door. "Open," he commanded, and it slid aside to reveal Jon and Ivan, dressed all in green and brown camouflage and carrying long fly-casting rods in their hands.

"Time's a-wasting," Jon said as he handed Derec a rod of his own.

"What about breakfast?" Derec asked.

"What do you think we're going fishing for? Come on !"

Waiting barely long enough for Derec to grab the rod, they turned and strode off down the hallway, ignoring his protests about showering and getting a camouflage suit of his own and telling people where they'd gone. He had no choice but to follow his two newfound friends through the corridors of the enormous mansion, out through a back door that opened onto a leaf-strewn footpath, and down the grassy hillside toward the pond. The cool ground against his bare feet woke him right up, and the sight of mist rising from the water, red-tinged in the morning light, stilled his babbling tongue.

Maybe Ariel was right, he thought as he watched the other two strip line out of their reels and make a few exploratory casts out over the water. Derec mimicked their motions and saw with delight that he evidently knew, on some instinctive level, how to cast a fly into a pond. He watched the fly settle through the mist and touch the water, sending a single ripple out like an ever-widening target for the fish to zero in on.

Yes indeed. Maybe Ariel was right. Maybe there was more to life than robots after all.